Praise for Jennifer Estep's thrilling Elemental Assassin series

"Gritty!" —*RT Book Reviews*

"Engrossing!" —*Publishers Weekly*

"This series kicked off with a bang, and the action hasn't let up since."

—*Fresh Fiction*

"A raw, gritty, and compelling walk on the wild side."

—Nalini Singh, *New York Times* bestselling author

"One of the best urban fantasy series going on the market. I cannot come up with a single thing about these books that I dislike."

—*Bibliopunkk*

"Jennifer Estep is a dark, lyrical, and fresh voice in urban fantasy. . . . Gin is an assassin to die for."

—Adrian Phoenix, author of *On Midnight Wings*

"A talented writer whose heroines are a wonderful mixture of strength, intelligence, and a deeply buried vulnerability that allows us to relate to them on every level."

—*Smexy Books*

"Man, I love this series."

—*Yummy Men & Kick Ass Chicks*

WIDOW'S WEB

"Most of the characters in Estep's riveting series suffer from serious emotional baggage. What makes this ensemble so compelling is their determined struggle to build new lives. Estep has found the perfect recipe for combining kick-butt action and high-stakes danger with emotional resonance."

—*RT Book Reviews* (Top Pick!)

"Filled with such emotional and physical intensity that it leaves you happily exhausted by the end."

—*All Things Urban Fantasy*

BY A THREAD
Goodreads nominee for Best Paranormal Fantasy Novel, and *RT Book Reviews* nominee for Best Urban Fantasy World Building

"Filled with butt-kicking action, insidious danger, and a heroine with her own unique moral code, this thrilling story is top-notch. Brava!"

—*RT Book Reviews* (Top Pick!)

"Gin is stronger than ever, and this series shows no signs of losing steam."

—*Fiction Vixen*

SPIDER'S REVENGE
A RITA nominee and an *RT Book Reviews* Editor's Choice for Best Urban Fantasy Novel

"Explosive . . . outstanding. . . . Hang on, this is one smackdown you won't want to miss!"

—*RT Book Reviews* (Top Pick!)

"A whirlwind of tension, intrigue, and mind-blowing action that leaves your heart pounding."

—*Smexy Books*

TANGLED THREADS

"Interesting storylines, alluring world, and fascinating characters. That is what I've come to expect from Estep's series."

—*Yummy Men & Kick Ass Chicks*

"The story had me whooping with joy and screaming in outrage, just as all really good books always do."

—*Literary Escapism*

VENOM

"Estep has really hit her stride with this gritty and compelling series. . . . Brisk pacing and knife-edged danger make this an exciting page-turner."

—*RT Book Reviews* (Top Pick!)

"Since the first book in the series, I have been entranced by Gin. . . . Every book has been jam-packed with action and mystery, and once I think it can't get any better, *Venom* comes along and proves me completely wrong.".

—*Literary Escapism*

WEB OF LIES

"The second chapter of the series is just as hard-edged and compelling as the first. Gin Blanco is a fascinatingly pragmatic character, whose intricate layers are just beginning to unravel."

—*RT Book Reviews*

"One of the best urban fantasy series I've ever read. The action is off the charts, the passion is hot, and her cast of secondary characters is stellar. . . . If you haven't read this series, you are missing out on one heck of a good time!"

—*The Romance Dish*

SPIDER'S BITE

"The fast pace, clever dialogue, and intriguing heroine help make this new series launch one to watch."

—*Library Journal*

"Bodies litter the pages of this first entry in Estep's engrossing urban fantasy series. . . . Fans will love it."

—*Publishers Weekly*

JENNIFER ESTEP

HEART
OF
Venom

AN ELEMENTAL ASSASSIN BOOK

POCKET BOOKS

New York   London   Toronto   Sydney   New Delhi

Pocket Books
A Division of Simon & Schuster, Inc.
1230 Avenue of the Americas
New York, NY 10020

This book is a work of fiction. Any references to historical events, real people, or real places are used fictitiously. Other names, characters, places, and events are products of the author's imagination, and any resemblance to actual events or places or persons, living or dead, is entirely coincidental.

First Pocket Books paperback edition September 2013

POCKET and colophon are registered trademarks of Simon & Schuster, Inc.

For information about special discounts for bulk purchases, please contact Simon & Schuster Special Sales at 1-866-506-1949 or business@simonandschuster.com.

The Simon & Schuster Speakers Bureau can bring authors to your live event. For more information or to book an event, contact the Simon & Schuster Speakers Bureau at 1-866-248-3049 or visit our website at www.simonspeakers.com.

Manufactured in the United States of America

10   9   8   7   6   5   4   3

ISBN 978-1-4516-8900-6
ISBN 978-1-4516-8904-4 (ebook)

To my mom, my grandma, and Andre—
for your love, patience, and everything else that
you've given me over the years

To my papaw—you will be missed

ACKNOWLEDGMENTS

Once again, my heartfelt thanks go out to all of the folks who help turn my words into a book.

Thanks go to my agent, Annelise Robey, and editors, Adam Wilson and Lauren McKenna, for all their helpful advice, support, and encouragement. Thanks also to Julia Fincher.

Thanks to Tony Mauro for designing another terrific cover, and thanks to Louise Burke, Lisa Litwack, and everyone else at Pocket Books and Simon & Schuster for their work on the cover, the book, and the series.

And finally, a big thanks to all of the readers. Knowing that folks read and enjoy my books is truly humbling, and I'm glad that you are all enjoying Gin and her adventures.

I appreciate you all more than you will ever know.

Happy reading!

❖ 1 ❖

"What do you mean, I can't come?"

I jerked my head down at the heavy weight swinging between us. "Do you really want to talk about this right now?"

"I can't *think* of a better time," he replied, then dropped his half of the load onto the ground.

I let go of my half of the weight, put my hands on my hips, and rolled my eyes at the whiny, petulant tone in my foster brother's voice. "You can't come because it's a girls' day at the salon. No guys allowed. That includes you."

Finnegan Lane sniffed, straightened up to his full six-foot-plus height, and carefully adjusted the expensive silk tie knotted around his neck. "Yes, but I am not just *any* guy."

More eye-rolling on my part, but Finn ignored me. His ego was pretty much bulletproof, and my derisive looks wouldn't so much as scratch his own highfalutin opinion of himself.

"Besides," he continued, "I'd get more enjoyment out of a spa day than you would."

"True," I agreed. "I don't particularly care how shiny my nails are or how well conditioned my hair is."

Finn held out his manicured nails, studying them with a critical eye, before reaching up and gently patting his coif of walnut-colored hair. "My nails are good, but I could use a trim. Wouldn't want to get any split ends."

"Oh, no," I muttered. "We wouldn't want such a horror as *that*."

With his artfully styled hair, designer suit, and glossy wing tips, Finn looked like he'd just stepped out of the pages of some high-end fashion magazine. Add his intense green eyes, chiseled features, and toned, muscled body to that, and he was as handsome as any movie star. The only thing that ruined his sleek, polished look was the blood spattered all over his white shirt and gray suit jacket—and the body lying at his feet.

"Come on," I said. "This guy isn't getting any lighter."

The two of us were standing in the alley behind the Pork Pit, the barbecue restaurant that I ran in downtown Ashland. A series of old, battered metal Dumpsters crouched on either side of the restaurant's back door, all reeking of cumin, cayenne, black pepper, and the other spices that I cooked with, along with all of the food scraps and other garbage that had spoiled out there in the July heat. A breeze whistled in between the backs of the buildings, bringing some temporary relief from the sticky humidity and making several crumpled-up white paper bags bearing the Pork Pit's pig logo skip down the oil-slicked surface of the alley.

I ignored the low, scraping, skittering noises of the bags and concentrated on the sound of the stones around me.

People's actions, thoughts, and feelings last longer and have more of an impact than most folks realize, since all of those actions and feelings resonate with emotional vibrations that especially sink into the stone around them. As a Stone elemental, I have magic that lets me hear and interpret all of the whispers of the element around me, whether it's a jackhammer brutally punching through a concrete foundation, rain and snow slowly wearing away at a roadside marker, or the collective frets of harried commuters scurrying into an office building, hoping that their bosses won't yell at them for being late again.

Behind me, the brick wall of the Pork Pit let out low, sluggish, contented sighs, much the way the diners inside did after finishing a hot, greasy barbecue sandwich, baked beans, and all of the other Southern treats that I served up on a daily basis. A few sharp notes of violence trilled here and there in the brick, but they were as familiar to me as the sighs were, and I wasn't concerned by them. This wasn't the first person I'd had to kill inside the restaurant, and it wouldn't be the last.

"Come on," I repeated. "We've had our body-moving break. You grab his shoulders again, and I'll get his feet. I want to get this guy into that Dumpster in the next alley over before someone sees us."

"Dumpster? You mean the refrigerated cooler that Sophia hauled in just so you could keep bodies on ice close to the restaurant with at least a *modicum* of plausible deniability," Finn corrected me.

I shrugged. "It was her idea, not mine. But since she's

the one who gets rid of most of the bodies, it was her call."

"And why isn't Sophia here tonight to help us with this guy?"

I shrugged again. "Because there was some James Bond film festival that she wanted to go to, so she took the night off. Now, come on. Enough stalling. Let's go."

"Why do I have to grab his shoulders?" Finn whined again. "That's where all the blood is."

I eyed his ruined jacket and shirt. "At this point, I don't think it much matters, do you?"

Finn glanced down at the smears of red on his chest. "No, I suppose it doesn't."

He grumbled and let out a few put-upon sighs, but he eventually leaned down and took hold of the dead guy's shoulders, while I grabbed his ankles. So far, we'd moved the guy from the storefront of the Pork Pit, through the rear of the restaurant, and outside. This time, we slowly shuffled away from the back door of the Pit and down the alley.

Finn and I had moved bodies before, but the fact that this dead guy was a seven-foot-tall giant with a strong, muscled figure made him a little heavier than most, and we stopped at the end of the alley to take another break. I wiped the sweat off my forehead and stared down at the dead guy.

Half an hour ago, the giant had been sitting in a booth in the restaurant, chowing down on a double bacon cheeseburger, sweet potato fries, and a big piece of apple pie and talking to the friend he'd brought along. The two giants had been my last customers, and I'd been waiting for them to leave before I closed the restaurant for the night. The first guy had paid his bill and left without incident, but the second one had swaggered over to the cash register and handed me a fistful of one-dollar bills. I'd counted the bills, and the second my eyes dropped to the cash register, he'd taken a swing at me with his massive fist.

Please. As if no one had ever tried that trick before.

But such were the job hazards of an assassin. Yep, me, Gin Blanco. Restaurant owner by day. Notorious assassin the Spider by night. Well, actually, it was more like I was the Spider all the time now. Ever since I'd killed Mab Monroe, the powerful Fire elemental who'd owned a good chunk of the crime in Ashland, everyone who was anyone in the underworld had been gunning for me. I was a wild card in the city's power structure, and lots of folks thought that arranging my murder would prove their mettle to everyone else. Tonight's giant was just the latest in a long line of folks who'd eaten in my restaurant with the intention of murdering me right after sopping up the last bit of barbecue sauce on their plates.

Since Finn had been sitting on a stool close to the cash register, he'd pulled a gun out from underneath his suit jacket and tried to put a couple of bullets into the other man, but the giant had slapped Finn's gun away. The two of them had been grappling when I'd come around the counter, palmed one of my silverstone knives, and repeatedly, brutally punched the blade into the giant's back, sides, and chest until he was dead. Hence the blood that had spattered all over Finn—and me too, although my long-sleeved black T-shirt and dark jeans hid most of it.

"All right," Finn said. "Let's lug this guy the rest of the way. I need to go home and get cleaned up before my date with Bria tonight."

I'd just started to bend down and take hold of the giant's ankles again when a mutter of unease rippled through the stone wall beside me—a dark whisper full of malicious intent.

I stopped and scanned the alley in front of us. Sophia's rusty cooler stood at the far end, although several more Dumpsters and smaller trash cans crouched in between like tin soldiers lined up against the walls. It was after eight now, and what little lavender twilight remained was quickly being swallowed up by the shadows creeping up the walls. Another breeze whistled down the alley, bringing the scents of cooked cabbage, grilled chicken, and spicy peanut sauce with it from the Thai restaurant down the block.

Finn noticed my hesitation. "What's wrong?"

I kept scanning the shadows. "I think we have company."

He adjusted his tie again, but his eyes were flicking left and right just as mine were. "Any clue who it might be?"

I shrugged. "Probably our dead friend's dinner companion."

Finn shook his head. "But he left before the giant attacked you. Even if they were partners, once he realized what happened to his buddy, the second guy would have hightailed it out of here as fast as he could if he had even the smallest *shred* of common sense—"

A bit of silver stuck out from behind a Dumpster off to my right. I lunged forward and threw my body on top of Finn's, forcing us both to the ground.

Crack! Crack! Crack!

The bullets sailed over our heads, but I still reached for my Stone magic and used it to harden my skin into an impenetrable shell. I also tried to cover as much of Finn's body as I could with my own. I might be bulletproof when I used my magic, but he wasn't.

Footsteps scuffed in the alley behind me, indicating that our attacker felt bold and confident enough to move toward us. Then—

Crack! Crack! Crack!

More bullets zipped down the alley. The guy must have adjusted his aim, because I felt all three of the projectiles punch against my back before rattling away in the semi-darkness. They would have blasted out through my heart, killing me and maybe Finn too, if I hadn't been using my Stone power. My body jerked with the impact of the bullets; then I let my limbs go absolutely slack and still as I sprawled over Finn, as though I was as dead as the giant lying next to us.

I looked at Finn, who gave me a saucy wink, telling me that he was okay. I felt his hand reach up, then drop from my waist, taking a light, thin weight with it. Finn brought his hand back up, and I wrapped my fingers around his. When he pulled his hand away, he left me holding the knife he'd grabbed from against the small of my back. I slid the weapon partially up my sleeve, hiding it from sight, then closed my eyes and waited—just waited for my enemy to come close enough.

More footsteps scuffed in the alley, followed by the harsh, raspy sound of someone breathing in through his mouth. I cracked open my eyes. A pair of mud-covered boots were planted right next to my face. As I watched, one of the boots drew back, and I knew what was coming next.

Sure enough, a second later, the giant's boot slammed into my ribs.

Despite the fact that I was holding on to my Stone magic, the blow still hurt, like getting beaned in the chest with a fastball, but I kept my body loose and floppy as though I couldn't feel it at all.

Still, the force of the blow knocked me partially off Finn, who grunted as my elbow dug into his shoulder.

Silence. Then—

"Open your eyes, pretty boy, or I'll put a bullet through your skull," the gunman threatened.

Finn sighed, and I saw him open his eyes and slowly hold his hands up. "All right, all right, you got me. I'm still alive."

"I don't care about you," the giant snapped. "Is she dead? Or is she faking?"

"Of course she's dead," Finn snapped back, holding his hands out so the giant could get a better look at the bloody smears on his clothes. "Do you not see the blood all over the two of us? I'm lucky the bullets stopped inside her instead of going on through and into me." He shuddered. "And now I think I'm going to be sick. So can you please just roll her off me or something? I can't *stand* the sight of blood."

If it wouldn't have given me away, I would have snorted. Finn didn't have any more problem with blood than I did. He just didn't like it being splattered all over one of his precious Fiona Fine designer suits.

"But you're her partner," the giant said. "Everyone knows that. Shouldn't you be, you know, more upset that she's dead?"

"Actually, I'm more like her henchman," Finn corrected. "As for being upset that she's dead, well, she's not exactly the kind of woman you say *no* to, if you know what I mean. Trust me. I'm happy that she's gone. Thrilled. Ecstatic, even."

Silence. Then—

The giant kicked me in the ribs again. Once more, I pretended that I couldn't feel the sharp, brutal blow. The giant kept up with his attacks, plowing his foot into my ribs, my shin, and even my shoulder. I thought he might lean down, press his gun against the back of my skull, pull the trigger, and try to put a couple of bullets into my head just to make sure that I was dead. But for once, my luck held, and he didn't take that final step. Maybe he was out of bullets. Or maybe he just wasn't that smart. Either way, after about three more minutes of dithering around and petulant pleas from Finn to move my body off him, the giant seemed to buy my playing possum.

"I did it," the guy finally said. "I did it! I killed the Spider! Woo-hoo!"

Okay, I thought the *woo-hoo* at the end was a little much, but I let the giant enjoy his moment of victory.

It was going to be the last thing he ever enjoyed.

"All right, all right," Finn groused again. "Now, can you please get her off me? Seriously, dude, I'm about three seconds away from throwing up here. I know you don't want that all over your boots." He started making choking sounds.

"Fine, fine," the other man muttered. "Just quit your damn whining, already."

The giant reached down, grabbed my shoulder, and turned me over.

I surged up and stabbed him in the chest for his thoughtfulness.

The giant screamed in surprise and jerked to one side, making my knife skitter across his ribs instead of slicing into his heart. He staggered back, and my knife cut free of his chest, blood spraying everywhere. The giant brought his revolver up between us and pulled the trigger.

Click.

Empty. Well, too bad for him. Fatal for him, actually.

I scrambled to my feet, raised my knife high, and threw myself forward, but the giant was anticipating the move. He caught my arm in his hand. Given his enormous strength, it was easy for him to keep me from plunging my knife into his chest a second time. So I brought my free hand up, curved my fingers, and clawed at his face. The giant let go of my arm and craned his neck back, trying to protect his eyes from my prying fingers.

"Gin! Down!" I heard Finn yell behind me.

I immediately stopped my attack on the giant and dropped to the ground.

Crack! Crack! Crack! Crack!

Bullets punched through the air where I'd been standing, and the familiar acrid burn of gunpowder mixed with the stench of garbage in the alley. A second later, the giant's body hit the ground with a dull *thud*.

Knife still in my hand, I got to my feet and hurried over to him, but there was no need. Finn had put a couple of bullets through the giant's right eye and up into his brain. His body had already shut down; he wasn't even twitching.

I turned to look at Finn, who had a gun clenched in one hand. With his other hand, he was picking a piece of wilted cabbage off his jacket sleeve. He tossed the cabbage aside with a disgusted expression and moved over to me.

"You okay?" I asked.

Finn nodded. "You?"

I nodded back and gingerly touched my side. "I'll have some bruises from where he played kick-the-can with my ribs, but I'll stop by Jo-Jo's on the way home and get her to patch me up. No worries."

"Speaking of Jo-Jo's, I still say that I should get to come to your little soiree," Finn said. "Especially after I was so helpful here tonight."

I narrowed my eyes. "You start up with that again, and I'll be dealing with three bodies instead of just two."

Finn gave me a wounded look, but after a moment, he sighed and holstered his gun. "Well, at least this one's already halfway to the cooler," he grumbled.

I grinned at him. "See? We're nothing if not efficient."

Finn muttered some choice words under his breath, but he reached down and took hold of the dead giant's shoulders, and I grabbed his ankles. We lugged the two men over to the cooler to await Sophia and her body-disposal skills.

Not the first body dump we'd done—and certainly not the last.

✳ 2 ✳

Two days later, Saturday, the dead giants were still on ice in the cooler, but I found myself in much nicer, warmer confines: a beauty salon.

The salon took up the back half of an old plantation house, and the area had a homey and welcoming, if cluttered, feel. Tubs of nail polish and lipstick sat on a counter, along with bottles of hair dye, shampoo, and conditioner. Nestled in between the tubs and bottles were brushes, combs, curlers, rollers, scissors, and every other item you could think of that would untangle, tease, straighten, curl, kink, or cut your hair. Stacks of beauty magazines covered the small tables scattered here and there in the room, the models on the slick, glossy covers beaming as if they approved of all the beauty ministrations that could be had here.

I was relaxing in one of the cherry-red salon chairs when something warm, wet, and slightly rough touched my foot. I leaned to one side, and Rosco, Jo-Jo's basset hound, licked my toes again, then gave me a hopeful *woof.* I stretched out my foot and rubbed it against his side. Rosco let out a loud, contented sigh and collapsed in a wrinkled puddle of black and brown fur, perfectly happy to let me rub his round tummy for as long as I would.

"Hold still, darling," Jo-Jo drawled as she put another coat of paint on my fingernails. "I'm almost done."

Rosco and the salon were the pride and joy of Jolene "Jo-Jo" Deveraux, the dwarven Air elemental who healed me whenever I got banged up or almost shot, stabbed, beaten, or magicked to death as the Spider. Given my current notoriety in the Ashland underworld and the legion of would-be murderers targeting me, I was over here more days than not. Then again, I would have been over here anyway, since Jo-Jo was a mother figure to me and part of my extended family.

Since we were having a girls' day at the salon, I'd forgone my usual long sleeves, jeans, and boots in favor of a red tank top, some white cutoff shorts, and a pair of black sandals that immediately got kicked off over into the corner when I'd first arrived an hour earlier. Jo-Jo, however, enjoyed dressing up, and she had on one of her prettiest pink dresses, along with her usual strand of pearls. Her white-blond hair was curled just so, her soft, understated makeup would have put any beauty queen to shame, and her bare feet showed off the perfect raspberry pedicure that she'd just given herself.

"You know, you really don't have to give me a manicure," I said. "You should be relaxing today too."

Jo-Jo raised her head and gave me an amused look. Laugh lines fanned out from the corners of her clear, almost colorless eyes. "You did all the cooking, darling. That's more work than this is. Besides, I like pampering you, Gin. You don't take nearly enough time for yourself. Especially not these days."

"I know, I know," I said. "But it's a shame that you're doing up my nails so neat and pretty when they'll probably be chipped by this time tomorrow. Or probably before I leave here today. I never seem to be able to keep the polish on them for very long."

I held up my hand. Jo-Jo had painted my short nails a deep, dark red that was definitely my color. If nothing else, it would help hide the blood that was sure to get on my hands the next time some idiot tried to murder me.

"Well, I have to agree with Jo-Jo," a light, lilting voice chimed in. "I'd rather have your cooking than a manicure any day. This dark chocolate mousse pie is to die for, Gin."

I looked to my right where my baby sister was eagerly digging her fork into a piece of said pie. Like me, Detective Bria Coolidge had dressed down today, in a pale blue T-shirt, gray cargo shorts, and brown sandals, although she was still beautiful, with her blond hair, rosy skin, and cornflower blue eyes. But just because Bria was off the clock didn't mean that she wasn't armed. I knew that her gun and her gold detective's badge were stuffed into the oversize straw bag that she'd brought along, just like my knives were laid out on the buffet table within easy reach.

Bria took another big bite of the pie and made the

same sigh of contentment that Rosco had a minute ago. "What all did you make besides the pie?" she asked, her eyes going from one covered dish on the table to the next.

"Well, since it's girls only today, I decided to go all out," I replied. "There's the dark chocolate mousse pie you are currently enjoying, along with some chocolate truffles, double-chocolate-chip cookies, and dark- and milk-chocolate-dipped strawberries, kiwis, pineapples, and mangoes."

Bria gave me a wry grin. "I'm sensing a chocolate theme."

I returned her grin with one of my own. "You might say that. But there's some real food too, in case we get tired of dessert. Plus, Roslyn is bringing some fresh veggies from her garden."

Jo-Jo glanced at the clock on the wall, which was shaped like a puffy cloud, her rune and the symbol for her Air magic. "Where is Roslyn?"

Roslyn Phillips, another one of our friends, was also supposed to come to the salon today, along with Sophia Deveraux, Jo-Jo's younger sister.

Bria waved her fork in the air. "She called me this morning and said that she'd be a little late, that we should go ahead and start without her."

"And you went for the food first. You're picking up some of Finn's bad habits," I teased. "How was your date with him the other night?"

Bria's fiery blush told me everything that I needed to know. "I plead the Fifth," she murmured, and took another bite of pie.

"Well, when you're finished with that, come over here, darling, and tell me what color you want on your nails," Jo-Jo said.

My sister nodded, but her eyes were fixed on the glass cake stand that was filled with the chocolate-dipped fruit. Bria turned her attention back to the buffet, while Jo-Jo put the cap on the polish she'd used on my nails. She had started to lean over and put the bottle back into a tub with the others when she paused and frowned. She stared at the bottles of nail polish, but her eyes were cloudy and unfocused, as though she wasn't really seeing what she was looking at.

"Jo-Jo?" I asked. "Is something wrong?"

The dwarf used her magic to heal wounds, but her power also gave her a bit of precognition, as it did with most Air elementals. While the stones whispered to me of all the things that people had done in a certain spot, the breeze whistled in Jo-Jo's ear about all the things that folks might do in the future.

Jo-Jo shook her head, making her soft, springy curls bounce around before they settled back into place. The cloudy, vacant look vanished from her eyes, although she put her hand up against her right temple and started massaging a small spot there, as if she suddenly had a headache.

"I can't put my finger on it exactly," she said. "I've just . . . I've had a bad feeling these past few days. Actually, it's been more than a few days. More like ever since that mess at Briartop a couple of weeks ago."

I grimaced. Jo-Jo was being kind. *Mess* didn't adequately describe what had happened at the Briartop art museum, when a ruthless giant named Clementine Barker had decided to use her army of underlings to rob the exhibit of Mab Monroe's loot—and try to murder me to boot.

Of course, I'd killed good ole Clem and her gangster family, but my victories had come at a price: Jillian Delancey, the innocent woman who'd died because she'd had the bad, stupid, fatal luck to be wearing the same dress that I was wearing that night, causing one of Clementine's men to mistake her for me and shoot her.

Jo-Jo noticed me frowning, and she leaned over and patted my hand. "Don't worry, darling. It's probably nothing. Sometimes I take these spells where it seems like something bad is going to happen at any second. Most of the time, it turns out to be nothing more than a little bit of heartburn." Despite her words, her clear eyes grew cloudy and troubled once again. "I'll just . . . I'll be glad when Sophia's here."

Like Roslyn, Sophia was running a little late this morning, since she'd wanted to get rid of the two dead giants in the cooler. I'd given all the restaurant staff the day off with pay, so both Sophia and I could enjoy our time at the salon, and I'd told Sophia that the giants' bodies could wait another day, or at least until after our salon time, but she had insisted that she was going to dispose of them this morning. Or maybe she was simply being practical. Odds were that someone else would jump me at the Pork Pit sometime in the next few days, and, well, that cooler could only hold so many bodies. As it was, Finn and I had had to pack the two giants in like pieces of a jigsaw puzzle just so we could close the lid.

Sophia had disposed of dozens of bodies for me and

for my mentor, Fletcher Lane, before I'd taken over the assassination business from the old man. She could handle two giants with her eyes blindfolded and one hand tied behind her back. But Jo-Jo looked so worried that I wrapped my hand around hers and gave it a gentle squeeze, careful not to smear the polish that she'd put on my nails.

"Do you want me to call Sophia and see where she's at?"

Jo-Jo shook her head. "No, that's all right. Like I said, it's probably just heartburn. I think I had one too many cups of Finn's chicory coffee this morning. That stuff will knock your teeth plumb out of your mouth, it's so strong."

She gave me a chipper smile, grabbed the plastic tub, put it on her lap, and started sorting through the many bottles of polish. Jo-Jo held up first one pink, then another, trying to find one that she thought Bria might like, but the cheery colors did little to brighten my mood.

Maybe it was the way Jo-Jo's sculpted eyebrows were pinched together in worry, or maybe it was how quickly her smile slipped back into a frown when she thought that I wasn't looking at her anymore. I couldn't see the future like she did, but Jo-Jo had been right about too many things in the past for me to dismiss her dread as nothing more than caffeine overload. If she thought something ominous was gathering on the horizon, then no doubt, the wind was blowing storm clouds in our direction right now.

Despite my unease, the next half hour passed by in a blur of cheery conversation and good food. Jo-Jo opened one of the doors set into the back wall of the salon, and Rosco dutifully heaved himself to his feet and slowly waddled outside to do his doggy business. Bria finally finished her pie and sat down in my spot in the salon chair so Jo-Jo could do her nails while we waited for Roslyn and Sophia to arrive.

I wandered over to the buffet table, piling my plate high and then taking a bite of everything in turn. The fried chicken salad on the mini sourdough rolls. The salty, crunchy, homemade potato chips. And then, of course, the mousse pie, which melted on my tongue bite after sinfully rich, decadent, delicious bite, as though I were eating a light, frothy cloud made of dark, luscious chocolate. I'd gotten up early that morning to put everything together, but it had been worth it. Cooking was a passion of mine, a chance for me to show the people I cared about exactly how much I loved them—and a way for me to deal with whatever was bothering me.

Like Jillian Delancey's death.

Not for the first time, Jillian's face flashed before my eyes. Dark brown hair, dark eyes, great smile. All gone because of me, because of the dumb luck that seemed to delight in messing with me and mine time and time again.

"What are you thinking about, Gin?" Bria asked, walking over to me and waving her strawberry-pink nails in the air to help dry them.

I looked away from the patch of wall that I'd been aimlessly staring at and down at my plate of food, which I'd set on the table. "I'm thinking that I should have put some more kosher salt on the potato chips."

Bria shook her head, causing her blond hair to glimmer like strands of spun gold in the sunlight streaming in through the windows. "No, you're not. You're thinking about something else, something important. What happened at Briartop? Or is it Owen?"

I grimaced at the mention of Owen Grayson, my, well, I didn't know exactly what Owen and I were these days. Not together but not as far apart as we'd been. Owen had brought Jillian to the museum for Mab's gala. She'd been his friend and business associate and had wanted to be more, although Owen had told me that he didn't think of her like that. Either way, Jillian had still ended up dead because of me—the second woman associated with Owen to meet that particular fate in a matter of weeks.

Bria laid a hand on my arm. "You know you can talk to me, right? About anything?"

I nodded. I did know that, although it always amazed me. After years of thinking that Bria was dead, she'd reappeared in my life several months ago. It wasn't easy, her being a cop and my being an assassin, but we were making it work, and we were closer now than ever before.

"I know, and I appreciate it. What can I say? I like to brood over my food."

Bria laughed, but then her face turned serious, as if she wanted to ask me something. She started toying with the silverstone pendant around her throat. A primrose, the symbol for beauty, her rune.

Watching her fiddle with her necklace made my fingers curl into my palms, touching the scars on my skin there, a small circle on either hand, each mark surrounded by eight thin rays. The same symbol was also stamped into the middle of the silverstone ring that I wore on my right index finger. My rune, a spider rune, the symbol for patience—and so many other things to me.

It too had once been a necklace, until Mab had used her Fire magic to superheat the silverstone and melt the pendant into my hands, her brutal, effective way of torturing me and marking me in more ways than either one of us had known at the time.

"Gin?" Bria asked.

I snapped out of my memories. "I'm sorry. I spaced out there for a minute. Was there something that you wanted to ask me?"

Bria drew in a breath, but before she could tell me whatever was on her mind, the sound of a door banging open at the front of the house cut her off. A moment later, footsteps sounded. I recognized the heavy tread as belonging to Sophia, but the odd thing was that it didn't sound like she was walking normally. Instead, a series of *scrape-scrape-scrape*s screeched across the hardwood floor, as if Sophia was dragging one of her feet yet moving fast at the same time. Before I could puzzle out why she would be walking that way, she appeared in the salon doorway.

Jo-Jo might be a sweet Southern lady with her pink dresses, polish, and pearls, but Sophia had a different style altogether: Goth. Today, as usual, she wore black from head to toe—boots, jeans, and a T-shirt with a big pair of puckered crimson lips on it. A crimson leather collar spiked with silverstone ringed her throat, and her lipstick was a flat black that matched her hair.

Normally, I found Sophia's style to be dark but also cool, quirky, and funky. The problem now was that her black clothes kept me from noticing the blood on her arm and leg for several crucial seconds.

"Sophia?" I asked.

Her black eyes met mine, and I saw something there I'd never seen before: fear.

"Run," Sophia rasped in her low, broken voice.

Then she collapsed without another word.

⁂ 3 ⁂

"Sophia?" Jo-Jo said. "Sophia!"

Jo-Jo dropped the bottle of nail polish she'd been holding. The glass shattered on the floor, splattering the bright, glossy, strawberry liquid everywhere, but Jo-Jo didn't notice as she ran past us to where Sophia lay. Bria and I started forward too, but we'd only taken two steps when the front door banged open again, as though someone had kicked it wildly and sent it flying into the wall. A second later, more footsteps sounded, multiple sets, all heavy, loud, and determined, all headed our way.

Whatever trouble Sophia had gotten into had followed her home.

Bria and I glanced at each other, then both lunged for the buffet table. Bria went for the gun in her straw bag underneath the table, while I reached for my silverstone knives atop its far end. But before we could get to our weapons, six men burst into the salon, all carrying guns.

Two of the men grabbed Jo-Jo and hauled her away from Sophia. The dwarf tried to fight back, but the men were strong, and they easily lifted her off her feet and pinned her against the closest wall. Two more men stood over Sophia, pointing their guns down at her, while another stepped forward, dug his hand into Bria's golden hair, and yanked her up against his body. The sixth man grabbed my left arm and leered at me, but he didn't drag me away from the buffet table. His first mistake—and his last.

If it had just been me, I would have instantly gone on the attack, grabbing my knives and using them to cut into the men until there was nothing left of them but bloody chunks. But I couldn't do that, not while they were holding guns on Bria, Jo-Jo, and Sophia. My Stone magic would let me survive being shot in the chest, but Bria's Ice and the Deveraux sisters' Air power wouldn't. No, I'd have to be smart about things and wait for the right time to strike. Maybe I'd even keep one of the men alive long enough to question him. Because I wanted to know whom these bastards worked for and who'd sent them after me. That was the only reason I could think of for why they'd stormed into Jo-Jo's salon: because they knew that the Spider was here, and their boss wanted my head as a prize.

I coldly eyed the men. They were of varying shapes, sizes, and coloring, but they were all fit, trim, and tanned, as though they spent a lot of time outdoors. My gaze dropped to their hands, which were also rough, tan, and callused. Whoever they were, these guys were used to hard physical labor, which seemed at odds with the formality of their dress. They all wore old-fashioned brown suits, along with starched white shirts, heavy brown boots, and matching brown fedoras. All put together, they reminded me of some sort of Roaring Twenties gang, the kind that ran mountain moonshine back during Prohibition.

My gaze dropped to the gun the man holding me had shoved into my side, an old-fashioned revolver. The sort of large, sturdy hand cannon that would put a good-size hole in anyone—dwarf, giant, vampire, elemental. They weren't messing around when it came to their weapons. Good for them.

Bad for them that they'd used the guns to burst into Jo-Jo's salon. It was one thing to attack me at the Pork Pit or even at Fletcher's house. I expected that these days. But my friends, my family, were off-limits—period. Perhaps I'd let one of the men live long enough to crawl back to his boss and tell him that. Or maybe I'd deliver the message in person—along with the men's bodies.

One of the guys standing over Sophia turned and yelled over his shoulder. "We've got 'em, boss! It's all clear now!"

So the boss was here too. Good. That would save me the effort of tracking him down later or letting any of his men live.

This time, instead of banging against the wall, the door at the front of the house slowly *creaked* open. More footsteps sounded—slow, deliberate, and cautious—and another man stepped through the doorway and into the salon.

He was six feet tall, and his body was so dense it looked like it was carved out of granite. His muscles rolled with every breath he took, while his broad chest seemed solid enough to bounce a quarter off. He wasn't tall enough to be considered a giant, and his body had the stocky, sturdy construction that was associated with dwarves. Unless I missed my guess, he had both races' blood in his family tree, giving him the best of both worlds, a giant's larger size and a dwarf's tough musculature.

Unlike the other men, he was wearing a snazzy gray suit with a pair of red suspenders that peeked out from beneath his jacket. A gray fedora with a fluffy red feather tucked into the brim topped his head, casting his face in a bit of sinister shadow. Smoothly, he swept off his hat, revealing thinning black hair that was slicked back in a vain attempt to hide a burgeoning bald spot. His eyes were dark brown, and his skin was dusky olive. Lines furrowed his forehead and grooved around his mouth, but I couldn't get a real sense of his age. He could have been fifty. He could have been a hundred and fifty, or older, depending on how much dwarven blood he might have.

But the most disturbing thing was the fact that he was giving off magic.

Dozens of small, hot, invisible bubbles started bursting against my skin the second the man stepped into the salon, like matches being lit close to and then stabbed out on my bare arms. The annoying, burning sensation told me that he was probably quite strong in his Fire power, given the way the hot bubbles kept on popping and popping against my flesh. I ground my teeth together to keep from snarling at the horrible feel of his magic.

The leader surveyed his men. He nodded, apparently

satisfied with how they'd taken control of the situation. Then he stepped to one side, and I realized that he wasn't alone. A woman had followed him into the salon.

The woman wore an old-fashioned red wrap dress that could have come straight out of some gangster movie, with a pair of black patent-leather kitten heels. Her black hair was curled into tight waves against her skull, and a couple of thin diamond pins sparkled in her dark locks. She had the same brown eyes and dusky olive skin as the leader, and it was obvious that they were related, although she seemed a bit younger. Her body was also taller and much slimmer than his, as though she'd gotten more of the giant than the dwarven blood from the family tree. Plus, she was giving off the same sort of Fire magic as the leader, and her power felt even stronger than his.

The woman looked first at Sophia, then at Jo-Jo. She didn't even bother glancing at Bria or me. Her gaze went back to Sophia and stayed there, and she smiled, her teeth as white as paper against her scarlet lips.

Meanwhile, the leader smoothed his black hair back that much more and plastered a pleasant smile on his face, as though he'd dropped by for a polite visit. He stepped forward, and a curious thing happened. Instead of walking over to me and spouting off about how he was finally going to kill the Spider, he too ignored me completely and moved toward Jo-Jo.

He stopped right in front of her and smiled even wider, revealing a row of perfect white teeth. "Ms. Deveraux, what a pleasure to see you again. It's been a long, long time." His voice was cool and cultured, but I could detect a faint twang in it, as though he had some hillbilly accent that he was working hard to hide.

"Not long enough," Jo-Jo snarled. "I know why you're here, and you, your men, and that twisted sister of yours can get the hell out of my house."

He sighed and shook his head, as though her violent reaction saddened him. "I thought that the past fifty years or so might have made you more reasonable, but I can see that's just not the case."

Jo-Jo didn't bother responding. Instead, she spat in his face.

Everyone froze, except for Jo-Jo, who spat in the leader's face again. She started to do it a third time, but one of the men holding on to her shoved his gun even deeper into her side and thumbed back the trigger. Jo-Jo stopped spitting, but she did lift her head and give the leader a look that was total, murderous hate.

Jo-Jo prided herself on her manners, and it shocked me to see her do something so crass, so vicious and out of character. Bria raised her eyebrows at me, as surprised as I was, but I shook my head a tiny bit in response. I didn't know who the man was or why Jo-Jo would look at him that way. But one thing was clear. This wasn't about me, but I was going to end it.

The woman in the red dress moved closer and raised her hand so that it was level with Jo-Jo's face. She rubbed her thumb and forefinger together, and red-hot embers hissed out from between her fingertips as though she was holding a sparkler. More and more of those invisible bubbles popped against my skin as the woman reached for even more of her Fire magic.

"Let me kill her," the woman snarled in a voice that was even twangier than the leader's. "Or at least put out one of her eyes. She deserves it for insulting you like that."

"No, Hazel," the leader said, pulling a gray silk hand-kerchief from his pants pocket and using the fabric to wipe the spit off his face. "Leave her be—for now."

Hazel gave him a sour look, but she reluctantly let go of her magic, dropped her hand, and stepped away from Jo-Jo.

The man tucked his handkerchief back into his pants. He pulled his hand out, and a small piece of paper flut-tered out of his pocket and drifted to the ground. He didn't seem to notice it, though. Then again, it was most likely just a bit of trash. Just like he was.

"You'll have to forgive me. I would have been here sooner, but I've been busy these past few months. Busi-ness has been booming ever since Ms. Monroe died, as I'm sure you can imagine."

Business? What sort of business was he in? And what did it have to do with Mab?

He paused, as if he expected Jo-Jo to respond, but she kept silent.

"Anyway," he continued, "I finally managed to get myself in gear and come on back down to Ashland. I'd been meaning to for a while now. Ever since I heard that our mutual friend Mr. Lane had passed away last year. A shame, him being tortured to death like that."

I frowned. Fletcher's murder was no secret, but there was something ominous about the way the leader talked about him, as though the old man's death was something he'd been waiting for and looking forward to for a long,

long time. He said that he'd known Jo-Jo some fifty years ago. Had he known Fletcher back then too? Had the two of them been enemies all these years?

Even more hate burned in Jo-Jo's eyes, making it look like she had two chunks of white quartz glowing in her face. "You're no friend of mine, Harley Grimes. You never were, and you never will be. So get out of my house. You weren't welcome back then, and you sure as hell aren't welcome now."

I kept my face blank, but my mind was spinning at the man's identity. Harley Grimes. I'd heard that name before, when Jo-Jo had told me how he'd kidnapped and tortured Sophia years ago. Grimes had even forced Sophia to breathe in elemental Fire, ruining her vocal cords.

My gaze snapped to Sophia, who was still lying on the floor. She stared back at me, and once again, I saw the fear in her eyes—fear not just for herself but for all of us. She knew what Harley Grimes was capable of better than anyone.

So I turned my attention to the men surrounding us, looking for any weaknesses that I could exploit. A few seconds of inattention, a tremor in a gun hand, something, anything, that would give me an opening to attack—or at least let me put myself between Grimes and everyone else.

Grimes smiled again and let out a soft, sinister laugh. "Of course I'll leave you in peace, Ms. Deveraux. I'm not a monster, after all. Besides, I've finally gotten what I came for—what you and Mr. Lane took from me all those years ago."

He turned away from Jo-Jo and jerked his head at

the two men guarding Sophia. They reached down and hauled the Goth dwarf to her feet. Sophia winced and clutched a hand to her left thigh. Blood had soaked into her black jeans there, and more blood trickled out of the gunshot wound on her left arm, which peeked out from beneath her T-shirt sleeve. Grimes, Hazel, and their men must have jumped her somewhere, maybe in the alley behind the Pork Pit, and put a couple of bullets into her, trying to subdue her so they could kidnap her. Sophia must have managed to escape and had come to warn Jo-Jo. But Grimes had known exactly where she would go, and he'd followed her to finish what he'd started.

"Oh, Sophia," Grimes purred. "How I've missed you."

He stretched out a hand, as though he was going to caress her cheek, but Sophia snapped out, trying to bite off his fingers. Grimes snatched his hand back at the last second, his face full of disbelief, as though he didn't understand why she wouldn't welcome his touch after he'd had her shot and threatened her sister. He regarded her for a moment, then casually flung his hand out and slapped her across the face.

The sharp *crack* reverberated through the room like a clap of thunder, and the hard, brutal impact made Sophia stagger back, along with the two men holding her. Oh, yes. Grimes was definitely strong, thanks to his giant and dwarven blood.

But even worse, he put a bit of his Fire magic into the blow, and flames flashed between them as his skin touched hers. The stench of burning flesh filled the salon. After a moment, Sophia slowly raised her head. The imprint of Grimes's hand had been seared into her left cheek like a brand.

Even more Fire magic flickered in his eyes, making them burn a dark, dangerous brown. "I'd hoped that we would start out on better terms this time, but I'm going to enjoy teaching you to mind your manners around me once again. It seems that you've forgotten."

Sophia's nostrils flared with rage, but that was her only response.

The man holding on to my arm winced at Grimes's threat, as though he'd been on the receiving end of his leader's wrath in the past. He was so busy staring at Grimes that he didn't notice when I eased my right hand behind me, reaching back toward the buffet table. My fingers slid across the smooth surface until I felt something cold, hard, and metal. I stretched back a bit more, hooking a fingertip on the edge of the metal and dragging it toward me.

My hand closed around my knife a second later. I tightened my grip, feeling the spider rune stamped into the hilt pressing against the larger, matching scar on my palm. Owen had made this knife for me, and I was going to enjoy putting it to good use on Grimes, Hazel, and their band of miscreants.

"You leave her alone, Grimes," Jo-Jo snarled. "Sophia doesn't belong to you. She never has, and she never will."

Grimes turned to face her again. "It seems that you've forgotten something too, Ms. Deveraux. That I take whatever I want, and that whatever I want is mine. And I've been missing Sophia for a very long time now."

"You aren't leaving here with her," Jo-Jo snarled again. "Not as long as I'm still breathing."

Grimes regarded her for a long moment. "Well, I have to admire your protective instincts, if nothing else. But this problem has a very simple, very easy solution."

"And what would that be?" Jo-Jo asked.

He smiled, showing off his perfect teeth again. I knew what he was going to do, but before I could move, before I could react, before I could fucking *stop* it, Grimes reached into his suit jacket, pulled out a gun, and shot Jo-Jo in the chest.

✶ 4 ✶

The bullet punching into Jo-Jo's body tore her loose from the men who'd been holding her. She gasped in pain, and her head snapped back against the wall, but she didn't go down.

So Grimes shot her again.

This time, Jo-Jo's bare feet slid out from under her, and she crumpled to the salon floor.

Bria, Sophia, and I all surged forward, struggling to get free of the men who were guarding us, but a ball of Fire magic flashed to life in Hazel's hand. She spun around in the middle of the salon, laughing, the skirt of her red dress rippling out around her like waves of blood.

"Give me a reason," she said, smiling at us all in turn, her magic making her eyes gleam with a dark, sadistic light. "Any reason at all."

I looked at Sophia, but she shook her head at me. She didn't want Bria or me to get shot—or worse, if Hazel had her way. I ground my teeth together in frustration, but I stopped fighting. I had my family to think about, and there was too much danger of Hazel burning Bria or Sophia to death before I could kill her. Not to mention the fact that Grimes and the rest of his men could start shooting at us at any second.

Sophia realized that I was standing down—for now—and she carefully pointed her right index finger at Jo-Jo, then raised her black eyebrows at me in a silent question. She wanted me to save her big sister, no matter what happened to her in the meantime. Sophia was willing to sacrifice herself for the rest of us. She knew that the sooner Grimes and his men left with her, the sooner Bria and I could help Jo-Jo. My heart squeezed tightly, but I nodded back at her, telling her that I understood.

Grimes stared down at Jo-Jo, his face perfectly calm and composed. She was slumped against the wall, her skirt up over her knees, her legs sprawled out at an awkward angle. Her breath puffed out in short, painful, ragged gasps, and her hands pressed tightly over the two gunshot wounds in her chest. Blood oozed out between her fingers, dripping down and painting ugly crimson roses on her pretty pink dress. Scarlet specks also covered the white pearls around her throat.

I hoped that she might reach for her Air magic and heal herself with it, but I realized that I didn't know if she could actually do that. Even if she could, maybe the pain was simply too great for her to concentrate on her magic, or maybe using her Air power now would sap what little strength—and life—she had left.

When Grimes was sure that Jo-Jo wasn't going to get

up, he gestured at some of his men. "You four, stay behind and make sure that Ms. Deveraux dies, then follow us back in the second car. I'm rather tired of knowing that she's alive."

His gaze focused on me, then on Bria, and he smiled again. "There's no hurry, though. I got what I came for, so take a few minutes to amuse yourself with these two, if you want. Just be sure they won't be able to speak to anyone about it after the fact."

The four men let out dark, delighted chuckles at the thought of raping and killing Bria and me, but they weren't nearly as cold and sinister as the black rage beating in my heart. I ignored the men and looked at Bria. My sister's blue eyes blazed with anger. I nodded at her, and she nodded back. We knew what we had to do now.

Grimes stuffed his gun back under his suit jacket, then gallantly flipped his gray fedora back up onto his head. He leaned forward and mockingly tipped his hat at Jo-Jo. She glared at him as best she could, but her eyes were glassy and slightly unfocused with pain.

"I would say until we meet again, but we both know that's not going to happen," Grimes said. "But don't you worry, Ms. Deveraux. I'll take real good care of Sophia for you. Just like I did before. In fact, I plan to give her my full attention in the days and weeks ahead. After all, we've got a lot of lost time to make up for."

Jo-Jo made a strangled sound, but Grimes had already turned his back on her.

He stepped through the salon doorway and crooked his finger at the two men still holding Sophia, who tightened their grip on her and started dragging her toward the doorway. Hazel stood to the side and watched, that ball of Fire magic still burning in her hand.

But Sophia wasn't going without a fight. She grabbed on to one side of the doorframe, holding on with one hand and stretching the other out to her sister.

"Jo-Jo!" she rasped, a plaintive wail to her low hoarse tone that I'd never heard before. "Jo-Jo!"

"Sophia!" Jo-Jo screamed in return, holding out one hand and reaching for her.

The two men had their hands around Sophia's waist, trying to drag her away, but the dwarf was stronger than they were, and she could have held on forever—if the wood hadn't cracked.

One second, Sophia was hanging on to the doorway. The next, the wood had splintered off into a long shard, sending her flying back into the hallway with the men. They landed in a tangle of arms and legs, the men shouting and Sophia snarling.

"Now, now. We'll have none of that," Hazel said.

Stepping into the hallway, she grabbed Sophia by her hair, jerked her up, and slammed the ball of Fire magic into her back. Sophia screamed, but after a moment, the flames licking at her T-shirt were snuffed out. Sophia had Air magic, just like Jo-Jo did, and she was using her power to push back against Hazel's Fire.

But it didn't work.

As soon as the flames disappeared, more Fire flashed to life in Hazel's palm, and she shoved it into Sophia's back, causing her to scream once more. That gave the two men she was fighting a chance to latch onto her again and start dragging her down the hallway.

Sophia fought them—she fought them with all the strength and magic she had, but it wasn't enough. Not with Hazel burning her over and over again and laughing the whole damn time. The more Sophia struggled, the more magic the Fire elemental used on her, and the more she cackled with glee, until her light, pealing chuckles rang through the entire house.

Sadistic bitch.

As difficult and painful as it was, I shut the sound of Sophia's screams and agony out of my mind and focused on the four men left in the salon. They weren't at all concerned about the elemental battle raging in the hallway. The two men who'd been guarding Jo-Jo started kicking the dwarf, adding to her injuries, while the two men holding Bria and me decided to listen to Grimes's advice and have some fun with us.

The man guarding me tightened his grip on my arm, his fingers digging into my skin. "Don't you worry, honey," he said, leering at me. "I'll treat you real good."

"Really?" I said. "Is that so?"

He pulled me up flush against his body. "Oh, yeah. I'll give it to you so good that you'll be begging me for more."

I coldly smiled into his face, then whipped my right hand out from behind me and stabbed him in the throat with my knife. I yanked the weapon out as brutally as I had driven it in and followed up my first fatal blow with another furious punch to his heart. He was dead before he hit the floor.

He wasn't going to be the only one, though—not by a long shot.

I shoved the dead man away, grabbed another knife

from the buffet table behind me, and headed toward Bria's man. He was so surprised by what had happened to his buddy that he gaped at me. He didn't notice Bria drop her hand down to her side or the bluish white light that flickered in her palm as she reached for her Ice magic.

Bria drove her elbow into the guy's side, making him grunt, release her, and stagger back. But she wasn't about to let him get away. Instead, she whipped around, grabbed his jacket, pulled him forward, and shoved her hand into his face with one smooth motion.

Then she unleashed her magic on him.

The bluish white glow of her Ice power intensified, burning as brightly as a star, and a frigid sensation blasted through the salon, colder than any winter day. A second later, the light faded, and Bria let go of the man. He thumped to the floor, his whole head encased in two inches of elemental Ice. If he wasn't dead already from the extreme, sudden frostbite, he'd suffocate soon enough. I was already turning to the two men kicking Jo-Jo, but I made a mental note to tell Bria how impressed I was by the creativity—and viciousness—of that display of her power. I'd have to remember that particular trick.

The last two men finally noticed that Bria and I were fighting back. A little smarter and quicker than their friends had been, they raised their guns and fired at us.

Crack! Crack!

Bria and I both dived for cover behind two of the salon chairs. The bullets hit the chairs, sending bits of fluffy white fabric puffing up into the air like snow. Bria had managed to snag her straw bag in the confusion, and she quickly upended it and grabbed the gun that came tumbling out. She clutched the weapon with her right hand as another ball of elemental Ice pulsed to life in her left palm.

Crack! Crack! Crack! Crack!

The men continued to fire at us.

"Go!" Bria shouted. "Get Sophia! I'll cover you!"

I hated to leave her in the middle of a fight, but she was right. We had to save Sophia.

I nodded at Bria. "Now!" I screamed.

We both rose from behind the salon chairs. The men raised their weapons to fire at us again, but Bria reared back and threw her Ice magic at them, causing them to duck down out of the way of the chilly blast. She followed that up by raising her own gun and firing it at the men while I sprinted for the doorway.

Hazel and the other two men had already managed to drag Sophia outside. Knives in hand, I sprinted through the house and ran out the open front door. I leaped down off the porch and hurried across the lawn, my bare feet squashing the grass.

A large white van sat in the driveway, parked at a haphazard angle behind Sophia's classic convertible and a beige sedan that I didn't recognize. Hazel had already gotten into the driver's seat of the van and had cranked the engine. Sophia was still struggling with the two men at the back of the vehicle as Grimes looked on, apparently unwilling to get his suit or his hands dirty. I didn't bother screaming at the men to let go of Sophia. They'd do that as soon as I killed them—and Grimes and Hazel too.

Grimes must have seen me racing toward him out of the corner of his eye, because he turned in my direction.

He frowned and considered me a moment, as though he was surprised that I'd managed to get past his men and make it all the way outside.

Then he threw his Fire magic at me.

The flames streaked through the air, seeming to burn hotter and brighter as they zoomed across the lawn. I didn't have time to duck them, not if I wanted to save Sophia, so I used my Stone magic to harden my skin as the elemental Fire engulfed me.

The searing strength of the heat stopped me in my tracks, and it took all my concentration to keep holding on to my own power so I wouldn't be incinerated. Grimes wasn't quite as strong as Mab had been, but his magic still packed a hell of a wallop.

I didn't want to waste precious seconds dropping to the ground and rolling around to smother the flames, so being one of the rare elementals who was gifted in not one but two areas, this time, I grabbed hold of my Ice power. I sent out a blast of magic and used my cold power to douse the Fire trying to scorch my skin. The flames immediately froze into weird twisted shapes, cracked off my body, and plummeted to the ground like icicles falling off a roof. The cold Ice hissed as it came into contact with the hot embers and smoldering grass underfoot. I darted forward again.

Apparently impatient with his men's lack of progress, Grimes was now wrestling with Sophia himself. He didn't bother to look at me to see if I was still standing. He seemed confident enough in his magic to believe that one fiery burst was enough to toast me to ashes. Fool.

Grimes grabbed Sophia and rammed her head into the

side of the van. She kept fighting him, so he slammed her head into the metal again, hard enough to leave a dent behind. She collapsed on the driveway, unconscious. Grimes easily picked her up and tossed her into the back of the van.

"Stop!" I screamed, trying to distract him long enough for me to get to Sophia. "Stop!"

He glanced over his shoulder at me and frowned again, as though I were some bothersome bug he thought he'd already swatted away. He gestured at his men, and they moved from the driveway over to the edge of the lawn in front of the house. I headed toward Grimes, but his men put themselves in between the two of us, and I had no choice but to go through them to get to him.

So I tightened my grip on my knives and threw myself into the fight.

The men pulled out their weapons, but I didn't give them the chance to fire. I sliced one of my knives into the gun hand of the man on my right, then pivoted and did the same thing to the second man. They both grunted with pain and surprise, but they snapped their hands up, ready to beat me to death. I didn't care. I moved back and forth between them, whirling this way and that, cutting into the first man, then the second, until they resembled a couple of piñatas, only with blood and guts pouring out instead of candy.

I finally managed to cut down one of the men in front of me. The other followed a moment later, giving me a clear path to the van and Sophia trapped inside.

"Sophia!" I screamed, running toward the vehicle. "Sophia!"

Hazel threw the van into gear and whipped it into a U-turn right in the middle of Jo-Jo's lawn. The tires threw up grass and dirt, and the van fishtailed, but Hazel managed to get it under control. She gave me an evil grin before flooring it.

I dropped my knives and chased after the van, throwing myself forward, trying to use my speed and momentum to latch onto one of the rear door handles, but I just wasn't quick enough to catch the vehicle, and my fingers missed the handles by several inches.

I fell flat on my face instead.

My Stone magic softened the landing, but I still felt the jarring, bruising impact through my whole body. Still, I pushed the pain away, rolled forward, and surged back up onto my feet. I wasn't giving up yet—

But I was too late.

The van zoomed down the driveway, screeched through a hard right turn, and raced out of sight—taking my friend along with it.

☙ 5 ❧

I sucked down a breath and started running again. Maybe I could catch them before they got out of the subdivision—

"Gin!"

I pulled up short and whirled around. Bria stood on the front porch, covered with blood.

"It's Jo-Jo!" she screamed again. "Get in here! Quick!"

I looked over my shoulder. By this point, the van was gone. I couldn't catch Grimes and Hazel, and I couldn't save Sophia.

I couldn't save her.

"Gin!" Bria yelled again.

My heart burned with rage and guilt and shame, but there was nothing I could do about that right now. So I sucked in another breath, grabbed my knives from where they had fallen on the driveway, and ran back toward the house.

Once Bria realized that I was headed in her direction, she darted back inside. Dread tied my stomach into tight, aching knots, and I forced myself to move even faster. I leaped up onto the porch, raced down the hallway, and burst into the salon. Bria was already crouched down by Jo-Jo's side. Rosco was there too, his furry head resting in the dwarf's lap. He must have come back inside while I'd been chasing after Sophia. He let out a low, plaintive whine when he saw me, begging me to help the mistress he loved so much.

Jo-Jo was in the same spot as before, slumped against the wall, her head lolling to one side, her clear eyes open, blood all over her chest.

Fear, guilt, and grief roared to life inside my chest, bubbling up like lava about to erupt from a volcano. My knives slipped from my numb fingers and clattered to the floor. I bent over double from the cruel, searing pain, from the thought that Jo-Jo was gone, dead, murdered—that I'd failed her just like I had failed Fletcher when I hadn't been able to save him from being tortured to death inside the Pork Pit.

Then Jo-Jo slowly turned her head in my direction and looked up at me, her eyes bright and cloudy with pain, confusion, and fear—for her sister.

"Sophia . . ." Jo-Jo whispered, her voice faint and weak. "Grimes . . ."

Relief surged through me, so sharp, cold, and bitter-sweet that it took my breath away. My knees buckled, and I stumbled down onto the floor beside her.

"Don't you worry about that right now," I finally said in a rough, ragged tone. "Just try to relax."

I peered at Jo-Jo's wounds, and my relief vanished, replaced once more by that hot, churning wad of fear, guilt, and grief. Grimes had shot her twice, and he'd made both bullets count. Two ugly holes marred her flesh, close to her heart. Each one a kill shot. The only reason Jo-Jo was still alive was that she was a dwarf, and her dense muscles had kept the bullets from tearing into her heart. But she was losing blood with every shallow breath that she drew in, and it wouldn't be long until she ran out of it entirely.

Bria picked up a towel she'd grabbed from somewhere and pressed it against Jo-Jo's wounds, trying to stem the blood loss. I got back up onto my feet, stepped over the dead men, and started rummaging through all of the pink plastic tubs on the counter, knocking bottles of shampoo, tubes of lipstick, and bags of pink sponge curlers off the surface in my hurried, desperate frenzy to find something that would help Jo-Jo. Finally, my fingers closed over a small metal tin, with a puffy cloud rune painted on the top in white and outlined in a deep, vibrant blue.

I popped the lid off the tin and dropped down beside Jo-Jo again. "Here," I told Bria. "This will help."

She pulled the towel away from the wounds, picked up Rosco, and moved him out of the way. I grabbed one of my knives from the floor and used it to cut open Jo-Jo's dress so I could have better access to her injuries. Then I dipped my bloody fingers into the tin, which was full of a clear ointment that had a soft, soothing vanilla scent. I leaned forward and carefully smeared the substance all over Jo-Jo's chest, trying not to cause her any more pain than was absolutely necessary, but she still winced with every brush of my fingers against her skin.

Not only could Air elementals heal folks with their magic, but they could also imbue things like lotions, liquids, and creams with their power, as Jo-Jo had done to this tin of ointment. Now I was hoping that she'd put enough of her healing magic into the clear salve to help save her.

I held my breath as the ointment slowly soaked into her skin. It didn't pull the black, ragged edges of the gunshot holes back together, but it did slow and then finally stop the blood loss—for now. Jo-Jo's injuries were deep and serious, and it wouldn't be long before the Air magic in the ointment faded away and the wounds started to bleed once more, and that was if one of the bullets didn't continue its journey on into her heart in the meantime.

Once again, that hot, agonizing fear that I was going to lose her rose in me, but I ruthlessly squashed it, focusing on what we needed to do next to save her.

"We've got to get her to a healer, to another Air elemental," I said. "Right now."

"But who?" Bria asked.

Rosco eased back over to Jo-Jo's side and whined again, as if he was asking the same question.

Who indeed? Air elementals weren't all that rare, but they didn't exactly grow on trees either. Not to mention the fact that not every Air elemental used his or her power to heal. Some, like Sophia, used it to destroy, to rip apart skin and bones and sandblast molecules into nothingness. My heart clenched again at the thought of Sophia and what she could be experiencing at Grimes's hands right now, but I pushed those sick, guilty feelings away. First, I had to save Jo-Jo. Then I could go after Sophia and rain down all of my cold, cold wrath on Harley Grimes for what he'd done to the Deveraux sisters.

Jo-Jo coughed, as though she was trying to say something. I leaned closer so I could hear what she was telling me.

"Coop . . ." she finally whispered. ". . . er."

It took me a moment to put the syllables together. "Cooper?"

Jo-Jo's head lolled to one side, which I took as a *yes*.

Bria frowned. "Cooper? Cooper Stills? Do you think that he can heal her?"

Cooper was Jo-Jo's gentleman friend. Well, I suspected that they were a little more than friends, but that didn't matter right now. All that did was the fact that he had Air magic. Cooper was a blacksmith by trade, so I didn't know how good at healing he was. Still, I knew that he'd do his damnedest to save Jo-Jo any way he could.

At around five feet, Jo-Jo was tall for a dwarf, and she was heavy, because of her stocky physique. All of her thick, strong muscles had saved her from being immediately killed by Grimes's bullets, but they weren't doing her any favors now, because Bria and I didn't have the upper-body strength to move her as quickly as we needed to. All we could really do was carefully shuffle forward with her a few steps at a time—time that Jo-Jo didn't have.

Since Bria had Jo-Jo's shoulders and I had her ankles, I grimaced, thinking about how Finn and I had moved those giants' bodies a few days before behind the Pork Pit. And now here I was, doing the exact same thing to Jo-Jo.

It was one of the cruelest, sickest feelings of irony that I'd ever experienced.

And another thing that I was going to kill Harley Grimes for.

"We aren't getting anywhere like this," Bria finally said. "Put her down. I have an idea."

I bit my lip, wanting to scream at the delay, and she noticed my hesitation. Rosco let out another whine, mirroring my frustration.

"Trust me," she said.

I nodded, and we slowly lowered Jo-Jo to the blood-spattered floor. Once that was done, Bria moved in front of the dwarf, as though she was going to leave the salon and step out into the hallway, although she ended up crouching down beside Jo-Jo's bare feet. She put her hands flat on the floor, and the bluish white light of her magic leaked out from underneath her palms. A blast of power filled the salon and rolled outward through the entire house, and my own Ice magic stirred in response to the welcome, familiar feel of my sister's cold, frosty power. A second later, the light and the feel of her magic vanished.

"There," she said, getting to her feet. "Maybe this will help make it easier to move her."

I peered out into the hallway, which now resembled some sort of crystal cave. My sister had used her magic to coat the floor from the salon all the way to the front door with an inch of elemental Ice.

"We can drag her along the Ice easier and faster than we can carry her," Bria explained.

I grimaced again at the thought, but then I nodded. "You're right. It's not pretty, but I think it will work."

We moved back over to Jo-Jo, picked her up again, and shuffled forward until she was in the hallway. Then we put her down on the sheet of Ice. The cold crystals seared the bottoms of my bare feet, but I didn't care. All that mattered was saving Jo-Jo. Bria and I leaned down, each of us grabbing one of Jo-Jo's legs.

Then we pulled her across the Ice.

Bria had been right. With the slick surface, we were able to move farther and faster than if we'd still been trying to carry Jo-Jo. Rosco trotted along beside us, his black toenails digging into the Ice for traction.

We were still careful, though, trying not to jostle her any more than necessary. I hated doing this to Jo-Jo, dragging her along like she was just another body that I needed to dispose of, but we didn't have a choice, not if we wanted to get her to Cooper before it was too late.

Jo-Jo didn't utter a sound the whole time, although I knew how much pain she had to be in, not only from her wounds but also at the thought of what Grimes would do to Sophia. Instead, she fixed her gaze on the ceiling. The clouds that had been painted up there matched the white mist that filled her eyes.

But what made my stomach clench were the scarlet smears left behind on the Ice, like long, thin talons trying to tear into the crystals. I couldn't tell if the stains were from all of the blood that covered Jo-Jo's clothes or if her wounds had started bleeding again. It didn't much matter, since I couldn't do a damn thing about it either way.

Not one damn *thing*.

Jo-Jo wasn't going to die, I vowed. I wasn't going to *let* her. I'd already lost my mom; my older sister, Annabella;

and Fletcher. I wasn't going to lose Jo-Jo too. Not like this and not to a piece of scum as twisted, dirty, and rotten as Harley Grimes.

When we reached the end of the hallway, Bria bent down and sent another wave of Ice crystals rolling out in front of her, coating the front porch.

We had managed to tug Jo-Jo out onto the porch and started to pick her up again to carry her down the stairs when a car pulled up the driveway and stopped in front of the house. I tensed, thinking that maybe Grimes and Hazel had come back for their men, after all, or maybe even for Bria and me. But after a moment, I recognized the silver Audi and realized who it belonged to.

A woman opened the driver's-side door, got out, and stepped around the car. Like Bria and me, she was dressed down, in a black T-shirt, khaki shorts, and black strappy sandals, but the simple clothes only seemed to enhance the generous swell of her breasts, her toned legs, and all of the lush, lovely curves in between. She pushed her sunglasses up onto her head to hold back her black hair. The bright morning sun brought out the rich color of her toffee skin and eyes, further enhancing her beauty.

Roslyn Phillips gave us a happy wave and headed toward the porch, somehow not noticing the two dead men lying in the grass off to her left.

"What are y'all doing out here?" she called out. "I thought that y'all would be back in the salon where it was cool—"

What she did finally notice was the blood on Bria and me and the fact that Jo-Jo was lying on the porch between us. The smile slipped off her face, her eyes widened, and her mouth dropped open in surprise and growing horror.

"Gin?" Roslyn asked in a hesitant voice.

"Open your car door!" I yelled at her. "Now!"

Roslyn didn't ask any questions as she hurried around the car, yanked open the back passenger door, and pulled out the basket of vegetables that had been sitting there. Tomatoes, peppers, cucumbers, and more tumbled out of the container and rolled across the driveway. Once that was done, she ran over to the porch. Bria and I started to lean forward to grab Jo-Jo's shoulders and ankles again, but Roslyn waved us away.

"Don't worry," Roslyn said. "I've got her."

She crouched down and scooped up Jo-Jo like the dwarf didn't weigh any more than a small child. It was bizarre, seeing svelte Roslyn holding stocky Jo-Jo in her arms, but it wasn't entirely unexpected. Roslyn wasn't an elemental, not like Bria and I were, but she was something that was even better in this situation: a vampire.

My eyes narrowed. "You've been drinking Xavier's blood."

Like all vampires, Roslyn had to drink blood to live, but she got more than just vitamins and nutrients from it. Depending on whose blood she was chugging down, a vampire could absorb everything from an elemental's Fire magic to a dwarf's toughness from a frosty glass of O-negative. Even regular old human blood was enough to give most vamps enhanced senses and above-average strength. Since Xavier, Roslyn's significant other, was a giant, it only made sense that she was strong enough to pick up Jo-Jo.

Roslyn nodded. "Xavier says that my drinking his blood makes him feel better about me working at the club so late. He figures that if I have his strength, or at least a portion of it, then it's the next-best thing to him being there on nights when he's out working the police beat with Bria."

"Remind me to thank him for that," I murmured.

Roslyn quickly carried Jo-Jo over to her car and maneuvered her into the backseat, while Bria raced back inside the house. I climbed in beside Jo-Jo, and Rosco squeezed into the footwell, covering my bare feet with his warm, plump body. A few seconds later, Bria reappeared and slid into the front passenger seat, her arms full of towels.

"Where to?" Roslyn asked as she jumped into the driver's seat.

"Cooper Stills's place," I said. "Start heading north. I'll give you directions as we go along."

"You got it."

I took Jo-Jo's bloody hand in mine as Roslyn threw the car into gear, backed up, turned around, and zoomed down the long driveway.

✳ 6 ✳

While we raced toward Cooper's place, Bria passed me the towels that she'd grabbed from the salon. I used the cloth to keep steady pressure on Jo-Jo's wounds, which had started bleeding again, despite the healing ointment that I'd slathered on them.

"Who did this?" Roslyn asked, smoothly zooming her car around a sharp curve. "And why?"

Bria shook her head. "I don't know. We were in the salon, eating and talking, when these guys burst into the house. It looked like they'd followed Sophia there. They took her and shot Jo-Jo. Gin and I killed some of the men in the salon . . ." She looked over her shoulder at me.

"And I took out two more outside the house," I said, finishing the story. "But they still managed to get away with Sophia."

Roslyn eyed me in the rearview mirror. "Gin?"

"His name is Harley Grimes," I snarled. "And he's a fucking dead man."

I didn't say anything else, but Roslyn and Bria exchanged a glance. They had heard the vengeance in my voice, and they knew exactly what it meant.

At the sound of Grimes's name, Jo-Jo let out a low moan and weakly thrashed against me. I put a bloody hand on her forehead and smoothed back a few strands of her hair, trying to calm her down. Despite the violence that she'd suffered, her white-blond curls were still as perfect and springy as ever. So was her makeup, except for the drops of blood on her face.

"Shh," I said. "It's okay. Don't try to talk. We're on our way to Cooper's right now. He'll be able to heal you."

At least, that was my hope. The only thing I'd ever heard of Cooper doing with his magic was using it to help him build weapons, sculptures, and fountains in his blacksmith's forge. But he had Air magic, and he was Jo-Jo's best chance of making it through this alive.

Her *only* chance.

Jo-Jo let out another low moan, but the clouds that were still drifting through her eyes slowly parted, and she fixed her gaze on me.

"Gri . . . Grimes . . ." she whispered. "It was . . . him. He's finally . . . come back . . ."

I smoothed back another one of her many curls, this one stiff and matted with blood. "Shh. Don't worry. I remember what you told me about Grimes. I'm going to get you settled at Cooper's, and then I'm going to go get Sophia back, lickety-split. Believe me when I tell you that Grimes will wish that he'd stayed away."

"Prom . . . promise?" Jo-Jo rasped, her voice sounding eerily like Sophia's.

I bent down so she could see the cold determination in my wintry gray gaze. "Promise."

Jo-Jo nodded, and her eyes fluttered closed, as though that one simple word had solved all of her problems, including the bullets in her chest.

Roslyn steered around the curvy mountain roads with all the skill and speed of a race-car driver, and we made it to Cooper's faster than I thought we would. Good thing, since every minute, every second, counted for Jo-Jo—and Sophia too.

Roslyn turned off the road and eased the car onto a driveway, which was really little more than a bumpy dirt track that seemed to lead to nowhere in particular. Roslyn slowed down, crawling up the hill, but the car still rocked from side to side. I grabbed hold of Jo-Jo and tried to keep her from jostling around too much. Rosco whined at my feet. He didn't like the roller-coaster ride either.

Finally, Roslyn rounded a curve, and a large, sprawling house came into view. It was a beautiful structure, made out of smooth gray river rock and topped with a coal-black A-line roof. To my surprise, a car was parked in front of the house, a silver Audi that could have been a twin to the one we were riding in. It looked like Cooper had a visitor. Odd, given how far up in the mountains we were and how much the dwarf liked his privacy. But I didn't care who was here or what they saw, as long as Cooper managed to heal Jo-Jo.

Roslyn parked the car. As soon as the vehicle stopped, she, Bria, and I were in motion, opening our doors and pulling Jo-Jo out of the backseat as quickly and gently as we could. Bria and I passed Jo-Jo over to Roslyn, so the vamp could carry her toward the house.

"C'mon," I said. "Cooper will probably be around back. That's where his forge is."

Bria and I led the way, with Roslyn behind us, cradling Jo-Jo in her arms. Rosco trotted alongside the vampire, his stubby legs churning to keep up with her, staying as close to Jo-Jo as he could.

"Cooper!" I yelled. "Cooper! We need you!"

We rounded the corner of the house and stepped into the backyard. A series of wide, flat stones made out of the same gray river rock as the house had been set into the grass, forming a patio. A stone path wound from the patio over to a large forge, which was also made out of gray rock.

But the forge was dark and empty. Two men were sitting in wrought-iron chairs on the patio, drinking frosty glasses of sweet iced tea from the tall pitcher sitting on the glass-topped table between them. One of the men was tall and strong-looking, with piercing blue eyes and blond hair slicked back into a ponytail. He wore an expensive, impeccably tailored business suit that added to his sleek good looks. The other man was a dwarf, wearing a gray cotton work shirt and matching pants, both blackened here and there with the embers and ash that had shot up out of countless fires in his forge. His hair was a soft, shiny silver, shot through with patches of peppery black, while his eyes were an unusual rusty color.

Phillip Kincaid and Cooper Stills stared at us. Both men froze, their mouths open and glasses halfway to their lips.

"Gin?" Cooper finally said, lowering his iced tea to the table.

"Hello, Cooper," I said in a grim voice. "Jo-Jo needs your help."

Cooper led us through a den cluttered with tools, sketches, and bits of metal and into a kitchen. A long rectangular table divided the room in two. It too was covered in sketches, along with pencils, erasers, rulers, and several panes of blue, red, and green stained glass. Cooper darted forward, put his arm down, and shoved everything off the wooden surface and onto the floor at the far end. I winced at the clatters, crashes, and cracking glass, but the mess wasn't important right now—Jo-Jo was.

"Put her down here," he said.

Roslyn gently laid Jo-Jo down on the table and arranged her arms and legs so that she would be as comfortable as possible.

Jo-Jo stirred and opened her eyes. "Cooper?" she rasped.

He bent over so she could see him and clasped her hand in his. "I'm right here, doll. Don't you worry about anything now."

Jo-Jo nodded, and her eyes slid shut again. Cooper stared down at her another moment, then ran a hand through his hair, causing it to stand up as high as if he'd stuck his finger into a light socket. He let out a breath and went over to the sink to wash his hands. He quickly dried them off, then moved to stand beside Jo-Jo again. Cooper hesitated, then picked up her hand once more, smearing her blood right back onto his own clean fingers.

"What's wrong?" I asked.

"I don't . . . I don't know where to start," he admitted.

A hard fist of fear wrapped around my heart. If Cooper couldn't heal Jo-Jo, then she was *dead*. There wasn't time to find another Air elemental to heal her, not given how bad her wounds were and how much blood she'd already lost. But screaming at Cooper wouldn't help, so I swallowed my fear and frustration and forced myself to stay calm and focused.

"Have you ever done this before, used your magic to heal?"

Cooper shook his head. "Not exactly. I healed a few cuts and bruises for Eva, Owen, and Phillip when they were younger. But nothing . . . nothing like this."

He frowned. "Although . . . it's strange. Jo-Jo and I have been talking about our magic quite a bit lately. I've been telling her how I use my Air magic to help superheat the fire in my forge, making the flames burn as hot as they can for as long as possible so I can get better and quicker results when I'm working with various metals."

"And Jo-Jo?" Bria asked. "What has she told you?"

"Mostly about how she uses her magic to heal," Cooper answered. "I had a cut on my hand the other day, and she talked about her power while she used it to fix me right up."

Jo-Jo had said that she felt like something bad had been about to happen for weeks now. I wondered if that sense of dread included a suspicion that she might get hurt, if that was why she'd starting showing Cooper how she used her Air magic to heal.

"You can do it, Coop," Phillip said in a hearty, cheery voice, clapping him on the back. "I know you can."

He didn't add that Cooper simply *had* to figure out a way to make his magic work if Jo-Jo were to survive. We all knew that.

Some of the worry and uncertainty smoothed out of Cooper's lined features at the vote of confidence. He gave Phillip a grateful wink. Then he tightened his grip on Jo-Jo's hand and leaned forward.

"Well," Cooper murmured. "Here we go. Ready or not."

His eyes began to glow a bright copper as he reached for his Air magic.

I just hoped it would be enough.

☀ 7 ☀

Cooper's Air power surged through the kitchen, ruffling my hair and sliding across my bare arms before settling over Jo-Jo.

Even though his magic wasn't directed at me, it still felt like there were dozens of tiny invisible needles stabbing into my skin, and I gritted my teeth to keep from snarling at the uncomfortable sensation. Two elements always complemented each other, like Air and Fire, and two elements always opposed each other, like Fire and Ice. With Cooper's Air magic being the antithesis of my own Stone power, it simply felt wrong to me, the way that fingernails screeching down a chalkboard drove some folks plumb crazy. Bria grimaced too. She didn't like the sensation of Cooper's Air magic any more than I did.

For the longest time, all I was aware of were the uncomfortable pricks of Cooper's magic, the coppery glow of his eyes, and the steady *tick-tick-tick* of the clock on the wall. One after another, the minutes slipped by, but we were all frozen in place, not daring to move or even speak for fear of breaking Cooper's concentration.

I stood right behind the dwarf, while Bria and Roslyn were on the other side of the table next to the sink. Phillip leaned against a cabinet full of mismatched dishes in the corner, his arms crossed over his muscled chest, his jaw clenched so tightly that I could see the muscles standing out in his neck. Rosco lay at Phillip's feet, his blood-smeared head resting on one of Phillip's black leather wing tips.

Still, as I stared down at Jo-Jo, I couldn't help but think back to another place, another time, and another woman lying so very still . . .

The dwarf was totally weird.

That was the thought that kept running through my mind as Sophia closed down the Pork Pit for the night. Fletcher had left me in his restaurant an hour ago, saying that he had some business to take care of.

In other words, he had to go kill someone.

That's what Fletcher did as the assassin the Tin Man, and that's what he was going to teach me how to do too. I hadn't been staying with Fletcher long, just a couple of months, but he'd already showed me lots of ways to defend myself. He said that I was making good progress, mastering the basics. I didn't really think it was all that difficult. All you had to do was hit your enemy hard and long enough, and he'd eventually go down. All Fletcher was really teaching me to do was to find those weak spots and exploit them to the fullest.

I was disappointed that he'd had a job, especially since he'd promised me that he'd start showing me how to fight with weapons soon, including knives. That was what I was most interested in, since Fletcher used silverstone knives on most of his jobs, and I wanted to be just like him. I had been hoping that this was finally the night, but it hadn't turned out that way.

So here I was, sitting behind the counter, my schoolbooks spread out in front of me, even though I'd already finished my homework, watching Sophia mop the floor. The last customer had left thirty minutes ago, and Sophia had pulled out a radio that Fletcher kept in a slot under the cash register and flipped it on. The radio was tuned to some oldies station, and she swiveled her hips in time to the snappy, upbeat music as she pushed the wet mop across the faded blue and pink pig tracks on the floor and then underneath the matching vinyl booths in front of the windows.

Sophia was dressed completely in black, from her boots to her jeans to her long-sleeved T-shirt. Even her lipstick was black. The only bit of color on her was the grinning white pirate skull in the middle of her shirt, which featured crimson flames shooting out of its eye sockets.

Someone took the whole Goth look a little too seriously, if you asked me. Oh, yeah. She was totally weird.

"So," I said when the song ended and some boring commercials came on. "What do you and Jo-Jo like to do at night for fun? Cook? Watch TV? Play board games?"

Since Fletcher was out on a job, I was going home with Sophia and spending the night at Jo-Jo's house.

Sophia let out a soft snort at my question. I rolled my eyes. Okay, okay, so the dwarves were probably a little old for board games, but I was just trying to make conversation. It wasn't like I knew a lot about them, especially not Sophia.

Sure, she worked at the Pork Pit, but she never seemed to pay much attention to me, except to pick me up and move me out of her way whenever I got between her and the stoves. Literally, Sophia would put her hands under my armpits, hoist me up into the air, carry me around the counter, and plop me down on a stool, like I was some dumb kid who didn't know any better than to touch a hot stove or put my hand in the french fryer when the grease inside it was bubbling away. Whatever. I was thirteen, not a complete idiot.

"You don't talk much, do you?" I asked.

Sophia looked at me out of the corner of her eye, but she didn't even deign to answer me with so much as a grunt this time. She kept right on mopping as if I hadn't said a word.

I huffed, letting her know how much she annoyed me, but I gave up trying to talk to her. Instead, I cracked open the book of fairy tales that Fletcher had given me and started reading.

Twenty minutes later, I had finished the first two stories. Why did giants and witches always get such a raw deal? They were just defending themselves from bratty kids who wanted to steal their stuff and eat their property. If someone tried to swipe my golden goose or nosh on a piece of my gingerbread house, well, I'd unleash some of my wicked new self-defense moves on them and show them what was what. And so would everyone else in Ashland. Nobody took kindly to thieves in this city, especially not the folks over in Southtown.

Thinking about gingerbread houses made my stomach rumble, so I slid off my stool and went over to the cake stand sitting in the middle of the counter. I'd helped Fletcher make some sugar cookies earlier. There were only five left, and I knew that he wouldn't mind me eating them.

I lifted the glass top, set it aside, and grabbed one of the cookies. The sugary, buttery concoction melted on my tongue, bringing with it the sharp, sweet tang of the almond extract that added extra flavor to the dough. I sighed with contentment and reached for another one—

The bell over the front door chimed, signaling that we had a customer. I quickly chewed and swallowed the rest of my cookie, then wiped the crumbs off my hands, ready to tell the person that the restaurant was closed for the night.

But there was no need, since Jo-Jo stepped inside.

The dwarf was wearing a long pink coat, and her pearls peeked out from underneath the collar. Gloves the same cotton-candy color as her coat covered her hands, and a matching, fuzzy hat perched on top of her head, hiding most of her white-blond curls from sight.

At the sound of the door chime, Sophia came out of the bathroom, which she'd been cleaning. "Problem?" she rasped.

Jo-Jo shook her head. "I've got to go get Finn. The boy's at some party over in Southtown. Apparently, he decided to flirt with the girlfriend of the guy who brought him, and now he doesn't have a ride home."

Sophia snorted. *Me too.* With Finn, there was almost always some girl involved.

"Anyway, I thought I'd stop and see if you needed anything before I headed in that direction."

Sophia shook her head. Jo-Jo turned her clear gaze to me.

"What about you, Gin?" she asked. "I've got to swing by the grocery store on the way home. How about I get you some of that spearmint hard candy that you like so much, since you'll be spending the night with us?"

"Sure," I said in a soft, hesitant voice. "If it's not too much trouble."

"No trouble at all, darling."

Jo-Jo smiled at me, causing the laugh lines around her mouth to deepen and making her face look that much warmer and more inviting. I found myself grinning back at her. Jo-Jo was one of those folks you couldn't help but like.

Sophia, not so much. Especially since she was frowning at me—again. She probably didn't like Jo-Jo bringing me a treat. Then again, Sophia didn't seem to like anything about me.

Well, the feeling was definitely mutual.

"Actually, before I forget, Finn said that he left his coat in the back of the restaurant," Jo-Jo said. "He asked me to bring it to him. Gin, can you go get it for me, please?"

"Sure."

I pushed through the double doors and went into the back. It took me longer to find the coat than it should have, but then again, I didn't know why it was in one of the walk-in freezers to start with. Maybe Finn had been in there making out with one of the college-age waitresses. You'd think those girls were old enough to know better, but they all giggled whenever they saw Finn. I didn't know why.

I grabbed his coat, which was cold and crusted with ice, and headed toward the front of the restaurant—

"You don't approve of what Fletcher is doing with Gin," I heard Jo-Jo say.

I froze, my hand against one of the double doors. One good push, and it would swing wide open, and I could step into the storefront with the sisters. But instead, I found myself leaving it shut and peering through the small round window set into the top.

Jo-Jo and Sophia stood in the middle of the restaurant in

the same position as before. Even though I knew that I didn't have to hide from the dwarves, I remained perfectly still. An old habit from living on the streets and trying to make myself as invisible as possible to all of the big, bad people out there.

"Why don't you like the thought of him training her?" Jo-Jo asked, even though Sophia hadn't answered her first question yet. "He just wants to teach her how to defend herself. The way he taught you."

Silence.

"Too young," Sophia finally said in her eerie, broken voice. "Too innocent. Too soft."

Soft? Too soft? I seethed. I wasn't soft. Not anymore. Not since my family had been murdered, and especially not since I'd been living on the streets. I'd seen things, done things, that couldn't be unseen or undone. Like eating garbage on a regular basis, scrounging through Dumpsters for enough newspapers to stay warm at night, and running away from the vampire pimps so they wouldn't try to force me to be one of their girls. So if there was one thing that I was not, it was soft.

"Well, I guess we'll see," Jo-Jo said. "Now, where is Gin with Finn's jacket—"

"Right here," I said, finally pushing through the doors to the other side.

I handed Jo-Jo the coat.

"Thank you, darling. I'll see you two at home." Jo-Jo winked at me, then left.

I turned to Sophia, but she'd already disappeared back into the bathroom to finish cleaning. Of course she had. Anything would be better than having to talk to me.

I had started to go back over to the counter and eat

another cookie when the bell over the door chimed again. Jo-Jo must have forgotten something.

But it wasn't Jo-Jo. Instead, a skinny blond kid whose height suggested he was about my age hurried into the restaurant and ducked down behind one of the booths. He stayed like that for a few seconds before slowly rising, peering over the table, and staring through the windows and out into the street.

"Can I, uh, help you?" I asked.

He whirled around at the sound of my voice, and that's when I saw all the blood on him. His face looked like someone had taken a hammer to it. Every part of it from his chin to his cheeks to his forehead was bruised and puffy. Both of his lips were split open and dripping blood all over the floor that Sophia had just mopped. A pair of glasses clung to his nose, although the frames were bent out of shape, probably by whoever's fist had plowed into his face so many times. But perhaps worst of all, several red, angry burns dotted his neck, as though someone had lit a whole pack of cigarettes and then stubbed them out one by one on his skin there. More cigarette burns marred his thin arms, but those looked older, since they had already scarred over.

Sophia had heard the bell too and stepped into the storefront. She saw the kid and frowned. "Sorry. Closed—"

The kid whipped his head in her direction. Sophia blinked, as surprised by his battered face as I had been.

"Please don't kick me out!" he said, scrambling to his feet. "You gotta help me! They're after me!"

"Who?" she asked.

"Two giants," the kid said, his blue eyes wide and frightened behind his glasses. "All I did was pick their pockets while

they were smoking in the alley. I swear. And only because I needed some money for food. They only had, like, twenty bucks on them, but one of the giants chased and grabbed me anyway. He would have put my eyes out with his stupid cigarettes, if I hadn't kneed him in the balls and taken off. He didn't care about the money. Not really. He just wanted to hurt me. You know? They both did. Please, please, just let me hide in here a few minutes."

Sophia stared at the kid, taking in his bruised face, the blood dribbling down his chin, and the old tattered clothes that covered his body. Her gaze lingered on the burns on his neck. Her lips flattened out into a hard, thin line, and a spark of anger burned in her black eyes.

"Okay," she rasped.

He blinked. "Okay?"

She nodded. "You're safe here."

She reached out and gently put a hand on the kid's scrawny shoulder. He was so thin that his collarbone jutted up against the top of his ratty T-shirt. The kid flinched at Sophia's touch, and her mouth turned down, as though she was suddenly sad for some reason.

"Gin, get a cloth. Clean up."

I knew that it was for the kid, to wash the blood off his face, but I eyed the dwarf, wondering at the sudden change in her. I'd never seen Sophia go from being so gruff to so angry to so sad before, all in the matter of a minute.

But I went into the back, got a clean dishrag, and wet it with warm water. By the time I returned, Sophia had sat the kid down at one of the tables and had put the rest of the sugar cookies on a plate for him to eat, and he was gulping them down as fast as he could. Annoyance spurted through me, but he looked like he could use the calories more than I could, so I shrugged it off. Besides, I knew exactly what it felt like to be that hungry.

I handed Sophia the rag, and she managed to get the kid to stop eating cookies long enough for her to start wiping off his face. Once again, I stared at Sophia, amazed at how tender she was being and the care she took in dealing with him. She certainly wasn't that gentle with me whenever she picked me up and moved me out of her way. Then again, I didn't look like I'd just had my face run through the bottom of a blender either.

"More," she said a minute later, holding the rag out to me.

The kid used the lull to stuff another cookie into his mouth.

I rolled my eyes at her command, but I took the dirty rag, went into the back, exchanged it for a new, clean one, and soaked it with warm water. I had started to push through the double doors to step back out into the storefront when the bell over the front door chimed—and two giants burst into the restaurant.

"There he is!" one of the men screamed, stabbing his finger at the boy. "You dirty little thief!"

Sophia surged up onto her feet, stepping in front of the kid and trying to protect him, but the first giant was in a rage, and he rammed right into her, driving her all the way across the restaurant and back up against the counter.

I gasped, my hand strangling the warm rag that I was still holding.

The boy let out a frightened squeak. He got up to run, but the second giant snatched him by the back of his neck and drove a fist into his ribs. The boy dropped like a stone to the floor.

Sophia let out a bellow of rage at the sight. She snapped

first one fist, then the other, up into the giant's chin, driving him back. And she didn't stop there. She threw punch after punch at the giant, driving her fists, fingers, and even her elbows into his chest, throat, and groin.

My mouth fell open a little more at her quick, brutal, efficient assault. I knew that Sophia was strong—she was a dwarf, after all—but I had no idea that she was such a total badass too. I wondered if this was a result of the training that Jo-Jo said that Fletcher had given her.

Sophia threw another punch at the giant, but this time, he managed to catch her hand in his. He squeezed her fingers, and I heard her bones pop from the brutal pressure. Sophia grunted with pain, and the giant slammed his fist into her face. She staggered back, her legs going out from under her and her head snapping against the counter. She too fell to the floor, unconscious.

The giant loomed over her, but when a minute passed and she didn't stir, he glanced over his shoulder at his buddy.

"What do we do now, Mason?" he asked.

The giant who'd hit the boy, Mason, grinned back at him. "I say we see how much is in the cash register, grab everything we can from the back of the restaurant, and then dump their bodies outside on our way out the back door. What do you say, Zeke?"

The other giant returned his friend's evil grin with one of his own. "Sounds like a plan to me."

Mason grabbed the kid's leg and dragged him over to where Sophia lay, while Zeke went around the counter and started messing with the cash register.

I held my position behind the door and tried to think how I could stop them.

Because I was *going to stop them.*

Sure, Sophia might not be my favorite person, but she was Jo-Jo's sister, and Jo-Jo dearly loved her. Besides, I couldn't let the men kill her, much less a kid they'd already beaten and tortured, without trying to stop them. That would go against everything that Fletcher was teaching me about how to protect myself and especially the people that I cared about.

Through the door window, I risked another glance into the storefront, but the men were still busy with the cash register. My gaze kept going back to their massive fists. There was no way that I was a match for their strength. No, I needed a weapon if I had any chance of taking them down—I needed a knife.

I turned away from the door and ran back toward the storage room where Fletcher kept the extra vegetable knives, wondering if I could really do it, if I could really save Sophia, or if I'd end up being beaten to death along with her and the kid—

A soft *thunk* snapped me out of my memories.

One second, I was running through the restaurant on that night so long ago. The next, I was back in Cooper's kitchen, the stench of Jo-Jo's blood saturating the air like the foulest sort of perfume.

Cooper reached down and picked up something small and metal off the table. He held it up so we could all see the bloody bullet that he'd fished out of Jo-Jo's chest.

"One down," he murmured, setting it back down on the table. "One to go."

A few minutes later, another *thunk* sounded as Cooper used his magic to pull the second bullet out of Jo-Jo.

"Now comes the hard part," he muttered.

Cooper reached for even more of his Air magic, so much of it that a strong, steady breeze gusted through the kitchen, whipping up the sketches that he'd shoved onto the floor and whirling them around and around like a tornado. Cooper let go of Jo-Jo's hand and held his palm up over her chest, right above the two bullet holes, his hand and fingers glowing a rich, warm bronze.

Slowly, very, very slowly, he started moving his hand back and forth over the wounds. And slowly, very, very slowly, the ugly black holes in Jo-Jo's skin started to pucker up and draw in on themselves. Several minutes later, her injuries had sealed up completely.

If Jo-Jo had been healing someone, his or her skin would have smoothed out, as though that person had never been shot in the first place. But the marks on Jo-Jo's chest remained red and puffy, like two large, angry blisters on her skin. Cooper strained and strained with his magic, causing more and more Air currents to whip through the kitchen, but he couldn't get the wounds to fade out. Maybe he couldn't figure out how to do it, or maybe that level of finesse was simply beyond him.

Finally, Cooper let go of his magic.

"There," he said, letting out a breath and wiping a sheen of sweat off his forehead. "That's the best that I can do."

"Will she live?" I asked in a low voice.

He kept staring at her, exhaustion and uncertainty etching deep lines into his face. "I got the bullets out, but she lost a lot of blood, and there was a lot of damage inside her that I didn't know how to fix. That I was afraid to try to fix, in case I ended up making everything worse instead. So I don't know. I just . . . I don't know."

He stepped back and staggered as his feet went out from under him. He would have fallen to the floor if Phillip hadn't stepped forward and grabbed him. Roslyn hurried to take Cooper's other arm, and together they led him into the den so he could sit down and rest. He'd used up all of his Air magic, all of his great dwarven strength, trying to heal Jo-Jo—and it still might not have been enough to save her.

Bria moved over and gave my arm a sympathetic squeeze before following the others into the den, leaving me alone with Jo-Jo. Well, Rosco and me. The basset hound got to his feet, walked over, and plopped down beside the table, guarding his mistress once again. Normally, the dog spent most of his time snoozing in his basket in the salon, only deigning to get up for treats and tummy rubs. I couldn't ever remember seeing him this active. Then again, this was anything but an ordinary day.

In the den, the low murmur of voices sounded. No doubt Bria was filling Cooper and Phillip in on what had happened at the salon.

I carefully took Jo-Jo's hand in mine. Normally, she had the softest, warmest, gentlest hands of any person I knew, but right now, her skin was cool and clammy to the touch. Still, her breathing came easily enough, her chest rising and falling in a slow but steady rhythm. I slid my fingers down against her wrist, searching for her pulse. It too was slow but steady. The tight, tense pain that had pinched her brow had vanished, and her features were slack and relaxed.

I leaned down and put my mouth close to her ear. "You rest easy, sweetheart. Because now that you're safe,

I'm going to go get Sophia back—and put Harley Grimes in the ground for good."

I didn't know if Jo-Jo could hear me or not, but I'd made my promise to her, and I was going to keep it, no matter what.

But I couldn't do it standing around waiting for her to wake up. She wouldn't want that anyway. No, she'd want me to go after Sophia as soon as I could.

So I leaned down and kissed Jo-Jo's bloody cheek, then left her behind.

* 8 *

Rosco stayed in the kitchen with Jo-Jo while I headed into the den. Cooper was sprawled across a worn, sagging, brown-striped sofa that had seen better days. He must have run his hand through his hair again, because his salt-and-pepper locks were standing straight up over his forehead.

"She seems to be resting comfortably," I said. "Thank you."

Cooper nodded, and some of the tension eased out of his body, making him sink even deeper into the couch cushions. He cared about Jo-Jo too. We all did.

The patio door opened, and Roslyn stepped inside, holding a glass of iced tea. She must have poured it from the pitcher that had been left on the table outside. She handed the drink to Cooper, and he slugged it down in one long swallow. He set the glass on an end table next to his elbow and leaned back against the couch once more.

"Now what?" Phillip asked, standing in front of the TV.

"Now I go get Sophia back."

He nodded. "Bria said Harley Grimes and Jo-Jo know each other?"

"Yeah," I said. "He, Sophia, and Jo-Jo have a history together. If you could call it that."

"What sort of history?" Cooper asked.

"Grimes kidnapped Sophia years ago. He beat her, tortured her with his Fire magic—including ruining her voice—and then did a whole lot of other unspeakable things to her before Jo-Jo hired Fletcher to rescue Sophia. And when Fletcher did, he made sure that Grimes knew that if he ever bothered Sophia and Jo-Jo again, he would wish he hadn't."

"But Fletcher's dead," Bria pointed out.

"I know. Grimes must have found out about his death and figured that the coast was clear. That's why he came to the salon today, and that's why he took Sophia again."

No one spoke for a moment.

"I've heard of Grimes," Phillip said. "Lives up on some mountain above Ashland, along with a bunch of his men."

Phillip Kincaid was more than just a pretty face. He was also the owner of the *Delta Queen* riverboat casino and one of the major underworld bosses in town. So Phillip knew practically everyone who was involved in anything illegal in Ashland.

I fixed my gaze on him. "Tell me everything you know about Grimes."

He shrugged. "Not much. Just that he lives out in the woods in some sort of camp up on Bone Mountain. Grimes and his men sell guns in and around the city, hire themselves out as muscle, things like that. Someone also told me that they even make their own moonshine, get all liquored up on it, come roaring into Ashland every once in a while, and tear shit up, despite some halfhearted attempts by the police to stop them. Only Grimes doesn't run from the law so much as put bullets in anyone who gets too close to his camp and his operations."

Now that Phillip mentioned them, I realized that I'd heard some of the same stories about a moonshine-swilling, gun-running gang holed up on top of one of the mountains. I just hadn't realized that it was Grimes and his crew. The guns must have been the mysterious business that he'd been talking about earlier. The one that had been booming ever since I'd killed Mab. Yeah, I could imagine that a lot of underworld folks had bought a lot of guns in their efforts to kill one another these past few months.

Good to know, but I needed more information if I had any chance of rescuing Sophia, like exactly where this camp was. I had a feeling that I'd find all that info and more at Fletcher's house. The old man had kept files on everyone who was up to no good in Ashland, and Harley Grimes would have been sure to be at the top of Fletcher's watch list, given what he'd done to the Deveraux sisters all those years ago.

"Thanks for the info, Phillip. I appreciate it, but I'll take it from here."

I started toward the patio door, but Bria moved to block my path.

"What are you going to do now?" she asked.

I shrugged. "What I do best. Kill Grimes, Hazel, and everyone else who gets between me and Sophia."

Bria lifted her chin. "Fine. But I'm coming with you."

"No, you're not."

She slapped her hands on her hips in defiance. "Yes, I am—" Bria suddenly winced and dropped her hands to her stomach, as though she'd pulled a muscle.

My eyes narrowed. "What's wrong with you? Are you hurt?"

She grimaced, but she didn't answer me.

"Bria . . ."

She sighed and pulled up her T-shirt. A large, nasty, fist-shaped bruise blackened her side to the left of her belly button. "While you were chasing after Sophia, one of the guys in the salon hit me a few times before I put a couple of bullets in his chest. It's no big deal."

"Oh, no," I sniped. "Probably just some cracked ribs from the looks of that."

"I don't think they're cracked," she said in a defensive voice. "They weren't even bothering me until a few minutes ago."

"That's because the adrenaline hasn't completely worn off yet. Believe me, even if they're not cracked, they're still going to be plenty sore soon enough. Now, come over here, and sit down."

Bria grumbled, but she let me guide her over to a blue recliner in the corner and sank down onto it. She winced again. If that simple motion hurt, it wouldn't be long before her bruised body stiffened up more, and she wouldn't be able to do anything without feeling the pain of the fight.

"You're staying here," I said. "You're in no condition to fight, especially not against someone like Grimes."

Bria's face scrunched up with mulish determination, and she opened her mouth to argue, but I cut her off.

"Please?" I asked in a soft voice. "Sophia's already gone, and I almost lost Jo-Jo. I don't want to lose you too."

Her lips flattened out into a thin line, but she reluctantly nodded. That alone told me how much she was already hurting. "All right, all right," she said. "What do you want me to do?"

"Call Finn, and tell him what happened, then stay here and watch over Jo-Jo. I don't think that Grimes will come after her again, but I don't know that he won't either."

Bria nodded, and she squeezed my hand. "Just promise me that you'll be careful."

I squeezed back. "I promise."

"I'll stay too," Roslyn volunteered. "And I'll call Xavier and let him know what's going on."

"Thank you. And I need one more favor from you."

"Name it."

I looked at Roslyn. "Can I borrow your car?"

She reached into her shorts pocket, pulled out her keys, and tossed them over to me. "Only if you promise to ram it over the bastard who took Sophia."

I grinned. "Consider it done."

I didn't tell Roslyn that running over Harley Grimes with her car was too good, too quick, and far too merciful a death for him. Oh, no. I was going to give Mr. Grimes my personal brand of attention—Spider-style.

The others agreed to stay put, keep an eye on Jo-Jo, and hold down the fort in case Grimes or any of his men showed up at Cooper's. It was a long shot that they would, but I hadn't thought armed men would burst into the salon this morning either.

I headed outside, but I wasn't alone. Phillip followed me. He matched me stride for stride as I stepped off the patio and started around the house.

"What do you want, Phillip?"

"I want to go with you."

I stopped and gave him a flat look. "Not going to happen. Jo-Jo's not out of the woods, Cooper's exhausted, and Bria's injured. Someone needs to stay here and help Roslyn with them, and that someone is going to be you."

"And you need someone to watch your back," Phillip countered. "Look at you. You're a bloody mess right now. Hell, you don't even have any shoes on."

I glanced down, my toes curling into the soft grass. He was right. I'd been so focused on getting Jo-Jo out of the salon that I hadn't even stopped to grab my sandals on the way out. I shrugged and started walking again.

"What do you think you're going to do?" Phillip continued, moving with me. "Get a couple of knives, go up to Grimes's camp, and take him out?"

"That's *exactly* what I'm going to do," I said. "Except that I'm not going to be so nice as to merely kill him. No, after I get there, I plan on carving up Harley Grimes like a Thanksgiving turkey and leaving pieces of him all over the mountain for the buzzards to find. If they can stomach the likes of him."

Phillip didn't bat an eye at the cold promise of violence in my voice. "I can't say that I disapprove, but Grimes is a bad, bad guy, Gin. He's someone that even I would think twice about taking on. I didn't tell you half of the things I've heard about him."

"Like what?"

"Well, for starters, he's ruthless."

"And I'm not?"

Phillip ignored my snide comment. "Grimes kills anyone who tries to cut in on his gun-running market in the slightest way. Mab herself used to get weapons for her giants from him, and even she paid what Grimes asked for them. A couple of the Southtown gangs made moves against him in the past, but he killed them all—and their family members. Mothers, sisters, brothers, cousins." He hesitated. "Apparently, Grimes also fancies himself a ladies' man. And if he sees a lady he likes—"

"He takes her," I finished. "No matter who gets in his way. Yeah, I knew that already. I got a close-up view of Mr. Grimes doing that in the salon."

Sophia! Jo-Jo! Sophia! Jo-Jo!

The Deveraux sisters' screams echoed in my head, and the memory of Sophia hanging on to that doorframe, stretching one hand out to Jo-Jo, rose in my mind, blocking out everything else. I blinked, and the image vanished. But left in its place was my dark desire to end Harley Grimes's miserable existence. Once again, that cold, black rage pulsed through my body, beating along like an ominous song keeping time with my heart.

I rounded the front of the house, stalked over to Roslyn's car, and wrenched open the driver's-side door.

"Gin?"

I turned to face Phillip. Concern darkened his blue eyes, and his golden eyebrows were drawn together, as if he was still trying to think of some way to talk me out of this. His hands were curled into fists, and I got the distinct impression that he was considering tackling me to keep me from leaving. But nothing short of death would stop me, and if I had to hurt Phillip to make my point, well, I wouldn't like it, but I'd do it, the way I had done so many other terrible things over the years.

Phillip must have sensed my thoughts, because he made himself loosen his fists and step back, although his jaw was still clenched so tightly it made his chiseled cheekbones stand out like arrows pushing against his skin.

Phillip and I weren't friends, not exactly, but he was trying to look out for me in his own way. So I decided to put his mind at ease—so to speak.

"You're forgetting one thing, Phillip."

"And what's that?"

"Harley Grimes might be a bad, bad guy, but I happen to be a bad, bad bitch. And this bastard has hurt my family for the second time. He's not just going to pay for that—he's going to *die* for that. Believe me when I tell you that nothing you do or say is going to stop me from going up to his camp and killing anyone and anything that looks at me cross-eyed."

Phillip's lips pinched tight with frustration. "Well, if you won't let me go with you, at least let me call Owen."

"No. No way. Absolutely *not*. This doesn't have anything to do with him."

Phillip snorted. "You're involved in it, which means that he is too. He'll never forgive me if I let you go off and get yourself killed. He loves you, Gin. He always has, despite what happened with Salina."

What happened was that I'd killed Owen's ex-fiancée, Salina Dubois, even though he'd asked me not to. Of course, Salina had been trying to kill me and a whole bunch of other people at the time, but Owen had still had a hard time dealing with her death, especially since it had been at my hand. Needless to say, our relationship hadn't exactly been a bed of roses since then.

Still, Owen and I weren't as estranged as we had been. Since seeing each other at the Briartop museum, he'd come into the Pork Pit a few times to have lunch. We were still dancing around each other, though, still trying to figure out how or even if we could move forward. That was frustrating enough, but I didn't want Owen involved in this.

"Gin?" Phillip asked. "Did you hear what I said?"

"Owen and Salina have nothing to do with this," I snapped. "Jo-Jo and Sophia are my family, and nobody—*no damn body*—hurts my family. Ever. Even if they weren't my family, I wouldn't leave anyone to the likes of Harley Grimes. Not after what I saw him do this morning."

Phillip hesitated again, like he wanted to tell me something else, but I didn't let him.

"Look," I said. "The best thing that you can do for me right now is see to Cooper. Make sure that he's resting and getting his strength back. I don't know how well his magic worked on Jo-Jo, and he might need to try to heal her again. He knows that you believe in him. That will give him more confidence that he can save Jo-Jo if she takes a turn for the worse. And I'm also asking you to believe in *me*. Because I didn't earn my reputation as the Spider by chance."

"I know," Phillip said. "But you shouldn't have to do it alone."

I gave him a grim smile. "I appreciate the concern, but in the end, we're all alone—especially me."

"Just . . . be careful, okay, Gin? I don't fancy getting an ass-kicking from Owen over you."

"Why, Philly," I drawled, using Eva Grayson's childhood nickname for him. "It almost sounds like you care."

"About you?" He snorted again. "Never."

"Good to know. Now, if you'll excuse me, I have a date with the devil that just can't wait."

I got into Roslyn's car, pulled the door shut, and cranked the engine. Phillip waved at me, telling me good-bye or maybe even wishing me good luck. I waved back, then hit the accelerator and raced down the driveway.

⁂ 9 ⁂

I drove Roslyn's car back to Jo-Jo's house. I would have called Finn and told him what was going on, but I'd left my cell phone at the salon, along with my knives. The first time that I could remember forgetting my weapons and leaving them behind in years.

As the miles passed, I tried to remember everything that Jo-Jo had ever told me about Grimes. It wasn't much. He'd kidnapped Sophia, taken her to his camp, and done terrible things to her before Jo-Jo had hired Fletcher to rescue her. The old man had saved Sophia, and he and Grimes had fought to a standstill, but Fletcher hadn't been able to finish the job and kill him. Still, Grimes had kept his distance from the Deveraux sisters since then, on the threat of death from Fletcher. End of story.

I'd definitely have to swing by Fletcher's house and see what else I could dig up. Despite what I'd told Phillip, despite my rage and how painfully aware I was of how much Sophia was probably suffering this very second, I wasn't going to go rushing into Grimes's camp blind. No, I wanted to be as prepared as possible when I attacked him. I'd have to be, in order to get Sophia out of there alive.

I drove even faster than Roslyn had, so it didn't take me long to reach Jo-Jo's house. Despite the earlier gunshots and flashes of elemental violence, no police cars sat in the driveway. The house was on higher ground and set back from the road much farther than the others in the subdivision, so you'd really have to look to notice anything out of the ordinary. Besides, gunshots weren't uncommon in Ashland, not even out here in the 'burbs. When they did erupt, most folks hurried to lock their doors and grab their own weapons, rather than calling the cops, most of whom would take their sweet time responding.

From a distance, Jo-Jo's home looked the same as always. A three-story white plantation house perched on top of a hill, a grassy lawn spread out around it like the rippling skirt of an emerald dress. It was only when I got out of the car and walked closer that I could see the damage that Grimes, Hazel, and their men had done.

The front door, left wide open, had a muddy boot print planted in the middle of it, and a sheet of water from Bria's melted elemental Ice covered the hallway, soaking my bare toes. A long, splintered piece of wood floated in the water like the plank of a wrecked ship, the part of the doorway that Sophia had pulled off in her desperate attempt to stay with Jo-Jo.

The inside of the salon wasn't any better. The men Bria and I had killed lay where they had fallen, blood pooled under their bodies, their sightless eyes fixed on the ceiling. I went through their pockets, rifling through their wallets for clues about Grimes, but all I found were driver's licenses, credit cards, and a few crumpled bar receipts. Nothing useful. I threw the last wallet aside in disgust.

But the worst part wasn't the water or the bodies or the kicked-in door. No, the worst part was the blood that had splattered against one of the walls. Because I knew that it was Jo-Jo's blood, that I hadn't been able to protect her from this horror in her own home, that I'd stood by while she'd been shot and Sophia had been kidnapped. If I could have, I would have killed the men all over again for destroying Jo-Jo's salon. Because it was more than a business—it was a sanctuary. More than once, I'd shown up on Jo-Jo's front porch late at night, covered with blood and bruises. And every time—*every single time*— she'd welcomed me with open arms and healed me with no questions asked. More than that, she'd made me feel wanted, protected, loved. I'd always felt safe here—until today.

Harley Grimes would live just long enough to rue the moment he'd ever decided to come after the Deveraux sisters again.

My knives were still where I'd left them, two on the floor and three on the buffet table with all the food. The dark chocolate mousse pie, the fried chicken salad sandwiches, the chocolate-dipped fruit. All spoiled now and covered with hungry, humming flies that had invaded the house along with the heat. More sad reminders of how horribly wrong the day had gone.

I grabbed my knives, sliding one into its usual spot

against the small of my back before tucking the others into the pockets of my shorts. I glanced around, wondering if there was something that I'd overlooked, and I spotted a piece of paper on the floor next to Rosco's basket in the corner. I went over, picked up the paper, and unfolded it.

An image of Jo-Jo sitting on the steps at the Briartop museum stared back at me.

I recognized the photo as one that had run in the newspaper a few weeks ago, one of many that the media photographers had snapped after Clementine's botched heist that night. The rest of the story had been carefully cut away from the photo, along with the other people in it, leaving only the image of Jo-Jo behind. The paper had been folded into a small square, and the edges were soft and worn, as though Grimes had been carrying it around in his pocket for a while.

This must have been the thing that had finally fully reignited his interest in Sophia, even more so than Fletcher's death. The reason Jo-Jo had been shot.

My surprise quickly faded away, but a sick, sick feeling lingered in my stomach. Because Jo-Jo wouldn't have even been at the museum if not for me, if I hadn't asked her to come and heal Phillip after Clementine had shot him.

My fault—it was *my fault* that Grimes had come after the Deveraux sisters again. I'd put Jo-Jo in the spotlight without even meaning to, and now she and Sophia were paying the terrible price for it.

My fingers curled around the clipping, crushing the newspaper into a small, round wad. Not for the first time, I cursed Clementine Barker and then Jonah McAllister, who'd hired her in the first place. McAllister couldn't have possibly realized that this would be one of the consequences of his actions, but I knew that he would enjoy it all the same, should he ever learn of it. There were few things the weasely lawyer liked better than causing trouble for me and mine.

I let myself fume about McAllister for a moment before I tossed the wadded-up newspaper clipping aside. My eyes scanned the ruined salon a final time, but there was nothing else to see or do here, so I grabbed my sandals from the corner and slipped them on.

I'd just started to leave when my cell phone rang.

It was such a loud, jarring, unexpected sound that I whirled around, a knife in my hand, ready to kill whatever was making that noise. But after realizing that it was only my phone, which I'd left on the buffet table, I let it ring until it went to voice mail. I picked it up and had started to slip it into my pocket when it began ringing again. I had a sneaking suspicion who was calling and that he wouldn't give up until I answered.

"What?" I growled into the receiver.

"Finally!" Finn practically shrieked in my ear. "There you are! I've been calling and calling you!"

"Yeah, well, I've been a little busy, in case you haven't heard."

"I got off the phone with Bria a few minutes ago," Finn said. "Tell me what happened."

I quickly filled him in on everything that had happened. While I talked, I left the salon and walked down the hallway, my sandals sloshing through the puddles of water. I stepped out onto the front porch, stopping to shut the door behind me. At least, I tried to. Its hinges had come loose from the frame, and it wouldn't quite close all the way. Another thing that Grimes had broken—and something else that he was going to pay for.

When I finished, Finn was silent for a moment. Then he let loose with a very long, very loud, very imaginative string of curses that quickly devolved into a raging manifesto about how Grimes should be brutally tortured, stitched back together, and then tortured again for everything that he'd done to Jo-Jo and Sophia.

"Well," I drawled when Finn had finally calmed down enough to let me get a word in edgewise. "I second all that. In fact, I'm getting into the car right now to go make it happen."

"I'm up in Cypress Mountain meeting with a client, but I can leave right now and be down there in a few hours," Finn said. "Then we can go after Sophia together."

"There's no time. I need to get to her as soon as possible. There's no telling what Grimes will do to her."

I didn't tell him that it might already be too late. Finn knew that as well as I did.

"You can't go after Grimes alone," Finn said. "Who knows how many more men he has on that mountain of his? At the very least, you'll be outnumbered."

"I can, and I'm going to. I don't care how many fucking men he has. I'll kill every single one of them if that's what it takes; you should know that."

"I do know that. I also know that you're upset, but going up there on your own isn't a smart move," Finn said. "You know it too, deep down inside. You're just not thinking clearly right now because you're so angry."

Sophia! Jo-Jo! Sophia! Jo-Jo!

The sisters' screams echoed in my head again, and once more all the images, all the terrible memories, of the day overwhelmed me. Sophia stumbling into the salon, telling us to run. Jo-Jo stretching her hand out toward her sister. Sophia hanging on to the doorframe with all her might. The coppery smears of Jo-Jo's blood on Bria's sheet of elemental Ice. The agony in her eyes at the thought of Sophia in Grimes's clutches. The cold touch of Jo-Jo's hand at Cooper's house.

Finn was right. I was angry. But I was determined too. And waiting simply wasn't an option, no matter how dangerous doing this alone was going to be.

"My thinking is crystal-clear," I snapped. "Save Sophia. Kill Grimes. It's pretty cut-and-dried. Save your breath, Finn."

"Gin, wait—"

I hung up on him. The phone started ringing a second later. No doubt, Finn thought that he could talk me out of it. He should have known better.

* 10 *

With my phone turned off and tossed onto the passenger seat of Roslyn's car, I left Jo-Jo's salon and drove over to Fletcher's house, my house now. I zoomed up the driveway, making the tires spit out gravel in every direction, crested the ridge, and parked.

The ramshackle structure looked a bit odd, since it featured a mishmash of white clapboard, brown brick, and gray stone, all topped off by a tin roof. But to me, it was simply home. To the right of the house, the yard stretched out before abruptly dropping off into a series of jagged cliffs. To the left, the woods formed a solid line of green, gray, and brown.

I got out of the car and headed for the front porch. Normally, I took a moment to reach out with my magic and listen to the stones around me, in case anyone had decided to lie in wait to ambush the Spider at home. But today I didn't even bother. If someone was out there, then today was the unluckiest day of his life, because the idiot would be my warm-up for Harley Grimes.

But as I opened the heavy black granite front door shot through with thick veins of silverstone, nothing seemed out of the ordinary in the chirping of the birds in the trees or the rustle of the rabbits in the underbrush. Good. I didn't want anything else to slow me down and keep me from reaching Sophia as quickly as possible.

I stepped inside, shut the door behind me, and headed straight for Fletcher's office. I hated delaying even a second, but I needed more information before I went after Grimes, and this was the one place I was sure I could get it.

A large maple tree shaded this part of the house, and even with the day's sun, Fletcher's office was dark enough that I had to turn the lights on to see what I was doing. The room was a mess, with papers, pens, and folders stacked everywhere, from the desk in the back to the bookcases standing against the walls to the file cabinets that squatted on either side of the door. But there had been a method to Fletcher's madness, and I'd slowly been figuring out his system.

In fact, I'd been spending more and more time in his office over the past few weeks, trying to track down the mysterious M. M. Monroe, the long-lost relative that Mab's will had listed as heir to all of her earthly possessions. I hadn't had any luck so far, but going through the files had finally nudged me into straightening up the old man's office. At least a little bit. I left most of his things where Fletcher had kept them, though. In a way, it made me feel like he was still here, still guiding me, even though he'd been dead since last fall.

I hadn't run across any information about Grimes, Hazel, and their men, but there had to be *something* here. Fletcher and Grimes had almost killed each other over Sophia, and the old man had made Grimes stay away on his mountain ever since then. Plus, Fletcher had liked to keep tabs on everyone who was up to no good in Ashland, and there was no way that he wouldn't have tracked Grimes through the years, especially if he thought that Grimes might be a threat to the Deveraux sisters again someday.

I started with the file cabinets beside the door, flipping through all of the folders inside. No file on Grimes. I moved over to the bookcases, rifling through the items on every shelf. No file. I went over to the desk, sorting through all the papers on the battered surface and then all the ones in the various drawers. Still no file.

Frustrated, I slammed the last drawer on the desk shut, then swiveled Fletcher's chair back and forth, making the wheels go *screech-screech-screech*. I studied every part of the office, wondering if there was anything that I'd missed, any possible place that Fletcher might have stashed some information on Grimes that I'd overlooked.

And that's when I noticed the sticker on one of the bookcases.

It was a small sticker, stuck on the bottom right corner of the case, a few feet away from the desk. Odd that Fletcher would put a sticker on the wood way down there where no one was likely to notice it. But what was odder still was the sticker itself: a couple of white scythes crossed over a red heart, all on a black background. It wasn't Fletcher's style at all . . .

But it was definitely Sophia's.

My heart quickening, I got down on my knees and ran my hands all over the bookcase, searching for a secret compartment, but there wasn't one. The case was just a case, solid wood from top to bottom. Puzzled, I rocked back on my heels, wondering where the file could be, since it wasn't actually sitting on one of the shelves.

Then I remembered something that Fletcher had always said: *Simpler is better.* I let out a laugh, leaned forward, and reached *under* the bookcase. A second later, my fingers closed around a folder, and I pulled it out into the light. Unlike the manila folders that Fletcher used for everything else, this one was black and simply had *Sophia* scrawled across the front in silver ink. I sat on the floor, leaned my back against the desk, and opened it.

Hello, Gin. If you are reading this, then I am dead, but Harley Grimes is not.

I recognized the old man's handwriting, and the distinctive flow and cadence of his words made it feel like he was sitting here right beside me, slowly, carefully, quietly reviewing the information with me.

If Harley Grimes has any sort of heart at all, then it is a heart of venom—cold, cruel, and delighting in the suffering of others. Sophia wasn't the first girl he took, and she certainly wasn't the last . . .

Fletcher went on to detail everything that Jo-Jo had told me. How Grimes had seen Sophia, wanted her, and kidnapped her. How Jo-Jo had reached out to Fletcher and hired him as the Tin Man to rescue Sophia. Fletcher's journey up Bone Mountain to where Grimes had his camp. The guerrilla tactics that he had used to pick off

Grimes's men one by one. And finally, his last battle with Grimes.

I had already killed Horace and Henry, Grimes's older brothers, and wounded Hazel, his younger sister, and I managed to trick Grimes himself into using up all of his Fire magic before I finally confronted him face-to-face.

We fought. He used his fists. I had my knives. It was a long, hard battle, but I was wearing him down and moving in for the kill when Hazel snuck up behind me and gutshot me with a pistol. I stabbed Grimes in the chest, but he ran away, and I knew that the wound wouldn't kill him—but that mine would if I didn't get to Jo-Jo in time.

So I left. I regret that. I should have stayed and finished the job, even if I would have died up there on the mountain with Grimes. At least then I would have known that Sophia and Jo-Jo were safe from him forever . . .

Fletcher went on to describe how he and Sophia had helped each other down the mountain and how they'd gotten back to his car and then over to Jo-Jo's house so she could heal them both. He also detailed some other skirmishes that he'd had with Grimes over the years, but by then, he'd had other things to think about—like me and Mab.

But the file contained other useful things, including a map of the mountain where Grimes made his home and detailed sketches of the camp itself. Apparently, Fletcher had trekked up there every single year to see what Grimes was up to. His final trip had been in May of last year, several months before his death. That meant that the map and the sketches were more than a year old, but they would have to do. Besides, given the old-fashioned suit that I'd seen him wearing earlier and the fact that Fletcher's own maps didn't vary much year to year, Grimes didn't strike me as the kind to change a lot about his home or his operations.

Still, as I read through all the information, it almost seemed like there was something missing. Some gap in his narrative, some small piece of information that Fletcher had decided not to include, for whatever reason. In certain places, it almost seemed as though someone else had to have been with Fletcher and Sophia on the mountain, helping them, for him to be able to do what he did. For the life of me, though, I couldn't imagine who it would have been or why the old man would have left that person's involvement out of the file. I couldn't puzzle it out, so I moved on.

Finally, I came to the last thing in the file, a letter addressed to me. With shaking hands, I unfolded the single sheet of paper.

Grimes won't let Sophia go a second time. And he doesn't deserve to live after what he's done to her and so many others over the years. Finish what I started. Kill him, Gin. For Sophia, for Jo-Jo—and for me too.
   Be careful.
   Love,
   Fletcher

Those were the last words in the file, and I traced my fingers over them. The paper was smooth, but touching it calmed some of my anger and worry and made me feel like Fletcher was watching over me.

"Consider it done," I murmured.

The old man didn't respond, of course, and the quiet of the house soaked up my whispered words, but I knew that he would have approved of what I was going to do. Like I had told Finn, my plan was simple.

Save Sophia. Kill Grimes. Stab to death anyone who got in my way.

I showered just long enough to wash the blood off me. Then I geared up for my rescue mission.

Black hiking boots with reinforced steel toes, dark blue jeans, a tight fitted red tank top under a long-sleeved dark green T-shirt. In a few minutes, I'd transformed myself from spending a summer day at the salon into tackling a dangerous job in the forest as the Spider. Despite the fact that it was ninety degrees outside, I also put on a gray vest lined with silverstone. I'd seen how well-armed and trigger-happy Grimes and his men were, and the magical metal in the vest would stop any bullets that came whistling in my direction, along with absorbing some of Grimes's and Hazel's Fire magic, should they get the chance to use it on me.

I also made sure that I had plenty of knives. One up each sleeve, one at the small of my back, one tucked into each boot. My usual five-point arsenal, which I supplemented by sticking a couple more knives into the various pockets on the front of my vest. I had a feeling that I'd need every single one of the weapons before this was all said and done.

When I was properly outfitted, I went downstairs to the den. It was a comfortable room and one that I spent a lot of time in, but I moved past the worn furniture and over to the fireplace. I reached up inside the chimney and pulled down a black backpack that I kept there in case of emergencies—like this one.

I unzipped the bag, which contained more knives, a couple of guns, silencers, and plenty of ammunition. Making sure that the weapons were in working order, I inventoried the other items inside. Climbing rope, some packets of dried food, a bottle of water, a few small tools, a hand-cranked flashlight, a pair of binoculars, waterproof matches, a couple of tins of Jo-Jo's healing ointment. Everything I should need to get up the mountain to Grimes's camp, rescue Sophia, and get back down again.

I threw Fletcher's folder of information into the top of the bag, then zipped it shut. I hefted the backpack onto my shoulder and started to leave the den, but a couple of sly wink-winks of silverstone caught my eye. I stopped and stared at the mantel above the fireplace.

A series of framed drawings were propped up there, the runes of my family, dead and alive. A snowflake and an ivy vine for my mom, Eira, and my older sister, Annabella. Bria's primrose rune. The neon pig sign outside the Pork Pit that I'd drawn in honor of Fletcher. A hammer, Owen's rune, representing strength, perseverance, and hard work.

The drawings were the same as always, but there were new additions on the mantel: two silverstone pendants, one snowflake and one ivy vine. My mother's and Annabella's runes. I'd draped the necklaces over their matching drawings, so that the two snowflakes and the two ivy vines were resting next to each other.

For years, I'd thought that the pendants had been lost forever, buried in the rubble of our mansion the night Mab had murdered my mother and Annabella. But Mab had had the runes the whole time, and they'd been on display at Briartop, along with all of the Fire elemental's other treasured possessions. At least, until Owen had swiped them from the museum and had given them to me, something that had touched me more than he knew. Probably more than anyone knew.

I reached out and touched first one rune necklace, then the other, my fingers trailing over the smooth, hard, cold metal. I'd already lost too many people I cared about. I wasn't losing Sophia too. No matter what I had to do, what I had to suffer through, or what I had to sacrifice to get her back.

I looked at all the drawings and the necklaces in turn, fixing the runes in my mind, letting them remind me of exactly who and what I was fighting—and killing—for.

Then I left the den and the symbols of my family behind.

I'd almost reached the front door of the house when the phone in the hallway started to ring. I thought about answering it but decided not to. It was probably Finn again, trying to talk me into waiting for him.

I glanced at the clock on the wall. More than two hours had passed since the men had stormed into the salon, and Grimes and Hazel were probably back up on their mountain by now, thinking that no one was coming after Sophia. I'd already spent enough time going to the salon and then coming home. Necessary trips, but every minute that ticked by was another one that Sophia spent with Grimes, another one that he could be torturing her.

So I walked right on by the ringing phone. It wasn't until I was outside and had stepped off the front porch that I realized that I wasn't alone. Another car sat in the driveway, with a man leaning against it: Owen Grayson.

Owen had on the same sort of clothes as mine—brown boots, brown pants, black T-shirt. His arms were crossed over his muscled chest, while the bright sun brought out the blue highlights in his thick black hair. He was as ruggedly handsome as ever. Or maybe I just thought so because I knew that he wasn't mine, not anymore. Not for weeks now. And he probably never would be again.

"Owen?" I asked, stopping short at the sight of him. "What are you doing here?"

Instead of answering me, he reached into his car and grabbed a black backpack that was eerily similar to mine. He shut the car door and walked toward me. A series of *clink-clank-clink-clank*s drifted over to me as whatever was in his bag shifted back and forth. The sounds of guns, knives, and other sharp bits of metal jostling together was as familiar to me as a lullaby—and much more comforting.

Owen stopped in front of me and hoisted the backpack onto his shoulder. His gaze met mine, his violet eyes dark, somber, and serious. "I'm here to help."

* 11 *

Words just . . . failed me.

For a moment, I was completely speechless. Of all the people who would offer to help me with something like this, I hadn't thought that Owen would be one of them. Not anymore. Not after I'd killed his first love. But here he was anyway, despite everything that had happened between us. And it felt . . . good. It felt . . . *right*.

"Phillip called and told me what happened," Owen said. "I tried to call you, but your phone kept going straight to voice mail, so I called Finn. He said that he was driving back to Ashland but that he wouldn't be here for a couple of hours and that you were determined to go after this guy Grimes immediately. So I came to help."

Anger sizzled in my chest, but I couldn't blame Phillip and Finn for their actions. Like Phillip had said, they were just trying to make sure that I didn't go off and get myself killed out in the middle of the woods. I would have done the same thing if they, Bria, or anyone else I cared about had been bound and determined to go after a dangerous criminal by herself. Well, actually, I probably would have hog-tied them and gone in their place.

Still, Owen and I . . . we weren't exactly together these days. Sure, I'd gotten him out of the vault and away from Clementine and her giants at the Briartop museum, but I didn't want him to think that he owed me anything for that, because he didn't. Not one damn thing. I would have gladly battled Clementine a thousand times for him, even now, after he'd broken my heart. Because that's what you did for the people you loved. You fought for them no matter what—and no matter how terribly they hurt you.

"You don't have to go with me," I said. "It's not your fight."

"Yes, it is," Owen replied. "I care about Jo-Jo and Sophia too. More important, I care about *you*, Gin. I know how much this has to be hurting you right now."

That was the one thing about Owen that continually surprised and scared me, just how well he could see past my usual indifferent mask and suss out my true, buried emotions.

Still, I kept that mask up and locked in place as I stared at him, trying to see if he really meant what he said. But his eyes were clear, his stance tall, his jaw tight and determined. He seemed like the Owen of old, before Salina had wreaked such havoc on us.

But there was something else lurking in his face, a wariness that I hadn't seen before. It almost seemed as if he was holding his breath and waiting for the other shoe to drop. As if I was about to say or do something that would injure him so greatly that he would never, ever recover from it. But I had no idea what that could possibly be.

"You don't owe me anything, if that's what this is about," I said, struggling not to show anything of what I was really feeling. "Not for what happened at Briartop and not for Salina either."

Owen did the last thing that I expected him to: he smiled. A great, big, beautiful smile that brightened his whole face. "I knew you were going to say that."

"Okay," I said, not quite sure what he was getting at. "But that doesn't make it any less true."

Owen nodded. Then he blew out a breath and raised his eyes to mine. "Look," he said. "I've been an idiot about a lot of things—a *lot* of things. You, me, and especially Salina and everything that happened with her. But I'm not being an idiot about this. Finn said that you told him that Sophia was injured. At the very least, you'll need some help getting her off the mountain. At the very worst, well, we both know how bad that could be. And we both know that this Harley Grimes isn't just going to let you leave with her."

"No. But then again, I didn't plan on asking his permission."

Owen's grin widened. "I didn't figure that you would."

His voice had taken on a sly, teasing tone, and I found myself grinning back at him, despite the seriousness of our discussion.

"What can I say? I am rather headstrong that way," I quipped.

"Headstrong is one way of putting it," he drawled. "Mule-headed stubborn is another."

"That sounds like something Jo-Jo would say."

The words slipped out before I could stop them, wiping the grin off my face and snuffing out the easy banter between Owen and me. A shadow enveloped me once more at the thought of Jo-Jo and how she was laid out on Cooper's kitchen table, still fighting for her life. Owen's smile vanished too, as if he shared in my dark thoughts. He probably did. No doubt Phillip had told him how much blood Jo-Jo had lost and how hard Cooper had had to work simply to stabilize her.

"Listen, I'm going with you whether you want me to or not," Owen finally said in a quiet, determined voice. "And not because of Salina or Briartop or anything like that."

"Then why?"

"Because I've spent too much time lately not having your back, and you need that today more than ever."

Our gazes locked, gray on violet, with so many emotions, so many memories, so many words spoken and unspoken ebbing and flowing between us. Once more, I looked at Owen—*really* looked at him—as if I could peer through his eyes and see all the deep, dark secrets of his heart and soul lurking underneath. Trying to determine if he really meant what he said. But his eyes remained clear, his stance stayed tall, and his jaw was as tight as it had been before. I didn't sense any hurt in him. No anger, no blame, no accusation of any kind. Just the quiet determination to stand by me through this, no matter how bad it was already and no matter how much worse we both knew it was going to get.

Still, I decided to give him one last chance to back out.

"I don't think that you understand what I'm going to do now," I said. "Because Harley Grimes is pure evil, and I'm going to have to be that way too in order to rescue Sophia. Violent. Vicious. Vindictive. With no quarter asked for and sure as hell none given. Not to Grimes, not to his men, not to anyone who gets in my way."

"I know," Owen replied in a quiet voice. "I know, and I don't care. Not anymore. You do what needs to be done to save Sophia. I'll be right there with you, every step of the way. No matter what. I promise."

His words touched me more than he knew. Because *this* was what I'd wanted him to say when everything had gone so horribly wrong with Salina. That he understood why I'd killed her even as he asked me not to. Because it simply had to be done before she hurt anyone else Owen cared about, including himself. By killing Salina, I'd been trying to protect Owen from, well, Owen. And more important, from being responsible for the death of someone he'd once loved.

I had carried that burden around every single day, ever since I hadn't been able to save Fletcher from being tortured to death inside the Pork Pit, so I knew how very heavy, how very *wearisome*, it was. Now it seemed like Owen wanted to return the favor by going with me into Harley Grimes's lion's den and helping Sophia and me however he could.

"Trust me on this, Gin," Owen said. "Please."

It was that soft, final *please* that did me in. Because I could see how hard he was trying and how much he meant what he said.

"All right," I said. "All right. You win. If you're so

bound and determined to go with me, then let's get moving. We have a long way to go before we reach Grimes's camp."

After another quiet moment, we both shouldered our gear again. Owen started to head back over to his car, but I shook my head and gestured for him to follow me to Roslyn's vehicle.

"This one already has blood all over the inside. No reason to mess up anyone else's ride today."

Owen opened the back door, stopping a moment to stare at stains forming all across the leather seats. He dropped his backpack onto the floorboard, on top of one of the bloody towels that I'd used on Jo-Jo's wounds. I put my bag down next to his, then slid into the driver's seat. A minute later, we were headed down the driveway.

As I drove, I told Owen everything that I knew and suspected about Grimes. While I talked, he leaned over into the backseat, unzipped my backpack, fished out Fletcher's file on Grimes, and started reading through it.

Owen frowned. "The name sounds familiar. Why do you think Grimes came after Sophia again after all these years?"

That newspaper clipping of Jo-Jo flashed through my mind. Guilt twisted my stomach, but I made myself shrug. "Probably for pure meanness. Fletcher took her away from him, and Grimes didn't like that. So he finally decided to do something about it. The coward just waited until after Fletcher was dead to make his move."

"Do you think that he knows about you?" Owen asked. "That Fletcher trained you?"

I thought of the way Grimes had so casually thrown

his Fire magic at me, then walked away, so sure in the knowledge that the flames would roast me where I stood.

"I don't think so. Otherwise, he would have brought more men, at the very least, and he wouldn't have left me alone with the ones he did bring."

Owen nodded his agreement, then hesitated. "I haven't said this yet, but I should have. I'm glad that you're all right, Gin."

I nodded, keeping my eyes on the road and my face blank, not letting him see how much his words meant to me, how much they would always mean to me.

I left the suburbs behind and wound my way up through Northtown, the rich, fancy, highfalutin part of Ashland, where the wealthy, social, and magical elite lived. We passed mansion after mansion, all with tasteful yards that were as lush and green as they could be, despite the scorching summer sun beating down on them. I drove fast, and we soon left the immaculate estates behind and started winding our way up through the mountains above Ashland.

Our route took us by Country Daze, an old-timey store owned by a friend of Fletcher's. Several cars were parked in the gravel lot that fronted the store. But that wasn't what caught my attention—the man standing by the stop sign did.

He was an older man, with a bit of wispy white hair that stood straight up as if in defiance of the wilting humidity of the day. Despite the heat, he wore brown boots, along with blue pants and a long-sleeved blue cotton work shirt, and his dark, burnished skin hinted at his Cherokee heritage. An old, weathered brown satchel sat at his feet.

But the most interesting thing about Warren T. Fox was the rifle that he had casually propped up on his shoulder, as though it was perfectly normal for him to be standing by the side of the road holding a gun. Well, this was Ashland. I would have been more surprised if he didn't have a weapon.

Warren peered at our car as it approached him. He must have spotted Owen and me, because he grabbed his bag, straightened up, and started walking in our direction, rifle and all.

"What is he doing?" I asked. "Has Finn made some pass at Violet that I don't know about, and Warren is finally going to shoot him for it?"

Violet was Warren's college-age granddaughter and the best friend of Eva Grayson, Owen's sister. Finn liked to flirt with Violet as much as he did with every other woman who crossed his path, despite his involvement with Bria.

Owen shifted in his seat. "After Finn called me, I made a few calls myself."

"To Warren? Why?"

"Because nobody knows these mountains better than he does," Owen said. "Warren's told me more than one story about his hiking and hunting adventures, and I thought that we could use his help finding Grimes's camp."

It was a smart idea, something that I should have thought of myself. Sure, I had Fletcher's maps of Grimes's camp, but there was nothing like firsthand knowledge. As much as I would have liked to tell Owen that we didn't need Warren, I couldn't. I didn't like putting Warren in danger, but Owen was right. If Warren knew the area around Grimes's mountain hideout, then that gave us an even better chance of finding and rescuing Sophia as quickly as possible. Besides, even I had no desire to tangle with an irate old coot like Warren T. Fox.

So I rolled down my window, slowed, and stopped in the middle of the road. Warren ambled over to my side of the car and leaned down so he could peer inside at us.

"I'm looking for a guide," I drawled. "Or maybe a hunting buddy, depending on your point of view. Know where I might find somebody like that?"

A grin creased his face, adding more layers of wrinkles to his features. "I think that I know just the fella for you, Gin." His smile vanished. "I only wish the circumstances were different."

"Me too, Warren. Me too."

I unlocked the car, and Warren opened the back door. He paused a moment, staring at all the blood staining the backseat, just like Owen had. Warren harrumphed, as if the sight offended him, or maybe it was because he knew that it was Jo-Jo's blood. But he got in anyway and shut the door behind him.

"How is Jo-Jo?" he asked in his high, thin, reedy voice.

"Hanging on—for now. I figure that having Sophia there when she wakes up will make all the difference."

He nodded. "That it will. So why don't you stop lolly-gagging in the middle of the road, and let's get on with it."

"Why, Warren," I drawled again. "I thought you'd never ask."

I put the car back into gear, eased forward, and made a turn at the stop sign, going even deeper into the mountains and drawing that much closer to Grimes's camp— and Sophia.

❖ 12 ❖

Once again, I recapped the morning's events at the salon. Warren listened to my story, nodding his head here and there.

When I'd finished, I added, "Owen says that you like to go hiking and hunting up in the mountains and that you might know the area around Grimes's camp."

Warren's lips puckered, as though he'd bitten into a lemon. "It's more than just a *might know*. I've been there before."

My eyes shot up to the rearview mirror. Warren stared back at me, his mouth still twisted into that sour expression.

"When?" I asked.

"The last time Grimes took Sophia."

Suddenly, I realized what had been missing from Fletcher's writings on his battle with Grimes: that mysterious third person he'd tried so hard not to mention.

"You . . . *you* helped Fletcher rescue Sophia all those years ago? I thought that you and Fletcher had a falling out over a woman when you were young and that the two of you didn't speak after that."

Warren looked at me in the mirror another moment before he turned his head and stared out the window. "Well, that might be a bit of an exaggeration. Fletcher and I used to go hunting in the mountains together all the time when we were young. After he left and moved down into the city, I kept on going without him."

"So when Jo-Jo approached him about getting Sophia back, Fletcher needed you to guide him."

"Actually, Jo-Jo came into my store one day, covered in mud and crying up a storm. I'd never seen her before, so I asked her what was wrong, and we got to talking. She told me how Grimes had kidnapped Sophia and how she'd been out in the woods trying to find her sister with no luck." Warren cleared his throat. "So I told her about Fletcher being the Tin Man."

I could picture it all in my mind. Jo-Jo stumbling into Country Daze, Warren sitting down with her, Jo-Jo sobbing out her story, Warren realizing that she had a problem that only his former friend could solve—

The right tires hit a rumble strip on the side of the road, jolting me out of my musings. I turned the wheel, edging the car away from the dangerous curve. The road straightened out for several hundred feet, so I looked at Warren in the rearview mirror again.

"That was how the two of them met? Because of you?"

Warren nodded. His dark eyes met mine in the mirror again. "I knew that he could help her, that he was probably the *only* one who could help her. Even back then, Harley Grimes had a reputation for being an evil, vicious, crazy son of a bitch."

"Half giant, half dwarf, and all mean," I murmured, echoing what Jo-Jo had once told me about Grimes.

Warren nodded his agreement. "But I didn't think that Fletcher would ask for my help too. At first, I refused, but then Jo-Jo came back to the store and begged me to guide him up there. I couldn't turn her down then—or now."

"Thank you, Warren," I said in a soft voice. "For everything."

"Bah," he said, waving his hand. "Don't thank me until it's over, Sophia is back where she belongs, and that bastard Grimes is finally dead."

He stared out the window again, his eyes distant, his lips pinched together, the lines on his face grooved even deeper with old memories, old hurts, old heartaches. I wondered what Warren was seeing, what he was remembering, what he was feeling. If he was reliving the trip he'd taken with Fletcher so very long ago or if he was thinking ahead to the danger he was going to face for a second time.

Either way, there was nothing for me to do but keep on driving and hope that I could get us all back down the mountain again in one piece after we rescued Sophia.

Warren directed me to one of the many scenic overlooks on the narrow, curvy, switchback roads of this section of the Appalachian Mountains. Unlike the others that we'd passed, which were little more than gravel pits squeezed in between the road and the sheer edge of the mountain, this overlook was actually a park with a paved lot. I stopped Roslyn's car in front of a sign planted in the grass that read *Bone Mountain Nature Preserve.*

I stared through the windshield at the wooden sign and realized that maybe I wasn't as unfamiliar with the area as I'd thought.

"Is something wrong?" Owen asked, noticing me eyeing the sign.

I shook my head. "No, not wrong. But I've been here before. I should have remembered when I first heard the name. Fletcher brought me here years ago. Not to the park but to this mountain."

I didn't add that the old man had taken me out only to desert me on our hike, just to see if I had the strength and smarts to get back down the mountain on my own. One of the many tests he'd given me over the years. I wondered how much I'd be tested today. Didn't much matter. Like I'd told Finn and everyone else: Harley Grimes was a dead man. He just didn't know it yet.

"Gin?" Owen asked. "Are you okay?"

I shook my head to clear away the memories. "Yeah. Let's move. I want to get eyes on Sophia and Grimes's camp as soon as possible."

Owen, Warren, and I grabbed our gear, locked the car, and walked up a series of steep, narrow stone steps that led from the parking lot to the top of a ridge that curved and bulged out like a half-moon. A few blue and green fiberglass picnic tables perched in the grass, along with a couple of dented metal trash cans. A three-foot-high stone wall marked the edge of the grass and separated the tables from the steep drop below. The ridge offered a sweeping view of the cluster of mountains that surrounded us. Trees and rocks stretched out as far as the eye could see, like green and gray ribbons unspooling in every direction, crowned by the deep, vivid blue of the sky and the burning orange citrine jewel of the sun so very high above.

Roslyn's had been the only vehicle in the parking lot, and no one was eating lunch at the picnic tables, stretching their legs after being cooped up in the car, or walking their dog through the grass for a quick potty break. Good. I didn't want anyone to see us, especially with Owen and me looking like commandos out of some action movie, Warren our grizzled, rifle-toting sidekick. Besides, if someone saw us, there was always the chance that word would reach Grimes that we were coming.

Warren pointed to the right, and I realized that the park featured more than picnic tables and a pretty overlook. Several wooden signs shaped like arrows were stacked on top of one another where the grass gave way to the trees. Three faint paths started at the signs, then curved off in three different directions into the green and brown canopy of the forest beyond.

"The eastern trail leads to the next ridge over," Warren said. "That's where Grimes's camp is. From what I remember, Grimes and his men often use this little park as a meeting spot. Most folks in these parts know better than to stop here, day or night."

"Let me guess," I said. "Grimes and his men bring the guns, and other folks show up with suitcases full of cash."

Warren nodded. "Cash, gold, even diamonds on occasion. Fletcher told me that he found an old-fashioned safe and a stash of valuables in one of the outbuildings at

Grimes's camp. He said that he also saw some of Grimes's men burying metal boxes full of cash and guns in the woods all around the camp."

That didn't surprise me. A lot of folks in Ashland didn't trust banks—with good reason. Sometimes the people working for the financial institutions were even more crooked than the criminals who called the city home. Finn was a prime example of that, given his day job as an investment banker. He didn't swindle his clients, but he thoroughly enjoyed playing shell games and hoodwinking the government out of all of the tax money that his clients owed. And he was amazingly good at it; Finn could hide money better than a squirrel storing nuts for the winter.

And Grimes wasn't the only one with caches of money and weapons hidden here and there. I had stashes of cash, knives, clothes, and other supplies all over Ashland. Fletcher's house. Bria's house. Finn's apartment. Behind a freezer in the back of the Pork Pit. In Roslyn's office at her nightclub, Northern Aggression. In a bathroom vent in the English building at Ashland Community College, where I took so many classes. Even in a fireplace at Owen's mansion.

I glanced at Owen, who'd been quiet while Warren and I were talking. I hadn't thought much about the duffel bag that I'd left at his house a few months ago. But that had been back before Salina had come into our lives. I wondered if he still had my things or if he'd thrown them out.

The last notion made my heart twinge with pain, but I ignored it and focused on the signs and trails again. "C'mon. We need to get moving."

I slid my backpack onto my shoulders and headed for the eastern trail. Owen and Warren did the same with their gear, then fell into step behind me.

With myself in the lead, we walked a good distance in silence with only the sounds of the forest around us. The high, cheery *chirp-chirp-chirp* of the birds in the trees, the low, lazy drone of bees and other bugs, the sharp, crackling *rustle-rustle-rustle* of lizards, frogs, and other critters in the underbrush of dry leaves.

This was a pretty patch of woods, and if we'd been out on a summer hike, I would have taken my time and enjoyed the scenery. The dark brown soil of the forest floor gave way to the lush, vibrant green of the leaves, and the arching branches of the trees stretched high into the cloudless sky above. The thick canopy dappled the forest in shifting shadows, which provided some welcome relief from the July heat, although the humidity was as muggy and oppressive as ever. Despite the shade, sweat trickled down my neck and the small of my back, making my clothes stick to my skin like patches of soggy tape. I could have used my Ice magic to help cool myself, but I didn't want to waste my power like that. Not when I had a feeling that I'd need every ounce of my strength to go up against Grimes.

His combination of giant and dwarven blood made him tough enough, but add his Fire magic to that, and you had a truly dangerous enemy. Not to mention the fact that Hazel had the same sort of strength and Fire power that her brother did and how much malicious glee she took in using her magic to hurt other people.

But what worried me the most was Sophia. She'd been shot at least twice before she'd stumbled into the salon and then was burned with Hazel's Fire when she'd been dragged away. I didn't know how many more injuries Hazel and Grimes might have inflicted on her in the meantime or how much blood she might have lost.

So there was a very real chance that Sophia wouldn't be well enough to leave the mountain under her own power. Since she had an even more muscular body than Jo-Jo's, she weighed more and would be even harder to move. But if we had to carry her all the way down the mountain, so be it.

After about half an hour of following the trail, the three of us stopped. We all chugged down some bottled water, and then I drew out the maps of the area that had been in Fletcher's file and showed them to Warren and Owen.

Warren tapped his finger on one of the maps, then pointed up ahead. "The edge of Grimes's property, at least what he likes to think of as his property, starts about another two miles up the trail, beyond that next big curve."

I eyed the sharp bend, where the trail made a hard right and disappeared behind a thick stand of oaks. "Will he have guards posted around the perimeter?"

Warren tapped another spot on the map. "Not way down here but definitely farther up the trail. There's another path, well, more like a deer track, that runs parallel to the main trail. We can follow that. It leads to a ridge that overlooks Grimes's entire camp. We can get our bearings there and decide where to go to next."

And see whether Sophia is even still alive.

He didn't say the words, but we all knew that it was a possibility, that Sophia might already be dead. That maybe all Grimes had wanted was to kidnap her so he could torture her to death.

Owen must have seen the worry in my face, because he gave my arm a gentle squeeze. "We'll find her, and we'll get her out of there. Jo-Jo can fix the rest. That's what you always say, right?"

"Right."

I echoed the word back to him, but my voice sounded faint and hollow, even to me. Because there were some wounds, some hurts, some sorrows that even Jo-Jo's Air magic simply couldn't fix, and Sophia had them, She had ever since the first time Grimes had taken her. Her raspy, broken voice, the sadness that glimmered in her black eyes, the way she sometimes tensed up when a new customer entered the Pork Pit. And now her worst nightmare, her deepest, darkest fear, had come to life and was happening to her all over again. Sophia had barely survived what Grimes had done to her the first time. I didn't know what—if anything—would be left of her after this new round of horrors.

"Gin?" Owen asked in a soft voice.

"C'mon. Let's find this trail of Warren's. The sooner we set eyes on Sophia, the sooner we can rescue her."

Owen gave my arm another squeeze. Then he grabbed his backpack, while Warren hoisted his rifle onto his shoulder again. Together, the three of us started back up the trail.

We'd only gone about fifty feet when a man rounded the bend in front of us.

He wore brown boots and pants, a short-sleeved white button-up shirt, and an old-fashioned brown fedora that was an exact match for the ones that Grimes's men had on when they'd swarmed into Jo-Jo's salon. He also had the same sort of large, old-fashioned revolver strapped to his side as they had. All of that marked him as one of Grimes's men—and as good as dead.

The man spotted us at the same time as we saw him, and he stopped in his tracks in the middle of the trail. His eyes widened in surprise, and his hand dropped to the gun on his belt. The man's fingers curled around the hilt of his revolver, but he didn't immediately yank it out and start shooting at us.

His first mistake—and his last.

❉ 13 ❉

Instead of palming a knife, surging forward, and killing the man where he stood, I held my hands out to my sides, gave him a bright, friendly smile, and slowly ambled toward him.

"Oh, thank goodness! *Finally*, we see another hiker out here in the middle of nowhere. Can you help us? Because my friends and I, we are *totally* lost."

I jerked my thumb over my shoulder at Owen and Warren. All the while, though, I kept moving closer and closer to the man. He kept his eyes trained on me, his suspicious gaze flicking over my clothes, as if he was wondering why I was wearing jeans and long sleeves when it was ninety degrees out, but he still didn't make a move to draw his gun. Even if he did, it wouldn't much matter. The silverstone in my vest would catch any bullets he sent flying my way.

I drew even nearer to him. The guy must have decided

that I wasn't all that much of a threat—long dark clothes notwithstanding—because he cocked his head and leaned to the side, trying to get a better look at Owen and Warren on the trail behind me.

He frowned, and then his eyes bulged again. He must have spotted Warren's rifle and finally realized that we weren't lost hikers after all.

But it was already too late.

Even as the guy fumbled for his gun, I stepped forward and slammed my fist into his face. His head snapped back, and I sucker-punched him in the gut. I followed up those first two blows with hard, brutal jabs to his chest, stomach, and groin.

After the last few hours of worrying about my family, driving all over Ashland, and gathering supplies and intel, it felt good to finally *act*, to finally *do* something that would actually get me closer to rescuing Sophia.

So I kept hitting him, over and over again, driving my fists into his body with quick, precise, debilitating strikes. He was listing from side to side and about to topple over when I finally grabbed his arm, turned my body to his, and flipped him over my shoulder and onto the ground.

He rocked back and forth on the trail, coughing, sputtering, and trying to suck down as much oxygen as he could, since I'd pummeled all of the air out of his lungs. I had a knife out and up against his throat before he knew what was happening or could even think about reaching for his gun again.

He froze, his mouth gaping like a fish's as he stared up at me.

"If you make one sound, one fucking *sound*, I will slit

your throat and leave your miserable carcass out here for the crows to pick over," I snarled.

He snorted, like he didn't believe that I'd actually make good on my threat, so I nicked him with my knife. He hissed with pain and surprise, so I cut him again, a little deeper this time.

"What did I say about making a sound?"

The guy finally realized that I was as mean, heartless, and crazy as I claimed to be and swallowed down the scream that was rising in his throat. Pain filled his hazel eyes, along with fear. Good. That would make this easier.

"Gin?" Warren asked. "What are you doing?"

"There's some duct tape in my backpack," I said, not really answering his question. He'd figure it out soon enough. "Hand it to me, please."

Owen stepped forward and walked around me. A zipper sounded, and he reached into the bag, which was still on my back, and rifled through the items inside. A moment later, he zipped the bag back up and handed me the duct tape. He didn't say a word the whole time. Good. I didn't want him to. I didn't want anything to distract me from what I had to do now.

I kept my eyes on the guy on the ground. "If you make one sound that I don't like, one small snort or grunt or fart, I will cut your throat quicker than you can blink."

The guy started to nod but thought better of it as my knife kissed his throat again. He swallowed, his Adam's apple scraping against the blade.

Warren kept his rifle trained on the man while I wrapped the tape around the guy's hands and ankles, trussing him up so he couldn't run away.

When the guy was secure and no longer a threat, Owen helped me haul him up and onto his feet. By this point, the guy was shooting daggers at me with his eyes, but I ignored his sullen glares. He had no idea how much more he was going to hate me before this was all said and done.

"As you've probably guessed by now, we are not hikers," I said. "We're here for the woman Grimes kidnapped this morning. We want her back, and you're going to help us with that."

The guy snorted again. I casually swiped my knife across his left arm. His mouth opened, and he started to yelp with pain, but I slowly waggled the bloody blade in front of his eyes.

"Not a *sound*. Remember?"

He winced, but he choked down his scream and slowly nodded.

I flipped the knife over, so that I was holding it by the blade, then held the weapon up where he could see it, along with the spider rune stamped into the hilt. "Now, tell me, have you ever heard of the Spider?"

The guy's gaze flicked over me again, taking in my dark clothes, his blood on my knife, and the cold, cold expression on my face. His eyes widened again, and he nodded much faster this time.

"Good. So I can assume that I don't have to bother explaining exactly who I am and what I do?"

Another nod, this one even quicker and more enthusiastic. Sometimes it was good to be notorious and feared.

"Well, this is your lucky day, because you get to see me in the flesh. More important, you get to be helpful. You *do* want to be helpful, don't you?"

By this point, the guy's head was snapping up and down faster than I could talk, and the rest of his body trembled in time to the rapid, jerky motions.

"Excellent. Because now we're all going to go for a little walk in the woods." I looked at Warren. "Where's this other trail you were talking about?"

He pointed to the west.

"Lead the way, then."

Warren nodded and stepped off the main trail and into the woods. Owen stopped long enough to pull a gun out of his backpack, then followed him. I slapped a piece of duct tape over my prisoner's mouth, so he wouldn't scream for his buddies and give away our position. Then I gestured toward the trees.

"Move."

The guy hesitated.

"Walk or die—your choice."

Maybe it was the threat of violence, or maybe it was the absolute chill in my eyes, but the guy swallowed, shuffled forward, and slowly fell into step behind Owen. I kept my knife out and ready to strike in case he got any stupid ideas, then headed into the forest after the others.

We left the main trail behind and walked due west for about twenty minutes. The landscape grew more rugged the farther we hiked, as the thick stands of trees and rich soil gave way to more high, open balds made out of layered sheets of limestone and other rock. I reached out with my magic, listening to the stones, but they only sleepily murmured of the blazing sun that was slowly baking them and the afternoon thunderstorms that whistled over the mountains, bringing a bit of cooling rain with them before quickly giving way to the hot, brutal sun once more.

I'd always enjoyed hiking with Fletcher in the mountains. It was a special treat, being surrounded by so much of my own element, these steep ridges, flat plateaus, and rocky landscapes that I felt such kinship with. I would have enjoyed this outing too, if not for the horrible circumstances that had brought me here.

Warren slowed, then finally stopped. He gestured to the top of the rock-strewn ridge that we'd been climbing up.

"Grimes's camp is about another hour beyond that crest," he said. "But we'll start running into the traps he has set up around the perimeter soon. Maybe even more guards. So I figured that you might want to stop and do whatever it is that you're going to do with that fella before we go any farther."

I looked at Warren, and he stared right back at me, his expression carefully devoid of emotion. He knew exactly what I was planning to do, and so did Owen, who also had a blank look on his face. The only one who wasn't clued in was Grimes's man. His head kept swiveling back and forth between us.

"Thank you for letting me know. You guys might want to take a walk for a few minutes."

Warren snorted and flapped his hand at me. "Bah, I've seen more blood and violence in my lifetime than you have, Gin. So don't try to coddle me."

"I'm staying too," Owen said in a quiet voice.

I stared at them both again, but their shoulders were

set, their mouths fixed in flat, determined lines. They knew what I was going to do now, what I had to do in order to have the best possible chance of saving Sophia.

"All right," I said. "But don't say that I didn't warn you."

I turned to my prisoner and ripped the duct tape off his mouth. The guy hissed with pain, but that was the only sound he made. He'd learned that much, at least.

"It's finally time for you to be useful," I drawled. "Tell me about Grimes's camp and what he did with the woman he kidnapped this morning, the one with the black hair and clothes."

The guy shook his head. "I'm not telling you a thing, not one damn thing."

"Sure you are," I replied in an easy voice. "Everyone talks eventually. Even me. The only question is how much it has to hurt first. And believe me when I tell you that I'm very, very good at inflicting massive amounts of pain on people in a very, very short amount of time."

He gave me a surly look. "You think I'm scared of you? Please. You couldn't possibly be the Spider. That ruthless bitch would have killed me the second she saw me. Not dragged me halfway up the mountain instead."

"You're right," I replied. "So maybe I should get on with things. Wouldn't want to disappoint my fans."

I slid my backpack off and set it on the rocks. Then I started rolling my shoulders and swinging my arms from side to side, limbering up for what was to come. I even did a couple of squats, just for kicks. Yeah, it was a show more than anything else, but sometimes a little show was all you needed to get someone to see things your way.

But the guy kept quiet through my warm-up routine, so I decided to up the ante by palming a second knife and turning toward him.

He let out a harsh laugh. "Oh, look, she has another knife. What do you think you're going to do with that, honey? Cut me up a steak for dinner?"

I kicked the guy's right knee out from under him, and he landed awkwardly on his ass on the rocks. Before he could yell with pain, I slammed my boot into his ribs, driving the air out of his lungs again.

And I didn't stop there.

Again and again, I kicked him in the ribs, chest, and stomach, until he got the message. He groaned and rocked from side to side, trying to find some position where his body wouldn't ache, but there wasn't one. I'd made sure of that.

When his moans finally died down, I straddled him and crossed my blades over his throat. "Now, sugar, I'll show you *exactly* what I intend to do with my knives—unless you start talking."

The guy glared at me, still defiant. "Go to hell. You won't get anything out of me. I'm more scared of what Mr. Grimes will do to me than some bitch with a couple of knives."

"Your mistake, sugar."

"Why is that?"

I leaned down so he could see exactly how cold and empty my eyes were. "Because Mr. Grimes isn't here right now—but I am."

Before he could protest, I slapped the piece of duct tape back over his mouth.

And then I started cutting him.

I used small, shallow cuts at first. A nick here, a thin slice there. Little more than paper cuts, really. But the longer I worked on him, the deeper I went, slowly sawing into his neck, his arms, and the thick muscles of his chest.

I didn't particularly enjoy torturing people. In fact, it went against everything that Fletcher had ever taught me about being an assassin. No kids, no pets, no torture. But Sophia's life was at stake, and there was nothing that would keep me from rescuing her, not even Fletcher's killer code of honor.

Owen and Warren stood a few feet away, watching the whole thing. Every slice I made, every bit of blood that spurted out of the guy's wounds, every muffled scream he let out through the tape over his mouth as I dug my blades deeper and deeper into his tender flesh. They didn't say a word, and they didn't try to interfere. Even if they'd wanted to, Owen and Warren couldn't have stopped me. Not from doing whatever it took to save Sophia. Not even from this.

The guy writhed on the ground, trying to buck me off, but I dug my knees into his chest and used my weight to hold him in place.

And then I cut him some more.

It went on for about three minutes before the guy started shaking his head up and down, as though he was trying to scream, *Yes! Yes! Yes! I'm ready to talk!*

I rocked back onto my heels and coldly considered him. "I'm going to take the tape off your mouth now. You'd better be ready to tell me everything I want to know. Because if this is a trick and you even *think* about screaming, then I'll bury my knife so deep in your throat that you won't let out so much as a whistle before you die. Understand?"

The guy furiously nodded again, his head moving even faster than before.

I leaned forward and yanked the tape off his mouth. "Now, where is the woman Grimes took? What does he plan on doing with her?"

"She's—she's at camp!" he sputtered. "It's about another hour away, just like the old man said!"

"Is she still alive?" I had to ask the question, even though my heart felt as hard and heavy as a brick in my chest, dreading the answer.

"Yes! Yes, she's still alive!" the guy said, the words tumbling out of his mouth one after another. "Grimes wants her for himself! He told the rest of us not to even think about touching her!"

I didn't have to ask him any more questions, because the guy started babbling all about Sophia, Grimes, and the camp. He told me everything that I wanted to know and a few things that I didn't. Apparently, in his free time, Grimes liked to go trolling through Ashland, especially around the community college. Once he saw a girl he liked, he grabbed her off the street, out of one of the parking lots, or even right off campus and brought her up to his mountain camp, and he didn't let her go until she died from the torture, rape, and abuse that he subjected her to. Occasionally, Grimes would get bored with a girl before he killed her, and he'd give her to the rest of his men as a reward for their loyal service. The girl always died real quick after that.

The whole thing made me sick, but it matched up with the information in Fletcher's file.

But what was especially revealing was that Grimes wasn't the only one in on the act. Hazel enjoyed torturing the girls even more than Grimes did, beating them, berating them, and using her Fire magic on them again and again for no real reason other than the fact that she could. Sometimes she was the one who would go trolling and bring back whatever young man caught her eye to meet the same sad fate as the kidnapped girls.

"How many men does Grimes have?" I asked. "Where are they stationed? What kind of weapons do they have? Do any of them have elemental magic?"

The guy hesitated, so I cut him again to encourage him to keep talking. After a few more slices with my knife, he sang like the proverbial canary.

According to my new best friend, Grimes currently had around three dozen men working for him—a mix of dwarves, giants, vampires, and humans, all armed with guns, knives, and whatever other weapons they could make or scrounge up. But Grimes and Hazel were the only ones with elemental magic. A few guards patrolled the camp perimeter, but Grimes counted on his ruthless reputation to keep most folks away, along with the booby traps that surrounded his camp.

Apparently, my guy was a relatively new recruit and had been sent down to do a sweep through the park and make sure that no one was hanging around who shouldn't have been and that no one had tracked Sophia to Bone Mountain.

"Grimes said that some woman tried to stop him," the guy babbled. "Some chick who got lucky and took out a couple of our guys. He said that once he had the dwarf under control, he was going to go back for the other chick—and that he was going to teach her a lesson that she wouldn't forget."

"Well, Grimes doesn't have to worry about finding me," I said. "Because I'm going to find him first. Anything else you want to add?"

The guy didn't say anything, so I casually twirled my knives in my hands to motivate him one final time.

"That's it! That's it!" he sputtered again. "That's all I know. I swear! I swear! I wouldn't lie, not to you." He stared at the knives in my hands—knives stained a bright, glossy crimson with his blood. He shuddered, but a desperate, hopeful light still flared in his eyes, despite what I'd done to him. "So . . . I was helpful, right? I mean, like, really, *really* helpful. I told you practically everything there is to know about Grimes and his operation."

"Oh, yeah. You sang your sweet little heart out for me."

I didn't add that it had been a foregone conclusion. Few people could resist more than a few minutes of torture, even me.

"So . . . you . . . you're going to let me live, right?" the guy asked.

Behind me, Owen and Warren remained still and silent. They hadn't said a word while I'd carved up and questioned the guy, and they didn't speak now. It wouldn't have done them—or him—any good. Because I had a promise to keep to Jo-Jo and Sophia—and Fletcher too.

"You said that you've been working for Grimes for, what, six months now?"

The guy nodded his head.

"Tell me," I asked. "Of all those poor women Grimes

has kidnapped and brought to his camp in the time that you've been there, exactly how many of them did you rape and torture along with the others?"

He winced, as though I'd caught him with his hand in a cookie jar instead of talking about the horrible brutalization of so many innocent victims. "Um . . . well . . . you see . . ." His voice trailed off, and he gave me a sheepish grin, followed by a shrug, as if to say that he was just one of the guys.

"Yeah," I said. "That's what I thought."

I plunged my knife into his heart. The guy opened his mouth to finally let out a good, long, loud scream, along with all the others he'd been holding back while I'd been cutting him. But I denied him even that much mercy. I ripped the blade out of his chest and sliced it across his throat before he could utter a single sound. He bled out quickly after that, which was a far more merciful death than what his vile gang had given all those young women and men.

When I was sure that he was dead, I wiped my knives off on his pants leg, then got to my feet. Warren and Owen stayed silent.

Warren finally turned to one side and spat on the rocks. "That's one of Grimes's men that we won't have to worry about getting between us and Sophia."

Well, I supposed that was one way of looking at things, instead of the cold, hard fact that I'd just tortured and killed a man. Warren nodded at me, then shouldered his rifle and satchel and started back up the ridge.

And finally, even though I dreaded it, I turned to face Owen.

I expected to see censure stamped all over his features, along with disgust, disapproval, and disappointment. But I didn't find any of those things. Instead, Owen stared right back at me, his violet gaze level and steady on my gray one. There was no judgment in his eyes, no wariness, no hurt or pain or anger.

Instead, he squared his shoulders and faced the truth of the situation head-on, just like I did. Because the other cold, hard fact was that Harley Grimes wasn't the only one who had a heart of venom. I did too.

Owen had just seen me at my most violent, my most vicious, my most vindictive, and he wasn't disgusted by my actions, and he wasn't turning away from me because of them. I wondered at the change in him. Maybe he only felt this way because this was some random stranger who lay dead at my feet and not someone he had loved.

Not Salina.

"Warren's right," Owen finally rumbled. "One down. And good riddance."

He nodded at me, then hefted his backpack onto his shoulder, turned, and headed after Warren.

If the situation had been different, if we'd had more time, I might have called out and asked him if he really meant what he'd said and what he really thought about everything that I'd done. But Sophia was waiting, and this was no time to be selfish and think about Owen and me and what was or wasn't happening between us. Not when Sophia was in so much danger and especially not when she could be in so much pain right now because of Grimes.

So I slid my knives back up my sleeves, grabbed my own bag, and followed Owen and Warren up the ridge.

❖ 14 ❖

We'd been hiking for about thirty minutes when we came across the first trap.

I only noticed it because the trap was emanating the faintest bit of magic. I was scanning the forest, a knife in my hand, on the lookout for Grimes's men. I took a step forward, and hot, invisible bubbles started popping against my skin.

"Stop," I said. "Nobody move."

Warren and Owen both froze in their tracks.

After a moment, Owen frowned. "Is that . . . Fire magic?"

Owen had an elemental talent for metal, which was an offshoot of my own Stone power, so he could sense magic just like I could.

"Yeah," I said. "I feel it too. Now, let's see if we can find out where it's coming from."

We peered into the woods around us, eyeing the trees, leaves, rocks, even the dirt under our feet.

"There," Warren said.

He pointed at a slender poplar about three feet ahead on the faint track we'd been following. It took me a few seconds to realize that a small rune had been scorched into the tree trunk a couple of inches off the ground, a small circle surrounded by several dozen wavy rays. A sunburst, the symbol for Fire.

Runes were more than fancy familial symbols or flashy business logos. Elementals could also imbue runes with their magic and get them to perform specific functions. Lots of folks used the sunburst symbol for magical trip wires and booby traps.

Warren got down on his hands and knees, laid his rifle and satchel aside, and carefully crawled forward. "What do we have here?"

He hooked his finger under something and gently pulled it up so Owen and I could see the thin, translucent fishing line that had been strung ankle-high between the poplar and another tree on the opposite side of the track. The left end of the line was wrapped around a wooden peg that had been driven into the ground, while the right end was merely taped to the tree, right on top of the sunburst rune. As soon as you walked through the fishing line, the tape would rip off the rune, and the sunburst would flare to life and explode with elemental Fire. Simple but effective.

Warren pulled out a pocket knife and carefully cut through the part of the line that was attached to the peg, disabling the trap.

"From what I remember, we'll run across more than a few of these. Best to clear a path now," he said. "While we're not being chased."

"Agreed," I said. "But let's also leave a few of them intact. We don't want Grimes's men realizing that all of the traps have been disarmed and that strangers are near the camp. They probably know where the traps are, but if we're lucky, they might forget about them in their haste to get to us. And wouldn't it just be a shame if they tripped them and got a face full of elemental Fire instead of us?"

"Sneaky." Warren's face creased into a devilish grin. "Fletcher would have done the exact same thing."

I grinned back at him. "I know."

Warren was right. We found several more traps after that. Most were set dozens, if not hundreds, of feet apart, but some were clustered together so tightly that if you tripped one, you'd set off three more in rapid succession. You wouldn't even realize what was happening until the multiple jets of elemental Fire hit you from all sides and scorched you to ashes on the spot. I had to admire Grimes's slyness, if nothing else.

But not all of the traps were magical. In fact, many were crude, simple devices. More fishing line strung ankle-high between two trees that would send a spiked club swinging in someone's direction. Snares hidden under piles of dry leaves that would haul you up into the air when you stepped into them. Even a six-foot-deep pit lined with sharp, pointed wooden stakes, complete with a body lying at the bottom of it.

At one time, the body had been a young woman, judging from her slender form and the pale purple dress she wore. She'd run right into the pit, which was hidden behind a bush, and had fallen stomach-first onto the stakes, one of which had driven all the way through her body and punched out her back. Like she was a piece of meat skewered on a kebab. Really, that's all she was now.

I didn't know how long she'd been dead, but the stench of rotting flesh wafted up out of the pit, turning even my stomach. The bright sun only intensified the putrid scent, making it shimmer up like sickening heat waves. Flies swarmed all over the woman, and bits of her flesh hung in tatters on her arms, where the crows and other carrion birds had picked and raked at her skin with their beaks and talons. Other animals had been nibbling on her too, judging from the bits of bone that peeked out here and there among the rest of her decomposing skin.

All around her, the rocks in the bottom of the pit alternated between shrieking with all of the terror, fear, and agony the girl had endured and chuckling with the sly, dark malice of the people—the monsters—who'd done this horrible thing to her. Both sounds made me sick to my stomach.

I wondered if she'd been one of the college girls Grimes had kidnapped, how long he'd tortured her, and if this grisly death was her reward for finally escaping him. Well, at least the poor thing wasn't suffering anymore—but I was going to make damn sure that Grimes did. For her and all the others he'd done this to.

Owen stared down at the body. "Eva has a shirt that same color. She had it on the other day when she went to class."

Warren and I didn't respond. We all knew that ours was a dark, dangerous, violent city, but this—what Grimes did to these girls—was cruel, even by Ashland standards.

Owen shook his head, as though that simple motion

would fling away his troubling thoughts and the horrible sight before us. He bent down and studied the ground around the trap. "There are a lot of boot prints here. We must be getting close to the camp."

"Close enough." Warren spat on the ground again. "Close enough."

There was nothing that we could do for the woman, so we left her where she was, staked at the bottom of the pit. Maybe when this was all over, I'd come back and give her a proper burial.

We walked for ten more minutes before Warren put a finger to his lips and crouched down on his knees. He held his rifle and satchel down by his side and slowly started moving forward. Owen and I tightened our grip on our own weapons and bags, stooped down, and followed him. The three of us crawled up to the top of a stone ridge, then got down on our bellies and slithered forward so that we could peer over the edge of the rocks.

Harley Grimes's camp lay below us.

This particular ridge dipped down into a steep, rocky hillside that ran for about two hundred feet before flattening and spreading out into a clearing in the middle of the forest. The camp looked to be about half a mile wide from west to east and also that deep from north to south before the trees took over again on the far side of the clearing.

A large rectangular building perched on the far west end of the camp, and the gray cinder block structure had the low, squat, utilitarian feel of a barracks. From what I remembered from Fletcher's file, that was where most of Grimes's men stayed, each one with his own little cot, like they were in the military instead of a vicious mountain gang. Another building to the right was made out of the same cinder blocks, although it was a much smaller square. Steam escaped from a couple of metal pipes set into the roof. I breathed in deeply, and a whiff of cooked meat and some sort of stewed vegetable drifted over to me. Grimes's version of a kitchen or mess hall.

My suspicions were confirmed a few seconds later when a couple of men pushed out of the double doors that fronted the building. Both were carrying tin cups and matching plates of food that they took over to some wooden tables that had been set up between the kitchen and the barracks. Like the rest of Grimes's men, they wore old-fashioned suits, and they took the time to remove their hats and shrug out of their jackets before they sat down to eat. Murmurs of their conversation drifted up the ridge, but the words were indistinguishable, so I examined the rest of the area, comparing it with the maps in Fletcher's file.

Not much seemed to have changed since the last time the old man had been up here to spy on Grimes. A couple more cinder block buildings dotted the landscape, some used to store the guns that Grimes ran, while others housed the cash, gold, and valuables that he took in exchange for them. At least a dozen men moved in and around the structures, chopping wood, hauling boxes here and there, and doing whatever other chores they'd been assigned. I even spotted two guys tinkering with a rusty old jalopy that had been parked to one side of the kitchen, as though they were trying to get the ancient car to rumble to life.

At the east end of camp was another, larger building made out of gray clapboard, with snakes of copper wiring peeking out from the sides and back like the quills on a porcupine. More steam drifted up from that area, and I breathed in again. This time, I got a whiff of something sour. No doubt that was the spot where Grimes and his men brewed up their mountain moonshine. It didn't surprise me that they made their own hooch. In fact, it seemed to fit in perfectly with Grimes's old-fashioned gangster mentality, and I was willing to bet that his homegrown moonshine was stout stuff, all the better to rile up his men when they went down into Ashland on one of their tears.

But it was the structure in the center of the camp, directly across from us, that held my attention, a three-story plantation house. Unlike the other plain, faceless structures, it was a beautiful building, with an elegant, airy design. The white paint gleamed like a pearl in the midday sun, while the glass windows glimmered like diamonds next to the black shutters. A porch wrapped around the front of the house, which was surrounded by a wide, grassy yard and a white picket fence. A variety of pink, red, and white roses twined through the fence slats, their delicate petals and thick green vines providing vivid splashes of summer color.

If it hadn't been for the plain, grim, depressing look of the rest of the camp, I would have thought the house was a beautiful mountain hideaway. But the more I stared at the structure, the more something about it bothered me, like I'd seen it somewhere before.

Three stories, plantation style, white paint, front porch. My stomach turned over at the wrongness of it . . .

"Is it just me, or does that house in the middle look like Jo-Jo's place?" Owen whispered.

"It's not just you," I replied in a low voice. "I wonder when Grimes built *that*."

According to Fletcher's maps, there had been a house in that spot the last time he'd been up here, but he'd sketched it as a much smaller structure, and he hadn't made any mention of it resembling Jo-Jo's. That wasn't the sort of thing that he would have overlooked.

"It certainly wasn't here the last time Fletcher and I were," Warren chimed in. "But that was some fifty years ago. It's definitely new—in fact, it doesn't look to me like it's more than a few months old. See how fresh the paint still looks? And how thin the yard is in places?"

"Do you think . . . do you think that he built it for Sophia?" Owen asked.

That was exactly what I thought, that Grimes's sick obsession with her had led him to do that very thing. I wondered how long he'd been planning to kidnap Sophia again and when he'd started construction on the house. If Warren was right, and the structure had only been finished for a few months, then Grimes must have started building it as soon as he heard that Fletcher had died back in the fall.

I kept scanning the clearing, fixing the locations of all the buildings in my mind and watching the men go about their chores. No one glanced up at the ridge, and no one realized that we were watching them. No doubt, they felt perfectly safe and secure in their mountain camp. Well, that was going to change—and soon.

I was about to tell the others to draw back down away from the edge of the ridge, when the front door of the plantation house opened. I put the maps away, then rustled around in my backpack, grabbed my pair of binoculars, and held them up to my eyes so I could get a better look at things.

Harley Grimes stepped out onto the front porch, then ambled down the steps and out into the yard. He'd traded in his gray suit for a fresh one in an off-white. A matching fedora with a black feather stuck in the brim topped his head, and I could see the shine of his black wing tips from all the way up here. Once again, he was dressed like some gangster straight out of the Prohibition era. According to Fletcher's file, that's when Grimes had grown up. Apparently, he enjoyed clinging to his youth. That, or he just liked his look to match his occupation.

The door opened again, and a woman stepped outside. She hesitated, then followed Grimes down the porch and out into the yard. I recognized her, but this person was the exact opposite of what I *knew* her to be.

She wore a short-sleeved white sundress patterned with tiny pink roses—instead of her usual black jeans and T-shirt.

A black ribbon was cinched around her waist, and black patent-leather heels gave her a few more inches of height—instead of her old, battered black boots.

Her black hair was pulled back into a high ponytail tied with a long white ribbon—instead of the colored streaks and glitter that usually highlighted her hair.

Pale pink lipstick covered her lips—instead of the darker, bolder colors that she normally wore.

Grimes held out his arm. The woman hesitated again, then stepped forward and took it.

Sophia.

❖ 15 ❖

I blinked and then blinked again, wondering if I was really seeing what I thought I was. But the picture didn't change, no matter how much I adjusted the focus on the binoculars or how hard I squinted through the lenses.

Sophia standing with Grimes, wearing a dress, dolled up like a gangster's moll from some old-fashioned mob movie. It was *bizarre* seeing her like this, looking so different and not at all like her usual dark, fierce, Goth self. It was wrong. Just . . . *wrong*.

After a few seconds, I lowered the binoculars and passed them over to Owen.

"Is that . . . Sophia?" he asked, peering through the lenses. "What's she doing? Why is she wearing a dress? And why isn't she trying to get away from him?"

"Look past them," Warren said, using the binoculars he'd pulled out of his own satchel. "There on the porch."

I'd been so shocked by Sophia's appearance that I

hadn't noticed that three men had also stepped out of the house behind her—and that they all had guns in their hands.

"No doubt, Grimes will have them shoot her, but not kill her, if she steps out of line," I said. "She's still injured, though. See how she's limping?"

Sophia favored her right leg with every step that she took, dragging her left one along behind her in an awkward shuffle. Her left arm also hung limply by her side, and one of her cheeks was red from where Grimes had slapped and burned her in the salon. I didn't see any blood on her, though, so Grimes must have at least bandaged her wounds. Well, that was something, although he was still going to suffer for everything that he'd done to her and Jo-Jo.

Owen handed me back the binoculars, and I focused in on Sophia again. Grimes squired her around the yard, dragging her over to the picket fence and pointing out the roses to her. Sophia hobbled along beside him as best she could. But through the binoculars, I could see exactly how cold, hard, and flat her expression was and the way her black eyes kept darting around, desperately looking for an escape.

But there was nowhere for her to go.

Even if she could have gotten away from Grimes, there was nothing but clear space all around her, which would make it all too easy for one of the men on the porch to step forward, take aim, and put a bullet in her back.

Still, she tried.

Sophia waited until Grimes turned his head, and then she brought up her good arm and punched him in the face, making his spiffy white hat fly off his head. She kept hold of him, spun him around, and hooked her arm around his throat, using Grimes as a shield between her and the guys with guns on the porch. She also plucked Grimes's revolver out of the holster on his belt, thumbed back the trigger, and held the weapon up to his head.

Sophia didn't say a word, but she didn't have to. Her meaning was crystal-clear. If any of the men followed her, she'd shoot Grimes in the head with his own gun. I thought she should go ahead and do that anyway.

Apparently, Sophia had the same idea, because she pulled the trigger.

Click.

Click. Click.

Click.

I could hear exactly how empty the revolver was all the way up here on the ridge.

"Really, Sophia," Grimes drawled, his voice drifting up to our location. "You didn't think that I'd keep a loaded gun anywhere you could get your hands on it, now, did you?"

Sophia growled and smashed the weapon into the side of his head. She shoved Grimes forward, then turned and ran away as fast as she could on her injured leg.

Sophia hadn't gone ten steps before a ball of elemental Fire streaked through the air and slammed into her back.

One second, Sophia was hobbling across the yard as quickly as possible. The next, she'd fallen to the ground, rolling around in the dirt and trying to smother the flames that scorched her skin.

Hazel walked out from around the side of the house,

where she must have been waiting for Sophia to make a break for it. She had swapped the red wrap dress that she'd had on in the salon that morning for a similar one in the same off-white as Grimes's suit. She stopped in the yard long enough to help Grimes get to his feet and retrieve his white hat. Then she walked over to Sophia, who was on her back on the ground. Hazel gave her an evil grin, then started kicking her.

Thwack.

Thwack. Thwack.

Thwack.

Over and over again, Hazel drove her foot into Sophia's body. Sophia grunted with every blow, but she didn't give Hazel the satisfaction of screaming. Still, every vicious kick that Hazel inflicted on her was like a knife slicing into my own heart.

"Warren," I asked between gritted teeth. "Please tell me that you can shoot that bitch from here."

He shook his head. "I could, but you know that will give away our position. The second I fire, Grimes will know that we're here, and it'll all be over."

"All right, then. I'll take care of it."

I started to get to my feet, but Owen grabbed my arm.

"Stop," he said. "Stop and think for a second. Warren's right. We need to hold on to the element of surprise as long as we can. Going down there right now is suicide. We all know it. Grimes's men will cut you down before you get halfway across the clearing. Or worse, they'll capture you along with Sophia."

"I know," I said, choking out the words. "But I can't stay here and do nothing. Not while they're hurting her—"

"Enough!" Harley Grimes's voice rang out through the clearing as he strode forward. "That's enough!"

Thwack.

Hazel gave Sophia one more hard, vicious, brutal kick, then reluctantly backed away.

I held my breath, waiting to see how badly injured Sophia was. But after a few seconds, she rolled over onto her right side, then slowly pushed herself up. It took her a few more seconds to stagger back up onto her feet. Dirt, leaves, and grass stained the skirt of her white dress, while the back was scorched from Hazel's elemental Fire. Her hair had come loose from its ponytail, and the white ribbon lay crumpled in the dust. Sophia shoved her black locks back off her face, leaving a bloody streak on her cheek on top of the burn that was already there, and fixed her cold gaze on Hazel.

"Wimp," she rasped. "That didn't even tickle."

Anger mottled Hazel's face, and she started forward, fists clenched, ready to hit Sophia some more. But Grimes held his arm out, stopping his sister.

"I said that's *enough*, Hazel."

She put her hands on her hips and glared down her nose at her brother. "You're not going to let her get away with this, are you?" Hazel demanded. "I *told* you that she would try something like this. She would have put a bullet in your head if she could have. You should just kill her. I've never understood your fascination with her. She's always been more trouble than she's worth."

"Sophia has always been high-spirited," Grimes said. "That's one of the qualities that I admire most about her."

Grimes moved forward. He held out a hand, as though

he was going to caress Sophia's cheek, but she jerked back out of his reach and curled her lips at him in disgust. Grimes regarded her for a moment, then slapped her across the face, just like he had in the salon. He was much stronger than Hazel, and the brutal blow sent Sophia spinning to the ground again.

"But you're right, sister," Grimes said in a calm, cold voice. "Sophia does need to be punished for her insolence, and I know exactly how to do it."

He gestured at the men still standing on the porch. They hurried into the clearing. Two of them grabbed Sophia's arms and hauled her to her feet, while the third kept his gun trained on her.

"Bring her," Grimes said.

He pivoted on his heel and strode off toward the east end of camp. The men forced Sophia to follow him, while Hazel brought up the rear.

I looked at Warren. "Do you know where they're taking her?"

He nodded, his face dark, grim, and troubled. "I have a good idea. And if I'm right, then it's the same wretched place that Fletcher and I rescued her from before."

Warren crawled away from the edge of the ridge, got to his feet, swung his satchel over his shoulder, clutched his rifle in front of him, and moved out.

The pine trees that clung to the crest screened us from any prying eyes below as Warren led Owen and me along the top of the ridge. With everyone focused on Sophia and her impending punishment, no one noticed us darting along the parallel path high above their heads.

Gunshots rang out through the camp, three blasts of three, for nine shots total. They must have been some sort of signal, because more men appeared in the clearing below. They left whatever they'd been doing behind, stepped out of the various buildings, and fell into step behind Grimes, Hazel, Sophia, and her guards. Every new man who appeared made my heart sink a little more, because each of them would make it that much more difficult to save Sophia from whatever terrible thing Grimes had in mind for her.

Warren, Owen, and I moved as fast as we could, but it was still slow going, running up and down the ridge, having to stop to skirt around or climb over the rocks and fallen trees that sporadically blocked the path.

Finally, after ten minutes, we had left the rocks behind and plunged back down into the forest. Warren didn't follow a set path but instead led us through one gap in the trees after another, still keeping an eye out for traps and circling around to the extreme eastern side of the camp.

We hadn't gone far when the stench of death hit me.

One moment, all I could smell was my own sweat as the July sun baked me in my long clothes and silverstone vest. The next, the stench of rotting, putrefied flesh hit me like a punch in the nose, forcing its way down my mouth and throat and choking me from the inside out. Behind me, Owen let out a low, strangled cough, as disgusted by the horrid scent as I was. Warren stopped long enough to pull a blue bandanna out of his pocket, knot it around his neck, and use the cloth to cover his nose and face as best he could before moving forward again.

Three minutes later, Warren stopped, crouched down low, and gestured for Owen and me to do the same. Together, we eased up to the edge of the tree line and peered through the screen of leaves, branches, and bushes.

Another clearing lay before us, much smaller than the spot where the buildings were located and only a couple hundred feet from end to end and top to bottom. At the western end, a narrow trail curved into a sharp bend before disappearing into the trees and leading back to the main camp.

Grimes was already here, along with Sophia, Hazel, and the rest of his men. Several worn, weathered tombstones dotted the landscape, like faded brown and gray daisies that had sprouted up out of the bed of dead leaves, twigs, and grasses. But Grimes ignored the markers and strode forward until he was standing on the edge of what looked like a trench about seven feet deep and fifteen feet square. If there had been any water in it, it would have been a bona fide moat. At first, I thought that perhaps it was another trap and that there were sharpened stakes lining the bottom.

I was right, and I was wrong.

Because it was a pit. Only there weren't stakes at the bottom. There were bodies.

* 16 *

Owen, Warren, and I were on a slight rise, and our higher vantage point let me see down into the pit. There must have been close to twenty bodies, maybe more, all in various stages of decay. Hence the overwhelming stench.

The bodies must have been tossed down into the trench and left to lie where they landed, because they were all sprawled on top of one another, tangled together in an awkward pile of arms and legs. I spotted a couple of bodies wearing brown suits, probably some of Grimes's men who'd pissed him off and paid the price for it. But most of the victims seemed to be women, judging from the bits of light blue, pink, purple, and green fabric that I spied among the broken, bloody, rotting limbs.

A cloud of flies churned over the pit, and for a moment, their hungry hums were the only sounds.

Finally, Hazel stepped forward. "You know the drill. In you go," she said with gleeful malice.

Then she grabbed Sophia's injured arm and shoved her down into the pit.

Sophia landed awkwardly on her left side and let out a sharp gasp of pain. Slowly, she got to her feet. Even though she was standing on the foulest sorts of things imaginable, *covered* with the foulest sorts of things imaginable, flies buzzing in the air all around her, the men hooting and hollering at her, Sophia still squared her shoulders, lifted her chin, and glared at Hazel with murder in her eyes.

It was one of the bravest things I'd ever witnessed.

I'd seen a lot of horrors in my time. Seen them and done some of them myself. Blood, guts, screams, tears, terror, torture, murder. But I don't know that I would have been able to do the same in Sophia's place—to face my enemies with such grace, bravery, and poise. I don't know anyone else who would have. In that moment, I admired, respected, and loved Sophia more than ever before, and once again, I vowed to do whatever it took to save her from this nightmare forever.

One of Grimes's men stepped forward and handed Hazel a shovel, which she threw down to Sophia. The shovel skittered across a couple of bodies, scattering the flies for a few seconds, before finally coming to a stop a few feet away from her.

"You know the drill," Hazel repeated. "Pick it up and start digging."

"Yes, Sophia," Grimes said, gesturing out at the pit. "Please start digging. As you can see, we need some more room. I've been very . . . displeased with people lately."

I frowned. Sophia had done this before? Buried bodies

in a pit? When? The first time Grimes had taken her? I looked at Warren, who gave me a grim nod, confirming my worst suspicions. My heart clenched. Poor Sophia. Of all the things that Grimes had done to her back then, of all the things that he could do to her now, I'd never thought it would be anything like *this*.

Because this was what Sophia did for *me*. She got rid of all the bodies that I left behind as the Spider. I never asked where she took them or what she did with them, although I could guess. Dropping them in out-of-the-way spots like the Ashland Rock Quarry. Heaving them into the Aneirin River to float downstream. Burying them in graves in the woods.

Was this . . . was this pit where Sophia had learned to dispose of bodies in the first place? It had to be. But if so, why would she willingly get rid of bodies for me now? Why had she gotten rid of them for Fletcher for all those years? Why continue to do something that had to remind her of all the horrors she'd suffered at Grimes's hands?

Guilt and shame joined the shock and disgust in my heart. All these years, I hadn't given a second thought to Sophia cleaning up my messes or the toll it might take on her. But now that I'd seen this, witnessed this horrific vision of her past, I felt sick inside to think that I'd asked her to do the same thing over and over again through the years. No, I hadn't even asked; I'd just assumed she would do it.

In a way, that made me worse than Grimes, Hazel, and their men. Because I was supposed to care about Sophia, not subject her to something like this. I wasn't supposed to benefit from her pain, but I had all the same.

Sophia glanced at the shovel that Hazel had tossed down to her, then slowly, carefully, deliberately crossed her arms over her chest.

"Pick it up, Sophia," Grimes said in a soft but deadly voice. "You'll only be punished more if you don't."

Sophia glared at him, showing her defiance, but after a few more seconds, her shoulders slumped in defeat. She let out a tired sigh, leaned down, and picked up the shovel. She shuffled over to the opposite side of the pit, as far away from Grimes, Hazel, and their men as she could get, stuck the shovel into the earthen bank there, and started to dig, widening the trench.

For several seconds, the only sounds were the steady *scrape-scrape-scrape* of Sophia's shovel stabbing into the earth and the soft *squish-squish-squish* of the bodies, maggots, and more under her feet.

But it apparently wasn't enough that Sophia had already been shot and kicked and was now wading through death. Grimes and Hazel decided to torture her with their Fire magic too.

The two siblings reached for their power, and flames sparked to life on their fingertips, dancing back and forth like molten-lava butterflies in the soft summer breeze. Their magic moved in perfect harmony, the flames undulating in time and even burning at the same intensity. Then, together, they threw their magic forward. Sophia's hands tightened around the shovel, and she stopped digging, knowing what was coming next, but she didn't hunker down or try to move out of the way. Instead, she stood there straight and tall as two balls of elemental Fire raced through the air and exploded into the bank, one on either side of her.

The scorching heat from the twin blasts blew back into Sophia, knocking her down onto the bodies again. I could feel the intensity of the elemental Fire all the way over where we were in the woods, and I could imagine how excruciating it must have been for her to be so close to it.

But once again, Sophia slowly picked herself up and staggered back onto her feet. The skin on her face, neck, hands, and arms had reddened from the blast, although I couldn't tell if it was only temporary from the heat or if her skin had been that badly burned.

But maybe the worst part was that the shifting cadavers beneath her feet actually ignited—at least, their clothes did. Oily smoke boiled up from the torn, bloody fabrics that were still clinging to the rotten limbs, adding to the horrible stench in the air.

Sophia glared over her shoulder at her two tormenters. Hazel cackled and threw another ball of her Fire magic into the bank close to the dwarf, the flames exploding and washing over even more of the corpses. More wretched smoke bubbled up around her, until it hung over the pit like the foulest sort of fog. After another moment, Sophia turned around and went back to her digging, the flames of Hazel's magic licking at her and the dead all around her.

The men who'd come to watch hooted with delight through the whole horrible thing. A few even stuck their revolvers up into the air and fired off some shots. The sharp *crack*s rattled around the clearing, punctuating the men's mocking laughter. Hazel played to the crowd, holding her long off-white skirt out to one side and elegantly bowing to the men before sending little bursts of Fire straight into Sophia's back. Not enough to kill the dwarf but more than enough to hurt her. Grimes tipped his white fedora back from his forehead, as though he wanted an even better view. Then he simply stood there and watched the whole thing, his lips curved up into a small, sinister smile.

The searing heat from the elemental Fire. The foul, rotten stench from the swollen, bloated bodies. The acrid aroma of burned flesh. The bugs humming through the air, hungry for whatever blood and bones they could find. Hazel preening. The men jeering. Grimes grinning.

And Sophia in the middle of it all, dressed up like a pretty, if stained, porcelain doll, as though she should be having tea in some summer garden instead of digging a mass grave.

It was one of the most disturbing things, one of the most sickening things, one of the cruelest forms of torture that I'd ever seen—and there wasn't a damn thing that I could do about it.

More than once, I started forward, determined to slash my way to Sophia, no matter how suicidal that would be. But every single time, Owen put his hand on my arm and kept me from giving in to my murderous rage. Even though I wanted nothing more than to leap out of the trees and cut down every single person I saw, I couldn't. There were just too many men between her and me, not to mention Grimes and Hazel and their damn Fire power. They'd cut me down with their guns and magic before I could even get close to Sophia, much less rescue her.

Besides, I had Owen and Warren to think about too. They'd come with me of their own accord, but I was still responsible for them. I might be okay risking my life but not theirs.

So I crouched there in the woods, and I watched the torture of someone I loved.

More than that, I *memorized* it—every gleeful yell, every crackle, pop, and sizzle of dead, smoking flesh, every foul smell that oozed through the air, every hiss of pain that escaped Sophia's burned, blistered lips.

Oh, yes, I watched, and I memorized every single dirty deed, every horrible thing, every bit of agony that Sophia was enduring. One by one, I embraced all of the sadistic terrors and the cold, black, unending rage that went along with them.

"What do you want to do, Gin?" Owen asked.

Hazel sent another blast of Fire magic into Sophia's back, causing Grimes and the rest of the men to howl with laughter again. The force of it made the dwarf clutch the shovel and hunch over in pain, but after a few seconds, she straightened back up and started digging again.

"The second that there's an opening, we rescue Sophia and get her the hell out of here. And while we're at it, we take these bastards out along the way," I said, my voice dripping with all the venom in my heart. "Every last one of them. No survivors—and absolutely no mercy."

❖ 17 ❖

Eventually, Hazel grew tired of her gruesome game and quit throwing her Fire magic at Sophia. The bodies continued to smolder, though, and I didn't see how Sophia kept from retching at the gruesome graveyard stench—or breaking down entirely.

"We've got some business to attend to back at camp. You five, stay here and watch her," Grimes ordered some of his men. "She's a clever thing. Don't let her out of your sight, and don't go near her, no matter what. She's killed more than one man with a shovel."

Sophia spun the shovel around in her hands and gave the men on the bank a dark, toothy grin. More than one shuddered and looked away from her. Nobody wanted his skull bashed in, and they especially didn't want to end up in the pit with all of the other bodies. But the men did as Grimes ordered, drawing their guns and lining up on the dirt bank opposite her, making sure to keep well away from the edge of the pit.

Sophia studied them, considering her options, looking for any sign of weakness, just like I would have. But the men had the high ground and the guns, and she knew it. So Sophia shrugged and went back to her digging, stabbing the shovel into the black earth, then swinging the dirt away in sharp, vicious arcs. I wondered if she was imagining that the earth was Grimes and Hazel. I would have been.

"Good," Grimes said in a pleased voice. "You've decided to behave. You see? We're making progress already. I'll be back just as soon as I can, darling. Then we'll have a nice dinner and talk about our future here together."

Sophia kept her back to Grimes so he couldn't see the disgust on her face, and she kept right on digging, as if she hadn't even heard him.

But she wasn't the only one who didn't like his words. Jealousy pinched Hazel's face, and she gave her brother an incredulous look. A few flames sparked on her fingertips, further hinting at her anger, but Hazel quickly curled her hand into a tight fist, smothering the Fire before anyone else noticed it. It seemed that Hazel didn't like it that Grimes was planning to devote so much of his time and attention to Sophia. I imagined that Hazel enjoyed playing queen of the mountain, given that I hadn't seen another woman in the entire camp.

Ever the gentleman, Grimes held out his arm to his sister. Hazel took it and shot Sophia a triumphant look, but the dwarf ignored her. Together, the siblings left the pit and headed back toward the main part of the camp, along with the rest of their men. The five whom Grimes had ordered to stay behind leaned against some of the sturdier-looking tombstones.

One minute slipped by, then another, then another. Still, I waited, wondering if this might be some sort of trick, if Grimes and especially Hazel might double back and hide in the woods so they could torture Sophia some more, should she try to escape again. But five minutes passed, and they didn't reappear. Maybe they really did have some other business to take care of, after all. I wondered what was so important that Grimes would leave Sophia for it, especially when he'd just captured her again.

"How do you want to do this?" Owen whispered.

I stared at Grimes's men, who were standing roughly parallel to our position in the trees, before studying the landscape around us. Because this wasn't just about killing the men in front of me; it was also about making sure that we got Sophia away from Grimes forever.

Finally, I turned to Warren. "What's the fastest way back down the mountain to the car?"

He pulled his blue bandanna down from around his nose so he could answer me. "The same way we came up."

"There are no other shortcuts? No way we could get there quicker?"

He shook his head.

"What about Grimes and his men? Is there another trail that they could take to get in front of us and cut us off?"

Warren shook his head again. "Not a direct trail, no, although they can always just cut through the woods."

I nodded. It wasn't ideal, but there was nothing that I could do about it.

"And how do you want to take out those guys guarding her?" Owen asked.

I unzipped my backpack, drew out one of the silencers inside, and held it up where he could see it.

"Quietly," I said, passing the metal over to him. "I'll approach them head-on, while you sneak around behind them. We should be able to take them out before they realize that they're surrounded. But whatever happens, we can't let them get a shot off. That's my main worry, that they'll signal Grimes, and he'll realize that we're here to rescue Sophia."

"That's a big chance to take," Owen said, screwing the silencer onto the end of his gun.

I let out a breath. "I know, but we're just going to have to risk it. This is our best, quickest chance to get close to her. It might be our *only* chance. I want to get Sophia out of here before Grimes and Hazel can do anything else to her."

Owen's face hardened, and anger sparked in his violet eyes, the same anger that I felt. He nodded.

"And me?" Warren asked. "What do you want me to do?"

"You stay here, and lay down some cover fire for us if things go wrong," I said. "I'd like to kill these guys and slip away before Grimes realizes what's happened, but Owen's right, and we probably won't be that lucky. So if worse comes to worst, we kill as many of them as we can here, then get Sophia to safety."

Warren patted his rifle. "You got it."

I stared at him, then Owen, wondering if I was about to get us all killed. If they had the same thought, they didn't show it. Their hands curled around their guns, and their gazes were steady, determined, and level with mine.

"Okay," I said. "Here's what we're going to do."

I looked at Owen, who had moved about thirty feet to the left of where I crouched at the edge of the trees. He nodded, and I threw a rock high overhead. It landed in the woods on the far side of the clearing, crashing into the underbrush beyond the pit. The men had been talking among themselves, but their heads snapped in that direction, and they straightened up and pushed away from the tombstones they'd been leaning against. A few of them raised their guns and took some tentative steps forward, as though they were thinking about investigating the noise, although they still kept away from the edge of the pit and out of Sophia's reach.

While the men were debating what they'd heard and whether it was some sort of animal, Owen used their distraction to sprint out of the woods behind them. I threw another rock in the same general direction as before. It too tumbled through the underbrush, keeping the men from noticing Owen crossing into the woods on the far side of the clearing.

Sophia noticed, though.

She glanced over her shoulder at just the right moment to see Owen disappear into the trees. She froze, her eyes wide, and I could almost see the wheels spinning in her mind as she wondered whether she'd actually seen what she thought she had.

"What are you looking at?" one of the men muttered. "Get back to work. That ditch isn't going to dig itself."

Sophia shrugged and went back to her digging, but she kept turning her head from side to side, peering into the trees that lined the clearing. She knew that something was up. Good.

After a few more minutes, the men settled down again, having decided that it was likely some animal creeping through the woods, after all.

Not an animal—the Spider. But they were going to find that out soon enough.

"Showtime," I whispered to Warren.

He nodded, dropped to a knee, and raised his rifle to his shoulder, getting a bead on the men.

I slid my knife back up my sleeve, pulled my vest down so that it covered as much of my chest as possible, crept down the hill, and walked out into the clearing.

I kept my pace steady and even, ambling along as though I was out for a nice, quiet walk in the woods, instead of deliberately heading toward a bunch of sadistic psychopaths with guns.

"Excuse me," I called out. "Yoo-hoo. *Hello*, over there."

This time, all of the men's heads snapped around in my direction. I smiled and gave them a bright, happy, cheery wave. Their mouths gaped even wider, as if they'd never seen a woman before. Then their eyes narrowed with wariness, and they raised their guns, aiming them at my chest.

"Hold it right there, lady!" one of the men barked, stepping in front of the others.

I kept right on waving and walking toward them, as

if their guns didn't concern me at all, making sure that all enemy eyes stayed on me. And it worked. The men didn't notice Sophia start creeping across the pit toward the bank where they were standing—or Owen sliding out of the woods behind them.

I kept my smile firmly fixed on my face as I neared the group.

The man in front thumbed back the trigger on his revolver. "I said *stop*. I mean it, lady."

"Whoa, now, boys," I drawled, doing as he asked and faking surprise. "Hold on there a second. There's no need to get violent. I'm just a little lost way out here in the woods, and I was wondering if you could help me. How do I get back to the Bone Mountain trail from here? Because I, like, totally lost my map back in the woods. One second, I had it. The next—poof!—the wind sent it sailing right over one of the ridges."

The leader frowned, his eyes scanning the woods behind me. "You're out here by yourself? Just you?"

"Yup, it's just little ole me," I said, making my voice even more syrupy-sweet and helpless. "All by my lonesome."

The man lowered his gun, his thumb tapping against the hilt as he tried to figure out whether I was telling the truth. Apparently, he wasn't concerned about one lone woman, because he holstered his gun.

"Did you hear that, boys?" he said, looking over his shoulder at his friends. "This poor little lady is lost. Lucky for her that she wandered into our camp, eh?"

He let out a dark chuckle, and all the men joined in his laughter, no doubt salivating over all the horrible things they wanted to do to me. They wouldn't be laughing in another minute, two tops.

I kept the empty, ditzy smile on my face and sidled even closer to him. "So can you help me figure out how to get back to the trail, then? Because I've got to tell you that it feels like I've been walking around out here in circles *forever*."

The man crooked his finger at me. "Sure, honey. Come on over here, and we'll fix you right up."

I went to him, my face all wide-eyed innocence, even as I surreptitiously palmed a knife and dropped it down by my side. Owen crept toward the man standing at the back of the pack, while Sophia eased a little closer to the side of the pit and hoisted her shovel up onto her shoulder as though she was taking a break.

The leader held his hands out to his sides, like he was welcoming me with open arms. I stopped in front of him and gave him another empty smile. He lunged forward, grabbed my arms, and yanked me up against him, grinding his body against mine.

"Hey!" I cried out in a mock-helpless voice. "What are you doing? Get your hands off me, you creep!"

"Oh, I'll be putting more than my hands on you in a minute. You go ahead and scream as loud as you want to, honey." The man sneered into my face, his breath smelling of sour moonshine. "We like it better when they scream, don't we, boys?"

"Really?" I purred. "That's funny, because I was thinking the exact same thing about you. No, that's not true. I actually like it better when you just *die*."

I brought my left hand up and slammed my knife into

his throat. He died with a choking gurgle, spraying blood all over my hand, face, and clothes, but I didn't care. Because the warm, sticky drops told me that I was finally doing something to help Sophia—like killing these bastards where they stood.

I shoved the dying leader away, stepped forward, palmed a second knife, and rammed both blades into the next man's chest. By this point, the others realized that I wasn't the innocent little Bambi that I appeared to be, and they raised their guns once more.

But Owen and Sophia didn't give them a chance to fire at me. Owen put his pistol up against the back of the man's head in front of him and pulled the trigger twice. Thanks to the silencer I'd given him, the gun barely made a sound, and the man was dead before he hit the ground. Meanwhile, Sophia whipped the shovel off her shoulder and slammed it into the knees of the guy closest to her, causing him to howl with pain. He toppled over into the pit, and Sophia whacked the shovel against his head, caving in his skull with a satisfying *crack*.

That left one man standing. He looked around at his fallen buddies, his eyes wide with confusion and fear, wondering how they'd all died so quickly. He drew in a breath to scream, but my knife in his throat cut off that concern.

Less than a minute after it had begun, it was over, and all five of Grimes's men lay dead at our feet. A good start but not enough. Not *nearly* enough.

I walked over to the edge of the pit, bent down, and held out my hand. Sophia clasped it, and I pulled her up and out of the trench. Up close, the stench was even more putrid and overpowering, the bodies bloodier and more rotten than I'd imagined. How had she managed to stand it? Both now *and* back then?

Sophia swayed forward, and I held her until she was steady on her feet. Owen stood off to one side, watching our backs.

Soot and ash flaked off Sophia's once-white dress, which hung in burned tatters on her back, while the heels had snapped off her shoes. Her black hair was a singed, tangled mess, while blood had soaked through the white bandages that had been placed over the gunshot wounds on her left arm and thigh. But the worst part was her skin, which was red, raw, and blistered, from her fingertips all the way up her arms. Her throat and face were as bright and shiny as a ripe tomato, her cheeks puffed up from the burns so that they seemed like they would pop if you so much as looked at them too hard.

Every single part of her had to just *hurt*. But she was still standing, still breathing, still in one piece. Everything else could be fixed—on the outside, at least.

"Jo-Jo?" Sophia rasped in her broken voice.

"Cooper healed her," I said. "At least, he tried to. I don't know how well he did. Maybe he'll know more about how she's doing when we get back to his place."

Worry glimmered in Sophia's black eyes, but she nodded.

Then the dwarf did something that she'd never done before in all the years that I'd known her: she threw her arms around me and hugged me tight.

"Thank you," she whispered in my ear.

I would have hugged her back if I didn't think that it would have caused her even more pain. "You are more than welcome. Now, come on. Let's get out of here."

Sophia nodded and pulled back. She leaned down, grabbed her shovel, and used it as a sort of walking stick. Together, with Owen, we headed toward the woods and our escape route.

✳ 18 ✳

Warren stepped out of the trees and met us at the edge of the forest, still clutching his rifle.

"Anything?" I asked.

He shook his head. "Not a peep so far. I don't think that anyone in camp heard what happened here, but it won't be too long before Grimes or some of his men come to check on the others. We need to disappear into the woods before they spot us—"

It was as if his words summoned up all the bad, capricious luck that I'd been expecting ever since we'd first set foot on Bone Mountain, because one of Grimes's men chose that exact moment to run into the clearing.

"Hey," he called out, still jogging forward and waving to someone behind him. "Go get Stewie, and come help me. Mr. Grimes changed his mind. He wants the woman brought back—"

He turned around and stopped short at the sight of

Owen, Sophia, Warren, and me standing to one side of the clearing. His gaze zoomed in on the dead bodies of his buddies sprawled among the worn tombstones. The guy sucked in a breath, but he did the smart thing and didn't approach us. Instead, he did something far, far worse: he pulled his gun out of the holster on his belt and fired three quick shots up into the air.

I cursed and started forward, ready to kill him, but Warren beat me to it. The old man raised his rifle to his shoulder and put a bullet in the other man's forehead.

But the sharp, staccato sounds of the revolver and the rifle echoed around the clearing, then bellowed through the trees and rattled farther out into the main camp. Shouts rose in the distance, indicating that Grimes, Hazel, and everyone else would descend on the area in minutes, if not sooner.

"What do you want to do, Gin?" Owen asked. "Make a stand here?"

I shook my head. "No. There are too many of them. They can easily outflank us, and they have more weapons than we do. Now we run."

Sophia hurried forward, but after a few yards she pulled up short and hissed in pain, despite the shovel that she'd been using to support herself. A bit of blood trickled down her bare leg.

"How bad is that gunshot wound in your thigh?" I asked.

"Just bandaged," she rasped. "Not healed."

That's what I'd feared, but there was nothing to be done about it. So I put an arm under Sophia's shoulder, taking some of her weight. Together, we headed for the trees.

Crack!

Crack! Crack!

Crack!

We didn't even make it into the woods before a couple more of Grimes's men raced into the clearing, guns out and firing at us.

"You take Sophia!" Owen shouted, raising his own weapon to fire back. "Warren and I will cover you!"

"Do it!" I yelled back. "But stay close to us! We can't afford to get separated!"

Owen nodded, and he and Warren let loose with another volley of shots. Their guns would be more effective than my knives at this range, even though all I wanted to do was turn around and throw myself at Grimes's men.

Together, Sophia and I hobbled into the woods and back up the faint path that Warren had made earlier when he'd led us down to the pit.

Crack!

Crack! Crack!

Crack!

Bullets zinged through the forest all around us as Grimes's men let off another round of shots. They put their stockpile of guns to good use, because the bullets slammed into the trees, cut through the leaves, kicked up wads of dirt, and pinged off rocks.

I put myself on the side of the trail where the bullets where coming from, protecting Sophia as much as I could, but I didn't reach for my Stone magic to harden my skin. I needed to save my power for something else that I had in mind, so all I could do was hope that Sophia and I wouldn't get shot in the meantime and that Owen and Warren wouldn't either.

Crack!

Crack! Crack!

Crack!

Owen and Warren returned fire, and several yelps of pain sounded as their bullets hit home. They had the advantage of using the trees as a screen, whereas Grimes's men were still standing in the clearing and firing blindly into the woods. Still, one of them could easily get in a lucky shot on any one of us.

Sophia limped along as quickly as she could, but it was slow going, especially since we were climbing back up to the top of the ridge that Warren, Owen, and I had used as a vantage point to spy on the camp earlier. Still, we trudged on and moved as fast as we could. That was all that we could do. Behind us, I could hear the *crunch-crunch-crunch* and *crackle-crackle* of Owen's and Warren's footsteps through the dry leaves as they stopped and started, firing, then moving up the trail, pausing to reload, then firing again, before repeating the whole process.

Sophia and I were about halfway up the ridge when a man stepped out of the woods in front of us.

Apparently, he hadn't thought that he would actually get ahead of us, because he seemed surprised by our appearance. He got over it real quick, though. He snapped up his gun and took aim at us.

Crack! Crack!

I pivoted so that my back was to the man, and the bullets punched into my silverstone vest with all the hard force of a jackhammer. The impact made me stagger forward, and I lost my grip on Sophia, who went tumbling down to the ground, her shovel flying from her hands.

Crack! Crack!

The guy put two more bullets into my back, both of which caught in my vest once again. I palmed a knife, whirled around, and threw it at him. The blade sank into his windpipe. He clawed at the blade, then foolishly pulled it out, essentially cutting his own throat. He waved his gun with one hand, while the bloody knife wavered back and forth in his other.

"That's mine," I hissed, darting forward, yanking the knife out of his hand, and shoving him away.

Letting out a high, whistling wheeze, he stumbled over the edge of the trail and rolled down the wooded hillside.

By this point, Owen and Warren had caught up with Sophia and me. My eyes locked onto Warren, who was limping and leaning on his rifle for support just like Sophia had been doing with her shovel. He was favoring his right leg, and my gaze dropped to his left thigh—and the blood and the bullet hole there.

"Warren?" I asked.

He waved his hand at me. "I'll live. Let's move!"

Owen darted forward, put his shoulder under Sophia's, and helped her to her feet. She grabbed her shovel to use as a walking stick once more. The four of us started back up the trail, with me in the lead this time, Sophia and Warren hobbling along behind me, and Owen in the rear, watching our backs.

Another man stepped out of the woods in front of us, but I was able to ram my knife into his chest before he even realized what was happening. I pushed him off the trail too, and we kept climbing, going as fast as Sophia and Warren could.

But it wasn't fast enough, not *nearly* fast enough.

Through the green wash of trees, I spotted more of Grimes's men running up the hill and converging on our position. Soon, enough of them would get ahead of us, cutting off our escape route, and more of them would swarm over us from behind. We'd be caught, trapped in the middle of a sticky web of death, and then we'd be executed, simple as that.

I couldn't let that happen—not to the others—and I knew what I had to do now. Maybe I'd always known that it would come to this.

I waited until we got to the top of the rocky ridge, hurried over to the edge, and risked a quick look down below. I counted around a dozen men, all with guns, in the main camp clearing. Some of them were running to the east, where the pit was and where we'd started our escape. A few others were staring up at the ridge, taking aim with their guns, and waiting for us to appear, although we were out of range of their revolvers way up here. Some of the smarter ones were running toward the west end of the camp, probably to another trail there that would lead them up to this location.

I didn't spot Grimes or Hazel, but I knew that they were out there somewhere searching for us, especially Grimes. He wouldn't let Sophia escape a second time.

Everything I saw only made me more determined to make sure that the others got off the mountain—even if I didn't.

"Get Sophia out of here!" I yelled, stepping away from the lip of the ridge and waving the others on past me. "Go! I'll hold them off!"

Sophia pulled up short. "No," she rasped. "Don't. Too dangerous."

"Somebody has to slow them down, and it's going to be me. I made Jo-Jo a promise that I'd rescue you, and I'm going to keep it. You wouldn't want to make a liar out of me, now, would you?" I grinned, trying to show her that I knew what I was doing—and what it would cost me.

Sophia didn't say anything, but fear filled her eyes, fear for me and of what Grimes and Hazel would do to me if I was captured. But that was something that I couldn't let myself think about right now. Otherwise, I wouldn't be able to do what needed to be done in order to save my family.

"She's right," Warren said, ripping the bandanna from around his throat and using it to make a crude bandage for his leg. "Now, come on. I'll drag you if I have to, but we both know that we don't have that kind of time right now."

Warren couldn't drag anyone, not with that bullet in his leg, but he was just stubborn enough to try, and Sophia knew it. She also realized that he was right.

Sophia gave me one more sorrowful look before she threaded her arm through Warren's. Leaning on each other, the two of them slowly crossed the ridge, stepped onto the trail on the far side, and vanished into the woods.

I shrugged the backpack off my shoulders and dropped it at my feet, along with the bloody knife that I'd been holding. I palmed my second knife, then pulled out the one from against the small of my back and the two from the sides of my boots. I grabbed a couple of guns out of the backpack and laid them on the rocks. Then I stuffed all five of my knives inside the backpack, zipped it up, and handed it to Owen.

"Here," I said. "Take this. I don't want Grimes getting his grubby hands on Fletcher's maps or the knives that you made for me. Don't worry. I've got plenty more weapons in my vest."

"Don't," he said in a low, strangled, anguished voice. "Don't give me your knives. Don't give up. Don't you *dare* give up."

"I'm not giving up. I'm being realistic."

More shouts echoed through the trees, along with a few more *cracks* of gunfire, as if to punctuate my words.

"I want to stay with *you*," Owen said, his words almost a snarl. "I want to fight with you and be by your side to the end—no matter what that is."

"I know," I said, my voice as calm as his was violent. "But you can't. Warren and Sophia are both injured, and they will never get off the mountain without help—*your* help. Grimes's men will catch up with them and drag them back here. He'll use them as leverage against us, and then we'll all be dead. So I want you to go, Owen. I *need* you to go. Please. For Sophia and Warren—and especially for me."

Owen closed his eyes a moment, his body shuddering, as though his heart was tearing in two as he accepted the truth of my words and what we both had to do now. Then he snapped them open, grabbed my arm, and pulled me close to his body.

"Whatever happens, you survive," he growled. "I'll come back for you as soon as Sophia is safe. I promise."

Stubborn determination blazed in his violet eyes, making them burn as brightly as amethyst stars, and my heart swelled with love for him. Despite everything that had happened between us and all the ways that we'd hurt each other, I still loved him. I would love him for as long as I lived.

I just didn't know how much longer that would be.

Because I didn't think that I would survive this fight. Grimes and Hazel had too many guns, too many men, too much magic, and I was all out of time—and options. This one precious moment might be all that I had left.

So I cupped Owen's cheek with one hand and stroked my bloody fingers over his face, smoothing out his worried frown and trying to memorize his features. I stared into his eyes, letting him see just how much I cared for him, just how much I loved him. Then I wrapped my arms around his neck and crushed my lips to his, wanting to feel his arms around me just one more time.

He returned my kiss with equal fervor, wrapping his arms even tighter around me. Emotions exploded inside me, one after another—heat, desire, need, want, love. For a moment, I gave myself over completely to it, this hot, burning, unending wave of emotion that threatened to pull me under and drown me with its intensity.

Crack! Crack! Crack!

Another round of gunfire burst out, closer this time, shattering the moment, and our kiss ended as quickly as it had begun, although the emotions lingered, sparking through my body like bolts of electricity, jolting every part of me and making me feel more alive than I ever had before.

Owen leaned forward and touched his forehead to mine, still staring into my eyes. "Survive," he whispered. "Promise me."

"I promise," I whispered, even though I knew the words were an empty lie. Then I stepped away from him. "Now, go. Before it's too late for all of us."

His eyes met mine, violet and gray, and the emotions roared over me again, even stronger than before—heat, desire, need, want, love. They made me want to fight, they made me want to survive—for him, for *us*—even though there was a slim chance of that, at best. Still, I grabbed on to those feelings, those emotions, those soul-wrenching jolts, and added them to the cold, black rage that was steadily beating in my heart, crystallizing my determination to protect him and the others, no matter what.

Owen nodded, shouldered my backpack, and started backing away across the ridge. He kept his gaze on mine the whole time. All too soon, though, he reached the trees on the far side. I grinned, trying to reassure him.

He returned my grin, although agony still burned in his eyes at the thought of leaving me behind. But War-ren couldn't get Sophia off the mountain by himself, not before Grimes's men caught up with them, and we both knew it.

"Go," I called out to him. "Now."

Owen gave me one more longing, solemn look before he turned and disappeared into the trees. I watched him go, wondering if I'd ever see him again.

I hoped so.

But hope was a useless emotion in this situation, so I set it aside and locked it down tight inside me, along with all of my other soft feelings, where they would stay safe and out of the way of what was to come. Instead, I embraced the blackness in my heart until there was nothing left but the icy rage to kill every single person who came within arm's reach of me.

Until I was no more and no less than the Spider once again.

Then I unzipped a pocket on my vest, grabbed one of my extra silverstone knives, and went to face my enemies.

* 19 *

When I was sure that Owen, Warren, and Sophia had a good head start on Grimes's men, I stepped out into plain view on the top of the ridge, my knife in my hand, making sure that everyone in the clearing below could see me.

Crack!

Crack! Crack!

Crack!

A few bullets pinged harmlessly off the ridge farther down the slope. Most of the men seemed to be armed with revolvers, so they weren't really in range yet, but they surged forward, scrambling up and over the rocks, trying to fix that. I stood there and let them come.

My gaze scanned over the men, and I counted at least a dozen headed my way, each armed with at least one gun. There were probably more of them at the east and west ends of camp, slogging through the woods and racing toward my position, but they wouldn't be a factor right now.

Twelve on one. Not bad odds, considering.

"This is for you, Fletcher," I said. "I hope that I make you proud."

Crack!

Crack! Crack!

More bullets pinged off the rocks, although they were slowly getting closer to hitting the mark. Still, I waited. Until finally—*crack!*—a bullet chipped into the stone at my feet.

I grinned. Now *that* was definitely close enough. Still, I waited until most of the men had climbed a few feet higher before I crouched down and held my hand up.

A silver light flared in my palm, centered on my spider rune scar, as I reached for the Ice magic flowing deep inside my veins. I studied the glowing circle and eight thin rays of silverstone embedded in my skin, watching the shimmer of magic grow and grow as I grabbed hold of more and more of my power. I wondered if this was the last time that I'd ever see my own rune.

Well, if it was, I was going to make it *count.*

I reached for the closest rock. The stone steamed and sizzled with cold as though I were searing my spider rune into it with the icy brand of my hand. In a way, I supposed that I was. It took less than a breath before cold crystals started spreading out from my palm, encasing the rock that I was touching, then flowing on to the next craggy stone and the one after that and the one after that.

Jo-Jo had always told me that I was one of the strongest elementals she'd ever seen, and I'd proven that to myself when I'd gone toe-to-toe with Mab and her Fire and lived through the fight. So it was easy for me to coat the rocks around me with an inch of elemental Ice. What wasn't so easy was pushing my power outward over the whole ridge and then even farther out into the woods beyond the rocks.

But I had a plan for that too: the silverstone spider rune ring on my right hand, the one that Bria had given me. I tapped into the magic that was housed in the metal there, adding it to the Ice power that was already flowing out of me. The reason silverstone was so prized was that the metal had a special property, the ability to absorb and store all forms of magic. That's why so many elementals wore rings, necklaces, and watches made out of silverstone, so they could have an extra boost of power when they needed it, say, for an elemental duel.

So many people had tried to kill me in the past few months that I'd taken to putting a bit of my Ice and Stone power into my ring every morning when I got up and again every night before I went to bed. As a result, the ring held more of my magic than it ever had before, and I intended to tap into every single bit of it.

It was a risk, using up all of my magic this way, but I wanted to give Warren, Owen, and Sophia the best possible chance to get off the mountain and back to Roslyn's car. I figured that turning the whole damn ridge into a field of elemental Ice was the best way to do that.

I kept reaching and reaching for my magic, watching the Ice crystals leapfrog from one rock and one patch of earth to the next, pushed forward by my Stone power like soldiers marching into battle. Below me, the men started shouting as the Ice approached and then rushed on past them like a cold crystal wave. A few weren't quite quick enough to let go of their handholds on the ridge, and their hands froze to the rocks and were trapped there by the thick layer of Ice. I hoped their fingers rotted, turned black, and fell off from frostbite. It would serve these bastards right for all the horrible things they'd done.

People thought assassins were evil, but at least my violence was mostly contained to my targets and whatever bodyguards they employed. Grimes and his men hurt everyone who'd ever crossed their path, whether they'd deserved it or not, like all those poor college kids they'd kidnapped and brought up here over the years. And Hazel, well, she liked to use her Fire magic for the sadistic little thrill that it gave her. I wondered how many folks had been innocently hiking through the woods when they'd stumbled across the camp, never to leave it again.

The thought made the black rage rise in me once more, and I dug down even deeper inside myself. It only took me a moment to release another cold blast of power, this one even stronger than before. The rest of the ridge Iced over, and the crystals kept right on going, spreading out into the woods beyond and the clearing below, until the rocks, trees, grass, and leaves glittered like polished glass.

Still, despite the elemental Ice, one man actually managed to climb all the way up to the top of the ridge. He stopped short of pulling himself up and over the crest. Instead, he held on to the cold, slippery rocks with one hand, while he raised the gun in his other hand to fire at me.

Before he could pull the trigger, I rose to my feet and kicked him in the face, smashing my boot into his nose. The sharp jab made his body arch back, and he lost his grip on the slick rocks. End over end, he plummeted to the clearing below. I'd hoped that he would plow into a few of his friends on the way down and knock them off the ridge too, but I'd kicked him too hard, and he fell clear of the rocks.

Snap.

I heard his neck break all the way up where I was. I grinned again. One down. Many more to go.

I crouched down over the ridge again, sending wave after wave of Ice magic out into the rocks and trees and grass below. Cold sweat soaked my clothes, my lungs burned, and my head began to pound from the effort of concentrating so long and so hard, from the sheer *will* that it took to force all of my magic out in all directions at once.

Steam rose from the Ice, shrouding the ridge, the woods, and the clearing below in a cold, eerie, misty fog. Well, that should give my friends a bit more cover as they trekked down the mountain.

Still, despite my best efforts, it wasn't enough.

If only it had been a cloudy day, my crystalline creation might have lasted a little longer, but the July sun was already beating down on the ridge and slowly baking it once more. I'd made the Ice as thick as I could, but it wouldn't be long before it melted away. But I'd done all that I could do to help Sophia, Owen, and Warren escape. The rest was up to them.

So I let go of the few remaining scraps of my Ice power. My spider rune ring was completely empty of magic. I had a bit of Stone power left, but it wouldn't do me much good now, unless I wanted to use it to harden my skin, protect myself from the bullets that were still coming my way, and dash off into the woods.

But I wasn't going to run. I might have given Sophia and the others a good head start, but her injuries, combined with Warren's, would make their escape a slow one. I still needed to give Grimes, Hazel, and their men something else to focus on for at least a little while longer: me.

I slid my knife up my sleeve, grabbed the guns from where I'd placed them on the rocks, and waited for Grimes's men to come.

After seeing what had happened to their buddy with the broken neck, Grimes's men quit trying to climb up the frozen rocks to get to me. But they had just as hard a time getting back down again, and several slipped off the ridge and fell to the ground below. Moans, groans, and high-pitched whimpers drifted up to me, along with the sharp, satisfying *snap-snap-snap* of bones breaking. My elemental Ice hadn't killed any more of the men, but I'd put at least a few of them out of commission. Hard to think about chasing after someone when your own femur was sticking up out of your skin like a lollipop gushing blood.

I looked down dispassionately at one man, who was crying, rocking back and forth, and clutching his leg. I could see the white of his bone from where I was. He wouldn't be getting up without an Air elemental to heal him. Even then, the process of being healed would be as excruciating as the broken leg itself. They should just shoot him. It would be kinder—

Crack!

A bullet zinged off the rocks to my right, and I realized that one man had already made the trek through the woods and up the side of the ridge.

Crack! Crack!

Too bad he had lousy aim. The bullets pinged off the rocks around me, but none of them actually came close to hitting me.

I ducked down behind a boulder, then scrambled on top of it and launched myself through the air. The man raised his gun, but I hit his body before he could pull the trigger, and we both went down on the ground. I was the only one who got back up.

Footsteps crunched through the leaves on the trail to my right, and shouts rose from that direction, like a pack of hounds baying out their location.

"Up here!"

"There she is!"

"Get that bitch!"

Men darted out of the woods and headed toward me. I raised the guns in my hands and took aim.

Sophia. Jo-Jo. Fletcher.

That was the mantra I chanted in my head as I fired off shot after shot, carefully aiming at every person who came within range of my weapons and trying to make every single bullet count. Man after man went down, tumbling to a stop at my feet with holes in their heads, necks, and chests, but all too soon, my guns *click-click-click*ed empty. I threw them away, palmed the knife that I'd tucked up my sleeve, and grabbed another one out of a pocket on my vest. More properly attired, I twirled the weapons in my hands and stepped forward.

Sophia. Jo-Jo. Fletcher.

I whirled first one way, then the other, cutting into every man who got within arm's and knife's reach of me, trying to make every single slice and stab as devastating as possible. Blood spattered everywhere, on me and especially on the rocks. Below my feet, the stone began singing a dark, rousing tune about all the death that I was dealing out, and I found myself merrily, loudly humming along in time to it, even though I was the only one who could hear the vicious chorus.

I sang, but the men screamed, the sounds rending the air like my knives did their flesh, the high, sharp echoes reverberating around the ridge and then rattling off into the trees and forest beyond. I hoped Sophia could hear these bastards' terror. I hoped it put the same hard, merciless smile on her face that it did on mine.

Sophia. Jo-Jo. Fletcher.

Time ceased to have any meaning. There were just enemies to cut down, one after another, as quickly, brutally, and efficiently as I could, before moving on to the next man standing. I stabbed arms and legs and chests. Drove my blades into throats and ripped them out again. Even punched my knife through one man's eye. His screams were among the loudest and most satisfying.

That man fell, and I whirled around to face my next foe—and realized that Grimes and Hazel stood behind me, flanked by several more of their gang.

Grimes's gaze scanned over his dead men at my feet, then flicked up to me. His expression was unreadable, but I knew exactly what I looked like. Strands of dark brown hair falling out of my ponytail and sticking to my sweaty, blood-covered face and neck. Even more blood spattered across my hands and arms, with still more soaked into my vest and the rest of my clothes. Even my socks squished with blood, and my boots had left behind an intricate pattern of dull brown stains on the gray rocks, as though I'd been tracing a complicated dance routine over and over again.

"Who the hell are you?" Hazel asked.

I grinned. "Your worst fucking nightmare."

The men standing behind Grimes and Hazel shifted uneasily on their feet. Their leaders might not be afraid of me, but they were—and with good reason.

I gestured at the dead men all around me. "You know, you really should get yourself some better help. All your boys are good for is target practice."

"Take her," Grimes ordered in a cold voice. *"Alive."*

I grinned even wider and twirled my knives, flinging fat drops of blood off the ends of the blades. "Please," I snarled, staring at the men behind him. "Step right up and die."

Nobody made a move toward me. I let out a dark, happy chuckle, then clucked my tongue. "So hard to find good help these days."

"Now!" Grimes screamed, his calm façade finally cracking.

Apparently, Grimes's men were more afraid of him than they were of me, because they rushed forward. Fools. I raised my knives again and stepped up to meet them. First, I'd take care of Grimes's men, then Hazel and the big man himself—

"Now, Hazel," I heard Grimes say.

A second later, thousands of hot, invisible bubbles brushed against my skin. I had just enough time to grab the man in front of me, turn him around, and use him as a shield before a ball of elemental Fire blasted into us.

The flames exploded on the man's chest, burning away his clothes and immediately turning the upper half of his body into a charred, blistered mess. He started screaming and didn't stop, so I shoved him out of the way and took a step toward Grimes and Hazel, who were holding hands, as if they were combining their magic.

That was all I saw before another blast of elemental Fire came my way. Then another one, then another one.

I managed to duck the first two balls but not the third one, which hit my shoulder like a red-hot sledgehammer and spun me around. Before I could move, before I could react, a fourth blast of Fire hit me square in the back.

This time, I screamed.

Because I was almost out of magic, and I didn't have any way to stop the elemental Fire washing over me. The silverstone in my vest heated up as it soaked up the worst of the flames, but it didn't absorb enough of the magic, not nearly enough.

The men attacking me fell back, as they started yelling and trying to get away from the flames before they leaped from my body and onto theirs. The stench and sizzle of my own charred flesh filled my nose, and smoke boiled up from my clothes, mixing with the lingering fog from my elemental Ice. The heat and pain were so intense that I couldn't tell which way was which, and before I could figure out where and whom to attack, a fist shot through the flames, slamming into my skull.

Mercifully, the world went black after that.

❄ 20 ❄

The sun woke me.

It streamed in through the open window, as sweet and innocent as could be, warming everything that it touched with its soft golden rays. Outside, birds trilled out high, happy notes, accompanied by the low, steady bass beat of bumblebees and other bugs.

I cracked my eyes open. A painting of puffy clouds drifting across a summer sky covered the ceiling above my head, like they always did whenever I woke up at Jo-Jo's house after a fight to the death. For a moment, I relaxed, even though part of me wondered why I was lying on the hard wooden floor instead of in the bed beside me. But the more I stared at the ceiling, the more it seemed like there was something slightly . . . off about it. Like the painting wasn't the same one that I'd seen so many times before.

A soft summer breeze fluttered in through the window,

ruffling the pretty, delicate lace curtains—and bringing the stench of death along with it. And I finally realized that I wasn't in Jo-Jo's house after all; I was in Harley Grimes's piss-poor substitute.

But instead of springing to my feet, I lay there on the floor and took stock of the situation, trying to force the rest of the fuzziness to fade from my mind. I still had on the same bloody clothes as before, although I could feel the breeze dancing over bare patches on my arms and legs from where Grimes's and Hazel's elemental Fire had seared through the fabric. The soft kiss of the wind made the burns and blisters that marred my skin start pulsing with pain, and I had to grit my teeth against the sensation. More cuts and bruises dotted my body, adding to my aching exhaustion. I'd put up a good fight, but it had left its mark on me.

Once I realized that I was more or less in one piece, I focused on my magic. My spider-rune ring was still empty and would be until I filled it up again, but being knocked unconscious had given my body a chance to regenerate some of my power, although it was still little more than scraps inside me, not nearly enough to let me go toe-to-toe with Grimes and Hazel with any hope of success—or survival.

I shifted on the floor and put a hand on my chest, patting myself down. I was still wearing my silverstone vest, and the front was largely intact. Then again, Grimes and Hazel had put most of their Fire power into my back. But all of my supplies had been fished out of the vest pockets, including my extra knives. Not surprising. I supposed I should be grateful they'd left my clothes on, burned and bloody as they were, instead of stripping me naked and shoving me into some sort of sundress and heels like they had done with Sophia. Actually, I wondered why they'd let me live in the first place. They should have grabbed one of my knives and cut my throat with it while I was still unconscious—

"Oh, good," a voice purred. "You're finally awake."

I raised my head to see Hazel standing in the doorway, along with three men, all with guns pointed at me.

Hazel gave me an evil smile, then held out her hand. Elemental Fire sparked to life on her fingertips, swaying back and forth like lanterns dancing in the wind. Even though she wasn't actively roasting me with the flames, I could still feel the intense heat blasting off them and brushing against my already burned skin, adding to my misery. The sensation made a snarl rise in the back of my throat, but I swallowed it down.

"Harley wants to see you," she purred again. "Now, are you going to come along quietly, or do I have to . . . encourage you?"

The flames on her fingers burned a little brighter and hotter in anticipation. They matched the cruelty flickering in her dark eyes.

I sat up and immediately had to put a hand down on the floor to keep myself from toppling right back over. After a moment, my head quit spinning, if not aching. Whoever had punched me had done an excellent job of it, judging from the pain that radiated out from my jaw and throbbed up into my right temple. Slowly, very, very slowly, I got up onto my knees and then onto my feet. The change in elevation made my head spin that much more, and I swayed from side to side until the white spots cleared from my vision and I found my balance. This was all not to mention how every single movement made my burned skin ache and how every shift of my singed clothes threatened to pop the blisters covering my arms, legs, and back.

So as much as I would have liked to have tackled Hazel, driven her to the floor, and strangled her to death with my bare hands, I didn't have the energy for it right now. Besides, she and Grimes had kept me alive for a reason, and I wanted to know what it was.

"I think I'll go with the first option," I finally said when I could open my mouth without hissing with pain.

Hazel pouted, obviously disappointed by my cooperation, but she curled her hand into a tight fist, snuffing out the flames and causing the resulting bit of smoke to drift toward the ceiling.

"Come on, then," she snapped. "Nobody keeps Harley waiting—or me either."

Again, I wondered why they'd bothered to let me live, but I supposed that I'd find out soon enough.

Hazel pivoted on her high heels and stormed out of sight of the doorway. The three guys with guns stepped down the hallway far enough for me to leave the bedroom and fall into step behind her, then followed us with their weapons pointed at my back. I thought about whirling around and going for one of their guns, but in the end, I decided against it. I might have been able to kill the three men, but they'd probably have managed to put a couple of bullets into me for my troubles. Not to mention the fact that Hazel would be quite delighted to roast me with her Fire magic, which I had little ability to defend against while my own power was still so low. So I decided to go along with them—for now.

We walked downstairs, and I was once again struck by an eerie sense of déjà vu. Grimes's house was almost an exact replica of Jo-Jo's, inside and outside. The floor plan, build, and construction were identical, right down to the dark cherry wood that had been used for the stairs and the curlicues carved into the railing that ran alongside them. Even the walls were painted the same soft blues, pinks, and whites as in Jo-Jo's house.

I wondered how Grimes had been able to match everything so exactly. He must have been inside Jo-Jo's house at some point. But when? I thought back. The only time the sisters had been away recently was when they'd come down to Blue Marsh to help me out with a particularly nasty vampire a few months ago. Perhaps Grimes had been in the sisters' house then without them realizing it; that was the only explanation that I could think of.

The only things that were different were the photos on the wall next to the stairs. Instead of shots of Jo-Jo, Sophia, Finn, Fletcher, or even me, pictures of Harley Grimes covered the wall. Most of the photos had the brown, faded, vintage look of old daguerreotypes, and almost all of them showed a grinning Grimes tipping his fedora, holding a glass jar of moonshine, or clutching a pair of revolvers crossed over his chest, as though he really was some romantic bootlegging outlaw mugging for the camera, instead of a sick psychopath who liked to kidnap and torture folks.

Other pictures showed Hazel in the same poses, along with one of her on a high ridge, looking off into the distance, queen of everything she surveyed, a set of diamond pins glinting like some sort of crown in her wavy black hair. There were even a few family portraits of Grimes and Hazel with a couple of other men who looked like them. Probably Horace and Henry, the brothers Fletcher had killed.

But there was one photo in particular that made me stop with one foot in midair: a picture of Sophia.

It was about halfway down the wall, right in the middle of a cluster of pictures of Grimes with his guns, and it looked like it had been taken with an old Polaroid camera. At first, I wasn't sure that it was Sophia. She looked so young in the photo, and she was wearing another white dress patterned with tiny red flowers. Her black hair was much longer and tied back into a pretty braid that trailed down over her right shoulder, but she was staring at the camera with the same flat, murderous expression I'd seen earlier at the pit.

The photo must have been taken the first time Grimes had kidnapped Sophia, which meant that he'd kept it all these years. Once I spotted the one, I noticed more photos of my friend. They lined the bottom of the wall, leading back up to the first.

All of those photos looked as though they'd been taken at a distance and featured a young Sophia in various spots: on the lawn at Jo-Jo's house, on the front porch of Country Daze, sitting in a library, reading a book. These pictures must have been snapped before Grimes had kidnapped her the first time. Because in all of them, she looked relaxed and happy and was sporting a variety of clothes in a rainbow of colors—white jeans, red tops, khaki shorts.

None of the photos showed Sophia in her dark Goth clothes. I wondered if she'd adopted the style after her first encounter with Grimes. I would have never wanted to see another dress, ribbon, or pair of high heels again either, if I'd been her.

Just how deep Grimes's obsession with her ran made the whole thing worse and reminded me that I needed to find some way to kill him before I died up here on the mountain. Otherwise, Sophia and Jo-Jo would never be safe.

"Come on," Hazel growled from the bottom of the staircase, realizing that I'd stopped to stare at the photos. "Keep moving."

One of the men behind me shoved his gun into my back, encouraging me. I stared at the first photo of Sophia in the white dress for a second longer before trudging the rest of the way down the stairs.

I wasn't terribly surprised when Hazel led me into the back half of the house. I steeled myself and stepped through the doorway after her, expecting to find some sort of twisted replica of Jo-Jo's salon, but the area was completely different. Instead of combs, curlers, and hair dryers, Grimes had set up a fancy, old-timey office and parlor in the space.

An antique desk trimmed with brass stood in the middle of the room, close to the back wall, with a variety of leather wing chairs arranged in front of it. A perfect place for Grimes to hold court and pontificate to his men. All of the seats were a dark green, except for the one behind the desk. It was the same vibrant cherry red as the salon chairs at Jo-Jo's.

A set of double doors to the left of the desk led out to what looked like a stone patio and then a fenced-in yard beyond. Grimes stood on the patio a few feet outside the open doors. He was dressed in a fresh suit, this one in a pale baby blue, and a blue fedora with a matching feather stuck in the brim perched on his head. I wondered how many of those old-fashioned suits he had hanging in his closets and in how many different colors.

But the surprising thing was that Grimes wasn't alone. Someone was on the patio with him. I couldn't see who it was, though, or even if it was a man or woman. A bit of black fabric was barely visible around the edge of one of the doors, telling me that the person was wearing some sort of dark pants, but that was all.

Grimes had his hands up and was gesturing. Bits of conversation drifted in through the open doors to me.

". . . bit of a problem . . . nothing that I can't handle . . . the shipment won't be delayed . . ."

Then the other person: "The guns had better not . . . that would . . . upset me."

I still couldn't tell whether the stranger was a man or woman. I was too far away, and the voice was too much of a low, smoky murmur.

I'd thought that Grimes would dress down the mystery person for his or her insolent tone and not-so-veiled threat, but the pleasant smile on his face tightened, his lips pulling back to show even more of his perfect teeth, as though he was grinding his molars together to keep the expression firmly in place. After a moment, he nodded. "Of course."

I frowned, wondering who this person was who could

intimidate Grimes with only a few words, especially since I, with my knives and my killing spree of his men, didn't seem to have had much of an impact. I tried to shift to one side, so I could get a better look at his mysterious guest, but a rough hand on my shoulder and a gun shoved against my spine made me stop.

Grimes's answer must have satisfied the other person, because he or she didn't say anything else. Grimes swept his fedora off his head and gave a low, elegant bow, but I couldn't see whether the other person returned the gesture with a polite nod of his or her own. Grimes turned, as if watching someone walk through the backyard. A second later, something creaked, like a fence gate being opened. Then . . . silence.

Grimes settled his hat on top of his head again, then strode inside the office and shut the double doors behind him.

Hazel looked at her brother. "Well?"

"There was a bit of . . . concern about all of the noise and commotion, and of course, we left the client waiting here in the house for far too long while we dealt with the situation," Grimes said. "All of which I apologized profusely for, in addition to offering a discount for all of the worry, waiting, and trouble, so I think that I managed to salvage the deal."

Hazel crossed her arms over her chest. "I *told* you that we should have waited until after this was done before you went after that haughty Deveraux bitch again."

Grimes gave his sister a cold, chilling look. "And I told *you* that I wanted Sophia back as soon as possible—back here with me, where she belongs."

Hazel's nostrils flared, and her jaw tightened, but she didn't argue with her brother any more. Still, it was obvious that she had no love for Sophia. I wondered why— well, beyond the obvious fact that she was a sadistic bitch. Was Hazel jealous because Grimes was still so fixated on Sophia all these years later? Because he'd apparently spent months building a replica of Jo-Jo's house for her to live in? Because he'd decided to bring her there despite the fact that it might jeopardize some big gun deal that the brother and sister had cooking? Or maybe it was a combination of all that and more. Grimes bringing Sophia in, even as his victim, would threaten the amount of time that he had for Hazel. Maybe that was why she liked torturing people so much, especially the young women Grimes kidnapped and brought here. Maybe Hazel didn't want any competition for her brother's attention—or anyone replacing her as queen of the mountain.

"Besides," Grimes said, "it's not my fault that our guest was left waiting. It's *hers*."

He pointed an accusing finger in my direction. All eyes turned to me, and I gave them all a cocky smile.

"Why, if I'd known that y'all had company, I wouldn't have bothered killing your men up on the ridge," I said. "I would have come straight on over here and shown your guests exactly how hospitable I could be—along with the rest of you."

Hazel stepped forward and backhanded me.

Pain exploded in my jaw, making every nerve ending in my face pulse with agony once more. White stars exploded in my vision again, and I rocked back on my feet, but I didn't give her the satisfaction of stumbling. Instead,

I blinked away the spots, stared back at her, and slowly swiveled my head from side to side.

"Thanks," I drawled. "My neck's been killing me all day, but that cracked it just right for me."

Hazel started forward to backhand me again, but Grimes cut in.

"Not now," he said. "You'll get your chance soon enough. I need some information from her first."

"Fine," Hazel muttered in a sullen tone. "We'll do it like usual."

I wondered what *like usual* was, but since it probably involved my screaming, bloody, torture-filled death, I didn't dwell on it too much. I'd find out soon enough.

Grimes moved over and sat down behind his desk, leaning back in his cherry-red leather chair. Hazel went over and perched on the corner of the wood. She'd also changed her clothes sometime while I'd been unconscious and was now wearing another wrap dress in the same baby blue as Grimes's suit and hat. She'd also stuck some different diamond pins, these shaped like small hearts, into her wavy black hair, although her lips were still the same bloody crimson as before.

In a bizarre way, the two of them seemed like two halves of a whole, yin and yang, with Grimes so strong and stocky and Hazel so tall and slender.

Hazel arranged the long skirt of her dress around her, as though she were some sweet Southern belle getting ready to host a genteel social, instead of the cruel, murderous psychopath that she was. She gave me a mocking smile. I ignored her and focused on Grimes. Despite how vicious Hazel was, he was the one in charge—even of her.

Grimes tipped his hat back from his forehead, leaned his elbows on his desk, and steepled his hands together, giving me a thoughtful look over the tops of his interlaced fingers. "Here's how this is going to work," he said. "You are going to answer my questions quickly and truthfully as soon as I ask them. Or there will be consequences."

"What sort of consequences?"

He gave me a thin smile. "I'll let Hazel use her Fire magic on you again."

"Oh, yes," Hazel purred in delight. "And Harley won't make me hold back this time like he did up on the ridge."

I threw back my head and laughed at her threat.

Smoke wisped out from between Hazel's clenched fists, and her brown eyes darkened with the fury of her Fire magic. She didn't like me mocking her. Too damn bad.

A minute passed, then another, and I kept right on laughing. Finally, when my ribs started to ache even more than they already had been, I let the last cold, mirthless chuckle die on my lips.

"Oh, sugar," I drawled. "I've been roasted, toasted, and tortured by some of the strongest, most vicious elementals this little corner of the world has ever seen. Not to mention all of the vampires, giants, dwarves, and regular folks who've gotten their hands on me over the years. Hell, I faced down Mab fucking Monroe herself and lived to tell the tale. Yeah, you're strong in your Fire magic, and so is your brother there, but you're nothing compared with Mab. *Nothing*. So I'd stop bragging and patting yourself on the back. You haven't earned it. You haven't earned a damn thing, especially not my fear."

Red splotches of anger bloomed like roses on Hazel's

cheeks, and more smoke boiled up from her fists, even blacker than before. If she'd been a cartoon character, matching clouds of steam would have been screeching out of her ears by this point.

"Careful, careful," I mocked. "You wouldn't want to singe that pretty dress of yours. Oh, wait. That's right. You only like doing that to other women. Or do you boil the clothes off all of the young men you kidnap before you kill them too?"

Fury flashed in her eyes again, but she slowly unclenched her hands, scooted off the corner of the desk, and stood up.

"Make her start talking, Harley," Hazel snarled. "Right now. Or I will."

I airily waved my burned, bruised, bloody hand at her. "Oh, there's no need to fret, now, sugar. I don't have any problem telling you why I'm here."

"And why are you here, exactly?" Grimes asked.

I stared at him. "I'm here because Fletcher Lane sent me."

Apparently, that wasn't the answer he'd been expecting, because Grimes's hands slid off his desk and into his lap. His eyes narrowed but not before I saw a flicker of emotion in the cold brown depths: fear.

"You *do* remember Mr. Lane, don't you?" I continued, mocking him with his own fondness for formal addresses. "He's the man who saved Sophia from you before."

"He's the man who *took* Sophia from me before," Grimes growled back. "One of my biggest regrets in life is that I didn't kill him years ago."

"Funny, because Fletcher felt the exact same way about

you," I drawled. "He didn't kill you way back then, but believe me when I tell you that I plan to rectify that now."

Grimes gave me an amused look. "Do you know how many people have tried—and failed—to kill me over the years? You're not the first person to come up to my mountain with a couple of guns and knives and try to take me out. I assume you saw the pit. That's not the first one that's ever been dug around my family's cemetery, and it won't be the last."

"Perhaps your other attackers weren't motivated enough," I quipped. "Believe me when I tell you that won't be a problem for me. I'm in it to win it, and all that."

Behind me, the three men with the guns shifted on their feet, making the floorboards creak and groan under their weight. Out of the corner of my eye, I saw the two men on my right exchange a nervous glance. They seemed much more concerned by my threat than Grimes did. Then again, I'd already killed a passel of their buddies, and the day was still young.

But Grimes had a different reaction from his flunkies. He ignored me completely. Instead, he swiveled around in his chair and reached for a decanter of clear liquid on a table behind his desk. Grimes unstoppered the bottle, and caustic fumes from whatever was inside assaulted my nose. Some of his mountain moonshine, I guessed, gussied up in fancy crystal. Mountain strychnine, from the harsh scent of it. That wouldn't just put hair on your chest; it would burn it clean off. And probably take a good portion of your esophagus along with it.

Grimes poured himself a couple of fingers' worth of moonshine into a crystal tumbler, then swiveled back around to face me again. Once he'd had a few sips of the foul brew, he set the tumbler aside and picked up a silver picture frame perched on the right side of his desk. He studied the photo for a moment, then set the frame down at an angle. The same sullen photo of Sophia that I'd seen earlier on the wall by the stairs peeked out at me.

"I knew that Sophia was mine from the first moment that I saw her," Grimes said. "Hazel and I were out getting supplies at this little country store down the mountain a ways. Sophia was there with her sister."

A jolt went through me. Country Daze—he had to be talking about Country Daze, Warren's store. No wonder the old coot had been so insistent on coming with Owen and me. Warren probably felt guilty that Grimes had first laid eyes on Sophia in his store, as guilty as I felt for Jo-Jo's picture being in the newspaper and leading Grimes back to her and Sophia all these years later. And especially for letting Sophia dispose of so many bodies for me over the years.

"Of course, I tried to do the right thing and court her proper," Grimes continued, still staring at the picture of Sophia, his eyes distant and dreamy with memories. "But Ms. Deveraux wouldn't have any of that. She thought that I was a bad influence on Sophia. She should have kept out of things that didn't concern her. But that won't be a problem now, will it?"

I thought of how casually Grimes had shot Jo-Jo in the salon and how cold, pale, and lifeless she had looked lying on Cooper's kitchen table. She could have taken a turn for the worse. She could have needed more healing magic than Cooper had to give.

She could have died in the time that I'd been up here on the mountain.

My heart squeezed at the thought, aching worse than any of my injuries, but I kept my face calm, as though we were talking about the weather, instead of a brutal attack on someone I loved.

"Oh, I don't know," I replied. "Jo-Jo is stronger than you think. She's a tough old bird. She might just surprise you—again."

"What do you mean by *again*?" Hazel asked.

My gaze cut to her. "Who do you think hired Fletcher in the first place? Jo-Jo wanted her sister back, and she decided to do whatever was necessary to make it happen."

"Yes, let's get back to Mr. Lane," Grimes said, leaning back in his chair and interlacing his fingers again. "I'm interested in why you said that he sent you, since I know that he's been dead for months now."

His voice and words were casual, but once again, a bit of unease pinched his face. Whatever Fletcher had done to Grimes all those years ago, however badly the old man had hurt him, however close the old man had come to killing him, it had left a lasting impression. Good. I wanted Grimes to be afraid. I wanted him to sweat and worry and wonder. But most of all, I wanted him to *suffer* for as long as possible before I ended him.

Even if I had no idea how I was going to accomplish that right now.

"Oh, you're right," I agreed. "Fletcher was killed last fall."

My gaze dropped to the floor, but I wasn't seeing the gleaming, pristine wood. Instead, blue and pink pig tracks spattered with blood filled my vision, along with a crumpled, ruined figure that had had the flesh peeled from his bones with Air magic. Fletcher. More memories rose in my mind of that horrible, horrible night when I'd realized that the job that I'd been sent out on was a trap and that I was too late to save Fletcher from being tortured to death inside the Pork Pit.

But I pushed the memories and the emotions back down into the bottom of my black heart and smothered them with a cold, icy layer of rage, just like I had done with the pain of my injuries. Because now was not the time to show any sort of weakness.

"If Lane is dead, then why are you here?" Hazel asked.

"Because he trained me," I answered in a voice that was even snider than hers.

"And who are you?" Grimes asked.

"My name is Gin, like the liquor."

They both gave me blank looks, apparently not getting the joke. Nobody appreciated irony these days.

I sighed. "My name is Gin Blanco," I replied. "But y'all probably know me by another one: the Spider."

The three men behind me sucked in a collective breath. They shifted on their feet again, backing away from me and making the floorboards *creak-creak-creak-creak* with their jerky, hurried movements. Well, it was good that my reputation had preceded me. Perhaps when it came time for me to kill Grimes and Hazel, these fools would cringe and cower instead of getting in my way. A nice thought, but I wasn't going to pin my hopes and dreams on it.

But once again, the brother and sister seemed completely unconcerned by my moniker.

"The Spider?" Hazel sneered. "Really? You're the big, bad bitch who took out Mab Monroe? I don't believe it."

I shrugged. "Believe it or not. Doesn't much matter to me."

"You're lying," Grimes said. "The Spider would never come here. She would never waste her time on some ill-advised rescue mission."

"Oh, I wouldn't say that it was so ill-advised, seeing as how I'm standing here and Sophia isn't." I grinned. "Y'all didn't catch her, did you?"

A muscle twitched in Grimes's cheek, but he returned my shrug with one of his own, as though the fact that I'd stolen Sophia right out from under his nose was of no consequence. "This isn't the first time that Sophia has escaped. She'll be back here where she belongs soon enough."

Hazel let out a derisive snort, then rolled her eyes. "All you've done for the past several months is talk and talk about Sophia Deveraux. I don't see what you find so fascinating about her. She's just a dwarf. Not even a very pretty one at that. Did you see those tacky clothes she had on? Not to mention that horrid spiked collar that she was wearing. You could do better, Harley. So much better. At the very least, we can find you a college girl who will clean up much nicer than Sophia Deveraux ever could."

From the evil glint in her eye, what she really meant was some poor girl whom Hazel would have an easier time torturing, an easier time breaking. It wouldn't surprise me if Hazel got even more enjoyment out of using her Fire magic on their victims than Grimes did. Sadistic bitch.

Grimes studied her a moment, as though he was considering her words, and a hopeful smile curved her crimson lips. Grimes stood up and walked around his desk, and Hazel turned to meet him. She held her hands out, reaching for his—

Grimes slapped her across the face for her trouble.

Hazel stumbled away, hitting the doors at the back of the office hard enough to make the glass rattle in the panes. She whirled around, her mouth open wide in surprise, a hand pressing against her cheek as if she couldn't believe the growing red welt there—and the fact that Grimes had hit her, his own sister, as casually as he would hit anyone else.

"Sophia is *mine*," Grimes growled, his brown eyes darkening with fury, as though the answer to Hazel's question should be obvious. "She's the only woman I've ever met who's *strong* enough to be mine. She's the only one who's never been cowed by me or backed down from me. All the others who have come through here over the years have been weak, foolish creatures, crying to go home, cringing at the smallest little thing, begging for mercy until I give them to my men just to be rid of their incessant whining. Every single one of them has displeased me, *disappointed* me with her weakness. But Sophia never has."

Fletcher had said in his file that Grimes was sick and twisted, but I was beginning to realize exactly how warped he really was. Harley Grimes imagined himself to be the king of this little mountain, and he took whatever and whomever he wanted, brought them here, and expected them to serve him in any way that he deemed fit. And when someone displeased him, when she cried, screamed, and sobbed at the terrible torture that he inflicted on her, then the fault was hers, and off to his men she was sent, to suffer that much more.

"You're right," I said. "Sophia is strong. She's certainly stronger than you, you sick son of a bitch. And as long as I'm alive, you will never lay one *hand* on her again, not so much as one fucking *finger*."

Grimes took a menacing step toward me. I clenched my hands into fists, bracing myself for what was to come. Because as soon as he was within arm's reach, I was going to lunge forward, grab the revolver out of the holster on his waist, and shoot him point-blank in the chest with it—even though I knew that I'd die in the attempt.

Either the men behind me would put a couple of bullets in my skull, or Hazel would scorch me to death with her Fire magic. And of course, there was always the possibility that Grimes's gun was empty of bullets, the way it had been when Sophia had tried to shoot him with it. But I didn't care. I'd bludgeon him to death with the thing if I had to. All that mattered was making sure that Sophia and Jo-Jo were safe from Harley Grimes forever. And if I had to sacrifice my life to save theirs, well, it was a trade that I was happy to make. For them and for Fletcher too.

But Grimes thwarted me without even realizing it, because he stopped and smoothed down his suit jacket, obviously trying to rein in his temper. His hands went to one cuff, then the other, pulling them down. As a final touch, he fingered the brim of his baby-blue hat and then the matching feather stuck there, as though making sure the fedora was still securely perched on his head, his peacock's plume perfectly on display. When he raised his eyes to mine again, he was cool, calm, and in control once more.

Grimes gave me a pleasant smile, the sort a shark would give a guppie before it snapped the smaller creature in two with its many teeth. "Well, then, Ms. Blanco, or whoever the hell you really are, it's a good thing that you won't be alive much longer, isn't it?"

I opened my mouth to tell him exactly what I thought about him, hoping to distract him long enough to surge forward, grab his gun, and end him. But Grimes snapped his fingers, and two of the men behind me stepped forward and clamped their hands on my arms, while the third shoved his gun into my back again.

"Take her outside to the usual spot," he ordered. "And call the men together. We all might as well have a little fun before we go back down to Ashland to find Sophia and bring her back here where she belongs."

✳ 21 ✳

Grimes turned his back on me, dismissing me from his thoughts, at least for the moment, and strode around behind his desk, putting himself well out of range of any desperate lunge that I might make at him.

Hazel moved over to Grimes and laid a possessive hand on his shoulder. She smirked at me. "Don't worry, now, *sugar*," she drawled, using the same mocking tone that I had used earlier. "We'll be with you in a few minutes."

There was nothing that I could do but grit my teeth in frustration as the three men forced me out of the office. All the while, though, I was thinking about distances and angles and how I could kill the men and then take on Grimes and Hazel.

But the three men didn't give me any opportunity to cause trouble. The first two guards kept their hands clamped on my arms, their eyes on me at all times, while the third guy hung back, his gun up and ready to pump me full of bullets if I so much as twitched funny.

They marched me down the long hallway, out the front door, down the porch steps, and across the yard. I thought that they might turn and head toward the pit, so I could join the other poor souls rotting there, but instead, they forced me to walk straight ahead. When we reached the middle of the clearing, they stopped. The two men holding on to my arms yanked me back and forth for a minute, until I was standing on a particular patch of dirt that had been worn smooth by the tread of so many feet on it over the years. Then those two and the third guy did a most curious thing: they slowly backed away from me.

The last guy with the gun raised his weapon high into the air and fired off nine shots, three bursts of three in rapid succession. That must have been Grimes's signal to gather 'round again, because more men started streaming out of the barracks, kitchen, and other buildings.

And they all had weapons.

Most carried guns, long, sleek rifles that could take down an enemy at a hundred paces, and the wooden stocks gleamed like polished bronze in the afternoon sun. Others held big old-fashioned revolvers, which they slowly twirled around and around on their fingers, as though they were cowboys right out of the old West, getting ready for a showdown at high noon. A few clutched knives, while some had crude, simple weapons like the sharpened stakes that I'd seen earlier in the forest.

My gaze went from one man's face to another. They all grinned, their eyes lighting up at the thought of my impending torture, whatever it was going to be. No one looked away, and no one had any spark of compassion, uncertainty, or unease in his face. No surprise there, given how many of their buddies I'd killed already. I was mildly surprised that they hadn't brought out the tar, feathers, and pitchforks, along with their other weapons. That seemed like something that Grimes would enjoy, given his seeming fascination with the past.

The men didn't speak, but a collective sense of anticipation and excitement rippled through them, as though this was some show that they'd witnessed many times before and were eager to see repeated. One guy even drew a silver lighter out of his pocket and lit a cigarette with it, as though this was some sort of smoke break before the main event started. He kept snapping the lid up and down on the lighter, ready to get on with things.

I wondered how many other folks had stood in this exact same spot, facing down Grimes's mob. Would these gangsters all raise their weapons and fire at once? Would they swarm me en masse? Or would they all throw themselves at me, drive me to the ground, and tear me limb from limb? No way to know, until they decided to attack.

I'd killed around a dozen men up on the ridge, but there were a dozen more gathered around me now. My gaze roamed over the crowd again, this time searching for any sign of weakness, any gap in the ring that might be big enough for me to fight my way through, any way that I could escape and live to kill another day. Or at least get back to Grimes and take him down before I died.

But there was nothing—no weakness, no gap, no hope of escape.

So I straightened my spine, stared back at the men, and braced myself for my impending execution.

I didn't have to wait long.

I'd only been standing in the ring of men for about two minutes when the front door of the house banged open, and Grimes and Hazel appeared. Hazel had her arm linked through his, and Grimes escorted her down the steps, through the yard, and out into the clearing in a show of gallantry as complete as any old-fashioned Southern gentleman ever could have managed.

The men parted enough to allow Grimes and Hazel to join in the ring. Once again, the big man kept out of arm's reach of me, but I swallowed my frustration. I couldn't kill Grimes, but I couldn't survive this either, despite my promise to Owen that I would. I'd known that the words were most likely a lie when I'd said them, but I'd at least hoped to destroy Grimes before I met my own end. Now I didn't even think that would happen.

My heart clenched at the thought of Owen, and I focused on the tightness in my chest, imagining it as a drumbeat and letting it steady me.

Live, live, live, live . . .

I could almost hear Owen's voice whispering that to me over and over again, and I seized onto that determination until there was no room for anything else. No doubt, no hesitation, no fear. Just the will to do what needed to be done to survive this.

Because if I couldn't kill Grimes now, that meant that I had to live to try again another day.

The Fire elemental swept his hat off his head and

bowed low to the crowd, before straightening back up and gesturing at me with his dapper fedora. "Allow me to introduce Ms. Blanco," he said in a loud, booming voice. "At least, that's what she says her name is. But we don't pay too much attention to names up here, do we, boys?"

The men all chuckled. Several wet their lips as they stared at me, while others slowly looked me up and down, their lecherous gazes trying to see my breasts through the blood-soaked vest that I wore.

"Now, we all know what we do to the folks we decide to bring up to our camp or those who wander in here by accident," Grimes continued. "We give them a choice. They can stay, or they can go."

A choice? I seriously doubted that, but I had no idea what he was babbling on about.

"Usually, that choice only involves a few of you, since it's a reward for those who have worked extra hard over the last few weeks. But I think that you will all agree that Ms. Blanco's . . . *antics* have earned her a special sort of punishment."

The men all hooted and hollered, their dark cheers rising in a swelling tide of impending violence. The guy with the lighter clicked it on and held it up as if he was at a rock concert, while a few of the others fired their guns into the air or stamped their feet, like they were bulls about to charge me. I really should have been wearing a red cape. It was my color, after all.

Grimes raised his hands, and the commotion slowly quieted down. "Now, you all know how many good men we lost today because of Ms. Blanco and her friends."

The crowd sobered at that, and angry, accusing gazes slammed into me from all sides.

"Rest assured that we will track down the other people responsible for the attack on our camp, and we will deal with them accordingly. But in the meantime, there is the question of what to do with Ms. Blanco."

Grimes looked at each man in turn. "Well, boys? What *should* we do with her?"

A chorus of shouts erupted from the crowd.

"Kill her!"

"Shoot the bitch where she stands!"

"Throw her in the pit!"

Naturally, that last screamed request came from Hazel.

Grimes grinned and cupped a hand to his ear, as though he were listening to each and every hoarse, murderous scream and was considering them all quite carefully. From Fletcher's file and what I'd seen, I'd thought that Grimes was just another bad guy, just another underworld thug, just another elemental who used his magic to keep his minions in line. But I had to admit that he had a certain charisma to him, a certain way of playing to a crowd, a certain cruel strength that others might admire and flock to. I had no doubt that his men feared him, but they respected him too.

After a few minutes, he raised his hands, and the men quieted down once more. "Well, those are all fine, fine ideas, but I have one that I think you'll like even better," Grimes said. "As some of you know, Ms. Blanco here claims to be the Spider, the most feared assassin in all of Ashland."

This time, derisive laughs and snorts rippled among the men.

"Now, I doubt that she's telling the truth," Grimes continued. "But let's say that she is. I know how much you boys like to go hunting, and I'd say that this is a prime opportunity to go up against the best of the best. Wouldn't you?"

More hoots and hollers. More stomping feet and lascivious grins. More fingers rubbing over the triggers of guns and the hilts of knives, itching to use the weapons on me.

"Now, we've all suffered a terrible loss here today," Grimes said, when the men had fallen silent once more. "This woman has taken our brothers in arms from us. Fine men and fine soldiers. She came up here, snuck up here in the shadows, and killed them, like a hunter shooting deer from a stand. Hardly sporting at all. So I say that we give her a taste of her own medicine and show *her* what it feels like to be hunted for a change."

Grimes fixed his gaze on mine. His eyes glowed a bright, almost golden brown, not from any Fire magic that he was embracing but from the strength and surety of his own crazy convictions.

"I like to think of myself as a sporting man, Ms. Blanco," Grimes said. "And the rules of this game are quite simple. You get a five-minute head start. After that, it's open season—on you."

When I didn't respond to his taunts or show so much as a flicker of fear, Grimes turned to his men once again.

"Bring her back dead, and you'll be richly rewarded," Grimes said. "Or, if you prefer, bring her back alive, and, well, the man who bags her can have her for an hour before we throw her in the pit and finish her off."

This time, the hoots and hollers were so loud that you could probably hear them on the next mountain over. Apparently, Grimes's boys were all about the thrill of the chase. Fools.

"Now, being the sporting man that I am, I will warn you that I'm not going to handicap Ms. Blanco in any way," Grimes said. "Some of you saw her fight up on the ridge, so you know exactly how dangerous she is already."

No weapons, no supplies, and a body full of aches and pains. Nah. I wasn't handicapped at all.

"Oh, yeah, she might have been tough up on the ridge," Hazel chimed in, cocking her hip to the side and striking a pose. "But that was when she had a couple of knives on her. I think the boys won't have nearly as much trouble with her this time around. Don't y'all agree?"

The men roared with laughter. They didn't notice Grimes arching a black eyebrow at Hazel and her cringing and quickly bowing her head in apology. Apparently, the big man didn't like anyone ad-libbing on his time.

So that's why he'd let me keep my clothes, boots, and vest—so I'd put up more of a fight and give his men a better show. The way things stood now, I'd either get gunned down in the woods like a deer or dragged back here and raped before being roasted like a pig in the pit by Hazel.

I flashed back to the dead woman whom Owen, Warren, and I had found in the stake-filled trap that morning. I wondered if this was the same choice that she'd been given: stay here and live a short, torture-filled life, or try to get away and die.

That black rage rose in me again, and I let the cold

seep into every part of my being, let it coat all the aches and pains in my body, let it fill in the hollow space where I'd used up so much of my magic, let it freeze out everything that might distract me from what had to be done now. Oh, yes. I embraced the rage until it was the only thing thrumming through my body—along with the will to survive.

Grimes's first mistake was not killing me while I'd been unconscious on the ridge. His second was this ridiculous blood sport. But his third and most egregious was the fact that he was giving me a chance, however small—because I was going to make the most of it.

While the men cheered and Grimes grinned at the adoration coming his way, I stared past the ring of jeering fools and scanned the camp, taking in all of the buildings and the woods beyond, comparing where I was with Fletcher's maps that I'd studied earlier.

After a moment, a cruel smile curved my lips. If Grimes and his boys wanted a show, I'd be more than happy to give them some fireworks that they'd never forget.

The hoots and hollers finally died down, and Grimes checked the watch on his wrist.

"Your time starts now, Ms. Blanco," he said.

"If I were you," Hazel said, giving me an evil smile, "I'd start running, bitch."

Hazel hadn't even finished speaking before I started moving. But instead of immediately breaking through the ring of men, I focused my sights on one particular target: the guy with the cigarette lighter.

He'd clipped the lid closed and was about to put the device in his pocket when I jammed my fingers into his throat and swiped the lighter from his hand. He dropped to the ground, wheezing. I hurdled over his body and started sprinting toward the east end of camp.

"Hey! She hit Bert!"

"She wasn't supposed to do that!"

Angry shouts rose behind me, but I tuned them out.

The smart thing would have been to start climbing up the rocky ridge, then find the path that Warren, Owen, and I had used to get up here in the first place. But I didn't know that I had the strength for such a quick, strenuous climb, given the burns and blisters on my hands, arms, legs, and back. Right now, it was all I could do to run through the pain.

And just because Sophia wasn't here didn't mean that she and the others were off the mountain yet. I didn't know how much time had passed while I was unconscious—maybe a couple of hours, maybe less—but I still wanted to give them as much time as possible to get away, so I headed in the opposite direction from how we'd approached Grimes's camp. Besides, there was something else that I wanted to do before I headed into the woods, one more little surprise I wanted to add to Mr. Grimes's show.

Instead of heading for the path that led to the pit or plunging into the woods, I veered to the left, straight toward the building that housed the moonshine that Grimes and his men made.

"Hey!" Another shout rose behind me. "You can't do that! You're supposed to run into the woods!"

I grinned. They wanted to play a game with me, but they didn't like the fact that I wasn't doing what they wanted me to, what they *expected* me to. Well, I wasn't some poor college girl who'd been kidnapped and was scared out of her mind and running blind. I was an assassin, and I was going to show them exactly how the Spider played this sort of twisted game.

I leaped up onto the front porch, threw open the door, and burst into the building. The inside had been gutted so that it was one big open space. Three copper stills had been set up in the middle of the area, with different lengths of pipe squatting in front of them, as though they were in the process of being hooked together. A table against the left wall bristled with more pipes, along with tools and rags.

My gaze snapped over to the right wall, which was covered with shelves and, more important, jars of moonshine. Hundreds of glass Mason jars of various shapes and sizes lined the wooden shelves, all sealed with shiny brass lids. The sunlight streaming in through the windows made the liquid glimmer like white gold. Well, I was about to change that.

I raced over, grabbed a jar of moonshine, and unscrewed the lid. Caustic fumes assaulted my nose, adding to the hot, sour stench of mash in the air and making me cough. Still, I rammed my shoulder into the shelves as hard as I could, making several dozen jars rattle, fall to the floor, and break. The inside of my nose felt like it was on fire, but I didn't care. At this point, it matched the aches and pains rippling through the rest of me.

I quickly stepped through the broken glass and moved to the opposite end of the shelves. I shoved my shoulder into this side too, making even more jars crash to the ground. Puddles of liquid started to ooze over the floor toward the stills, pipes, and supplies.

When I was sure that there was enough spilled moonshine for what I had in mind, I headed for a door set into the back wall. I also tipped over the open jar of moonshine in my hand, letting the liquid dribble out a little at a time. When the jar was empty, I tossed it away and took the final few steps to the door.

Grimes thought he was giving his men an advantage by taking away my knives, but he hadn't realized that I didn't need weapons or that the simplest thing could be the most dangerous in certain situations—like the cigarette lighter that I was still holding.

One of Grimes's men appeared in the doorway. His eyes locked onto the bit of metal gleaming in my hand.

"No!" he shouted, realizing what I was about to do. "Stop—"

I grinned again, clicked the lighter on, and tossed the flickering flame onto the floor.

WHOOSH!

The thing about mountain moonshine that made it so irresistible to some folks was the high alcohol content. I'd only been sucking down the fumes for a minute, and I already felt light-headed. In my case, I wasn't looking for a buzz so much as a burn, and I got one.

It only took a second for the fire to zip across the alcohol trail that I'd created on the floor and over to the puddles of liquor. It wouldn't be long before the flames would cause more of the glass jars to shatter, which would add even more fuel to the fire. I grinned into the heat of the flames even as the guy at the door turned and ran.

This should keep at least a few of Grimes's men busy and out of the hunt. Otherwise, the whole camp might go up in smoke—and wouldn't that just be a crying shame.

Shouts rose from the front of the building as smoke boiled up and the fire started edging toward the windows. The shimmering red-orange flames made the stills glow a bright copper.

Crack!

Crack! Crack!

Crack!

I ducked, thinking that the idiots outside were shooting at the building, but it was only the glass jars breaking. More moonshine spilled to the floor, and the flames arched higher.

"Burn, baby, burn," I murmured, encouraging the fire a final time before turning and running out the back door.

* 22 *

Several working stills squatted in the backyard behind the building, but they were far too big and heavy for me to tip over and add to the mayhem, so I raced past them, my eyes fixed on the woods ahead.

Crack!

Crack! Crack!

Crack!

Bullets pinged off the metal stills and pipes and rattled away into the trees. Apparently, my five minutes were already up. Or maybe I'd forfeited my laughable head start by not playing by the rules.

Apparently, not as many of Grimes's men as I thought were staying behind to fight the fire, because more shouts rose behind me.

"There she is!"

"I see her!"

"Get that bitch!"

I hopped over the white picket fence at the edge of the yard and darted into the woods. Despite the fact that men with guns were chasing me, I still made myself slow down and watch where I put my feet so I wouldn't fall victim to one of the traps strung up around the camp. I had no desire to escape the hunting party only to get a face full of elemental Fire from a sunburst rune seared into one of the trees.

But the good thing about nasty surprises like booby traps was that they could work both ways—like helping me thin out the murderous herd thundering through the forest behind me.

I darted through the woods as fast as I could, searching for anything that might trip me up—or at least injure one of my pursuers. More bullets crackled through the trees and leaves around me, but they weren't as close as they had been before, meaning that I'd managed to put a little distance between myself and my would-be murderers.

Out of the corner of my eye, I noticed the sun gleaming on something close to the forest floor, and I veered in that direction. Even though I knew it was there, it still took me a few seconds to spot the fishing line. The trap was identical to the first one that Warren had disarmed earlier. One end of the line taped to a sunburst rune that had been scorched into a tree trunk, the line running across the path at ankle level, then the other end wrapped around a small peg that had been pounded into the ground.

Perhaps Lady Luck had finally decided to smile on me, because this particular peg was actually hidden by a thick rhododendron bush. I stepped off the path and crouched down behind the bush, making sure that I was as hidden as I could be by the arching branches and green, glossy leaves. Then I carefully took hold of the fishing line and waited—just waited.

Ten . . . twenty . . . thirty . . . forty-five . . . sixty . . . I counted off the seconds in my head as I listened for sounds of pursuit. Finally, after about three minutes, two men came crashing through the woods toward me, rifles clutched in their hands. I peered through the branches at them.

"Did you see her?"

"Where did she go?"

"We need to find her!"

They shouted back and forth to each other as they moved through the woods. Grimes had trained them well. The two men stayed within sight of each other at all times so they could watch each other's back, and they were close enough together that they wouldn't miss me hiding in a clump of bushes between the two of them.

Slowly, they crept toward my position. I stayed still and quiet, my blistered, bloody fingers curled around the thin fishing line, as though I were a spider hanging on to a piece of my own web.

"Careful," one of the men said as they neared me. "You know this section is dotted with traps."

"What kind?" the other man asked. "Pits, snares, or Fire?"

"Fire, I think," the first man replied. "But you don't want to trip any one of them."

The other man nodded his head and started moving forward again, his eyes sweeping the forest floor, while his buddy kept a lookout on the landscape around them.

The men were fifteen feet away from me . . . ten feet . . . seven . . . five . . . three . . . one . . .

"Stop," the first guy said. "I see some fishing line. Be careful—"

I grinned and yanked on the line, pulling the tape free of the sunburst. The rune flared to life on the tree trunk on the opposite side of the path, burning an angry red in warning.

"What the—"

That was all the first guy got out before a ball of elemental Fire exploded all over him. He went down in a singed, smoldering heap, screaming and clawing at the flames that were melting his skin, hair, and eyes.

The second man stared down dumbstruck at his buddy, as if he couldn't believe that the other man had been careless enough to actually trip the trap. I surged to my feet. A branch crackled under my foot, but I didn't care. The man whirled around just in time for me to slam my fist into his chest. He staggered back, and I yanked the rifle out of his hands, flipped it around, and shot him in the throat with his own weapon. He was dead before he thumped to the forest floor—

The feel of hot, invisible bubbles popping against my skin was the only warning that I had that I wasn't alone. I threw myself down onto the ground.

A ball of elemental Fire slammed into the tree above me, showering me with hot sparks and smoldering splinters. Another gust of magic swept through the air. I grabbed the guy I'd shot and rolled him over so that he was on top of me. A second later, another ball of Fire hit the tree a few feet above my head. The flames washed over the man's body, burning through his clothes and leaving nothing behind but charred, ashy, flaky skin. The amount of Fire would have killed him had he not already been dead.

The stench of seared flesh filled my nose, along with noxious clouds of smoke. I coughed and shoved the burned body off me. The rifle still in my hand, I staggered to my feet and risked a glance through the trees. I didn't see any more men chasing me. They were probably busy putting out the fire I'd started. No, this time, Grimes and Hazel themselves were hunting me.

Grimes was carrying a rifle, which he raised to his shoulder and pointed in my direction. But I wasn't as concerned about him as I was about Hazel, who gave me a cruel grin even as more elemental Fire flashed to life in her hand. I could dodge bullets a lot longer than I could dodge magic.

Even as Hazel reared back her hand to throw her power at me, I fired off a few haphazard shots with my own rifle, then turned and started to run once more.

WHOOSH!

The Fire slammed into the spot where I'd been standing, and the heat from the blast nipped at my heels like a pack of hungry wolves, even though I was ten feet away and moving fast. Hazel wasn't holding back. She didn't want to take me back to camp alive. She just wanted me dead.

The feeling was mutual.

But with my magic still so low, there was no way that I could go toe-to-toe with her. And with Grimes by her side, I couldn't hope to hide in the woods, sneak up, and shoot her in the back either. That meant running away and coming back to fight another day. I wasn't ashamed by my retreat, though. I'd gotten Sophia away from here, so I'd kept that promise to Jo-Jo. Now I just needed to find a way to keep the one that I'd made to Owen to live through this.

So I ran and ran through the woods as ball after ball of elemental Fire tore through the trees, bushes, and rocks all around me. If Hazel wasn't careful, she was going to set the whole mountain ablaze with her magic. Or maybe that's what she wanted, for me to get trapped in the middle of a raging forest fire. Dead was dead, after all. I didn't think that Hazel would be too picky about how she accomplished my demise.

Either way, there was nothing that I could do but keep running. I needed to put as much distance between them and me as fast as I could, so I didn't have time to be cautious, slow down, and look for traps, not if I didn't want Hazel to roast me where I stood. So I had to hope that I wouldn't put my foot down in a snare, tug loose a bit of fishing line, or stumble into one of the stake-filled pits.

For once, my luck held, and I didn't encounter any more traps, but I still wasn't going to be able to escape Grimes and Hazel.

The fight at the salon, rushing Jo-Jo over to Cooper's, climbing up the mountain with Owen and Warren, killing the guards at the pit, using my Ice magic to freeze the rocks on the ridge; fighting Grimes's men, feeling his and Hazel's Fire slamming into my body. All of that had chipped away at me.

It was one thing to be without magic, but even more

troubling was the loose, rubbery feeling in my legs, the sweat streaming down my face, and the constant stitch in my side as I tried to suck down enough of the hot, humid summer air to keep putting one foot in front of the other.

I was about to turn and try to make some sort of desperate stand against Grimes and Hazel when I spotted a wide opening in the trees up ahead. I'd long ago lost track of where I was on the mountain, but maybe I'd managed to stumble onto some sort of forest service access road. There might even be an ATV nearby that I could flag down or hot-wire, if it came to that—

As I burst out of the trees, I immediately had to put on the brakes. The opening before me wasn't a road. It was a cliff.

I skidded to a stop just in time to keep myself from plunging over the edge. I stared down, and I remembered something important from Fletcher's maps that I'd forgotten: the river flowed through Bone Mountain.

The Aneirin River twisted and turned through Ashland and the Appalachian Mountains that ran around and through the city. I didn't know if this was the river itself or one of the many mountain streams that fed into it. Although *stream* was a bit of an understatement, given that the water was at least thirty feet wide and white and frothy with rapids.

Oh, yes, I remembered seeing the river on Fletcher's maps of the mountain. I just had no idea that I was this close to it—and no idea how to get across it.

Because this wasn't any old ridge that I was standing on top of; it was a bona fide cliff, with a sheer, vertical, three-hundred-foot drop to the water below. Not exactly your usual summer swan dive. Still, I might have considered it if I hadn't been so low on my magic. But I couldn't risk it. Not now. I'd have to find some other way off the mountain—

Crack!

While I'd been gaping at the rapids below, Grimes and Hazel had closed the distance between us. The first shot clipped the back of my left shoulder and spun me all the way around.

Crack! Crack!

The next two bullets *thunk*ed into the front of my vest, making me stagger back.

One of my feet slipped off the rocks, and I had to windmill my arms back and forth to keep from teetering the rest of the way over the side. Finally, I managed to catch my balance and stumble away from the edge, although I probably shouldn't have bothered, since Grimes and Hazel slowly approached me. He was still holding his rifle, while yet another ball of elemental Fire flickered in her hand. There was no way I could get a shot off with my own rifle without both of them unloading on me first.

"Well, well, well," Grimes crowed in a triumphant voice. "It looks like we've cornered us a pesky little varmint."

Instead of responding, I glanced over my shoulder at the rocks and rapids in the canyon below.

"Oh, now, don't be like that, Ms. Blanco," Grimes said, picking up on my train of thought. "We hunted you down fair and square. The least you can do is come on back to camp with us and hold up your end of the bargain."

"Why?" I snarled. "So I can be raped, tortured, and murdered?"

"Of course," Hazel chimed in. "That's your punishment for all the bad things that you've done. Besides, you jump, you die. Simple as that."

"I go back with you, I die anyway," I countered.

Grimes shrugged. "Not right away. Who knows? You might be able to escape . . . eventually."

It was probably the same line he used whenever he cornered someone in the woods like this. *Oh, come on back to camp,* I could just hear him saying in that soft, syrupy, twangy drawl of his. *It's better than dying out here in the middle of the woods. Who knows? You just might live through this, after all.*

But it was nothing but a damn, dirty lie. It had been a lie for all the people before me, and it would be for me too. Because Grimes and Hazel didn't have any intention of letting me live. No, I'd entertain them and their boys for a few days—if that long—and then they'd dispose of me in the pit, along with all the others.

"Besides," Grimes continued, thinking that I was wavering, "I'm starting to take a shine to you, Ms. Blanco. You're strong, just like you said Sophia was. And I do so admire the strong."

He didn't admire strong people; he wanted to break them to make himself feel stronger. That's what he had tried to do to Sophia all those years ago: break her spirit, break her strength, break her will to live, to survive all the horrors that he had visited upon her. But he hadn't broken Sophia, and he wasn't going to break me either.

"Come on, now," he said, his voice taking on a soft,

cooing note. "If you come back with us quietly, I'll keep you for myself. None of my men will touch you. I promise you that."

Hazel's mouth gaped open for a moment before her whole face tightened with rage and jealousy. The Fire flickering in her hand coalesced into a ball of molten lava that oozed out between her fingers and splattered onto the rocks at her feet, causing the stone to shriek in agony.

But Grimes didn't notice. He only had eyes for me. After a moment, he licked his lips, like his men had done back at camp, and his gaze flicked up and down my body. No doubt the bastard was thinking about how I'd look in a pretty white dress with my hair in a sweet little braid.

Well, he was never, *ever* going to find out.

My only regrets were that I wouldn't get a chance to tell my friends and family how much I loved them and that I wouldn't be able to stop Grimes once and for all.

I thought of Owen and how he'd kissed me on top of the ridge. There had been a desperate promise in that kiss, one that said that there was still a chance that things could get better between us, one that had kept me going through all of this. Just when it seemed like we'd finally turned a corner, we were going to be torn apart again forever.

But Owen would understand. He'd seen the pit. He'd seen what Grimes and Hazel had done to Sophia. He'd understand why I had to do this. I just wished . . . I just wished that I could have seen him once more.

But wishes were for fools. People made their own decisions, their own lives, their own fates. That was what Fletcher had always said, and it was certainly true in this case.

I'm sorry, Owen. So sorry. I wish that I had been able to keep my promise to you.

I slowly held the rifle out to my side, laid it down on the ground, and kicked it away, sending it skittering across the stones. Then I straightened back up, holding both of my hands out to my sides. Grimes smiled with hungry, sadistic glee, thinking that I was finally surrendering, that I was finally weakening, that I was finally giving up.

His grin lasted until I started walking backward toward the edge of the cliff.

"Don't be stupid," Grimes warned. "You'll never survive a fall like that."

"Probably not," I agreed. "But I have no interest in being your little torture toy either. I'd rather take my chances with the river and the rocks. Simple as that."

Before he could react, and still thinking of Owen, I turned and threw myself off the cliff.

❖ 23 ❖

It seemed as though I had a pair of cement blocks strapped to my boots. That's how quickly gravity yanked me down. The cliff rushed by my face in a swirling mix of grays and greens, and the wind tore at my hair and screamed in my ears.

Even as I plummeted toward the rocks, river, and rapids, I grabbed hold of what little Stone magic I had left and used it to harden my body as much as I could. I reached and strained and clawed for all those tiny bits of power, trying to weave the scraps into my usual solid shell, but I didn't know if it would be enough. If not, at least the end would be quick.

I hit the water a second later.

The impact knocked all of the air from my lungs and pulled me deep beneath the surface. For a moment, everything went cold and wet and black, and I thought that I was dead.

But then that pesky, determined, undeniable instinct to survive, to live, rose inside me, and I realized that the pressure in my lungs hurt too much for me to be dead.

It took me several sharp, hard kicks before I was able to break through to the surface. Even then, all I managed to do was swallow down a quick breath before the current dragged me under again.

I'd jumped into the Aneirin River twice before. Once from a balcony at the Ashland Opera House after a botched hit. Then again from the top of a moving train in order to escape Elektra LaFleur, an assassin with electrical elemental magic. But this was far more brutal an experience than either one of those previous adventures. In both of those cases, the water had only wanted to drag me down, down, down. But now it wanted to pull me every which way, dash me against the rocks, suck me down, push me up, and repeat the whole process over and over again until my mind was spinning around as much as my body was.

I quickly exhausted what was left of my Stone magic, and my skin reverted to its normal texture. That meant that I felt every single pull and grab and yank of the water, every slam of my body against a half-submerged rock or a gnarled fallen tree, every slash of a sharp stone across my skin. Good thing these weren't shark-infested waters, or I would have been their buffet, that's how much blood seemed to flow from the dozens of tiny nicks and cuts that crisscrossed my body. Still, I laughed at the thought. At least, I tried to. All I really ended up doing was swallowing more water.

Just when I was about to give in and let the water

sweep me under forever, the rapids surged forward, flowing even faster than before, as though they were building toward some grand finale. All that was missing was some wild, loud, bombastic music to go along with the steady surge. I blinked through the sheets of water stinging my eyes. Why was there so much blue? It almost seemed like the river was flowing into the sky—

I barely had time to suck in another breath before I plunged over the waterfall.

It wasn't a terribly steep drop, maybe thirty feet, but the force of the fall stunned me, and my mind went blank. Then my body slammed against the bottom of the pool below, snapping me out of my dangerous daze. Still, it took all the energy that I had left to kick my legs, claw my hands upward, and finally break free of the surface once more.

I blinked wearily and looked around, wondering what new challenge awaited me. But the waterfall must have been the end of the rapids, because the river formed a large, sedate pool before slowly flowing out of the other side of the wooded canyon that I was in.

The muddy bank was only about fifty feet away, but it took me much longer than it should have to flounder in that direction. At this point, I didn't even have the strength left to use my arms to pull myself through the water. All I could do was weakly kick, like a puppy that was in way over its head.

Eventually, though, I made it over to the bank. I tried to get to my feet, but they kept slipping and going out from under me. So I sank onto my knees and slopped forward through the mud, sending sprays of it in every direction. I got free of most of the water, although it still lapped at my ankles, bringing a bit of fresh misery with every slow, cold surge.

The sun beat down on my head, frying my scalp, but even that warmth seemed distant and far away. Finally, I couldn't go any farther. No matter how hard I tried, my arms and legs wouldn't cooperate, and I just lay there, panting for breath amid the mud, rocks, and dead limbs that formed a sort of driftwood fence on the bank.

I made sure that my face was out of the water as best I could. Then the blackness rose in my mind again, and this time, I didn't try to fight it as it blotted out everything else.

Sophia was in trouble.

That was the thought that hummed through my mind as I ran toward the storage room, grabbed a paring knife lying on a table there, and hurried back to the double doors that led into the front of the restaurant. I peered out through one of the windows, but the two giants had their heads down, counting the cash from the register. I opened one of the doors just wide enough for me to slip into the storefront, then tip-toed over to the end of the counter and hunkered down there, out of sight of our attackers.

I crept up to the corner of the counter and peered around it. The blond kid was still lying in front of the counter where Mason had dumped him, his thin arms and legs sprawled out at awkward angles. So was Sophia. I hadn't realized it before, but she'd cut her head when it had slammed against the counter, and blood had dripped down the side of her face and pooled on the floor. For a moment, I thought that she was dead, that I was too late to save her, that I'd failed her.

But I made myself keep staring at her, and I saw that her chest rose and fell in a steady rhythm. Some of the tightness in my own chest eased. As long as she was still breathing, Jo-Jo could fix the rest. That was what Fletcher always said whenever he came home with a knife, a gunshot, or some other wound he'd gotten as the Tin Man.

The giants finished counting the cash, split the bills between them, and walked around the counter so that they were looming over Sophia and the boy again. I thought that they might pick up Sophia and carry her into the back of the restaurant. That's what they'd been talking about before—taking her back there so they could kill her. The kid too.

But instead of trying to move her, the other giant, Zeke, got down on his knees on the floor. He leered at Sophia, even though she couldn't see him, then started unbuckling his belt.

"C'mon," the other man, Mason, growled. "Quit fooling around. There's no time for that. Besides, someone could always walk by and look in the windows at any second."

Not likely, given the late hour. Besides, the restaurant wasn't too far away from Southtown. Some nights, the vampire hookers and their pimps wandered over in this direction, so the street outside wasn't exactly a great place to linger after dark. Still, I held my breath, hoping that the possibility would be enough to get the giant to leave Sophia alone.

"Let 'em look." Zeke sneered. "I don't care."

"Well, I do," Mason snapped back. "So let's get them in the back out of sight before someone sees us. We got a nice little score from the cash register. Let's see if there's a safe in the back, then kill them and leave."

Zeke snorted. "No way. I say we have a little fun with this bitch before we off her."

"And I say that I don't plan on getting pinched by the cops over this . . ."

While the men continued to argue, I left the corner of the counter and darted forward, ducking down behind a table and some chairs. At this point, I was about fifteen feet away from the men. I could cross the restaurant in a few steps and be on top of them before they realized what was happening.

My hand trembled a bit, but I made myself clench my fingers around the hilt of the paring knife even tighter. The feel of the smooth steel handle digging into my cold skin steadied me. I drew in a breath. I could do this. I would do this. This was what Fletcher was training me for, so I could protect myself and the people I cared about. I didn't know if that included some random kid, much less Sophia, but Fletcher and Jo-Jo loved her, and I loved them. And that was all that really mattered to me.

"All right, all right," Zeke muttered. "Look at her. She ain't no great beauty. I'd rather have the cash from the register than her, anyway."

"C'mon, then," Mason repeated. "Quit whining, and help me carry her. She looks heavy."

Zeke rolled his eyes, but he rebuckled his belt and got back to his feet. Then both of the men leaned over. Mason grabbed Sophia's ankles, while Zeke took hold of her shoulders.

"On three," Mason said. "One, two—"

I didn't wait for three. *Instead, I rose from behind the table and raced across the restaurant. The giants were so focused on Sophia that they never even saw me coming.*

I rammed my knife into Mason's right side. He screamed

with pain and surprise, but there was nothing that I could do to keep him quiet, so I yanked the knife out and stabbed it into his other side. The paring knife wasn't quite as strong as I'd thought it would be, but I kept twisting and twisting it into his muscles, sawing through his ligaments and tendons. Blood spattered all over the blue and pink pig tracks on the floor, turning them a rusty red.

Mason pitched face-first onto the floor and started crawling forward, trying to get away from me. This time, I plunged the knife square into his back. I used my weight to drive the blade in as deep as it would go. I must have hit something vital, because he let out a choked scream that quickly died down into a raspy gurgle. He arched his back once, then slumped forward onto the floor, dead.

"You little bitch!" Zeke roared. "You'll pay for that!"

Before I could crawl off the dead guy, Zeke stepped forward, dug his hand into my hair, and yanked me up. This time, I yelped in pain and surprise. He held me out in front of him and gave me a vicious shake. Then he started hitting me.

Once, twice, three times, the giant backhanded me. My head snapped from side to side to side, and my world spun around and around and around from the blows. As a finishing touch, he rammed his fist into my stomach. He let go of my hair, and I dropped like a stone to the ground.

Zeke was strong, even for a giant, and the blows had hurt so much that I was having trouble fighting the black spots swimming at the edge of my vision. But I made myself focus and stay awake. Because if he knocked me out, he'd probably rape and kill me on the spot—if he didn't decide to go ahead and simply beat me to death.

So I pushed back at the black spots and focused on breathing. It took me a moment to realize that I'd managed to hang on to the knife while he'd been hitting me, and I tightened my grip on the bright, shiny silver handle, ready to use it on him the second that I got a chance.

But Zeke didn't give me one. He was in a rage now, and he drew back his boot to kick me in the ribs. I barely managed to reach for my Stone magic in time to keep him from caving in my chest with the vicious blow. And he didn't stop. Again and again, he lashed out at me.

I lay there and let him hit me, cradling the knife in my hand and trying to hide it as much as possible. I didn't really have another option. I needed the knife to kill him, and if he realized that I still had it, he'd kick it out of my hand and keep on beating me until I ran out of magic. Then he'd do the same to Sophia and the kid, and I couldn't let that happen.

Finally, after about three minutes of whaling on me, Zeke ran out of steam. He gave me one more vicious kick to the side.

"That'll teach you, you little bitch," he growled again.

I lay limp and still on the floor, as though he'd long ago knocked me out with his attack.

Zeke finally snapped back around to Sophia, who hadn't stirred the whole time. He focused his angry glare on her for a moment before turning to the boy.

"As for you two," he snarled, "you're both turning out to be more trouble than you're worth. And now I have to carry you all by myself."

Zeke kept grumbling as he leaned down and grabbed Sophia's shoulders again. Then he started dragging her around the counter and down the aisle. But he wasn't taking her anywhere. Not if I could help it.

I waited until he had reached the end of the counter and was trying to figure out some way to keep the double doors open long enough to shove Sophia through to the other side. Then I climbed to my feet and staggered after him. Every movement, every breath, hurt, but I put my hand against my ribs, gripped my knife even tighter, and hurried after Zeke as fast as I could. Lucky for me, he was having a hard time with Sophia's dead weight and the doors, so he was moving slowly.

He'd just managed to prop her up against the side of the counter when I crept up on his blind side and stabbed my knife into his back. But he was even bigger and stronger than his partner, and his punches had weakened me. So the knife didn't sink all that deeply into his muscles. I pulled it out, but before I could stab him again, he turned and punched me in the chest.

This time, I went down on the ground, and I didn't get back up. It hurt too much to do that.

Zeke loomed over me. "You are one determined little bitch, aren't you? Seems to me like someone should teach you some manners."

He reached for me, and this time, I knew that he wouldn't stop hitting me until I was dead. But the thought didn't fill me with dread. If anything, I got a sense of peace. At least, this time, I'd tried to do something. At least, this time, I'd tried to help, instead of cowering at the top of the stairs and watching Mom and Annabella disappear into balls of elemental Fire. That was something, I supposed—

A hand clamped around Zeke's ankle and yanked him

*down. I blinked, and it took me a moment to figure out what
had happened. Sophia had finally woken up.*

*Zeke put his forearms out in front of him, breaking his fall,
but he still went down on his hands and knees. Sophia scrambled to her feet, then threw herself onto his back, driving him
into the floor. He arched back, trying to throw her off him, but
she slapped his hands away, grabbed his head, and slammed it
into the door on one of the stoves. The giant kept fighting, but
Sophia kept her grip on his head and beat it into the oven—
again and again and again—until the metal dented.*

Thwack. Thwack. Thwack.

*She kept up a steady, furious rhythm, dashing his head
against the oven door, as though she wanted to shove it right
through the metal, each blow seeming a little harder and
more brutal than the last.*

*Finally, after about the sixth or seventh time, something
crunched, and the coppery stink of blood filled the restaurant. The giant quit struggling, and his muffled cries vanished altogether, although his arms and legs kept twitching
with small, disjointed spasms.*

*Sophia leaned back and rolled off him, breathing hard.
She swiped her black hair out of her eyes, leaving behind a
dark stain on her face—blood.*

*By this point, I'd managed to get back up onto my knees,
although I had the knife speared into the floor as I used it to
help hold myself up. Sophia noticed me watching her, grimaced, and dropped her hand, as if that would hide the fact
that she'd just caved in a man's skull with her bare hands.
Against Fletcher's favorite stove, no less. Then her black eyes
flicked over me, and she noticed the knife that I was still
clutching and the blood that covered me too.*

Sophia turned her head, looking for the other giant. Her eyes widened, then narrowed when he didn't appear, and she realized that I'd killed him.

"Not soft," I said, my voice coming out in a hoarse wheeze that didn't sound all that different from hers.

Sophia looked at me, her dark eyes almost sad. "No," she rasped. "Not soft anymore."

A low moan sounded in front of the counter. It took me a second to realize that it was the kid. Sounded like he was waking up.

Sophia got to her feet. It took her a moment to find her balance, but once she did, she leaned down and held her hand out to me. I took it, and she gently pulled me up. I wrapped an arm around my bruised, aching ribs. Sophia gently put her arm around my thin shoulder. Together, leaning on each other, we staggered around the counter and over to the kid—

The rest of the memory abruptly faded away. At first, I wondered why, but then I realized what had woken me out of my dream.

Someone was dragging me through the mud.

❊24❊

Apparently, I'd managed to pull myself far enough up onto the bank to keep from drowning. And now someone had put his hands under my shoulders and was pulling me the rest of the way up and out of the water.

I lashed out with my fists and legs, trying to get him to let go of me. But instead of being dropped, I felt a body slide down next to mine in the mud, and a pair of arms wrapped around me, holding me close. I kept fighting, kept struggling, but I was weak, and he was stronger than I was.

After a moment, I realized that I wasn't being hurt, that whoever this was held me close and *let* me beat at him with my hands. I breathed in, and a rich, familiar scent filled my nose, penetrating the last fragments of the dream and my disjointed ride through the rapids.

I let out a breath. "Owen?" I asked in a low, tentative voice.

He drew me even closer, and I felt his hand gently slide through my tangled hair. "It's me," he whispered. "It's me, Gin."

I finally managed to open my eyes, and I found myself staring into his bright, beautiful, violet eyes. I reached out and traced my fingers over his face, once again trying to smooth out the worry lines that marred his rugged features. He didn't wince, and he didn't pull away, despite the fact that my fingers were as cold as bony icicles, and I left smears of blood and mud all over him. Instead, he caught my hand in his and pressed a soft kiss to my palm, right in the middle of my spider-rune scar.

"I've got you, Gin," Owen said. "Just rest, baby. I've got you now. Nothing's going to happen to you. I swear."

I nodded and relaxed that much more. I knew that Owen would keep his promise, just as I'd managed to keep mine to him, despite all the odds. But before I could speak, before I could thank him for coming after me, the blackness rose again in my mind, swallowing up everything else.

Things were disjointed after that.

Every time I opened my eyes, I got a flash of something different. Owen picking me up and carrying me through the woods. Taking me to some sort of sheltered, rocky outcropping. Laying me down on a sleeping bag. Making me drink some water. Taking off my vest. Carefully pulling my clothes away from where they'd stuck to my arms and legs.

He cursed. At first, I wondered why, but then I realized that he must have seen the gunshot wound in my shoulder, the burns on my body, and all the other injuries that I'd gotten. I wanted to tell him that it was okay, that they didn't hurt too much, that I'd been through worse, but I drifted off once again.

The only things I remembered after that were the soft, soothing scent of vanilla and a few needles pricking here and there at my shoulder, arms, back, and legs. Owen must have brought some of Jo-Jo's healing ointment with him. That was the only reason I could think of why the pain of my injuries slowly lessened . . .

I don't know how much time passed before I woke up again. For a long while, I was drifting along in that peaceful blackness. Then I suddenly snapped awake.

I was lying on my side on top of a sleeping bag. A small fire crackled in front of me, the smoke drifting above the shelf of rocks and then disappearing into the night sky. Owen sat in front of the fire, idling poking a stick into the flames. I lay there and watched the play of light and shadow on his face. He'd actually done it. He'd actually come back for me just like he said that he would. I couldn't quite believe it, but it meant the world to me.

If it had been Finn or even Bria, I wouldn't have been so surprised. But Owen and I had been on such shaky ground lately. Still, despite everything that had happened between us, he'd come back for me. Even though it had been dangerous. Even though it would have been easier not to. Even though he could have been captured, tortured, and killed by Grimes and his men.

Despite all that, he'd still come back for me.

Owen must have sensed me staring at him, because he turned in my direction and smiled—a big, broad, beautiful smile that told me how happy he was that I was finally awake.

He started to get up and come over to me, but I waved him off.

"How are you feeling?" he asked.

I sat up and winced, as a hundred dull aches and pains shot through my body. "Like I'm a very small rabbit that's been shaken to within an inch of its life by a very large, very angry dog. Remind me never to go white-water rafting. At least, not without an actual raft."

He laughed, and the sound wrapped around me like a warm, welcoming hug.

I stared up into the sky; it was dark, except for a smattering of stars twinkling far, far away. "What time is it?"

Owen held his watch up to the fire. "Just after midnight."

I'd gone over the cliff sometime in the afternoon. I wondered if Grimes and his men were looking for me or if they'd assumed that I'd been dashed against the rocks and drowned in the rapids. Either way, there was nothing that I could do about it tonight.

I glanced around the camp he'd made, but I didn't see any sign of anyone else's gear.

"I came back alone," Owen said, noticing my curious gaze. "Finn hadn't made it back from his trip yet, and Bria wanted to come with me. Phillip too. But I didn't give them the chance. I slipped away while they were tending to the others. I didn't want to waste a second getting back to you."

"Sophia? Warren?"

"Both safe at Cooper's house," he answered. "It was

slow going, but I was able to get them off the mountain and over there without any problems. Whatever you did to Grimes and his men kept them from chasing after us."

I nodded. I'd tell him about how I'd Iced over the ridge later. Now came the question that I was dreading the answer to. "And Jo-Jo?"

"She's doing much better," Owen said. "Cooper was able to rest and replenish his magic while we went after Sophia. When he woke up, Jo-Jo was awake too, and she helped him use his Air magic to heal her more. She's not a hundred percent, but she should be fine in a few days. Cooper even had enough magic left to heal the worst of Sophia's injuries. Warren's too."

I let out a breath. Warren, Sophia, and Jo-Jo were all safe and on the mend—for now.

I thought of what Grimes had said, about how he was going to go after Sophia again. He wouldn't stop until he'd dragged her back up here to his twisted camp. He'd come looking for her sooner, rather than later, especially given what a mess I'd made of things. But Grimes was never getting his hands on Sophia again, I vowed. Because the next time I saw the bastard, I was going to end him.

"What about you?" Owen asked. "What happened?"

I told him everything that I had done to Grimes's men and everything that Grimes and Hazel had said to me.

Owen listened in silence. Then, after a moment, he grinned. "You really set fire to his moonshine operation? I would have loved to have seen the look on his face when he realized what you did."

"It was rather impressive," I said, grinning back at

him. "At least, what I saw of it was. I was hoping that the flames would spread and burn the entire camp to the ground, but that was probably too much to wish for."

"Probably," he agreed. "Men like Grimes always seem to have nine lives."

"Then I guess it's a good thing that I do too."

Owen returned my grin for a moment, but the expression quickly slid off his face, and his features turned serious once more. He stared at me before his gaze dropped back down to the fire. He started stirring the flames with his stick again. I wondered what he was thinking about, but I decided not to ask. He'd tell me in his own time, and there were other things that I wanted to know right now.

"How did you find me?"

"Well, when I hiked back to the ridge, I didn't see you anywhere in the camp. All I saw was a charred building and some guys putting out the smoldering remains of a fire. So I hiked back to the pit and the tombstones. I didn't know what was going on or where you were, but eventually, I was able to creep up and eavesdrop on a couple of Grimes's men. They were talking about how you'd jumped off a cliff and into the river. So I got out Fletcher's maps, since I'd brought them back with me, and I tried to figure out where you might have ended up downriver."

A piece of wood in the fire cracked, causing a few sparks to drift up into the air like fireflies. Owen watched them burn out before he continued his story.

"I hiked around the mountain until I reached the river, then followed it downstream for a few miles. I was searching for you, but I was also using my magic. I was just hoping that you still had on your silverstone vest."

"So you used your elemental talent for metal to see if you could sense any of it in the area."

He nodded. "And I finally did. I saw you half-submerged in the water in the canyon and fished you out. After that, well, here we are." He spread his hands out to both sides, gesturing at the fire and the dark woods beyond.

His story touched me. "You went to all that trouble for me?"

"I'd do all that and more for you," he said. "I'd do anything for you, Gin."

I looked at him, wondering at the sudden fervor in his voice. "Owen?"

He hesitated. At first, I thought that he wasn't going to say anything else, but then he squared his shoulders, lifted his chin, and looked me directly in the eyes. "I'm sorry," he finally said.

"For what?"

"For everything," Owen replied. "But especially for the way that I treated you after you killed Salina. It was stupid and inexcusable of me."

I thought back to everything he'd said at Fletcher's house when he'd told me that he was going to help me rescue Sophia. "Is this one of those things that you've been an idiot about?"

He gave me a rueful grin. "One of many. Isn't it obvious?"

"What changed?"

"I did," he replied. "I finally grew up. I finally *wised* up. And I finally realized just how much I love you."

I blinked, taken aback by his words—words that I

never thought I'd hear him say again. Hope blossomed in my heart that he really meant them, that we were finally dealing with our issues and making some real progress, but I tempered that warm, soft hope with cold, logical reason.

"But you loved Salina too," I said in a soft voice. "You were . . . upset when I killed her."

Owen grimaced. "That's putting it mildly, don't you think? I turned my back on you. I did the exact same thing to you that Donovan Caine did, even though I'd made myself a promise that I would never hurt you like he did, that I would never take you for granted, and that I would especially never judge you for being the Spider. But I did it all anyway, just like he did. Like I said, I'm an idiot."

I shrugged. Owen's reaction had hurt, but it hadn't been unexpected. It was always hard to watch someone you loved die, even when she wasn't the person you thought she was, even when she'd hurt the other people you cared about.

"You were just trying to protect me from Salina," Owen said. "From having to deal with her myself, from having to kill her myself. Because that's the kind of person you are, Gin. You take care of the people you love, no matter what. I think that's the thing that I love the most about you."

The words hung in the air between us, seeming as insubstantial as the smoke curling up from the fire. For a moment, the only sound was the cheery crackling of the flames. I didn't say anything, but I let him see the doubt in my eyes—doubt that he really meant what he said.

Owen threw his stick down close to the fire, came over, crouched down in front of me, and took my hands in his.

"I love you," he said. "I will *always* love you. Sometimes it scares me just how much I love you. I will never love anyone the way that I love you."

I couldn't help but ask the question. "Not even Salina?"

"Especially not Salina," Owen said. "I was a kid when I met her, when I loved her. I was young, and I was blind to the kind of person that she really was. I loved who I thought she was, who I wanted her to be, not who she actually turned out to be."

"But you still didn't like me killing her. So what changed?"

His lips curved up into a humorless expression. "I did. It was a small thing, really. I'd gone out to have drinks one night with Phillip at Northern Aggression. We got into . . . some trouble, but we managed to get ourselves out of it."

"Then what happened?"

"I took Phillip home to the *Delta Queen*, and he said something about how the fight that we'd gotten into was just like the good old days. He grinned at me, and I saw the scrawny kid he'd been back then. And I finally realized how much time Salina had cost me with him and with Cooper too. Time that I can never get back. How she'd ruined Eva's trust in me. How she'd hurt the people I'd cared about over and over again. I knew it all before, of course, but when he said that, it made me realize that I didn't want to waste any more time, especially not with you. That I needed to quit feeling sorry for myself and guilty that I hadn't been able to protect Eva, Phillip, Cooper, and you from Salina. That what I really needed to do was fix things between me and everyone else."

He stared at me. "I came up here today to help you rescue Sophia because it was the right thing to do. But I also came because I plan to spend the rest of my life making up for how much I hurt you . . . if you'll let me."

"And how long have you felt this way?" I whispered, my heart tightening painfully in my chest.

"I've always known it," Owen said. "I knew how much I loved you the night that you killed Salina so I wouldn't have to. I knew it at the Briartop museum when you burst into that vault to rescue me. And I knew it again today when you sacrificed yourself so that I could get Sophia and Warren to safety. The people you care about . . . you love them completely, no matter what. And that's the way that I feel about you too. I was just too much of a coward to admit it to anyone before. Not even to myself—and especially not to you."

I sat there, digesting his words. For a long time, Owen held my hands and waited—just waited. Finally, though, he spoke again.

"I know that I don't deserve it," he said. "Not after everything that I've put you through, but I want to try again. I want a second chance, Gin. Please."

These were the words that I'd longed to hear, that I'd longed for him to say to me for weeks now. And if he'd said them to me when I'd been facing down all those men on the ridge or Grimes and Hazel on the cliff, I would have said *yes* with no hesitation.

But words meant one thing in the middle of a life-or-death battle and sometimes quite another after the fighting was done.

He'd wounded me so badly, undermined all the trust that I had in him, in *us*—and especially in him not to hurt me the way that Donovan had. I loved Owen, had opened myself up to him, and he'd still hurt me. I'd had a lot of time to think these past few weeks that we'd been apart. Maybe too much time to think, to worry and wonder and obsess. Because when everything was said and done, I didn't know if I wanted to go through that again, not even for him. Owen wasn't the first person who'd broken my heart, but he was the one who'd done the most damage to it.

Maybe he wasn't the only one here who was a coward.

"Gin?"

"I don't know," I finally said in a soft voice. "You . . . you broke my heart, Owen."

"I know," he said, his face tight with guilt. "I know how much I hurt you. But I promise you this, Gin, I will spend the rest of my life making it up to you. And if it takes you some time to trust me again, to love me again, then that's okay. Days, weeks, months, years. I don't care. Because I'll wait for you. I would wait forever for you."

All the love that I had for him welled up inside me, blotting out everything else—except for a tiny, stubborn whisper of doubt in the deepest, darkest, blackest part of my heart. I almost said *yes* then, but I held back at the last possible moment.

Because I couldn't ignore that tiny whisper and all the dread and fear that it brought along with it. Because I still remembered how it had felt to lose Owen. Because I didn't want to go through that kind of heartbreak again. And it could happen—easily. Because I was the Spider, for better or worse, and I would *always* be the Spider. There would always be some sort of trouble headed in my direction, someone targeting me, someone wanting to murder me, and it would be all too easy for Owen and me to end up right back where we'd been after I'd killed Salina.

"I don't know," I whispered. "I just . . . I just don't know."

Owen gave me a small, understanding smile, although I could see the disappointment in his face. "And that's okay too."

We didn't speak for a moment.

"Come on," he said, his voice rough with emotion. "Lie back down. It's been a long day, and we still have to hike out in the morning. You need your rest."

He wrapped his arms around me, and together, we lay down on the sleeping bag and faced the fire. His rich, metallic scent once again filled my nose, mixing pleasantly with the woodsmoke, and the warmth of his body enveloped mine, driving away the last of my lingering chill.

I thought about everything that Owen had said and all the emotions that I'd seen flashing in his eyes—heat, desire, need, want, love, and hope. So much hope. A few hours ago, I'd thought that I'd never see him again, and I would have done anything to have had one more moment with him. Now here Owen was, proclaiming his love for me, and I suddenly couldn't let him back into my heart.

I could face down a psychopath like Harley Grimes any day of the week, but ask me to open up and risk my heart, and I reverted to that scared, angry, lonely little girl who'd lost her family and had vowed never to let anyone get too close again.

There was no maybe about it. I was *definitely* a coward. Tonight, at least.

* 25 *

A splash of sunlight on my face woke me early the next morning.

I squinted against the warm, golden glow. The fire was cold, but Owen must have covered me with the sleeping bag sometime during the night, because the fabric was tucked in all around me, making me feel like a mummy.

Even though I could have easily drifted back to sleep, I untucked one corner of the sleeping bag, threw the silky material aside, and sat up. I blinked a few times, trying to throw off the last comfortable, drowsy dregs of sleep.

"Owen?" I called out.

He didn't answer me, and I finally realized that he was nowhere in sight. Not sleeping behind me, not crouched over the remains of the fire, not stretching his legs by walking back and forth in front of the rocky outcropping that I was still lying under.

For a moment, I was confused, wondering if perhaps

I'd just dreamed that he was here the night before, but then I spotted his backpack, and I realized that he must be around somewhere. Maybe he'd gone to get some fresh water from the river, so we'd have something to drink on our hike back to the parking lot. Either way, I needed to answer the call of nature, so to speak, so I got to my feet—and then wished that I hadn't.

I was bruised, battered, and sore from head to toe. Blues, greens, purples, and yellows had blossomed like flowers overnight on my arms, mottling my skin from my shoulders all the way down to my fingertips. Given the stiffness in my muscles, I imagined that I had even more bruises on my back, chest, and legs, not to mention the burns and blisters from Grimes's and Hazel's Fire magic, which pulsed with tight, throbbing pain. Rolling down the river hadn't been my best idea, but it had gotten me away from Grimes, which was all that really mattered.

I gingerly touched the bandage over the gunshot wound in my shoulder. Lucky for me, it was a through-and-through, and Owen had rubbed plenty of Jo-Jo's healing salve on it. The wound was tender to the touch, but it wasn't bleeding, and it didn't have the hot, aching feel of infection. Maybe if Cooper was up to it, I'd get him to heal me when we got to his house.

Because the sooner I was better, the sooner I could kill Harley Grimes, Hazel, and every other person on this damn mountain.

With that cheery thought in mind, I staggered away from our camp, found a private spot behind a tree, and did my lady business. When I was finished, I went back to the camp, but I didn't hunker down under the rocks and curl back up on the sleeping bag. Instead, I stood by the remains of the fire and did some slow, careful stretches, trying to loosen up my stiff, sore muscles and get some blood flowing to them. Because it was still a long trek down the mountain, and we could still run into some more of Grimes's men—

Thwack.

The distinctive sound of flesh cracking against flesh made me stop in mid-stretch.

"Where the hell is she?" a man's voice growled.

Silence. Then—

Thwack.

"I asked you a question," the man growled again, his voice much louder and angrier than before. "I suggest that you answer me."

"Forget it," Owen snarled back. "I'm not telling you a damn thing."

Looked like Grimes's men had come looking for me after all—and they'd found Owen instead.

I scanned the ground around our camp, searching for one very specific item, but all I saw were Owen's backpack, a couple of empty tins of salve, and several crumpled, dirty rags that he'd used to wipe some of the blood and grime off me. No weapons.

"C'mon, c'mon," I muttered, dropping to my hands and knees and crawling around the fire ring. "Where did you put it, Owen? Where did you put it—"

Out of the corner of my eye, I spotted a piece of gray fabric sticking out from beneath the sleeping bag. I stretched out my hand, grabbed the edge of the fabric, and pulled my vest out into the light.

It looked worse for wear, just like I did. The whole thing was covered with blood, mud, and grass stains, while jagged cuts crisscrossed the gray material, exposing the gleaming silverstone underneath. But I shrugged into it anyway, even though the motion caused even more pain to unspool through my muscles, especially the two holes in my left shoulder, and ripple down my arms.

I zipped the bloody vest up over my chest, then hurried over to the fire ring. Most of the wood had been burned away, but I spotted one stick that hadn't been consumed by the flames, the one that Owen had been using to stir up the fire the night before. It was about a foot long and as wide as three of my fingers. The end wasn't as sharp as I would have liked, but I'd made do with worse before. I also picked up one of the rocks from the fire ring itself and hefted it in my hands. Smooth, round, and heavy. Perfect.

Crude weapons in my hands, I got to my feet and headed toward the sounds of Owen and his attackers.

I found them about two minutes later. They were definitely Grimes's men—three guys with guns, all dressed in brown boots, old-fashioned suits, and fedoras. Two of them held Owen up against a tree, while the third used his fists on him. They must have surprised Owen as he was coming back from the river, because I saw a couple of full water bottles that had been kicked to one side of the tree.

If they'd walked fifty feet more to the west, they would have easily discovered our campsite. They might have even come upon us while we were sleeping this morning and put a couple of bullets in our skulls where we lay. Too bad for them that they hadn't, because they weren't going to walk away from this spot.

The guy drove his fist into Owen's face, then hit him with a brutal one-two combo to his ribs. Owen hissed with pain, but he didn't give the guy the satisfaction of screaming.

"I'll ask you again, where is the woman?" the leader demanded. "Tell us where she is, and we might let you live."

By this point, Owen's face was bruised and bloody, but he gave the guy hitting him a haughty smirk. "Is that all you've got? My sister can hit harder than that."

"A wise guy, huh?" the leader snarled. "Have it your way. She can't have gotten far. Not after taking a plunge like that. We'll just find her ourselves. Who knows? Maybe we'll have a little fun with her before we drag her back to Grimes. Maybe we'll even let you watch."

The men laughed. Owen surged forward, but together the two men were stronger than he was, and they held him tight.

The leader chuckled at Owen's struggles, then drew back his fist for another blow. I hefted the rock in one of my hands and the stick of wood in the other, positioning them just so, then strolled out where they could see me.

"Are you boys looking for me?" I drawled. "Well, here I *am*."

Before they could react, I threw the rock from the fire ring at the leader. The stone zipped through the air and beaned him in the head like a baseball, leaving a bloody welt behind. Even as he stumbled away from Owen, I was already racing forward.

One of the men holding Owen turned to face me and yanked his gun out of the holster on his belt. I stabbed my stick into his hand, knocking the weapon away. The guy growled and lunged at me, but I stepped up and head-butted him in the face, crunching his nose with my forehead. The second his head snapped back, I raised my stick and drove it into his throat. It didn't sink all the way in, not like one of my knives would have, but it did enough damage, especially when I yanked it back out. The guy fell to the ground, gasping for air, and I fell on top of his back. I ground his face into the dirt and leaves until he quit fighting, and I knew that he was dead.

Owen had turned on the final man, pulled the guy's gun from his holster, and shot him in the chest three times with it, dropping him.

That left the leader, who had finally quit staggering around like a drunk. He gaped at Owen and me and backed up, as if to turn and run. I grabbed the second man's gun from the ground, and a couple of bullets solved that problem.

I got to my feet and scanned the forest, in case there were any more of Grimes's men lurking around who might come running at the cracks of gunfire. But a minute passed, then another one, with no signs or sounds of anyone heading our way. Those three must have been all that were in the area. So I shuffled over to Owen, who had his hands on his knees, trying to get his breath back.

"Are you okay?"

He wiped a bit of blood off his face, winced, and straightened up. "Yeah. Although now I think I know how you felt getting tossed around in the river yesterday."

I grinned at his black humor, but I still kept looking and listening at the woods around us. Just because no one had immediately appeared didn't mean that they weren't headed in our direction.

"C'mon," I said. "I don't know about you, but I'm ready to get off this damn mountain."

"I couldn't agree more," Owen quipped.

❊ 26 ❊

We packed up our things and headed out. Owen insisted on carrying his backpack and all of the supplies that he'd brought. He offered to carry me too, but I refused. I might be injured, but we'd make better time with both of us on our feet. So instead, he found a tall, sturdy branch that I could use as a walking stick to help me hobble along faster.

To my surprise, we made it back down to the parking lot at the foot of Bone Mountain without any problems. We hunkered down in the trees and watched Roslyn's car for several minutes, but no one was waiting to ambush us. Still, I made Owen check under the hood to see if one of Grimes's men had planted a bomb there, just in case. But the car was clean, and thirty minutes later, Owen had stopped the vehicle outside Cooper's house.

Quite a few cars were clustered together in the driveway now, facing out and forming a solid metal barricade in front of the house. I recognized Finn's Aston Martin, Bria's sedan, and Phillip's Audi. The battered gray pickup truck had to belong to Warren, given the rifle in the gun rack attached to the back window.

Owen and I got out of the car and shuffled up to the house. At this point, he was dragging his backpack along the ground with one hand, while I had both of my hands wrapped around my walking stick, despite the splinters digging into my palms. Neither one of us was in the best shape of our lives, but we'd made it back alive.

A few soft murmurs of conversation sounded as we headed around the side of the house and stepped into the backyard. The others were sitting around the table outside on the patio, almost as if they were waiting for us to show up. Finn in a perfect suit and tie, Phillip wearing the same thing, the two of them looking as cool as icebox pies, despite the sweltering afternoon heat. Bria in her usual jeans and button-up shirt, her badge and her gun both clipped to her black leather belt. Eva wearing shorts and a tank top. Roslyn in an elegant sleeveless sundress.

They were all leaning in toward the table and talking quietly, with Finn leading the conversation, judging by the wild way that he was gesturing. He was the first to spot Owen and me, and he stopped in mid-sentence to stare at us.

I grinned. "Honey, we're home."

The others scrambled to their feet. Eva raced over and gave Owen a long, tight hug, while Phillip clapped him on the back and almost sent him and Eva tumbling over. Bria came over and hugged me, along with Roslyn, and then the two of them stepped to the side so Finn could get in on the action.

He stopped in front of me, crossed his arms over his chest, and gave me a critical once-over, his green eyes as sharp and bright as emeralds in his handsome face. "You look like hell," he finally said.

My grin widened. "You should see the other guys."

Finn sighed and opened his arms. "Come on, come on, you know you want to hug me and get blood, mud, dirt, and who knows what else all over my brand-new suit."

"Why, I thought you'd never ask," I drawled.

I stepped into his arms, and Finn carefully hugged me, mindful of my injuries.

After a moment, he pulled back and sniffed in that haughty, superior way of his. "I *told* you to wait for me. You wouldn't be beat up *nearly* as badly if you'd done that." His tone was rough and grumbly, but I could still hear the worry in his voice.

"I know," I said, patting his shoulder and trying to soothe his ego and his concern. "Next time, I'll definitely wait for you."

"I'll hold you to that," he warned.

"I know you will."

Finn hugged me again, and then everyone changed places. Eva gently wrapped her arms around my neck, while Phillip stood by. Bria and Roslyn hugged Owen, while Finn went over to him and gave him a cuff on the shoulder.

"I thought that I told you to take care of Gin," Finn said. "Not bring her back half-dead."

His words and his face might have been stone-cold serious, but his tone was light with relief that I'd come back at all.

After a moment, Owen smiled. "Well, I tried, but you know Gin," he said. "She just *had* to kill a couple more guys before we finally left."

Finn returned his grin. "That I do."

Owen stayed outside on the patio to fill the others in on everything that had happened on the mountain, but I opened the door and stepped inside the house. I didn't have far to go, because they were all sitting in the den— Cooper, Warren, Sophia, and Jo-Jo.

Cooper and Warren were sprawled over two matching recliners, rocking back and forth and making the springs *creak-creak-creak*. I gave them both respectful nods, then turned my attention to Sophia and Jo-Jo.

The sisters sat side-by-side on the brown-striped couch, their fingers intertwined, and Rosco was sprawled across their feet, taking a nap. It looked like all of their injuries had been healed. I didn't see any blood on either one of them, no bruises, no burns, nothing that would indicate all of the terrible things that had happened over the past two days.

Sophia was once again in her black jeans and boots. A black T-shirt with a picture of a bloody, broken heart on it stretched across her chest. She looked like her usual self, right down to the black lipstick that slashed across her face. But I couldn't quite get the image of the photo that I'd seen in Grimes's house out of my mind, the one of a young Sophia wearing a white dress. I wondered what she'd been like before he'd taken her all those years ago. If she'd been a sweet Southern belle like Jo-Jo or something else entirely.

I had no way of knowing, so I focused on Jo-Jo instead. She too wore her usual pink dress and pearls, but her face was free of makeup, her blond hair hung limply around her shoulders, and her wrinkles were more pronounced than I remembered them being. For the first time since I'd known her, Jo-Jo seemed pale and thin and tired, not at all like the bright, vibrant, cheery force of nature that she usually was. I supposed that was to be expected, since she'd almost died from Grimes's bullets, but seeing her look so haggard and defeated made my heart hurt all the same.

Jo-Jo struggled to get up out of the soft cushions, but I went over to her instead. I dropped down to my knees, leaned forward, and gave her a gentle, careful hug, not wanting to undo any of the magic that Cooper had worked on her. Jo-Jo reached up and patted my back, despite the blood, dirt, and grime that covered me, and it seemed like I could feel each and every one of her bones, as delicate and fragile as a bird's under my fingertips.

I held on to her until I managed to blink back the scalding tears that had threatened to leak out of my eyes. "How are you?" I asked, finally pulling back.

"Better, now that you're here, darling," Jo-Jo said.

I looked at Sophia. "And you?"

"Fine," she lied, although she couldn't quite hide the flash of pain in her eyes.

"Grimes?" Jo-Jo asked.

"Not dead—yet."

She glanced at Sophia, and they clasped hands again,

even tighter than before. They were thinking the same thing that I was, that it wouldn't be long before Grimes came back for them again. But I had a plan for that, one that should take care of him, Hazel, and the rest of his men for good.

Cooper stopped rocking in his chair, leaned forward, and cleared his throat. "I hate to be rude, but you seem, um, tired, Gin."

"Tired?" Warren snorted. "What he really means is that you look like a survivor out of one of them zombie movies and almost as dead as one of those critters yourself."

Cooper shot Warren a sharp look, then turned his attention back to me. "Would you like me to, you know?" He gestured with his hands.

"Heal me?"

He winced. "If you want to call it that. I still feel like I'm fumbling around with my magic, more than anything else."

Jo-Jo gave him a soft smile. "You did just fine with Sophia and me. You'll get the hang of it. Practicing on Gin will be good for you."

Cooper grinned back at her, and his solid chest puffed up at her praise.

Well, I didn't know how I felt about being a test dummy for Cooper's Air magic, but Jo-Jo was obviously still too weak to heal me, and I didn't have any other options right now. Not if I wanted to be a hundred percent when Grimes, Hazel, and what was left of their miscreants came knocking on my door. In a day, maybe two tops, Grimes would find the bodies of the three men he'd sent to search for me along the river, and he'd realize that I'd survived after all. He'd want his revenge for me having the audacity to escape his evil clutches, not to mention all the death and destruction that I'd inflicted on his men and his camp. Grimes might have destroyed Jo-Jo's salon, but I'd paid him back in spades with what I'd done to his mountain hideaway. He wouldn't be able to let that stand, not if he wanted to hold on to the men he had left.

Besides, I'd seen the look of anticipation in his eyes on the cliff. He would want his revenge, but more than that, he would want to break me like he had all the other poor women and men that he'd kidnapped, tortured, and murdered. Grimes wanted to hear me scream and cry and beg for mercy. And the second that I did, he'd lose interest in me and toss me aside to Hazel and his men, just like he had with all the others. That's why he was still so obsessed with Sophia all these years later, because he simply couldn't fathom how anyone could be stronger than he was.

Well, let the bastard come. I was going to enjoy showing him exactly how wrong he was before I killed him.

"Gin?" Cooper asked, cutting into my dark, murderous musings. "Are you ready?"

"Yeah, I'm ready."

Warren got up, and I sat down in his chair. Cooper scooted his recliner close to mine, then reached out and took my hand. His fingers felt rough and callused, although his skin was pleasantly warm, as though the heat from all the fires in his forge had soaked into his body over the years. A moment later, his eyes began to glow a bright, familiar copper, and the prickly feel of his Air magic gusted through the den.

Cooper wasn't nearly as skilled in his magic as Jo-Jo was, not in this way, at least, so it took him far longer to heal me than it would have taken her, and it hurt a whole lot worse. Jo-Jo's magic had always felt like needles poking into my skin, uncomfortable but bearable. But Cooper's Air magic was much rougher and far more intense, as though my own knives were stabbing into my body, sawing through my muscles, and then haphazardly pinning everything back together again.

Still, I clamped my jaw down, ground my teeth together, and hoped that he wouldn't notice how I kept wiping my free, sweaty hand on my ruined jeans and digging my fingernails into the spider rune scar in my palm to try to take my mind off the fresh, clumsy pain raging through my body. Cooper was doing me a favor, so I couldn't complain. And I wouldn't, because that would hurt his feelings. Besides, I'd been through worse—much worse.

Ten minutes later, Cooper let go of his Air magic and dropped my hand. The copper glow was snuffed out of his eyes, and he sagged back against his recliner, causing the chair to creak weakly once more.

"There," he said, sounding as tired as I felt. "I reckon that's the best that I can do for right now."

I slumped down in my chair too and took stock of my body. The gunshot wound in my shoulder was completely healed, along with the burns on my arms, back, and legs, since those were the areas where Cooper had focused most of his magic. Cuts and scrapes still dotted my body, along with the rainbow clusters of bruises, but all of the open wounds had closed up, and the worst of the midnight blues and putrid purples had faded out to healing greens and not-so-sickly yellows. I wasn't in the best shape of my life, but Cooper had managed to put me back together again.

He looked at me with anxious eyes, so I pushed away my exhaustion, got up, and stretched this way and that, like a cat waking up from a long, satisfying nap. My muscles ached in protest, but I ignored the twinges of discomfort. It was worth it to see Cooper's face crinkle up and beam with pride.

"Well, thanks, Cooper," I drawled. "I feel just fine and dandy now. If you've got any magic left, you might want to go outside and check on Owen. Some of Grimes's men got hold of him and beat him up pretty good."

Cooper nodded, got to his feet, and hurried outside, his exhaustion seemingly gone.

Warren looked at Jo-Jo, then Sophia, then me. Without a word, he got up and followed Cooper, shutting the door behind the two of them. A minute later, another gust of Cooper's Air magic rippled through the room, although it felt much fainter, given the distance and the door between us.

I sank back into my chair, trying once again not to let my exhaustion show, and faced the Deveraux sisters. They both looked at me with somber eyes. Rosco continued to nap on their feet.

"Tell us what happened," Jo-Jo finally said in a soft voice.

I drew in a breath and started my story with the fight in the salon. I quickly moved on to my trip with Owen and Warren up the mountain, our rescue of Sophia from the pit, and my stand at the top of the ridge against Grimes, Hazel, and their men. After that, all that was left to tell was my run through the woods, my swan dive off the cliff, my ride through the rapids, and finally, Owen finding me and fishing me out of the river.

I tried to spare them the worst of it, glossing over a lot of the details, keeping my voice upbeat, and trying to make it seem more like a grand adventure than a brutal fight for my life. I didn't mention all of the sick, twisted things that Grimes had said to me about Sophia, the photos that he had of her, or how his house had been an eerie replica of Jo-Jo's inside and out. Of course, Sophia knew some of it, since she'd been in the house too, but I figured that those were her secrets to tell, not mine.

"I'm sorry, darling," Jo-Jo said, tears streaking down her cheeks like tiny rivers of crystal when I finally finished my story. "So very sorry that you had to go through all of that because of us."

I shrugged. Fighting for my life against evil psychopaths with personal vendettas wasn't anything new. In fact, it had become rather routine over the past few months. Mundane, even. Grimes's attack had just cut a little closer to home than some of the other ones.

"I wish that Fletcher had killed that bastard all those years ago," Jo-Jo said in a grim voice. "I wish that *I* had killed him all those years ago."

Sophia squeezed her hand, but the motion didn't comfort Jo-Jo. If anything, it made even more tears well up in her eyes, spill down her face, and drip onto her dress. She let out a small, squeaky hiccup and pressed her fist against her mouth, as though that would hold back her grief.

In all the years I'd known her, I could count on one hand the number of times that I'd seen Jo-Jo cry, and most of those had been before, during, and after Fletcher's funeral. My heart ached for her, but I didn't know what to do. I didn't know what to say or how to comfort her in the face of her tears, her trembling body, and the worry swimming in her clear eyes.

"Don't think about it right now," I said. "Sophia and I both made it back, and we're all safe now. Once Cooper gets the hang of his magic, he can finish healing you, and then we'll all be back to—"

I bit down on my lip, choking on my own words. I had started to say *normal*, but that wasn't the right thing to say, because we wouldn't be back to that for a long time, if ever. I'd never been one to sugarcoat things, but right now, I wanted to ease Jo-Jo's mind more than anything else. If I could have reached inside her, scooped out her hurt, and shoveled it into my own heart, I would have— and Sophia's too.

"It's not over," Jo-Jo said, finally wiping away her tears. "Not by a long shot."

"No," I replied. "It's not."

"He's never going to stop," Jo-Jo said. "Not now. Not after you got Sophia away from him again. Not after you've embarrassed him. He'll have to come after you to save face with his men and Hazel too. But more than that, he'll *want* to come after you. He'll want to teach you a lesson."

"I know," I said. "I know that he'll come after me, that he'll come after all of us."

"Now what?" Sophia asked, her voice even harsher than before and full of worry.

I leaned forward and looked at Sophia, then Jo-Jo, letting them see the determination in my wintry gray eyes—and the cold, cold promise of death.

"We let him come to us," I said. "And then we kill him."

☀ 27 ☀

Cooper finished healing Owen, and we all moved on to the things that we needed to do next. Finn and Phillip left to go see what they could dig up on Grimes from their various underworld contacts and to find out if anyone had heard a whisper of what had happened on the mountain. Bria headed to the police station to do the same. Roslyn went with her, so she could fill Xavier in on everything that had happened. Sophia helped Jo-Jo to one of the upstairs bedrooms, so they could both get some rest. Rosco finally woke up and followed them, his toenails clicking against the floor, and Cooper went to his own room to rest himself.

Meanwhile, I took a long, hot shower, slathered some more of Jo-Jo's healing salve onto my lingering wounds, and changed into a pair of shorts and a T-shirt that Bria had left at Cooper's for me. I headed back downstairs to find Owen in the den, staring through the glass door into the backyard. He too had showered and changed and looked as handsome as ever in a black T-shirt and khaki shorts.

He turned at the sound of my bare feet softly slapping against the floor. "You look more like your old self."

"So do you."

He nodded. "I was waiting for you to finish in the shower so I could tell you that I'm heading over to Country Daze with Warren and Eva. They're waiting in the truck for me. Warren wants to check on Violet and make sure that he's there in case any of Grimes's men come into the store for supplies."

I nodded. "Just be careful."

"We will."

He hesitated, then gestured at a case on the coffee table that I hadn't noticed before. The top of the case was open, revealing a layer of black foam and my five silverstone knives gleaming inside. The ones that Owen had made for me, the ones that contained my magic, the ones that I'd given to him on the ridge.

The ones that I never thought I'd see again.

"I thought you might want these back," Owen said in a low voice. "Especially if Grimes somehow tracks Sophia and Jo-Jo here."

I hadn't cried when Jo-Jo had been shot and Sophia had been kidnapped. When I'd seen Sophia being tortured. When Grimes and Hazel had thrown their Fire magic at me. When their men had chased me through the woods like an animal. I hadn't even cried when I'd jumped off that cliff, knowing that I would probably die from the fall.

But the simple sight of my knives and the spider runes glimmering on the hilts made my throat close up, and I had a hard time holding back the hot tears that pooled in my eyes. I went over, sat down in front of the table on the floor, and traced my fingers over the blades, letting the cold, smooth feel of the weapons ground me and help me get my emotions back under control.

"Thank you," I finally managed to whisper, still hunched over the knives and staring at them instead of him. "For keeping them safe for me."

"You're welcome," Owen said, his own voice rough and hoarse. "But don't you *ever* give them to me like that again."

I nodded, the knot in my throat preventing me from speaking.

"I found this too."

His hand appeared at my elbow, and I realized that he was holding a small rock, one with my spider rune seared into the stone.

The smooth, round rock was light gray, with my rune etched on it in a slightly darker silver, almost like a brand. I knew that if I compared it with the scar on my palm, it would be a perfect match.

"I found it on the top of the ridge that overlooked Grimes's camp," Owen said. "It was just lying there, along with all of the bodies of his men. From what you told me, I think this is the first rock that you touched, the one you started building all of that elemental Ice with."

I nodded and took it from him. The stone was surprisingly light in my hand and felt slightly chilled, as though it had absorbed some of my Ice magic. Perhaps the rock had a bit of silverstone running through it. After a moment, I set it down on the table, right next to the case of knives. I still didn't speak, though. I couldn't.

"I'll be back soon," he promised.

Owen touched my shoulder, giving it a gentle squeeze. Then he opened the door and left. A minute later, an engine rumbled to life in the front of the house before the sound slowly faded away.

I shuddered out a breath, reached into the case, and pulled out one of my knives. The metal felt cool to the touch, given the Ice and Stone magic stored inside the silverstone. I rubbed my thumb over the spider rune stamped into the hilt, that small circle surrounded by eight thin rays.

When I felt calm enough, I grabbed another knife out of the case and got to my feet. Then I started twirling the weapons, spinning the metal blades around and around, tossing them up into the air, and catching them as they plummeted back down to earth.

Faster and faster, higher and higher, I tossed the knives, until the blades seemed to float through the air like slender silver clouds. My gaze was locked on the spinning bits of sharp metal, but my mind was focused on something else entirely: the best way to go about killing Harley Grimes.

It was something that Fletcher had taught me to do. Keep my hands busy while I let my mind wander free. I moved from one side of the den to the other, all the while juggling the knives, thinking about angles, approaches, and when Grimes might show his face in Ashland.

And when I'd gone through it all, when I had a plan

that I thought would work, I tossed the knives up into the air one final time, caught them, and twirled them around in my hands. Ta-da.

I tucked one of the knives against the small of my back, comforted by the familiar, solid weight of it there. Then I slid the other one back into its slot in the foam and headed into the kitchen. I left the case open on the table, though.

I'd use the knives again soon enough.

Despite my juggling act, my emotions were still raw and far too close to the surface for my liking, so I spent the next few hours indulging in my own sort of therapy: cooking.

I raided Cooper's fridge and cabinets, pulling out flour, sugar, salt, pepper, and all of the other staples that I would need. Then I went to work. Mixing, stirring, measuring, chopping, mashing, sautéing, frying, baking, roasting. The familiar motions soothed something deep inside me, and I quickly lost myself in the rhythms of cooking. The smells of melted butter, sugar, cheese, and more blasted out of the oven and drifted up from the pots and pans bubbling on the stove top, and everything else faded away, except for the steady *tick-tick-tick* of the egg timer on the counter, counting down the seconds until my various dishes were ready to come out of the oven.

I figured that we could all use some comfort food, so I whipped up a succulent supper of country-fried ham, sharp cheddar mac and cheese, a crunchy summer salad of cucumbers and tomatoes, and mashed potatoes made with buttermilk, piled high with sour cream, and sprinkled generously with dill. For dessert, there were light-as-air buttermilk biscuits stuffed with some strawberry preserves that Jo-Jo had made for Cooper.

Drawn by the mouthwatering smells, Jo-Jo, Sophia, and Cooper came downstairs, and the four of us ate together, with Rosco sitting at our feet and looking on in anticipation of the scraps that were coming his way. Owen returned too, saying that Warren, Violet, and Eva were all safe at Country Daze. Eventually, Jo-Jo and Sophia headed back upstairs to try to get some more rest, taking Rosco with them, while Cooper relaxed in one of his recliners and flipped on the television in the den.

Owen fixed himself a plate of food, and I sat with him on the patio outside while he ate, sipping some of the sweet iced tea that I'd made to go along with the rest of the meal. By this point, it was late in the evening, and the sun was slowly descending behind the mountains. The oppressive heat of the day had finally broken, and the woods beyond the edge of the yard were starting to come alive with the scurrying, rustling, and *chitter-chatter* of various animals.

Owen was scraping up the last of his mashed potatoes when a car crunched through the gravel in the driveway in front of the house. He tensed, but I shook my head, telling him that it was okay. I recognized the smooth rumble of Finn's Aston Martin.

A few minutes later, my foster brother walked around the side of the house, followed by Phillip. The two of them must have ridden back over together. They sat down with us at the table, and I poured them both some iced tea.

Finn sniffed the air like a bloodhound. "Do I smell ham?" he asked in a dreamy voice. "With mashed potatoes *and* biscuits *and* mac and cheese?"

I shot my finger and thumb at him. "You got it."

Finn sighed in anticipation. He and Phillip went inside, fixed themselves plates, and brought everything out onto the patio. Actually, Finn carried three plates back outside, but I decided not to tease him about it. I waited until he'd polished off his first of four biscuits before I got down to business.

"So what did you find out?" I asked.

"Apparently, you put the fear of death into at least a couple of Grimes's men," Finn said through a mouthful of mac and cheese. "Because I've gotten not one, not two, but three different reports of Grimes's men drunk on moonshine and shooting their mouths off about what happened in a couple of the seedier bars over in Southtown. Given how news travels in that part of the city, I'd say that it's all over the underworld by now, that someone claiming to be the Spider went up to Grimes's camp and laid waste to a good portion of it. Apparently, the men talking you up in the bars deserted Grimes's operation. They didn't want to take a chance that you'd come back and kill what was left of them."

"And what was the reaction to the news?" I asked.

Phillip finished chewing a bite of ham, then stabbed his fork toward me. "From what I hear, Grimes has already vowed retribution, just as soon as he figures out who the woman pretending to be the Spider really is."

I snorted. The one time that my reputation as the Spider might have made somebody think twice about messing with me, my enemy didn't even really believe that I was the Spider to start with. Ah, the irony. Thumbing its nose at me once again.

"And what about the person I spotted at Grimes's house? The one buying all the guns?"

Finn shrugged. "I couldn't find out anything about who that was."

"Me either," Phillip chimed in. "Whoever they are, or whoever they're working for, they are keeping themselves off the radar, along with whatever they or their employer needs with all those weapons."

"The guns and who wants them doesn't matter anyway," I said. "Killing Grimes is what's important."

"How many men do you think he has left?" Owen asked.

I thought back to all the ones I'd killed on the ridge and in the forest, along with the first few men at the salon and the last ones who'd been beating Owen. "If he has a dozen men left, I would say that's a generous estimate. After the carnage I wreaked on his camp, it wouldn't surprise me if there were a few more deserters, just like Finn says there are already. But it's Grimes and Hazel and their Fire magic that I'm worried about. They're the ones who are really dangerous."

"How strong are they?" Phillip asked.

"Strong enough," I replied. "I actually think that Hazel might be a little more powerful than Grimes, but they both have more than enough Fire magic to be worrisome, even to me."

I didn't add that it was the sick, sadistic joy that they

took in using their magic that made them truly danger-ous, ruthless enemies.

Then again, so was I.

"So what do you want to do?" Finn asked. "Get some guns, go back up to their camp, and have it out with them?"

I shook my head. "No, Fletcher did that, and he al-most died up there on the mountain. And so did I. No, I think that it's time for Grimes to play on our turf—and on our terms."

Finn eyed me. After a moment, he sighed. "I know that look. What are you planning to do, Gin? And just how much is it going to wreck my wardrobe?"

I grinned.

Owen, Finn, Phillip, and I hashed out a strategy. Once we had everything nailed down, I called Bria and looped her in. Finn, Phillip, and Owen all went home for the night, but I decided to stay at Cooper's. I didn't think that there was any way that Grimes could find Jo-Jo and Sophia there, but I wasn't going to take the chance.

Cooper offered me his bed, but I refused and bunked down on the couch in the den instead. I'd managed to keep going for far longer than I should have, and as soon as I lay down, my exhaustion took hold of me once more. This time, I didn't try to fight it and fell into a dark, dreamless sleep.

I woke late that night. At first, I wasn't sure what had roused me, since I usually slept for several hours straight after being healed, as my mind tried to play catch-up and realized that my body was in one piece again. But after a moment, a series of soft, rumbling snores filled my ears. I looked down. Rosco had sprawled out on the floor beside the couch, his fat, stubby legs twitching in his sleep.

I snuggled back down into the groove on the well-worn couch, but try as I might, I couldn't go back to sleep. After I punched my pillow and failed to get comfortable for the fifth time, I got up, opened the patio door, and stepped outside.

It was a clear, cloudless night, the stars seeming almost close enough to touch, like glittering tiny apples hanging low on the black velvet tree of the sky. The full moon gave everything a pale silver tint, from the blades of grass in the yard to the tools hanging in Cooper's forge to the leaves in the woods beyond. The river rocks of the patio under my feet were still warm from the heat of the day, and the stones grumbled sleepily of the blazing sun that had baked them for hours and would do the exact same thing again tomorrow.

Apparently, I wasn't the only one who couldn't sleep, because another figure stood farther out in the yard: Sophia.

She still had on her black jeans and T-shirt, which only made her skin seem that much paler. Her face glimmered like a ghost's in the moonlight—pale, ethereal, eternal. Her feet were bare, just like Jo-Jo's always were.

I stepped off the patio and deliberately scuffed my own bare feet through the grass, letting her know that I was coming up behind her. Sophia looked over her shoulder and grunted.

"Couldn't sleep?" I asked, moving over to stand beside her.

She shook her head.

"Me neither."

We stared out into the silvery woods. Somewhere hidden in the trees, an owl let out a series of haunting *hoot-hoot-hoot*s, while a few crickets chirped in response. A breeze gusted through the yard, bringing with it the sharp, tangy scent of the wild onions that had sprung up among the grass.

Sophia bent down and plucked a daisy, one of several that had sprouted in the yard. She slowly, carefully, quietly started pulling the petals off the flower, then the leaves, until she'd stripped the whole thing bare. She tossed the stem aside and grabbed another one.

We stayed like that for a while, with Sophia plucking and stripping down one daisy after another, until she'd gone through a whole patch of them. I didn't ask her what she was thinking about. It was easy to tell that she was remembering everything that had happened in the last few days—and all the horrors that Grimes had visited upon her and Jo-Jo once again.

When Sophia finished with her final daisy, she threw the stem away, although she remained hunkered down in the grass.

"Thank you," she finally rasped, her voice seeming more broken than ever before. "For saving Jo-Jo. For coming after me."

"No thanks needed," I said. "My only regret is that I didn't finish off Grimes while I was there. Hazel too."

Sophia didn't respond. I started to ask her if she wanted to talk about it, but I held my tongue. Despite all those old, wise sayings, talking didn't always help. Not really.

All it did was drag all of your dark, messy, turbulent emotions out into the light for someone else to see. Besides, raspy voice or not, Sophia had never been much for chatting. So I stood there beside her, still and quiet, letting her know that I was here for her and that I would stay out here with her as long as she wanted me to.

To my surprise, after a few minutes, she began to speak.

"The first time he took me, I was so scared," Sophia said. "Grimes had been making threats for weeks, trying to get Jo-Jo to let him court me, but we could both tell that there was something wrong with him. They say that animals can sniff out evil. Well, I could sense it in him. But in the end, it didn't matter, because he took me and dragged me up to that damn mountain of his anyway. You can imagine what happened next."

Torture, beatings, rape. Jo-Jo had told me some of it, like how Grimes had forced Sophia to breathe in elemental Fire, ruining her voice. No doubt, that had happened in the pit when he and Hazel had been torturing her. So I didn't need her to fill in the gruesome details. It had been horrible, more than any person should ever have to endure, but Sophia had.

"It was ironic, Grimes taking me out to the pit again," Sophia continued. "Because that's the only place that I ever got a moment's peace from him and Hazel. They would drag me out there and make me dig at the sides, making it larger and larger so they could dump more bodies in on top of the ones that were already there. But I didn't mind it. Because after they had their fun with me, they would go and do other things. All I had to do was keep digging, and the guards left me alone. All those bodies shifting and rolling and squishing under my feet, they reminded me that I was still alive, and they helped me to keep going, even when all I wanted to do was just give up, lie down, and die. But I'd seen what happened to the other women who begged Grimes for mercy, men too, and I knew that I couldn't do that. Not if I wanted to live. I knew that I had to keep my mouth shut, endure it, and stay alive for myself—and for Jo-Jo too."

I could have told her how sorry I was for everything that she'd suffered back then and again these past few days too, but I kept quiet. Because this was Sophia's story to tell, and I had the sense that if I stopped her now, she'd never start it again. And I wanted to know all of it.

"I lost track of how long I'd been at Grimes's camp, and I'd almost given up any hope of ever escaping," Sophia said, her voice still low. "Until the day one of his men disappeared."

"When Fletcher came for you," I whispered.

She nodded, tugged a clover out of the grass, and started plucking the leaves off it. "Grimes didn't think too much of the guy's disappearance at first, just that he'd probably gotten drunk off the moonshine and fallen off a cliff or maybe even drowned in the river. But then another guy disappeared the very next day. Then another one the next day. And Grimes and his men started finding the bodies, all of them with their throats cut or stab wounds in their chests and all of them left right out in the open, almost like someone had declared war on them."

She stopped long enough to grab another clover and

start working on it. "Then I was out at the pit one day, digging, when I saw a man through the trees. He crept close enough to whisper that his name was Fletcher and that Jo-Jo had sent him to rescue me. Warren was there too. Fletcher told me that he and Warren were going to kill Grimes and get me out of there."

"But it didn't work out quite that way," I said, having an idea where the story was headed.

Sophia shook her head. "Grimes had figured out that Fletcher was really there for me. He, Hazel, Horace, and Henry, their other brothers, set a trap, and Fletcher walked right into it. He managed to kill Henry and Horace, wound Hazel, and he even got Grimes to use up all of his Fire magic. Fletcher and Grimes fought, but Hazel shot him, and Fletcher was too weak and wounded to finish Grimes off. At that point, I didn't care whether Grimes was dead. I just wanted to get off the mountain and go home. So I persuaded Fletcher to leave, and Warren and I managed to drag him down the mountain to where his car was. The three of us made it back to Jo-Jo's, and she healed him."

This time, she reached for a blade of grass and began tearing it into thinner and thinner strips. "After that, Grimes kept his distance, but I was always worried that he would come back someday, so Fletcher taught me how to fight, and in return, I helped him get rid of the bodies that he left behind as the Tin Man. I figured that it was more than a fair trade."

So that's why Sophia had disposed of all those bodies for Fletcher. Once again, my heart twisted at the wrongness of it, of the thought of her doing something over and over again that had to remind her of Grimes and everything she'd suffered at his hands.

"Fletcher never asked me to do it," she said, picking up on my thoughts. "He never asked me to get rid of the first body. But Grimes had made me good at digging graves, and it was the only way that I could think of to repay Fletcher."

"And me?" I whispered. "Why did you keep doing it for me? Why not at least stop when Fletcher died?"

"Because Fletcher loved you and trained you in his own image. And because I owe him everything. It wasn't just that he got me away from Grimes. It was all the years of peace that he gave me afterward."

Another thought occurred to me. "That's why you started working at the Pork Pit, isn't it? So Fletcher could keep an eye on you. So he could protect you from Grimes, in case he came after you again."

Sophia nodded again. "And Fletcher kept his promise, right up to the day he died. He was a good man that way."

She didn't say what we were both thinking: that Fletcher was gone now. That he wasn't around to protect her from Grimes anymore.

But I was.

I'd made a promise to the old man in his office, and it was the same one that I'd made to Sophia and Jo-Jo too, even if I hadn't said it out loud to them, even if they didn't realize it yet.

"Don't you worry about Harley Grimes," I said, reaching out and laying a hand on her shoulder much the same way that Owen had done to me when he'd given me back my knives earlier. "I'll make sure that bastard never hurts you or anyone else ever again. I'm going to finish what Fletcher started and kill him for good this time. That I promise you, Sophia."

She nodded, but the thick muscles in her shoulder bunched under my hand, and the tension in her face didn't ease. After a moment, she shuffled forward, keeping low and moving away from me and over to another patch of daisies. I let my hand fall away from her shoulder, but I didn't follow her.

Instead, I stood there with her in the dark of the night as she picked flower after flower, as though she could strip away all her bad memories as easily as she could separate the delicate petals from the stems.

But she couldn't, and we both knew it.

✳28✳

The next morning, I went to the Pork Pit and opened up the restaurant right on time, just like usual.

Despite the fact that I was being hunted by a couple of Fire elemental psychopaths, I still had a barbecue joint to run. Besides, Grimes was looking for a woman who said that her name was Gin Blanco, and everyone knew that the Pork Pit was mine. I only wondered how long it would take him to realize that I really was the Spider and come here to confront me.

The only thing missing from the restaurant was Sophia. She was still stashed away at Cooper's house, along with Jo-Jo. I'd told the sisters to take it easy and rest up, that nothing was going to happen today. That I had Finn tracking down some leads and was formulating a plan on how best to deal with Grimes.

I didn't tell them that I'd already worked everything out with Finn, Owen, Phillip, and Bria. I didn't want

Sophia and Jo-Jo involved in my scheme, and I didn't want them anywhere near me, not when I was waiting for Grimes to make the first move. They'd already faced him twice, which was two times too many. I was going to handle things from here, like I'd promised Fletcher. I didn't want Sophia and Jo-Jo to set eyes on Grimes ever again—at least, not until after I'd killed him.

I didn't think that the sisters really believed me, but they'd reluctantly agreed to stay put, especially since neither one of them was a hundred percent. Despite the fact that Cooper continued to use his magic on her, Jo-Jo was still weak, and Sophia, well, Sophia had been shot, kidnapped, and tortured. She needed some time to recover from that and from all the grievous wounds that she had on the inside, the ones that no magic could ever fix.

It made me a little melancholy, stepping into the restaurant and not seeing Sophia standing behind the counter, slicing up her homemade sourdough rolls for the day's sandwiches, or hefting a big pot of Fletcher's secret barbecue sauce onto a back burner to bubble away. But it was good that she wasn't here. If she was, all I would do was worry about her, and I couldn't afford to do that. I couldn't afford to be distracted for a moment, not when Grimes and Hazel were coming for me.

So I did my usual sweep of the restaurant for bombs, explosive runes, and any other nasty surprises that someone might have planted on the doors, inside the storefront, or even back in the restrooms overnight. When I was satisfied that no one had been inside the restaurant who shouldn't have been, I flipped the sign on the front door over to *Open*, tied a blue work apron on over my clothes, and switched on the appliances to start cooking.

The waitstaff showed up about half an hour later. A few were surprised when I told them that Sophia wouldn't be in for the rest of the week, but nobody said anything to me about it. They were all too worried about what I might do to them as the Spider to give me any lip about working a little harder because we were a man down.

But the day passed quietly. I cooked, waited on tables, cooked some more, and even managed to read a few chapters of *Dr. No* by Ian Fleming, which I was reading for a spy-literature class that I was going to start over at Ashland Community College in a few weeks.

People came and went, flowing in and out of the restaurant in a regular, familiar, comforting rhythm. No one entered the Pork Pit who shouldn't have, and no one tried to kill me. All in all, it was a rather boring day.

I knew that it wouldn't last, though. And I was looking forward to showing Grimes that I really and truly was the Spider.

Grimes's men showed up at the Pork Pit just before noon the next day.

Oh, they tried to hide who they were by trading in their usual old-fashioned suits in favor of jeans, cowboy boots, and western shirts, complete with pearl-button snaps. But their clothes were obviously new, judging from the stiff, starchy look of their shirts, the sharp creases in their jeans, and the fact that there wasn't so much as a speck of dirt on their fancy boots. Plus, one of them brought his brown fedora into the restaurant and threw it down onto the booth beside him, a hat exactly like the ones all of Grimes's men had worn.

For all intents and purposes, the two men looked like a couple of wannabe cowboys who'd come to the restaurant in search of a good, hot, greasy meal. But their eyes tracked my every movement, and they paid more attention to me than they did to their food. Pity. The strawberry-peach pie was quite excellent that day.

Either they were here to kill me and prove what badasses they were to the rest of the Ashland underworld, or they were watching me on Grimes's orders. Since they didn't try to murder me in front of the cash register or lie in wait and jump me in the alley when I took out the trash, that meant that they were most likely on a reconnaissance mission.

The two guys lingered in the restaurant for more than two hours, ordering second helpings of everything, including the pie. I hoped they enjoyed their last meal.

While the men were finally, slowly, finishing up their second servings of pie, I plopped down on my stool behind the cash register, pulled my cell phone out of my jeans pocket, and called Finn.

"Finnegan Lane, always at your beck and call," he answered in a cheery tone.

"It's on for tonight."

"Are you sure?" he asked.

I opened my book to the page that I'd marked earlier with a credit-card receipt, as though my conversation with Finn was so casual that I could read a few pages and talk to him at the same time. Out of the corner of my eye, I could see one of the men shoving a bite of pie into his mouth and staring at me.

"I'm sure. Let the others know. I'll keep to the schedule that we worked out."

"Roger that."

Finn hung up, and so did I. Now all that was left to do was wait and see exactly when Grimes would strike.

The men eventually finished their meal, paid up, and left. They didn't say anything to me, and they didn't approach me at the cash register, instead leaving more than enough money on the table to cover what they'd ordered. I dropped the change into the tip jar for the waitstaff to share.

But apparently, Grimes wasn't content simply to know where I was, because not ten minutes after the first pair of fake cowboys had left the Pork Pit, another set took their place. Same starched shirts, same creased jeans, same spotless boots. Their clothes were an exact match for the ones worn by the first set, and these two followed the same routine. Ordering lots of food, lingering over everything, not paying up until two hours later.

After they finally left, a third pair came in ten minutes later, just like clockwork, to rinse and repeat the whole process yet again.

Well, Grimes was definitely thorough. I'd give him that. He'd managed to keep at least two sets of eyes on me most of the day. I wondered if he really thought that I was stupid enough to lead him to Sophia and Jo-Jo and that I hadn't anticipated that he'd come after me in the first place.

"People sure must be hungry today," Catalina Vasquez, one of my waitresses, remarked as she grabbed a pitcher of water from the counter behind me. "Because those guys who just came in ordered a truckload of food. That's the third table that I've waited on today that's wanted practically everything on the menu."

"Must be the heat," I drawled. "Nothing works up people's appetites quite like being in the great outdoors, hiking up and down mountains, digging graves, things like that."

Catalina completely missed the sarcasm in my words. She gave me a puzzled look, like I was spouting nonsense. Perhaps the gravedigging remark had been a little over the top. But after a moment, she shrugged and went over to refill the watchers' water glasses.

I turned another page in my book, completely unconcerned by the sly, angry glares coming my way—and the violence that was sure to follow before the day was done.

I followed my usual routines, and the hours slipped by until it was finally time for me to close down the restaurant for the night. After Catalina and the rest of the waitstaff went out the back, I locked the door behind them, then headed into the storefront to turn off all of the appliances.

When everything was shut down, I flipped off the lights, went out through the front door, and locked that one behind me too. Then I stuck my hands into my jeans pockets, whistled a jaunty tune, and slowly ambled to the next block over, where I'd parked my car on the street.

The Pork Pit wasn't all that far away from Southtown, the part of Ashland that was home to hookers, pimps, gangbangers, and other desperate, dangerous folks. Two vampire hookers had left their usual hunting grounds a few blocks away and had wandered over here, trolling for customers. Sequined tube tops barely covered their breasts, while skirts that were all of six inches long clung to the tops of their thighs. They were wearing even less than usual, given the stifling heat.

The two hookers I passed gave me respectful nods and made sure to stay out of my way. Even their pimp, who was lurking behind a Dumpster in the alley, hunched down more at my appearance. Word had spread on this block and the surrounding ones about who I was and just how very dead I could make you.

Everyone else's deference to me made the two idiots following me stick out that much more.

It was the two men who'd come into the restaurant first today, still wearing their pearl-button shirts, jeans, and cowboy boots. They walked about fifty feet behind me. Since it was after seven, all of the commuters had left downtown for their nightly schlep out to the suburbs, and there wasn't that much foot traffic on the sidewalk or many vehicles coasting down the street.

Well, except for the two vampire hookers and the drivers who slowed down to ogle them. One man gave an appreciative *toot-toot* of his car horn. The hookers cocked their hips to the side and waved at him, inviting him to come get a closer look at everything they had to offer.

Other than that limited action, the area was largely deserted, and I'd have had to be blind not to realize how interested the two cowboys were in little ole me. Maybe Grimes hadn't trained his boys as well as I'd thought. Or maybe he was scraping the bottom of the barrel, given how many I'd killed at the camp.

Either way, I reached my car, got inside, cranked the engine, and drove away. I looked in the rearview mirror. The two men were hoofing it over to their own car, which was parked at the very end of the block. So I slowed down and stopped at the light, even though I could have easily coasted right on through it. I didn't want the idiots to lose track of me. It might take them hours to find me again, and that just wouldn't do, especially since I wanted Grimes dead before the sun set.

By the time the light changed, the men were pulling away from the curb and zooming up the street behind me. I went through the intersection, then drove over to Fletcher's house as though I didn't have a care in the world—and didn't realize that someone was following me.

And they did a piss-poor job of it too. Instead of hanging back at a safe distance, the men raced up until they were right on my rear bumper, then abruptly backed off. When they realized that they'd dropped too far behind and were in danger of losing me in the downtown loop, they roared right back up on my bumper again. And it was rinse and repeat, rinse and repeat, all the way over to Fletcher's house. I rolled my eyes. Good help truly was hard to find.

But I made it home without them rear-ending me and turned into the driveway. I took my foot off the gas, coasting forward, but the men didn't veer onto the path behind me like I thought they might. Instead, they drove right on past the entrance, as though they were going somewhere else entirely.

I sighed. I'd really wanted to get on with the business of killing them and confronting their boss. But good things came to those who waited, and I was very, very good at waiting.

So I steered my car up the driveway, parked it, and went inside the house to get ready for my not-so-unexpected visitors. It didn't take long.

Half an hour later, I was sitting in a rocking chair on the front porch, drinking some blackberry lemonade, when Harley Grimes finally made his move.

One minute, I was alone, sipping my beverage and wondering how much longer I'd have to sit out here before Grimes and Hazel took the bait that I was so thoughtfully dangling in front of them—me. The next, I heard a car start rumbling up the gravel driveway. Then another one. Then another one. Three vehicles total, all churning up the hill as fast as they could, as if they thought that I would run once I heard them coming and realized who they were.

I wasn't running, not tonight.

The cars left the driveway and skidded to a stop in the yard near the edge of the trees, spewing dirt and gravel everywhere, and cutting off any escape I might have thought of making to the woods. Men erupted out of the vehicles a second later. Guns drawn, they spread out in front of me. There were only eight of them, which was about what I'd expected. I recognized six as the watchers from the Pork Pit earlier, although they'd traded in their cowboy clothes for their regular old-fashioned suits, boots, and fedoras. But it didn't much matter what they had on. Because every single one of them was dead—they just didn't know it yet.

Finally, two more figures climbed out of the last car: Hazel and Harley Grimes.

Hazel marched over to join the group of men clustered on the lawn, but Grimes lingered by the car, staring up at Fletcher's house. I wondered if he was thinking about building some similar, twisted version of it up on his mountain. Well, he wasn't going to get the chance.

I put one foot up on the railing, tipped my rocking chair back a little farther, and took another long swig of my lemonade, completely unconcerned by all the guns pointed at me.

Finally, Grimes walked over and joined Hazel and his men, standing in the middle of them all. He too was wearing another old-fashioned suit, this one in a black that was as dark as his soul. His hat was black too, with a white feather jauntily perched in the brim just like usual. Hazel had on a white wrap dress with black ribbon piping down the seams. More diamond pins glittered in her wavy black hair, this set shaped like tiny roses. I wondered if the brother and sister had matching funeral outfits. I hoped so. They'd need them soon enough.

Ever so politely, Grimes lifted his hat for a moment before bowing his head to me. "Ms. Blanco," he said. "Please forgive me for my disbelief during our previous encounters at my camp. According to everything that my men have heard, you are indeed who you say you are, the Spider."

"Well, it's about time you figured that out," I drawled, and took another sip of my drink. "I would have thought that all of those dead bodies that I left up at your place would have clued you in to that simple fact. But I guess you're just a little slow on the uptake."

"And I see that you've picked up the same insolence that Sophia has," Grimes murmured. "But Hazel can quickly cure you of that."

Hazel smirked at me, elemental Fire flashing in her eyes in anticipation of the fight to come. She was looking forward to torturing me with her magic again. Good. Because I was looking forward to cutting her throat.

Grimes's gaze flicked around the yard again before scanning the front of the house, trying to see if there were any lights on inside or any hints of movement through the windows. "Where *is* Sophia? I thought that she would be here with you, given how . . . protective you've been of her."

"You might as well forget about Sophia, because she's somewhere where you will never, ever find her."

Grimes gave me a thin smile. "I rather doubt that, seeing how easily I found you. I've had my men watching you all day long at that restaurant you run downtown."

I returned his smile with an even colder one of my own. "You think I didn't know that? You really shouldn't have dressed them all up like cowboys. Or at least you should have made sure that their clothes weren't so obviously brand-spankin' new."

Grimes studied me, trying to figure out whether I was telling the truth. "If you knew that they were there, that they were watching you, then why didn't you try to slip away from them?"

"Because I'm not afraid of them—or you. You're a small, petty, mean little man who gets his kicks by hurting others. If I ran every time one of those came into the restaurant, well, I'd never be open for business."

His frown deepened, and anger sparked in his eyes. He didn't like hearing the truth about himself. Too damn bad.

I drained the last of my lemonade, put the glass down on the railing, got to my feet, and stepped off the porch. I walked out into the yard and stopped about twenty feet away from Grimes and Hazel. They stood in the middle of the eight goons they'd brought along with them. Not exactly the position that I'd wanted them in, but they were here, and that was all that really mattered.

"You should send your men away," I said. "Unless you want them to die in the cross fire. We all know that this is between you and me and Hazel."

Grimes gave me an amused look. "You really think that you can beat Hazel and me and our combined Fire magic? Is that why you let my men follow you home? Because you have some fanciful notion of defeating us in an elemental duel like you did Mab Monroe?"

I shrugged. "I didn't feel like hiking up your stupid mountain again. Besides, I figured that it was time for you to come to Ashland and see how we do things down here in the big city."

Grimes glanced around at the house and the clearing again, and his lips curved into a mocking sneer. "You mean living out here all by yourself in that run-down house? I prefer my camp. You'll come to love it there, too, over time, Gin. I just know that you will."

Once again, that greedy, lustful look flared in his eyes, and his oily, lecherous gaze tracked up and down my body, trying to see my curves through the jeans, long-sleeved black T-shirt, and matching black vest that I had on.

I gave him a flat look. "I said it before, and I'll say it again. I'd rather be dead than be one of your playthings. I managed to survive the mountain. I'll survive you, your twisted sister, and what's left of your little army too."

"You stupid bitch," Hazel snarled. "You think that you can take all of us on by yourself?"

"Why, sugar," I drawled, "who ever said that I was by myself?"

She looked at me, and I grinned back at her. Grimes frowned at my words, but it was Hazel who finally realized what I was up to and why I'd let them follow me home. She cursed, and a ball of elemental Fire flashed to life in her hand.

A perfect signal, if ever there was one.

❊ 29 ❊

Crack!

   Crack! Crack!

   Crack!

   Gunshots rang out from the woods to the left of the house. The first wave of shots took out two of Grimes's men. The others saw their buddies hit the ground, then ducked down and scrambled back behind their cars for cover. They raised their own weapons and started firing toward the trees where the bullets were coming from, but I didn't bother ducking or running for cover. The bullets weren't meant for me. I'd let Grimes and his men follow me back to Fletcher's so that I could lure them into my own trap, into my own sticky web of death, and Grimes had been arrogant enough to fall for it.

   While I'd been sitting on the porch, drinking lemonade, Finn, Bria, Owen, and Phillip had been getting into position in the woods, ready to snipe at Grimes, Hazel, and their men when they showed up.

Crack!

Crack! Crack!

Crack!

My friends fired another hail of bullets at the gangsters, shattering the windshields and denting the car doors that they were crouched behind. But I kept my eyes fixed on Grimes and Hazel, who were staring right back at me, as unconcerned by the bullets as I was. I stayed where I was, because this was the moment I'd been waiting for, my chance to finally take them out.

For Sophia, for Jo-Jo, and for Fletcher.

"What did you do?" Hazel spat out.

"Just made sure that you all get what you so richly deserve," I snarled back at her.

Hazel shrieked with rage, and the flames crackling in her palm intensified. I tensed, thinking that she might hurl her ball of elemental Fire at me, but instead, she turned and threw it into the woods. The Fire hit a tree and exploded, sending flames shooting into the air and licking at the leaves and grass along the ground.

In the distance, I could hear Finn yelling at Bria and the others to watch the Fire. He knew as well as I did that they couldn't afford to let the flames get out of control, or the whole ridge might go up, along with Fletcher's house—and then we'd all be dead.

Hazel laughed with dark delight when she realized that the flames were spreading. Bria left her hiding spot in the woods to rush over to the burning tree. Grimes's men drew a bead on her, but Finn and the others laid down another round of gunfire to cover her. A bluish-white light flared in Bria's hand, and she sent out a blast of Ice magic that quickly turned the flames into thick, twisted icicles.

Hazel's cackle cut off. Another ball of Fire popped into her hand, and she reared back, ready to throw it at Bria and roast my sister where she stood. I palmed my knives and charged at her, determined to keep that from happening.

Hazel saw me coming out of the corner of her eye. She waited until I was in range, then whirled in my direction and shoved her hand—and the flames flickering on her fingertips—right into my face.

I had just enough time to reach for my Stone magic and use it to harden my skin, head, hair, and eyes before the molten heat engulfed me, making me feel as though I was standing next to an open furnace. Hazel wasn't as strong as Mab had been, but she was still a powerful elemental in her own right, and it took me a moment to push back and snuff out the flames of her power with my own Stone magic. Smoke drifted up from my body, and sparks and ash fell from my clothes.

Hazel's eyes narrowed. "So it's true. You do have Stone magic, along with all that Ice you threw around on the ridge."

"You really should have listened to the rumors," I hissed. "Because now I'm going to kill you with it, just like I have all the others before you. Just like I will all the others after you who are stupid enough to mess with me and mine."

Another ball of Fire popped into Hazel's hand. "Not if I kill you first, bitch."

Instead of answering, I threw myself at her.

I stabbed out with my knives, trying to end Hazel once and for all, but she reached for even more of her magic, turning her fists into two flaming torches. Every time I swung at her, she thrust the flames of her magic into my face, making me retreat. So I reached for my Stone magic, used it to harden my skin, and went after her again.

Hazel realized that I was coming after her through the flames, and she stepped up to meet me.

Slash-slash-slash.

Whoosh!

Slash-slash-slash.

Whoosh!

Every time I swiped at her with my knives, Hazel reached for even more of her magic and tossed it in my direction. Since I didn't want to get burned alive on the spot, I kept my distance.

Finally, though, I grew sick of Hazel's game and stepped through the flames toward her. One knife to the heart, and she'd forget all about using her Fire power on me. She'd forget about everything except how much I'd hurt her.

And I did *so* want to hurt her.

But Hazel was as good a fighter as I was. Strong, quick, decisive, ruthless. Every time I lashed out with a knife, she managed to block the blow. She punched out with her fist, flames shooting out from between her fingers, and made me duck to one side. I came back up on the left with a knife, but she was already there, anticipating the blow.

Slash.

Punch.
Slash-slash.
Punch-punch-punch.

And on and on it went, with neither one of us able to do any real damage to the other. All we were really doing was wearing each other out and using up all of our magic in the process.

Out of the corner of my eye, I could see Grimes watching us while we moved in circles around the yard. Every once in a while, he would turn and throw a ball of Fire at the woods, forcing Bria to use her Ice power to counter it, and keeping the others pinned down there, but mostly, he watched me battle Hazel.

Yeah, he'd be the kind who liked to watch. I wondered if this was another way he got his kicks, besides torturing people in his pit of death or hunting them down like deer in the woods. I hoped he enjoyed the show, because he was going to get a front-row seat for round two. I was killing him as soon as I finished with Hazel.

I shut Grimes out of my mind and focused all of my attention on Hazel once more. Back and forth, we fought, kicking up dust, dirt, grass, gravel, and everything else that was underfoot, as though we were in the center of some whirling dust storm.

Finally, though, I saw an opening, and I took it. I raised both of my knives high and went in for the kill.

Hazel caught one of my hands in hers, then the other one. We seesawed back and forth, with me trying to drive the blades into any place on her that they would go and her easily using her mix of giant and dwarven strength to keep me at arm's length.

"What are you going to do now?" she hissed, the flames of her magic licking at my skin, trying to break through the protective shell of my Stone power.

"How about this?" I hissed back at her.

I head-butted the bitch as hard as I could.

I caught her square in the nose, the bone crunching like cereal under my forehead. *Snap, crackle, pop.* For the first time, one of my blows actually seemed to have an impact. Hazel staggered away, blood spraying all over her face, her eyes rolling up into the back of her head. The Fire dancing on her fingers dimmed down to a manageable level. I twirled my knives in my hands and went after her, pressing my advantage.

Slice.

Whiff.

I drew a knife across Hazel's right arm, making her yelp with pain. I ducked to one side, and her flaming fist sailed right on by my face.

Slice-slice.

Whiff-whiff.

A cut on her left arm this time, followed by a gash to her stomach. Hazel lurched forward, still swinging at me, but I easily sidestepped her blows.

Slice.

Whiff.

A deeper, more brutal strike went in and skittered off her collarbone before my knife slid free of her body. Hazel screamed and lurched forward again, but I ducked her awkward blow.

She shook off the rest of her daze and moved to block my next attack. I'd raised my knives as though I was going to try to stab her again, but it was a feint to disguise my real intention. Hazel stepped up to grab my arms once more, but I ducked down and lashed out with my foot, sweeping her legs out from under her. She let out a scream of surprise as she fell, and her head cracked against the ground.

Before she could recover, I threw myself on top of her. I raised my knife, ready to plunge it into Hazel's black, venomous heart—

A blast of Fire knocked me off her.

I'd been so focused on Hazel that I'd lost track of Grimes during the fight. He might have liked to watch two chicks rough each other up, but apparently, he drew the line at me actually killing his sister. I tried to get up, but another wave of Fire washed over me, even hotter and more brutal than before. I sucked down a breath in surprise, and I could feel the flames trying to force their way down my throat, but I managed to use my own Stone magic to block the attack.

This time, I was the one who was dazed, but I staggered to my feet anyway and turned to face my enemies.

Crack!

Crack! Crack!

In the distance, Finn, Phillip, and Owen were still firing at what remained of Grimes's men, while Bria worked to contain the bursts of Fire that Grimes had sent hurtling their way. But I pushed away all thoughts of my friends and the flames still licking at the edge of the woods. I couldn't afford to be distracted by anything right now, or I was dead.

Which was still a distinct possibility.

It was a risk, taking on two elementals at once, but it was a chance that I had to take. I hadn't wanted Sophia and Jo-Jo involved in this fight, but the truth was that I hadn't wanted Finn, Bria, Owen, or Phillip in it either. That's why I had insisted that they stay in the woods, instead of Bria and Owen standing with me and using their magic like they'd wanted to. I'd felt how strong Grimes and Hazel were in their magic on the ridge, and I hadn't wanted the others to be tortured with it if things went bad. This way, even if they used their combined power to kill me, my friends would still have a chance to snipe at them from the woods. I'd told Finn, especially, to kill Grimes—even if he had to sacrifice me to do it.

And it looked like that was what it had finally come down to.

"It doesn't have to be like this," Grimes said. "Tell me where Sophia is, and I'll let you live, Gin. You and Sophia. You can both come with me, stay with me. You're both strong. You both belong with someone who can handle that strength, tame it, shape it—someone like me."

He was so focused on me that he didn't see the evil glare that Hazel shot him. She'd make sure that I wouldn't live a week if I was stupid enough to take Grimes up on his offer.

"You'd better kill me now," I rasped, my voice rough and raw from the elemental Fire that I'd inhaled. "Because you will never break me, and I will never, *ever* stop thinking of ways to kill you. And sooner or later, I'll succeed."

Grimes shook his head, as though my threats of death deeply saddened him. "As you wish, then."

He held his hand out to the side. At first, I wondered why, but then Hazel stepped up and twined his fingers with hers. She gave me another evil grin, happy that her brother had reached for her. Elemental Fire hissed, sparked, and crackled where their hands met, and the flames there grew and grew. Grimes and Hazel lifted their free hands. Flames exploded there as well, burning as big and bright as twin bonfires. Once again, their magic was perfectly in sync, ebbing and flowing in time, yin and yang reunited. Or evil and more evil, in this case.

Separately, each of them was a strong elemental. But together, their combined magic rivaled Mab's. Hell, they might have even surpassed her. I'd gotten stronger myself since I'd fought Mab, but the intensity of their magic made me snarl and grit my teeth like a rabid dog. I reached for my Stone magic and used it to harden my skin once again.

Grimes and Hazel stretched their arms out in front of them. They let their Fire build and build.

Then they threw it at me—all their strength, all their power, all their hate.

Wave after wave of searing, smoking, unbelievable heat slammed into my body. I gritted my teeth much tighter to keep from screaming. It was all that I could do to use my power to block the combined strength of theirs.

I tried to get to them, tried to get close enough to cut just *one* of them with my knives, but every time I managed to stagger forward a few feet, another wave of Fire magic would send me sliding back. But I kept struggling, kept fighting, kept churning forward, even though all I was really doing was digging my heels into the burning grass underfoot. All I needed was to separate them, to stop them from sharing their magic and throwing the combined force of it at me, and then I could kill them.

At least, that's what I told myself, even if I knew that it wasn't true.

Because I'd already used up a fair amount of my magic fighting Hazel, and I didn't have enough left in the tank to stop them both. Even with the power I'd put back into my spider rune ring over the past two days and what was in the knives in my hands, I was still going to run out of magic before they did. Then their elemental Fire would wash over me and reduce me to soot and smoldering ashes on the spot.

And there wasn't a damn thing that I could do about it.

"Gin!" I thought I heard Owen yell. "Hang on! I'm coming!"

Crack! Crack! Crack! Crack!

My friends fired still more shots, but what was left of Grimes's men returned their fire, holding them at bay. They wouldn't reach me in time, and we all knew it. Still, I was going to hold on for as long as I could. Because if I couldn't kill Grimes and Hazel, then maybe they could. Because, magic or not, if Finn and the others pumped them full of enough bullets, then their magic would wane, and Finn could step up and finish the job—

Through the smoke and flames, I saw a figure slam into Grimes and Hazel, and I realized that it was Owen.

He threw himself at the brother and sister, and all three of them went down like pins knocked over by a bowling ball. Even though he had shattered their concentration, Grimes and Hazel were still holding on to their magic, and the flames washed over Owen, as though he were the wick in the center of a burning candle. His hoarse screams echoed all the way around the ridge.

"Owen!" I screamed, staggering toward him. "Owen!"

The three of them were still rolling around on the grass, but they finally came to a stop. Grimes's head snapped against the ground, stunning him, but Hazel positioned herself on top of Owen. She snapped her hand back and reached for her Fire magic once again.

I reached through the flames, dug my fingers into her hair, and yanked her off him. I tossed her aside as hard as I could, tearing clumps of black hair out by the roots. Hazel shrieked with pain, but I didn't give her time to recover. She hit the ground, and a second later, I was on top of her. Hazel reached for her Fire, throwing it into my face.

I ignored the flames searing my skin, raised my knife high, and buried it to the hilt in the bitch's black, burning heart.

Hazel arched her back and let out a bloodcurdling scream. I ripped the knife out and drove it right back into her chest, twisting and twisting and twisting it in. Muscles ripped, tendons snapped, and one of her ribs cracked under my brutal assault. Hazel slapped at me, her blows getting weaker and weaker with every passing moment, the Fire on her fingers giving way to smoking red and orange sparks. I tore the knife out of her chest once again.

And this time, I slit her throat with the blade.

Blood gushed out of the wound, spattering onto me, as hot as the flames still licking at my skin. Hazel's screams died down to gurgling wails, then were choked off altogether. She stared at me, the bright, shimmering Fire in her eyes slowly, stubbornly dimming and dulling as death crept up on her. Her head lolled to the side, and the last of the flames dancing on her fingertips vanished into smoke. After a moment, even that drifted up into the evening sky and dissipated.

When I was sure that she was dead, I crawled over to where Owen lay on his back on the grass. Deep, dark, ugly red burns and blisters covered every part of him that I could see—his chest, hands, arms, and face. His eyebrows had been singed off, and his scalp gleamed a baby pink in places where his black hair had been burned way. Bile rose in my throat at his devastating injuries.

"Gin . . ." he rasped.

"It's okay," I whispered, trying not to let him see how worried I was. "You're going to be okay—"

A shadow fell over me, blotting out the evening sun. I looked up. Harley Grimes had shaken off his daze and now stood over me, more Fire pooling in the palm of his hand. He reared back his arm, ready to throw it at me, ready to end me. I reached for what little magic I had and hovered over Owen, determined to protect him as much as I could—

A dark figure dressed all in black slammed into Grimes from behind. Sophia.

Sophia? What the hell was she doing here?

I blinked and blinked, wondering if my eyes and the clouds of smoke that filled the yard were playing tricks on me, but it was her. Sophia was here, and she was fighting Grimes.

With one hand, Sophia ground Grimes's face into the

dirt. With the other, she unleashed a series of sharp, brutal blows to his kidneys.

Grimes managed to raise his head and let out a delighted laugh. "Oh, Sophia," he purred. "Still trying to kill me after all these years. When will you ever learn?"

Grimes reached around with one hand and blasted Sophia with his Fire magic. She grunted with pain and rolled away from him, smothering the flames scorching her clothes and skin. A moment later, they were both back on their feet, fists clenched, staring each other down.

My gaze flicked past them. Sophia's classic convertible sat in the driveway behind the vehicles that Grimes's men had driven up here. I hadn't heard the car pull up in all the commotion. But she wasn't the only one who'd come. Jo-Jo was leaning against the side of the car, holding on to Cooper's arm to steady herself. I hadn't told them what was going down tonight, but they must have figured it out for themselves. That, or Finn had told them.

Finn, Bria, and Phillip came running up, having finally dispatched the last of Grimes's men. Finn took aim at Grimes. He looked at me, but I shook my head. Finn nodded and lowered his gun.

Grimes stared at Finn, Bria, and Phillip, then at Owen and me, and finally, at Cooper, Jo-Jo, and Sophia. For the first time, he seemed to realize that he was all alone and that Hazel and the rest of his men were dead.

But it didn't faze or worry him in the slightest. Instead, he reached for his Fire magic once again, more of it than ever before, until his eyes burned like dark liquid gold with his own power, and flames sparked and crackled like fireworks exploding on his fingers.

"Come with me now, Sophia," he ordered. "And I won't kill your friends."

Another damn lie, and we all knew it.

Sophia shook her head. "No. You're not killing any-one."

Grimes threw back his head and laughed—a wild, loud, crazy laugh that told us all just how far off his rocker he was. His plan to hunt me down, find Sophia, and drag us both back to his mountain had completely unraveled, and Grimes was coming undone at the seams right along with it.

"Really? And who's going to stop me, you?" He sneered. "Please. You're not strong enough to stop me. You *never* were. That's why you had to get that assassin to protect you all these years. Because you weren't strong enough to kill me yourself."

Sophia shrugged. "Maybe not then. But strong enough now."

Jo-Jo hobbled forward, helped along by Cooper, and went to stand beside her sister.

"We both are," Jo-Jo said in a clear, sharp voice. "My only regret is that we didn't do this years ago."

Grimes threw back his head and laughed again. Finally, when he realized that he was the only one who found it funny, he glared at Jo-Jo with pure hate in his eyes. "You won't kill me. You don't have enough magic to kill me. None of you does. None of you is *strong* enough."

Jo-Jo gave him a sweet smile. "That's the funny thing about Fire," she said. "No matter how strong it is, it sim-ply can't survive without Air—and neither can you."

She reached for her Air magic, her eyes glowing a

milky white. But instead of blasting Grimes with it, Jo-Jo did something even more clever and devious. She sucked all of the oxygen away from him.

The flames burning on his hand were immediately snuffed out. Grimes stared down at his hand in disbelief, then started snapping his fingers together, as though they were a cigarette lighter that he was trying to coax to life. He reached and reached for his magic, but without all that precious oxygen, he couldn't get so much as a single spark to flare to life.

Jo-Jo looked at Sophia, and the sisters nodded to each other. Sophia slowly approached him.

"Fine," Grimes muttered, finally giving up on his power. "I don't need magic to put you in your place, Sophia. I never did."

He let out a loud roar and charged at her.

And then they danced.

Despite all the years that I'd known her, I hadn't seen Sophia fight all that often. But she was as efficient and brutal with her blows as I was. More than that, she was motivated by all of the things that she'd suffered at Grimes's hands.

For a while, Grimes was able to block her blows, and all they did was exchange punch after punch after punch. But Sophia slowly wore him down. He missed a block, and she socked him square in the jaw. He missed the next block, and she slammed her hand into his sternum, cracking a rib, judging by the way he suddenly started gasping for air.

Grimes went on the attack, swinging, swinging, swinging, but Sophia swatted away his blows one after another after another. He overextended himself, and she slammed her boot into one of his knees. He howled with pain, but before he could stumble out of range, she clamped her hands on his arms and rammed her boot into his other knee. The cracking of his bones rattled through the entire yard.

Sophia let go, and Grimes dropped to the ground like a cement block. That's when we all knew that it was over.

Sophia positioned herself on top of Grimes and started hitting him, over and over again, as though she were working a heavy bag at the gym.

Thwack-thwack-thwack-thwack.

She pounded away at his chest, focusing on his ribs and driving all of the air out of his lungs, so that he couldn't even scream at what was being done to him—just like she hadn't been able to scream after he'd destroyed her vocal cords by making her breathe in elemental Fire.

Jo-Jo. Cooper. Finn. Bria. Phillip. They all stood there and watched Sophia beat Grimes to death, while I huddled on the ground next to Owen. Nobody said a word, although Bria winced at the brutality that Sophia unleashed. But she hadn't been up at the camp. She hadn't seen the pit, so she didn't fully understand his depravity.

But I did. More important, I understood Sophia's response to it and why she had to do this herself.

I'd wanted to spare her and Jo-Jo from facing Grimes again, but they'd come anyway because they needed closure. They needed to help defeat him. And most of all, they needed to know that the nightmare was truly, finally over.

Thwack-thwack-thwack-thwack.

And Sophia was making sure that happened with every single blow she landed.

Eventually, Cooper helped Jo-Jo over to Owen. The two dwarves settled themselves on the scorched earth, took Owen's hands in theirs, and reached for their Air magic, healing the horrible burns on his body. Then they used their power to heal me as well. Finn, Phillip, and Bria moved silently through the yard, their guns still drawn, checking on Grimes's men to make sure that they were all dead.

I got to my feet and went to stand close to Sophia. And I stayed right there, watching her, supporting her, through the whole thing.

I couldn't tell exactly when Harley Grimes died. One moment, he was still rasping for breath. The next, I realized that his eyes were focused on Sophia but that he wasn't seeing her anymore.

Sophia kept beating Grimes long after he was dead, but I didn't say anything, and I didn't try to stop her. She deserved all the time that she needed, for everything that he'd done to her and Jo-Jo.

Finally, though, her blows slowed, sputtered, then stopped altogether. Sophia sat back on her heels, breathing hard, covered in more blood than even I'd ever had on me. Her arms were completely coated with it, and it dripped off the ends of her fingertips like scarlet teardrops.

I looked down at Grimes—at least, what was left of him. It wasn't pretty. Sophia had used her dwarven strength to its fullest. His face was a bloody, pulpy, bony mess; his chest had caved in; and his knees were sprawled out at awkward, impossible angles where Sophia had broken them. If I hadn't known that it was the body of a man, I would have thought him no more than a pile of roadkill, bloated, bloody, and rotting on the side of some country road.

I stepped in front of Sophia where she could see me, then held out my hand, which was still covered with Hazel's blood. After a moment, she took it and let me pull her to her feet. She started to let go, but I tightened my grip on her hand.

"Not alive," I said. "Not anymore."

Sophia looked at me with a somber expression. But after a moment, she grinned, her smile wider, happier, and brighter than I'd ever remembered it being.

"No," she rasped. "Dead—finally."

❊ 30 ❊

We spent the rest of the night cleaning up the mess.

Or, rather, Sophia did.

One by one, she packed the bodies of Grimes, Hazel, and their men into the trunk of her classic convertible. When that was full, she stuffed the other ones into Roslyn's car, which I was still driving, since it was already such a lost cause. But instead of using her Air magic to sandblast away and dissolve all the blood into nothingness the way she normally would, Sophia left the stains where they were in the yard. The weather would take care of them soon enough. Besides, this wasn't the first blood that had been spilled in front of Fletcher's house, and it certainly wouldn't be the last.

Still, as I watched her work, I thought about what she'd told me at Cooper's house, about how being with the bodies in the pit had been the only peace that she'd ever gotten while she'd been Grimes's prisoner. I wondered what she was thinking now that his was one of the bodies that she was disposing of, but I didn't ask. We all had our own demons, and Harley Grimes was one of Sophia's, to deal with in her own way and time. Besides, for once, I rather enjoyed the irony of the situation.

Still, I went over to Sophia, who had a tape measure out, trying to determine how many more bodies she could stuff into the trunk of Roslyn's car. I put my hand on her arm. She stopped measuring and looked up at me.

"Are you sure you want to do this?" I asked in a quiet voice. "I can get rid of the bodies. You shouldn't have to do this anymore. Not for me. I don't *want* you to do it anymore."

Sophia stared at me, her black eyes thoughtful.

"It's who I am," she rasped. "It's what I do. For Fletcher—and for you too."

"But you shouldn't have to clean up my messes," I protested. "Not when I know what it reminds you of. Not when I know how much it hurts you."

Sophia stabbed her finger at her heart. "My choice. Not yours."

"But—"

She reached up and cupped my cheek with her bloody hand. "No buts. I love you, Gin. And this is how I show it."

Then she smiled, and I got a glimpse of the girl she had once been, before Grimes, before the pit, before everything.

"Not soft," Sophia rasped. "Neither one of us. Not anymore. Never again."

I blinked, surprised that she remembered the conversation we'd had in the Pork Pit so long ago after we'd battled those two giants. But she was right. We were definitely not that. Broken, maybe. But not soft.

"Okay?" she rasped, her black eyes searching mine.

"Okay."

I didn't like it, and I would always feel guilty about it, but it *was* her choice, just as it had always been. Sophia patted my cheek. Then she picked up another body, stuffed it into the trunk of Roslyn's car, and bent down to grab the next one.

And that was that.

"Gin!" Finn called out. "Come here and look at this!"

Before Sophia had started packing the bodies into the cars, Finn had quickly rifled through all of the dead men's pockets, including Hazel's and Grimes's. When he realized that they didn't have anything terribly interesting on them, Finn had gathered up their car keys and had started going through their vehicles one by one.

Now, he had reached the last car, that of Grimes and Hazel. He stood next to the open trunk, along with Bria. They both wore grim expressions.

"I thought that you'd want to see this for yourself." Finn gestured at the open trunk, then stepped to one side.

A couple of foam-lined cases sat inside the space, all with their lids hinged open to reveal the guns grouped inside. Rifles, shotguns, revolvers, even some semiautomatic weapons. It was quite an assortment. Another case held boxes and boxes of bullets.

"There are more guns and more ammo in the trunks of the other two cars," Finn said, his voice more serious than I'd heard it in a long time.

"So Grimes was going to deliver some guns to someone," I said. "So what? We knew that already. Remember, I told you about the person who was at his house. This is probably that order."

Finn and Bria glanced at each other, and then Bria leaned into the trunk and slowly closed the lid on one of the cases. A small yellow note was stuck to the top of the plastic. A name was scrawled on the paper: *M. M. Monroe.*

My mouth dropped open, but no words came out. I blinked and blinked, but the name on the paper didn't change. If anything, it seemed to loom even larger, as though the black letters were some sort of rune that was smoking with elemental Fire and about to explode in my face.

"We didn't think much of the guns either, until we found *that*," Bria said in a flat voice.

"The same note is on all of the cases in all of the cars," Finn added.

Once again, I wondered about the person I'd seen at Grimes's house. I still didn't know if it had been a man or a woman, but now I had a much more pressing concern. Had that been the mysterious M. M. Monroe? Or a hired hand whom M. M. Monroe had sent to deal with Grimes? It could easily be one or the other or some third option that I hadn't even considered yet. I had no way of knowing which one, only that it meant trouble.

I let out a long, loud, vicious curse. For the first and only time, I wished that Harley Grimes was still alive, so I could question him.

But he was dead, along with Hazel and the rest of his

men, which meant that there was no one left to give me any information about M. M. Monroe, who he or she was, and what he or she wanted with so many of Grimes's guns.

Finn and Bria watched me stalk back and forth in front of the trunk. Finally, Finn spoke up.

"Well," he drawled. "I guess your plan to draw M.M. back to Ashland worked."

"And I think we know that this person isn't here for anything good," Bria added. "There's only one reason you buy that many guns, at least in Ashland."

"Yeah," I said. "Because you're planning to start your own little criminal enterprise. Or not so little, in this case."

"It looks like M.M. plans to follow in Mab's footsteps after all," Finn said.

I stopped pacing. "Please tell me that there's some way that you can track these guns back to whoever ordered them."

Finn shrugged. "I can try, but it won't be easy. Grimes doesn't strike me as the kind of guy who kept meticulous records."

"Yeah," Bria said. "And the weapons that I've looked at already all conveniently have their serial numbers filed off, so I can't trace them in the system that way."

I bit back another round of curses. It wasn't their fault that we'd just killed off our best—and only—lead about M. M. Monroe.

As I looked at the guns, I couldn't help but think that I'd just traded one enemy for another.

Soon after that, Finn and Bria took off together, promising to check in with me later, both of them eager to work their sources and see if they could find out anything about the guns and M. M. Monroe.

I waited until Sophia had packed the last body into Roslyn's car and went inside the house with her, where we found the others in the den. Phillip was sitting in a chair in the corner, while Jo-Jo and Cooper were both sitting on the coffee table in front of the sofa where Owen was lying. I perched on the arm of the couch and watched Jo-Jo instruct Cooper on how best to use his magic to heal the remaining burns on Owen's body. Jo-Jo had taken care of the worst of the damage earlier in the yard, but it had quickly exhausted her, leaving Cooper to finish patching up Owen.

"Feel the Air around you," Jo-Jo said in a soft, patient voice. "Imagine it flowing through Owen's wounds, like a gentle breeze that takes all of his pain away with it."

Cooper gripped Owen's hand a little tighter and leaned forward, his eyes glowing a bright copper in his lined face.

"Good," Jo-Jo said, once he'd followed her instructions. "Now, picture the Air flowing through his wounds again, this time slowly smoothing out all of those nasty burns and pulling all of those cuts and scrapes together the smallest fraction. You need to do that again and again, until the wounds are completely healed . . ."

Cooper listened to Jo-Jo's instructions, and I watched as the remaining burns on Owen's body slowly grew soft and pink, then scarred out to white, then faded away altogether. I looked at Owen with a critical eye, but if I hadn't seen it for myself, I wouldn't have realized that he'd body-slammed himself into a couple of Fire elementals. With Jo-Jo guiding him, Cooper had done as good a job on Owen as she would have. He'd even fixed Owen's hair and eyebrows. No trace remained of his fight with Grimes and Hazel.

Jo-Jo nodded. "Good job, Cooper. We might make a healer out of you yet."

He beamed at her praise. Jo-Jo smiled back at him, but she couldn't hold back the tired yawn that escaped her lips. Cooper jumped up and took her arm. He helped the dwarf out of the den. Sophia followed them, and I heard their slow, steady tread on the stairs, then one of the doors of the guest bedrooms opening and closing. Sophia and Cooper would see that Jo-Jo was comfortable for the night, so I turned my attention back to Owen.

Phillip cleared his throat and got to his feet. "I need some fresh air. All this postbattle *rah-rah-we-lived* sentimentality is a bit cloying. I'll call you tomorrow, Owen."

"Thanks, Phillip," Owen replied.

I arched an eyebrow at Phillip, but he grinned and left the den. A moment later, the front door of the house opened, then closed.

When I was sure that we were alone, I went over and dropped down on my knees on the floor in front of Owen. He started to sit up, but I put a hand on his shoulder.

"Just lie there and rest a minute. You've definitely earned it."

Owen sighed. "I won't argue with that."

I took his hand in mine. "How are you feeling?" I asked, searching his face for any sign of pain or discomfort.

His lips curved up. "Like your barbecue, roasted low and slow."

His words made me chuckle, but the more I stared at him, the more I flashed back to how he'd looked lying in the yard, burned, bruised, and battered. The mere memory made my heart squeeze tight with pain and fear.

"You didn't have to do that," I finally said in a soft voice. "You didn't have to throw yourself into the middle of my fight with Grimes and Hazel. You could have shot one of them with your gun instead. What were you thinking? They could have easily killed you . . ."

"I wasn't thinking about my gun or shooting them," Owen replied. "I was thinking that I couldn't stand by and watch you die, Gin. That I was going to do whatever it took in order to save you."

"Well, I appreciate that, but I'm pretty good at taking care of myself." I tried to keep my voice light, but it didn't work. "More important, you don't have to prove anything to me. I know that you care about me. That was just a foolish risk to take."

This time, I couldn't stop Owen from getting up. He slid off the couch and onto the floor so that we were sitting side-by-side. Then he turned to face me.

"That's where you're wrong. I do have to prove something to you: that I'm as committed to you as you are to me. That I would do anything for you, *anything*."

I sighed. "You don't have to make up for what happened with Salina. That was a difficult situation. An impossible situation. I'm not going to hold it over your head."

Owen let out a breath. "I know you won't, because that's not the kind of person you are. But I'm holding it over my own head. *I* need to make up for it. Because you were only trying to help, only trying to protect me, Eva, Cooper, and Phillip, and I let you down in the worst possible way. I'm going to spend the rest of my life making up for it, if that's what it takes to win you back. To undo the damage that I did to you—to *us*."

It was more or less the same thing that he'd told me that night in the forest by the fire. His violet eyes locked with mine, letting me see how serious and earnest he was—and just how much he loved me.

Fletcher had always said that pretty words were all well and good, but people's actions were what really mattered in the end. In the past few days, Owen had climbed a mountain to help me rescue Sophia, searched miles of forest for me, fished me out of the river, and kept me safe from Grimes's men. Then he'd thrown himself into the middle of my fight with Grimes and Hazel, with no hesitation and no thought to the damage that he might do to himself. I hadn't asked him to do any of that—not one single thing—but he'd done it all anyway.

That told me everything that I needed to know, especially about how he really felt about me.

"I asked you before on the mountain, and I'm going to ask you again now," Owen said, his eyes still searching mine. "I want to try again, Gin. Please?"

My heart swelled with love for him, and this time, I didn't try to fight it, and I wasn't afraid of it, or him, or even of having my heart broken again. I might have lost sight of it in the forest, but if there was one thing that all my years as the Spider, all the battles, all the brushes with my own death, had taught me, then it was this.

That *this* was what was important. This moment right

now and all the ones that we were lucky enough to have after it. Today, tomorrow, hell, maybe even forever.

Me. Him. Us. Together.

Yeah, we'd hit a big bump in the road, and we still had some work to do. I needed to learn how to trust him fully again. He needed to forgive himself for Salina's crimes. And we both needed to learn how to let go of and move past the pain that we'd caused each other, learn how to work on our problems together.

"Gin?" Owen asked yet again, his eyes burning into mine.

I leaned forward so that my forehead was touching his. "Yes," I whispered. "Yes."

I cupped his face in my hands. Owen snaked his arms around my waist. Our lips met somewhere in the middle.

It was a slow, languid, lingering kiss, a perfect meeting of lips and tongues and mouths and breaths. That familiar spark of desire flared to life low in my stomach, then spread through the rest of my body, but this wasn't about giving in to that want. At least, not yet. No, this was about the silent, heartfelt promise that we were both making to each other, never to take this, us, for granted again.

Finally, the kiss ended, although I kept staring into Owen's eyes, wondering at all the love that I saw there.

I drew away from him, got to my feet, and held out my hand. He took it.

I led Owen to a bathroom on the other side of the house, where we would have some privacy. This was the largest bathroom in the house, with two sinks and an oversize, walk-in shower that took up most of one wall.

I shut and locked the door behind us, then turned the water on in the shower. Not too cold, not too hot.

We'd both be that, soon enough.

The steady hiss of the water was the only sound as we slowly undressed each other. I helped him shrug out of his shirt. He unzipped my vest. I unbuttoned his jeans. He did the same to mine. Our clothes quickly disappeared, until we stood there naked in front of each other. I smoothed my hands over his broad, muscled shoulders and then down his chest. He traced his fingers down my neck, before leaning forward and pressing a soft kiss to the hollow of my throat, making me shiver.

I held my hand out again. He took it, and I drew him into the shower.

Steam rose all around us as I grabbed the soap, lathered up my hands, and ran my fingers over his body, from his slightly crooked nose to his flat stomach and strong legs and all the way down to his toes. I went slowly and carefully, gently washing off all the blood and dirt of his battle with Grimes and Hazel. Owen had done the same thing for me once upon a time, and it seemed fitting to return the gesture. A fresh start, a clean slate, a new beginning, in more ways than one.

I kissed every spot that I cleaned, lightly nipping at some of the more sensitive areas with my teeth. By the time I'd worked my way down to his hard length, he was more than ready for me. I kissed that too, running my lips and tongue all over him.

Owen groaned. "If you keep doing that, this shower is going to be shorter than either one of us wants it to be."

I grinned and kept up with my ministrations a minute longer before kissing my way back up his body.

"Tease," he muttered in a hoarse voice, his violet eyes as bright as amethysts.

"And don't you love it."

He grinned and reached for the shampoo.

Owen turned me around so that my back was to him, then started washing my hair. I moaned at the feel of his fingers digging into my scalp. Soap suds cascaded down my body, and Owen's fingers quickly followed. Still behind me, he cupped my breasts in his hands, his fingers circling and massaging my nipples before moving lower. His fingers tangled in the curls at the junction of my thighs before sliding lower still. He dipped his fingers inside me, rubbing slow, lazy circles that made every part of me thrum with desire.

I arched back against him. "Tease."

"And don't you love it," he whispered, mocking me with my own words.

He stroked me until I was just as ready for him as he was for me. I turned around to face him, and we moved together with one thought. Our lips met and opened, our tongues stroking together, slow and soft at first, then quicker and more demanding as our hunger built. The water trailed down our bodies, and our hands followed suit, gliding, sliding, caressing, even as our kisses grew harder and greedier.

Owen left the shower long enough to grab a condom from his wallet. I took my little white pills, but we always used extra protection.

He stepped back into the warm spray of water. I

reached for him, but he was quicker. He picked me up, put my back against the wall, and slid into me with one smooth thrust. I groaned and wrapped my legs around his waist, my hands digging into his shoulders.

"Now, this would be teasing," Owen rasped against my lips.

He withdrew, then surged into me again, making me groan once more.

"I think I've had enough teasing," I said, nipping at his lower teeth with my lip. "Haven't you?"

He responded by thrusting into me again, even deeper than before. My nails dug into his skin. Oh, yeah. We were definitely done teasing.

What started out slow, soft, and sweet quickly boiled up into something quick, hard, and wickedly good. Owen thrust into me over and over again, and I matched him, rocking my hips against his. Our movements were so quick, so hard, so frantic, that my wet back slid down the shower wall. Owen growled and lowered me to the ground, the water pounding into his back even as he kept moving inside me, going deeper and deeper.

We rolled together, and then I was on top. I drew back, then rocked my hips forward in a long, slow glide that finally sent us both over the edge. Owen growled again, even lower and fiercer than before, and pulled me down on top of him. His lips met mine, both of us sucking the air out of each other's mouth, even as we moved together in that perfect rhythm.

And then . . . bliss—pure, white-hot bliss that blotted out everything else.

I collapsed on top of him. Owen pressed his lips to my temple and pulled me even closer, cradling me in the strong circle of his arms. I rested my face in the curve of his neck. No words were necessary. Not now.

And we stayed like that for a long, long time, the water cascading down all around us.

⁂ 31 ⁂

Three days later, the news broke about the grisly discovery of dozens of bodies at what looked like a small encampment in the mountains above Ashland. A couple of retired folks who were hiking part of the Appalachian Trail apparently noticed legions of flies in the clearing at Grimes's camp and went to investigate. They probably wished that they had just kept on walking.

But the hikers made a frantic call to the forest service, which in turn called in the po-po. Bria and Xavier were lucky—or unlucky—enough to be assigned to the case.

The po-po set up a staging area at the picnic tables in the park at the bottom of Bone Mountain, which was where I was right now. Bria had been practically living on the mountain for two days straight, and I'd brought her some food from the Pork Pit, along with enough for her to share with Xavier and her fellow boys in blue. I figured that it was only fair, since I'd created a good portion of the mess that they were dealing with now.

Bria, Xavier, and I were sitting at one of the blue fiberglass picnic tables, several feet away from everyone else. The two of them were scarfing down cheeseburgers with all the fixings, along with crispy steak-cut fries, coleslaw, potato salad, and some double-chocolate-chip cookies that I'd baked fresh that morning.

"We've got more than two dozen bodies in the pit alone," Bria said, washing down a bite of burger with some raspberry lemonade that I'd also made. "All in various states of decay. Not to mention all of the men that you killed."

Xavier nudged Bria with his elbow. "Tell her about the coroner."

She snorted. "Oh, he's having an absolute field day with all of this. You'd think that he was a kid, and it was Christmas morning, given how giddy he is. It's like he actually enjoys working on dead people."

Speaking of the coroner, he was taking a break too and standing in the food line with some of the other cops and crime-scene techs. He held out his plate, and Sophia dished him up some baked beans and fries, and a thick, hearty, barbecued-beef sandwich. He noticed me watching him. He smiled and gave me a cheery wave before scurrying over to take a seat at one of the tables.

"Maybe he just enjoys all the overtime that the city has to pay him and his assistants for schlepping all the way out here," I murmured in response.

Xavier looked at me over the tops of his aviator sunglasses. The noon sun beating down on his shaved head made his ebony skin gleam. "With all the bodies that you've dropped in and around Ashland in the past year, you've probably paid for a summer home for that man."

"Well, it's good to know that I have such a positive impact on our local economy," I drawled. "If not so much on its citizens."

Both Xavier and Bria grinned at my dark humor. We sat there and chatted about other things while they finished their food. Xavier excused himself, got up, and went to go get seconds from Sophia, but Bria stayed at the table with me.

I glanced around to make sure that no one was within earshot, then asked her the question that had been on my mind ever since Finn had shown me the note on the guns in the back of Grimes's trunk.

"Have you found out anything else about M. M. Monroe?"

Bria shook her head. "Nothing. I've scoured the main house and the building where Grimes actually stored his guns, but I haven't come up with anything. No pieces of paper with that name on them, no cell-phone numbers, no other indication that the guns were for M. M. Monroe. In fact, I haven't found so much as a date book or even an old-fashioned ledger of who bought guns from him. Say what you will about him, Grimes protected his clients' identities."

"Finn hasn't been able to find out anything on M.M. either," I said. "He's still horrified that Grimes did everything face-to-face and that he didn't even own a computer, much less use e-mail."

Bria chuckled and shook her head. Then she reached

down under the table and rifled through the backpack that she'd been carrying with her back and forth from the camp. She came up with a couple of towels and handed them over to me.

"I found a few things I thought you might like to have back."

I unrolled one of the towels to find a silverstone knife nestled inside, one of the extra weapons that I'd used to fight the men on the ridge. "Thanks. I am glad to see them again. You can never have too many knives."

Bria smiled a little, but then her face turned serious. "There's something else."

This time, she pulled a brown envelope out of her backpack and slid it over to me.

"I also took the liberty of going through Grimes's house and removing all those creepy pictures of Sophia that he had," she said in a soft voice. "I figured that nobody needed to know about Sophia except for us."

I nodded and pulled the envelope over to my side of the table. "I appreciate that, and I'm sure that she and Jo-Jo will too."

"How is Sophia? I've been so busy up here that I haven't had a chance to drop by the salon and see her or Jo-Jo."

"It's hard to tell with her. She keeps everything to herself."

Bria gave me a wry grin. "That sounds like someone else I know."

I stuck my tongue out at her, but I couldn't refute her words, because they were all too true. And I had my own nightmares about Grimes and his camp.

More than once in the past few days, I'd dreamed of

being down in the pit, clutching Sophia's shovel, and seeing nothing but tombstones looming over me. All the stones had been covered with my spider rune, drawn in my own blood.

Every time, I'd woken up in a cold sweat, thrashing against the sheets, gasping for breath, my skin stinging as though I'd been cut a hundred times with my own knives. I could only imagine how much worse Sophia's nightmares were.

"I think that Sophia will be okay," I said, finally answering Bria's question. "It'll just take some time, like everything does. The good news is that Jo-Jo finally has her strength back. She looked at her hair in the mirror yesterday morning and about had a heart attack. The next thing I knew, she was yelling at me to go get the car and take her to the salon so she could get the right kind of highlights to put on her hair."

Bria's grin widened. "Ah, the joys of having houseguests."

Sophia, Jo-Jo, and Rosco were staying with me at Fletcher's until we could fix the damage that had been done to their home. It was a little strange having them with me when it had just been me in the house for the past several months, but I didn't mind the company. In fact, it was rather nice, even if Sophia did stay up until all hours of the night watching old movies on TV, Jo-Jo muttered under her breath about the fact that I only had one kind of shampoo and conditioner, and Rosco kept scratching at the door to Fletcher's office, wanting to see what was in there and if he could eat any of it.

A bell rang, signaling that the lunch break was over

and it was time for the latest shift to hike back up to the camp. Xavier had Sophia wrap up his cheeseburger to go, while Bria reluctantly got up and threw her paper plates away before coming back over to me. I got to my feet too.

"Duty calls," she said.

"What will happen to the camp now?"

She shrugged. "There's been some talk by the forest service of renovating the camp and turning it into some sort of nature center. Maybe even establishing it as a getaway for folks hiking through the mountains."

"Do the forest guys really think that people will want to stay in a place where so many bodies have been found?"

Bria shrugged again. "Technically, it is their land, after all. I guess they can try, at the very least."

The thought of Grimes's camp made me think of another empty residence in Ashland: Mab's mansion. Now that M. M. Monroe was back in Ashland, or had at least turned his or her attention in this direction, the logical thing would be to take up residence there, since it belonged to him or her. But so far, the mansion remained empty, at least according to Finn's spies.

Like Bria, Finn hadn't been able to find out anything else about M. M. Monroe and what this person might be up to. But like we'd figured, it couldn't be anything good, not with M.M. buying so much ordnance. At least we'd thwarted that part of the scheme. I'd kept all the weapons and ammo that had been in Grimes's trunk and the other vehicles, moving them into the underground tunnel below Fletcher's house for safekeeping, and the po-po had seized all of the weapons that they'd found at the camp itself. So M.M. would have to get his or her guns somewhere else. A small inconvenience, more than anything else, but I was hoping that it would at least give Finn enough time to track this person down and figure out what he or she was really up to in Ashland.

That bell chimed again, telling folks to get their butts in gear, or else.

Bria hugged me and told me that she would call later if there were any updates or if she found anything else interesting at Grimes's camp. She went over to speak to Xavier, and then the two of them shouldered their gear and fell into step with the others. Bria waved at me a final time, then headed into the woods.

But she wasn't the only one. The coroner also gave me another jaunty wave before he followed her up the trail.

I grinned and waved back. What could I say? I was starting to like that guy.

The esteemed members of the po-po trudged back up to Grimes's camp, leaving Sophia and me behind to pack up the leftovers. We put the remaining food in the ice-filled coolers that we'd brought along, then moved through the picnic area, picking up the used paper plates, cups, and utensils and throwing everything into the trash bins.

We were about to grab the coolers and walk down the steps to our cars when I touched Sophia's arm and handed her the envelope that Bria had given to me.

"Bria found these at Grimes's camp," I said. "She said that they were all over his house and that she took them down before anyone else saw them. I thought that you might want them."

Sophia's fingers curled around the envelope, and she

hefted it in her hand, as though it weighed more than it actually did. Or maybe that was because of all the bad memories associated with what was inside.

Sophia sat down at one of the picnic tables, opened the envelope, and flipped through the photos, but I didn't join her. This was her pain, not mine, and I figured that she might want a few moments to herself. So I busied myself by going through the area one more time and making sure that we hadn't forgotten anything. Every once in a while, I would glance over to see how she was doing. Her expression was flat as she looked at first one picture, then the next, but I could see the pain shimmering in her eyes.

Finally, after she'd gone through them all, Sophia grabbed the photos and the envelope, got to her feet, and went over to one of the trash cans. She drew a long, thin lighter out of her jeans pocket, the one she'd used to light the sterno cans that warmed the baked beans and other food. She flicked the lighter on and held it up to the edge of one of the photos. She watched as the flames licked at the paper, then tossed it down into the trash can with the other garbage. I stood by, still and silent, and watched her.

One by one, Sophia burned all of the photos, until flames flickered out of the top of the trash can. The smell of burning paper filled the air, along with bits of ash.

Finally, Sophia got down to the last photo in the envelope, the one of her wearing that white dress that had been on Grimes's desk. She started to toss it in on top of the rest of the burning mess, but she hesitated. Instead, she stared at the photo for a long while, before finally sliding it back into the envelope.

Sophia noticed me watching her. "To remember," she rasped.

I nodded. I understood that sentiment all too well. It was why I had so many rune drawings on the mantel at Fletcher's house.

We stood there and watched the rest of the photos curl and burn, until there was nothing left of them but ash— and the memories, which weren't nearly as easy to get rid of.

❋ 32 ❋

A little more than a week after Harley Grimes had first stormed into Jo-Jo's house, I found myself back in the salon. Only this time, I wasn't getting my nails done. Instead, I was the one painting.

I stepped back, my eyes tracing over the wall and making sure that I hadn't missed any spots. Since the salon had been so damaged during Grimes's attack, Jo-Jo had decided to do a little remodeling. That meant a fresh coat of white paint everywhere.

However, not everyone was happy about being on paint duty instead of being pampered, like we'd first planned.

"Oh, sure," Finn muttered, dabbing his brush at the wall a few feet away from me. "*Now* you let me come. Now that there's work to be done and not just sitting around in your pajamas, drinking mimosas, and eating bon-bons."

I gave him an amused look. "Less whining, more

painting. Jo-Jo wants to reopen the salon next week, remember?"

Finn let out another huff, but he leaned forward and started some trim work around the doorframe.

"Well, I agree with Finn," Owen drawled from the opposite side of the salon, where he was working on another wall. "I could do with less painting and more pampering myself."

Beside him, Bria snorted. "Men. And they think that we're the weaker sex. At least we don't whine about every little thing, now, do we?"

Finn turned around and stabbed his paintbrush toward her. "I will have you know that I don't whine about every little thing. I only whine about the *important* things, my own comfort being chief among those."

Bria snorted again. I grinned and went back to my own painting.

Among the four of us, it didn't take long to finish painting the salon. Once we were done, I led everyone into the kitchen. While they settled themselves around the butcher-block table, I rustled around in the cabinets, coming up with plates, forks, napkins, and a large knife. Then I reached into the fridge and pulled out the key lime pie that I'd made early that morning.

Finn's eyes lit up. "You didn't tell me that there was pie."

"You would have quit painting and come in here."

"Absolutely," he agreed, grabbing the knife off the table and using it to cut into the dessert. "Why paint when you can eat pie instead?"

"Well, I can think of some things that are better than painting *or* eating pie," Owen rumbled.

He slid his arms around my waist and pulled me back

against his chest. That old, familiar electricity arched through my body, and my heart thrummed with desire—and love. Owen pressed a kiss to the side of my neck before stepping away from me. With everything that had been going on the past few days, we hadn't been able to spend a lot of time together, but the moments that we had shared had been wonderful. We weren't out of the woods yet, but I'd felt that we'd finally turned a corner and that we would come out stronger on the other side.

I turned around and tapped him on the nose. "Well, you'll have to tell me all about these mysterious activities later. Perhaps even give me a demonstration."

"It would be my pleasure," he agreed in a husky voice.

"Mine too," I murmured back. "But for right now, be a good boy, and eat your pie."

Owen made a face, but he took the plate that I offered him. I laughed.

Once Bria had gotten a piece of her own, I took what was left, along with some more plates, forks, and napkins, and stepped out onto the front porch, where Jo-Jo and Sophia were.

Jo-Jo was perched in a rocking chair, going through a brown cardboard box that was full of makeup, with Rosco snoring in a patch of sunlight at her feet. Sophia was sitting on the steps, her right index finger moving back and forth in a steady, deliberate pattern, carefully using her Air magic to dissolve all of the blood that had spattered there—Jo-Jo's blood.

"Y'all ready for a pie break?" I asked, and put everything down on a table next to Jo-Jo's elbow.

Jo-Jo grinned at me. "I don't know that I've done

enough work to have earned myself dessert already, but I won't pass it up."

I grinned back at her. "Good. Because I made that key lime pie that you love so much."

I cut her a big piece of the tart, tangy dessert. Sophia reached a stopping point and joined us, digging into her own slice. Rosco cracked open an eye, but when he realized that we weren't going to share, he huffed and continued snoozing at Jo-Jo's feet.

"You know," Jo-Jo said, after she'd finished her slice, "I don't think that Sophia and I ever said thank you for everything that you did on the mountain and everything that you're doing here now too."

I reached over and squeezed her soft, warm hand. "There's no need for thanks. Family takes care of family. Simple as that."

"Still, darling, you went above and beyond," Jo-Jo said. "I don't think that you know how much it means to Sophia and me."

"So much," Sophia rasped. "So very much."

I reached over and squeezed her hand too. "Well, I don't think that you know how much you guys mean to me. I'd take on Harley Grimes all over again for you—for both of you."

Both of their faces darkened at the mention of the Fire elemental, and for a moment, I wondered if I'd ruined the day. Jo-Jo and Sophia hadn't said much to me about Grimes, although more than once, I'd heard them whispering late into the night at Fletcher's house.

But after a moment, Jo-Jo looked at Sophia. They both grinned, and the mood lightened once more.

"Actually, I'm glad that we're finally getting started on fixing up the salon," Jo-Jo said. "I just got in a new order of makeup that I'm dying to test out on all my regular customers."

She bent over, rummaged through the cardboard box that was sitting at her feet, and came up with a bottle of scarlet nail polish, that deep, vibrant red that was so my color.

"It's called 'Heart's Desire.' Don't you just love the shade?"

"I think that it's just perfect," I said, meaning it. "What other plans do you have in store for the salon besides new makeup?"

Jo-Jo grinned at me. "Well, darling, I'm glad you asked, because . . ."

I sat back in my rocking chair and took another bite of my pie, letting Jo-Jo's words wash over me, enjoying the day and being with some of the people I loved most in the world.

My own heart's desire.

Turn the page for a sneak peek at the
next book in the Elemental Assassin series

THE SPIDER

by Jennifer Estep

A tale from Gin's past,
revealing how she became who she is:
Ashland's most notorious assassin, the Spider. . . .

Coming soon from Pocket Books

❉ 1 ❉

The day the box arrived started out like any other.

I opened up the Pork Pit, the barbecue restaurant that I ran in downtown Ashland, right on schedule. Turned on the appliances, tied a blue work apron on over my clothes, and flipped the sign on the front door over to *Open*. Then I spent the rest of the morning and into the afternoon cooking up burgers, baked beans, and the thick, hearty barbecue beef and pork sandwiches that my gin joint was so famous for. In between filling orders, I chatted with the waitstaff, wiped down tables, and made sure that my customers had everything they needed to enjoy their hot, greasy meals.

All the while, though, I kept waiting for someone to try to kill me.

Not for the first time today, my gaze swept over the storefront, which featured an assortment of tables and chairs, along with blue and pink vinyl booths. Matching, faded, peeling pig tracks on the floor led to the men's and women's bathrooms, respectively. A long counter with padded stools ran along the back wall, separating the cooking area from the seated customers.

Since it was after six now, the dinner rush was on, and almost every seat was taken. The waitstaff bustled back and forth, taking orders, fetching food, and refilling drinks, and the *clink-clank* of dishes filled the restaurant, along with the steady *scrape-scrape-scrape* of forks, knives, and spoons on plates and bowls. Murmurs of more than a dozen different conversations added to the pleasant mix of sounds, while the rich, hearty smells of cumin, black pepper, and other cooking spices tickled my nose.

Everything was as it should be, but still I looked at first one diner, then another. A few folks swallowed and quickly glanced away when they realized I was watching them, not daring to meet my gaze for more than a second. But most were happily focused on their food and companions and paid me no more attention than they should have. They were just here for the Southern treats the restaurant served up—not to try to murder me and cash in on my reputation as the Spider, Ashland's most notorious assassin.

"Gin?" A deep, male voice cut into my latest examination of the storefront and its occupants.

I looked over at the man perched on the stool closest to the old-fashioned cash register. Despite his slightly crooked nose and a scar that cut across his chin, he was ruggedly handsome, with intense violet eyes and black hair shot through with blue highlights. His navy business suit and white shirt highlighted the coiled strength in his chest and shoulders, and I wasn't the only woman in the restaurant who paused to give him an admiring glance.

"Is everything okay?" Owen Grayson, my lover, asked.

My eyes flicked left and right one more time before I answered him. "Seems to be. For the moment."

Owen nodded and went back to his meal, while I grabbed a rag and started wiping down the rest of the counter.

Actually, so far, the day had passed by in a perfectly normal fashion, with the glaring exception that no one had tried to murder me—yet.

Thinking that I might actually get through the workday unscathed for a change, I let myself relax, at least until the bell over the front door chimed. I looked over at the entrance, expecting to see a new customer, someone ready, willing, and eager to get their barbecue on.

Only this wasn't a customer—it was a tall, thin man wearing a delivery uniform of black coveralls and matching boots.

The guy glanced around the storefront for a moment before his eyes locked on me, and he headed in my direction. I tensed, eyeing the long white box in his hands, and dropped my right arm down behind the counter. A second later, out of sight, a knife slid into my hand, one of five blades that I had hidden on me. This wasn't the first time someone had dressed up like a deliveryman to try to get close to me at the restaurant. The last guy was still in the cooler out back, awaiting the skills of Sophia Deveraux, the head cook at the Pork Pit who also moonlighted as my own personal body disposer.

But to my surprise, the guy stepped right up to the cash register, as though this was a simple delivery.

"I've got a package here for Gin Blanco," he said in a bored voice. "Is that you?"

"Yeah."

"Here. Sign this."

He shoved an electronic scanner at me. I slid my knife into a slot below the cash register, where it would still be out of sight, and took the device from him. The man waited while I used the attached pen to scrawl something that sort of looked like my signature onto the screen. The second I was done, the guy snatched the scanner from me and shoved the white box into my hands.

He tipped his head at me. "Have a nice day."

He started to walk away, but I reached out and latched onto his arm. The guy stopped, looked at me over his shoulder, and frowned, as if I'd violated some sort of secret delivery guy protocol by touching him. Maybe I had.

"Yeah?" he asked. "You need something else?"

I carefully set the box down onto the counter. Thankfully, the seat next to Owen was empty, so I was able to slide it several precious inches away from us.

"What's in the box?" I asked.

The guy shrugged. "I don't know, lady, and I don't care. I just deliver 'em. I don't look inside."

He started to pull away, but I tightened my grip on his arm.

"You should really tell me what's in the box."

He rolled his eyes. "And why should I do that?"

"So I can make sure that there's nothing . . . nasty inside."

Confusion filled his face. "Nasty? Why would you think that there's something nasty inside?"

"Oh, I don't know," I drawled. "Why don't you check the name on the delivery order again."

He glanced down at his electronic scanner and hit a button on the device. "Yeah, it says deliver to Gin Blanco, care of the Pork Pit restaurant, downtown Ashland. So what? Is any of that supposed to mean something to me—"

Comprehension dawned in his eyes as he finally recognized my name and realized who and what I really was. Gin Blanco. Restaurant owner. And, more important, the assassin the Spider.

He swallowed, his Adam's apple bobbing up and down in his throat. "Look, I don't want any trouble, lady. I'm just a delivery guy. I don't know what's in the box, and that kind of info's not on my scanner. I swear."

I kept my grip on his arm and stared into his eyes, but I didn't see anything in them but a burning desire to get away from me as fast as he could. Smart man. Still, I let him sweat a few more seconds before I released him.

"Okay," I said. "You can go now."

The guy whipped around. He started to take a step forward when I called out to him again.

"Wait. One more thing."

The guy froze. He teetered on his feet, and I could almost see the wheels spinning in his mind as he debated making a break for the door. But he must have realized how foolish that would make him look, because he finally turned and faced me again. I crooked my finger at him. The guy swallowed once more, but he eased back over to me, although he made sure to stay out of arm's reach and keep the cash register between us.

By this point, my words and actions had attracted the attention of a few customers, who stared at me with wide eyes, as if I was going to whip out a knife and slice open the delivery guy right in front of them. Please. I preferred to be a little more discreet about such things, if only to keep up appearances.

I stared at the delivery guy for a few more seconds before reaching down behind the cash register and grabbing something underneath it. He swallowed a third time, and beads of sweat had formed on his forehead, despite the restaurant's air-conditioning. I raised my hand, and he tensed up that much more.

I reached out and tucked a hundred-dollar bill into the pocket on the front of his coveralls.

"Have a nice day," I said in a sweet voice.

The guy stared at me, his mouth gaping open, as if he couldn't believe I was sending him on his way without so much as a scratch on him. But he quickly got with the program. He nodded at me, his head snapping up and down, even as he backed away toward the door.

"Y'all come back now," I called out to him. "Sometime when you have a chance to sit down and eat. The food here is terrific, in case you hadn't heard."

The delivery guy didn't respond, but he kept his eyes on me until his ass hit the doorknob. Then he gulped down a breath, threw the door open, and dashed outside as fast as he could without actually running.

Owen raised an eyebrow at me. "I think you about gave that poor guy a heart attack."

A grin curved my lips. "Serves him right, for not being able to tell me what was in the package."

His gaze flicked to the white box sitting off to the side. "You going to open that?"

"Later," I murmured. "When we're alone. If there is something nasty inside, there's no use letting everyone see it."

"And if it's not something nasty?"

I snorted. "Then, I'll be pleasantly surprised. I'm not holding my breath about it, though."

Owen finished his cheeseburger and onion rings and had a piece of cherry pie with vanilla bean ice cream for dessert, while I spent the next hour working. Slicing up more potatoes for the last of the day's French fries. Checking on the pot of Fletcher's secret barbecue sauce that I'd set on one of the back burners to bubble away. Refilling drinks and ringing up orders.

I also took the package into the back and placed it in one of the freezers. I didn't know what surprises the box might contain, but I didn't want any of my staff or customers to get injured by whatever might be lurking inside.

Finally, a little after seven o'clock, the last of the customers paid up and left, and I decided to close the restaurant early for the night. I sent Sophia and the waitstaff home, turned off all the appliances, and flipped the sign over to *Closed* before locking the front door.

Now all that was left to do was open the box.

I carefully pulled it out of the freezer, took it into the storefront, and put it down on the counter in the same spot as before. I made Owen get up and move to the other side of the restaurant, well out of range of any elemental Fire or other magic that might erupt from the inside. Then I bent down and peered at the package.

A shipping order was taped to the top, featuring my name and the Pork Pit's address. But there was nothing on the slip of paper to tell me who might have sent the box or where it had come from. All of that information had been left blank, which only made me that much more suspicious about what might be inside.

And the box itself didn't offer any more clues. It was simply a sturdy white box, long, rectangular, and about nine inches wide. No marks, runes, or symbols of any kind decorated the surface, not even so much as a manufacturer's stamp to tell me who had made the box in the first place. I hesitated, then put my ear down close to the top and listened, in case someone had decided to put a bomb with an old-fashioned clock *tick-tick-tick*ing away inside. Stranger things had happened, in my line of work.

But no sounds escaped from the container. No smells either, and I didn't sense any elemental magic emanating from it.

"Anything?" Owen asked from his position by the front door.

I shook my head. "Nothing so far."

The lid of the box had been taped down, so I palmed one of my knives and sliced through the material, careful not to jiggle the package any more than necessary. Then I waited, counting off the seconds in my head. Ten . . . twenty . . . thirty . . . forty-five . . . sixty . . .

After two minutes had passed, I was reasonably sure

that nothing would happen until I actually opened the box.

"Here goes nothing," I called out to Owen.

As I slowly drew the top off the box, I reached for my Stone magic, using it to harden my skin, head, hair, eyes, and any other part of me that might get caught in a blast from a bomb or any rune trap that might be hidden inside. A sunburst rune that would make elemental Fire explode in my face; a saw symbol that would send sharp, daggerlike needles of Ice shooting out at me; maybe even some sort of Air elemental cloud design that would suck all of the oxygen away from me and suffocate me on the spot.

But none of those things happened, and all I saw was a thick layer of white tissue paper that was wrapped around whatever was inside.

So I drew in another breath and carefully pushed aside the paper, still holding on to my Stone power to protect myself from any possible problems. But to my surprise, the box held something innocuous after all: flowers.

Roses, to be exact—black roses.

I let go of my magic, my skin reverting back to its normal, soft texture, and frowned, wondering who would send me a box of roses. I picked up one of the flowers, mindful of the sharp, curved thorns sticking out from the stem, and turned the blossom around and around, as if it held some sort of clue that would tell me who had sent them and why.

And it did.

Because this wasn't your typical rose. The stem was a milky white instead of the usual green, and the thorns were the same pale shade. But really it was the petals that caught my attention, because they weren't black so much as they were a deep, dark, vivid blue—a color that I'd only seen one place before.

"All clear," I said.

Owen stepped over to the counter and peered into the box. "Roses? Somebody sent you roses?"

"It looks that way," I murmured.

A white card was lying on top of the flowers, so I picked it up. Only two words were scrawled across the front in black ink and tight, cursive handwriting.

Happy anniversary.

That was it. That was all the card said, and no other marks, runes, or symbols decorated the thick bit of stationery.

I ran my fingers over the card. Not what I had expected it to say. Some sort of death threat would have been far more appropriate. Then again, I hadn't thought that I'd get a package like this today either. But most troublesome was the fact that the two simple words gave me no clue as to the writer's tone, state of mind, or true meaning. The card, the message, the roses, could have been anything from a simple greeting to the most biting sort of sarcasm. If I were betting, though, I'd put my money on sarcasm. Or, perhaps a warning. Maybe even a promise of payback, retribution, revenge.

"Happy anniversary?" Owen asked, leaning over the counter and peering at the card in my hand. "Anniversary of what?"

I glanced up at the calendar I'd tacked on the wall near the cash register. August twenty-fifth. Ten years to the day it had happened. Funny, but right now, it seemed like ten minutes ago, given how hard my heart was hammering in my chest. I breathed in, trying to calm myself, but the sweet, sickening stench of the flowers rose up to fill my mouth and slither down my throat like perfumed poison. For a moment, I was back there, back with the roses, back in the shadows, beaten and bloody and wondering how I was going to survive what was coming next—

"Gin?" Owen asked. "Are you okay? You look like you're somewhere far away right now."

"I am," I said in a distracted voice, still seeing things that he couldn't, memories of another time, another place.

Another man.

Owen reached over and put his hand on top of mine. "Do you want to tell me about it?" he asked in a soft voice.

His touch broke the spell that the roses had cast on me, and I pulled myself out of my memories and stared at him. Owen looked back at me, his violet eyes warm with care, concern, and worry. It always surprised me to see those feelings reflected in his face, especially since we'd almost called it quits for good a few months ago. But we were back together and stronger than ever now. More important, he deserved to know about this. He deserved to know why I was the way that I was—and who had helped make me that way.

I gestured for him to take his seat on the stool again while I gently laid the dark blue rose back down in the box with the others. I kept the card in my hand, though, my thumb tracing over the words again and again. Then,

I sat down on my own stool, leaned my elbows on the counter, and looked at Owen.

"Get comfortable," I said. "Because it's a long story. Funny enough, it all begins with a girl—a stupid, arrogant girl who thought that she could do no wrong . . ."

More bestselling
URBAN FANTASY
from Pocket Books!

More Bestselling Urban Fantasy
from Pocket Books!